"If you got a battle, you can't expect the Lord to help you and not the other fella. Now can you? . . . No, son, you got to fight and hope God likes the way you're using your fists. And that goes for the boy you're fightin'. . . . I hope you won't have to stay here all your life, Newt. It ain't a all-good place and it ain't a all-bad place. But you can learn just as much here about people and things as you can learn any place else. Cherokee Flats is sorta like a fruit tree. Some of the people are good and some of them are bad—just like the fruit on a tree. . . . No matter if you go or stay, think of it like that till the day you die—let it be your learnin' tree."

So spoke Sarah Winger to her son not long before his thirteenth birthday, and this is the story of what happened to Newt Winger during his perilous climb out of childhood.

"THE STORY . . . HAS BEEN TOLD MANY TIMES. BUT NEVER HAS IT BEEN TOLD THE WAY GORDON PARKS TELLS IT . . . WRITTEN WITH POWER, SENSITIVITY AND TIMELINESS"

—ST. PETERSBURG TIMES

THE CREST IMPRINT ON OUTSTANDING BOOKS IS YOUR
GUARANTEE OF INFORMATIVE AND ENTERTAINING READING

THE LEARNING TREE

BY GORDON PARKS

A CREST REPRINT

FAWCETT PUBLICATIONS, INC., GREENWICH, CONN.
MEMBER OF AMERICAN BOOK PUBLISHERS COUNCIL, INC.

A Crest Book published by arrangement with
Harper & Row, Publishers, Inc.

Copyright © 1963 by Gordon Parks.
All rights reserved, including the right to
reproduce this book or portions thereof.

PRINTING HISTORY

First Harper printing, May 1963
Second printing, October 1963
Third printing, November 1963

First Crest printing, September 1964

The characters in this novel are fictional. Any
resemblance to persons living or dead is coincidental.

Crest Books are published by Fawcett World Library,
67 West 44th Street, New York, New York 10036.
Printed in the United States of America.

To Momma and Poppa

CHAPTER ✤ 1

NEWT WINGER lay belly-flat at the edge of the cornfield, his brown chin close to the ground, his eyes glued to a hill of busy ants. He singled out one struggling with tree bark twice its size, tugging it forward then sideways then backward up the incline. Being a veteran ant-watcher, Newt tracked its course near perfect over the rough and slippery terrain.

For five of his twelve years he had watched these creatures, remembering that his father often spoke of their energy and work habits in contrast to those of the listless blacks and whites in Cherokee Flats. ("Son, the only thing worse than lazy Negroes is lazy white trash—'cause they're born white, with a God-given chance from the start.")

This anthill was a special one, and Newt liked it better than most he'd seen. The sunny side of it glittered like diamonds because a chunk of sandy earth, washed down by the morning rain and held firm by a discarded plow, stuck to this portion of the mound. Newt pressed his chin even flatter, closing one eye, for now the ant with the bark was near the top and he got a clearer view with one eye shut. He moved his blunt nose close to what now seemed a big animal pulling a tree trunk up a mountainside.

As the ant reached the top, the glitter suddenly dimmed and bits of the mound blew into Newt's eye. He blinked and brushed out the dirt, but when he looked again, the whole mound was blowing apart. At the same moment he felt the cool Kansas wind rushing in, stinging his face and throat. Newt's prairie instincts told him this was no ordinary wind. Catlike, he jumped to his naked feet and looked to the sky. A great swirling black cloud was moving toward him from the southwest. It was broad at the top, gradually narrowing to a point at the bottom near the earth—looking every bit like a spinning top. He started to run, but this sight held him transfixed in the biting wind, his bare brown arms shielding his dark face. He leaned into the gale, looking much like a

7

small, wiry, broad-shouldered scarecrow, his tattered shirt and bib overalls flapping from the wind.

"Neewt! Neewt! Where is you? Neewt!" It was Big Mabel's voice somewhere down the cornfield. "Neewt! Neewt—!" As he spun about to answer, his foot struck the remains of the anthill, kicking the insects in every direction.

He jerked his foot up, afraid he had killed; then, falling to his knees, he began cupping the dirt and ants with his hands in an attempt to rebuild the mound. He kept pulling the scatterings together, only to see them blown away. Then frightened and confused, he fell to the ground and placed his body in the path of the wind to protect the rest of the hill. But the wind, mixed now with pouring rain, swept over and beneath him, swirling the loose pile into nothingness.

Big Mabel reached him just before the full front of the storm struck Cherokee Flats. As she yanked him to his feet, the wind-driven rain lashed her naked parts and flattened the wet gingham dress against her body. "What you doin' here, boy? Your maw and paw and all of us was worried 'bout you! Cain't you see the big storm comin'? What's wrong with you, anyhow? What you cryin' for? Come on now, git movin'! We got to hurry, boy! Come ahead!"

Newt pulled loose for a last look at the anthill, but as he did so a gust slammed him hard against Big Mabel and they both tumbled to the ground. As they went down, the girl twisted to break her fall and Newt fell beneath her, striking his leg on the sharp edge of the plow. They struggled to their feet and started off with the wind at their backs, blowing them into a weird slippery trot.

After several yards, Newt screamed in pain and dropped to his knees. "What's the matter, boy?" Big Mabel cried. Newt groaned and lay still. "Come on, boy. We cain't stop here! Come on, I'll help you! . . . My God, boy, where'd you git that slice in your leg? You bleedin' like a hog!"

Newt grimaced. "That old plow back there—shore does hurt, too."

Big Mabel looked about desperately. They were a good mile from the Winger house. Jim Pullens' place was a half mile closer, but still not close enough. She stared at the swirling blackness. "Too far to Jim's or your paw's place from here. Maybe we can make the killin' house to the other side of the field. Come on! Git on my back!"

She squatted in the mud and Newt clasped his arms about her neck, straddling her back, with his legs between her arms. She steadied him and began crawling along the edge of the field, seeking the protection of the cornstalks. But she changed her mind when she saw them bending crazily from their roots. "Cain't make it this way. Hang on, we'll skirt round the end!" She staggered up, balanced Newt's weight, then headed for the slaughterhouse across the field.

The high winds, rotating counter-clockwise, pushed, snatched and twisted them over the violent countryside, and Newt's concern for the ants and his gashed leg gave way to fear of thunder, lightning and screaming wind.

Suddenly Big Mabel yelled, "Dammit to hell, I'm stuck—cain't move!" She was sinking ankle-deep in mud. Freeing one foot then the other, she inched her way to higher and firmer ground.

The wind was behind them again, forcing Big Mabel into a crazy lope, and within a few minutes she was rounding the edge of the cornfield, from where she could make out the blurry image of the slaughterhouse. "We'll git there soon now, Newt! Hold tighter, boy! Hold tighter!" Newt whimpered and dug his face into the back of her neck, trying desperately to keep his wet hands from slipping apart—feeling pain from the cut, and the sticky warmth of blood between his toes.

Thunder rumbled over them and within a split second, in the blinding flash that followed, Newt saw the outline of the house off to their right. "There 'tis, Mabel! There 'tis!" A deafening crash echoed the thunder. He smacked his hands against his ears and lost his balance. "Hold on! Grab—" Big Mabel's warning was late. Newt was already falling.

His head struck first. Pain jolted through his neck to his belly and shimmied out to his toes. Then he was floating on a puffy white cloud fringed with orange and purple raindrops. The wind kept curling the cloud over him like a hot blanket. He tried pushing it off, but it kept covering him, so he kicked it with his foot, which punctured the cloud. He went tumbling through space with a chunk of cloud stuck through his leg. Down... down... down he fell.... "Help! Help! Momma, catch me! I'm fallin'—"

Big Mabel tore a strip from the bottom of her dress, bound it above the wound in his leg and began tightening. "Quiet, boy, you goin' to be all right now. You is safe in the killin' house—this'll stop the bleedin'." She secured the bandage, pulled a butcher knife off a rack, wrung water from her dress onto it, then placed the flat side of the blade against the lump on his forehead. "Why you let loose I don't know —with just a few feet to go." She ripped another piece off her hemline and began cleaning blood from his leg.

9

Newt's hazy awakening assured him of safety. Big Mabel's voice, which at first had seemed far away, was closer now. Slowly he made out the dark broad forehead, high cheekbones and sullen lips as she moved above him; the bare damp shoulders glistening in the weak light, the full breasts hanging free and swaying with each motion. His eyes caught patches of light in the roof where shingles were ripping away and water splattering through—except where he lay, for directly above him were sheets of tin he and his father had placed in early spring.

"You feelin' better now, boy?"

"My head hurts—and I'm kinda cold."

"Be warmin' you up in a minute. We's lucky to be inside. We's smack in the middle of a cyclone. Everything's gonna blow away if this keeps up."

"How'd my head git hurt?"

"You acted a fool and let loose and busted the ground with that noggin of your'n. That's how." Another patch of shingles tore from the roof. "Damn shore is blowin' to hell out there!"

"What you holdin' that knife on my head for?"

"Quit askin' so many questions, boy! I know what I'm doin'. It's to take swellin' out." She placed his hands on the cracked knife handle. "Here, hold it right there for a minute —gotta find somethin' to cover us up."

She went to an adjoining room used for smoking meat and groped about in the darkness for a moment or so. "Thank God—I know'd this old quilt was here somewheres!" She returned to Newt, took the knife and threw it aside, then spread the musty cover on the floor next to him. "Roll over here, boy." Newt propped himself up on his elbows and eyed the quilt.

"That thing's dirty!"

"You pick a hell of a time to git hinkty, boy. You's cold, ain't you? Well, this'll keep you warm. Git yore little black ass over!"

Newt scooted over on his backside, carefully dragging the injured leg behind the rest of his body. Big Mabel stood with hands on her broad hips looking down on him. "Better git them wet things off, too."

"What for?"

"There you go with questions again. Boy, I'm seven years older'n you, and I know what I'm doin'. Hadn't been for me you'd still be out there blowin' away with them damn ants!"

Newt scowled and began tugging at his overalls. Big Mabel

10

plopped down beside him and pulled them over his feet. Then she yanked the remains of the dress over her head and flung it in a corner.

"You oughta be feelin' better soon now," she said, fixing the quilt over them and, at the same time, pulling Newt hard against her naked body. "Come closer, boy, if you want to git warm." Her voice now was husky and low—so low that he could hardly understand her words.

And soon the warmth of Big Mabel brought a glow to his own body, and a hardness to his groin—one he had never felt before. Big Mabel felt the hardness too. She rolled over on her back, pulled him on top of her.

The killing house shook all over and the shingles kept flying away, but Newt felt even warmer. And the softness of Big Mabel cushioned the shaking; calmed his fears. And though the storm blew on, it was not long before Newt completely forgot its blowing.

Yet, outside over the prairie, groundhogs and skunks, jack rabbits and opossums took flight from the flooding lowlands. And sparrows, robins, bobolinks and swallows alike, trapped in the whirling wind, darted helplessly beneath the ominous sky. In the brush, cud-chewing deer knelt close together protecting their nervous young. And the dark sky drew darker.

Meanwhile, Jack Winger and his son Pete, keeping short distances apart, struggled through wind and rain over the countryside, combed all Candy Hill for Newt. Cutting across the river road, the two powerfully built men saw at the same time a large section of the road wash out and the bobbing headlights of a truck coming toward them. They rushed to the middle of the road, waving frantically at the onrushing vehicle; but the driver spotted the washout too late, and the big truck twisted off the road, jumped a ditch and crashed against a light pole, then slid back down the incline. Jack and his son heard the cracking, saw the upper part of the pole falling away. "Watch out!" Jack shouted. The power line snapped, and at once there was a showering of sparks and a zinging sound, followed by a great splash.

They made their way over to the truck, but the driver was already out of the cab when they reached it. "Damn near killed myself!" he hollered above the screaming wind.

"You hurt?" Jack bellowed.

"Naw—but that damned power line's down over the field there!"

"You betta warn somebody—we gotta keep lookin' for my kid! Didn't see a boy down the road, did you?"

11

"Nope, not a soul!" The two men started off. "Hope you find him!" the trucker shouted as they trudged away.

Bending almost double in the wind, Jack and Pete pushed along the slippery bank of Flynn's River, searching every crevice and cave along the way. Finally they reached the swimming hole.

"Newt! Newt!" Jack cried out. "Newt! Newt!" There was no answer, not even an echo as the wind whipped his voice away. Then Pete was hollering, "Neewt! Neewt!" His cry was all but silenced by a loud thunderclap. Jack shook his head dejectedly. Then they turned their backs to the punishing storm and headed toward home.

They could see the truck still straddling the ditch as they went back across the road, and when they passed beyond the washout, the man stuck his head from the cab. "D'ya see any sign of the boy?"

"No luck!" Pete yelled back, and they kept moving. They were alongside Jake Kiner's ranch now, hearing the hoofs of his frightened livestock pounding in the direction of the downed power line. The two men squinted through the driving rain. A bluish flash lit the prairie and several of the steers lurched grotesquely in sputtering death. The others shied, then plunged on over the tangled wire.

Sarah Winger jumped at the banging on the door. After a quick glance at her fourteen-year-old daughter Prissy, she hastened through the parlor, jerked open the door and watched as the two drenched, exhausted men staggered in.

"Jack?" Her voice was softly urgent and questioning.

He slammed the door, took a deep breath and walked to the corner where Pete was already shedding his wet clothes. For an instant Sarah stood motionless, her heart pumping. "Oh—oh," she moaned softly, "oh, my God." Then quickly she was through the door and into the open, her long black skirt whipping in the wind. But just as swiftly Jack was out beside her, coaxing and pushing her back into the house.

Pete rushed over and pulled them both in, banged the door shut, threw the bolt in place and gently grasped his mother's shoulders. "Ain't no sense in worryin', Momma." His tone was low and positive. "Newt knows this countryside better'n a squirrel."

"Prissy."

"Yessir, Poppa."

"Fix me and your brother some hot coffee."

"Yessir," she answered, and was off to the kitchen.

Sarah moved to the window and looked out at the stormy blackness. The clock on the wall showed three, and the wanging of the lead ball against the bell, chiming the hour, sounded incongruous to her ear, as if it were coming from some far-distant place, at some far-removed time. Her husband and son stood watching her, trying to share her thoughts, wanting in some way to banish the fear that held her. Jack took a chair to her and she sat down. And she remained there for an hour and a half more while the house shook under the twisting wind. She silently prayed for the safety of Newt—forgetting all else, peering through the lightning flashes for any sort of image that might miraculously be her son.

Near five o'clock the wind suddenly died, the sky began to pale and the storm was gone.

When Newt and Big Mabel left the smokehouse they could see the heavy clouds being suctioned off by the storm, swirling now into the distant northeast. And as they walked along, frogs leaped into the open and crickets made chirping noises with their wings, rubbing away the wetness. The late sun shimmered in the rivulets snaking through the muddy fields to streams and gullies in the lowland.

"Look'it there!" Newt suddenly shouted. He pointed at what was left of Jim Pullens' house.

"Lordy," Big Mabel blurted, "good thing we didn't try for here." They cut across the field to the crumpled house, seeing that there was no longer a roof and that the wall nearest them had caved in completely. "Lordy, what a mess!"

"Think he's all right?" Newt was tagging behind now, not only because of the pain in his leg but also from a fear of what they might find in the wreckage.

"Who, Jim?"

"Yeah. Don't see nobody stirrin' about."

"Well, come on, let's see." Now Big Mabel was slowing.

"Boy, lucky we didn't git here. We'd a—"

"Shush. What's that whinin' sound?" They stopped and listened.

"I don't hear nothin'."

"Sounded like—"

"It's Collie! It's Collie!" Newt blurted, limping faster toward the sound. "He must be under the roof!" Now he was down on his hands and knees, peeping under the fallen roof. "Here, Collie! Come on, boy! Here, Coll—" Then he recoiled in shock. "Mabel! Mabel! It's him! It's him! He's trapped under the roof."

13

"What? You shore, boy?"

"Yeh. Come see for yourself." Big Mabel flattened to the muddy ground, squinting beneath the tangled debris. "See?" Newt panted.

"It's Jim all right—he alive?"

"Mister Pullens! Mister Pullens!" Newt hollered. The dog whimpered and began wagging his tail. "Mister Pullens! Mister Pullens!"

" 'Tain't no use, Newt. See all the blood—he's prob'ly dead."

"We better git help. Maybe he's just knocked out."

By the time Newt and Big Mabel reached the Winger house, only a gentle breeze stirred the puddles in the yard. Prissy was skimming the water with her big toe when she saw them running toward her. "Momma! Momma!" she hollered. "Here comes Newt and Big Mabel!"

Sarah heard and ran from the kitchen. Pete, having just returned, disconsolately, from another search with his father, came down the path. "Poppa!" Jack Winger was in the back-yard eying his overturned henhouse, and the anxiety in Pete's voice made him wheel around. "Yep, boy! What is it?"

"Here's Newt and Big Mabel!" Pete called back on the run.

Prissy was already pouring questions. "Where was you? How'd you hurt your leg? Where'd you hide out?"

Before Newt could answer, he saw his mother in the door-way. The sight of her was heart-warming, and he wanted to go to her; but instead he turned to his brother. "Pete—Mister Pullens' house blowed down—he's trapped underneath it, and—and—" He was out of breath.

"He hurt bad?" Pete questioned.

"Looks to me he's—"

"Yeh," Mabel interrupted, "blood's all round his head."

Jack Winger was among them now. "What's the matter? Where you been, boy?"

"Jim's trapped under his house!" Pete burst out.

"Jim Pullens?"

"Yessir."

"Well, come on—let's git over there. Come on!" Jack shouted. Then he and Pete trotted off. Newt turned, too, and limped after them.

"Newt!" Sarah called halfheartedly.

He kept running, pretending not to hear his mother. She started to call again but changed her mind. "They may need him for somethin'. It's enough just to have him back! Thank

14

Jack spooned the thick gravy over a piece of cornbread before answering. "Your Uncle Rob's all right. Fact he's blind don't make him no difference. He prob'ly sensed the storm 'fore any the rest of us and got inside in time. The Simpson boy told me he seen him on his front porch right after the storm blowed over."

"How'd Mag take Jim's death?"

"She was plenty broke up when I told her. Her place got smashed up a little bit too. Jim was a good brother to her."

"Prissy," Sarah said, "you go help her git straight in the mornin'."

"Yessem."

"The little Johnson girl got burned real bad, I heard."

"Who told you that, Pete?" Sarah questioned.

"Doc Cravens. He told me they got her over at County Hospital."

"How'd it happen?"

"Her momma dropped a lamp or somethin' like that."

"Drunk, I bet," Jack moaned.

"You shouldn't be sayin' that, Jack. You—"

"You know well as I do, Sarah, that Lucy stays drunk offa canned heat and Chappie's likker."

"That still don't give you right to say it here at the table in front of these kids."

"Well—"

Pete broke in to save his father. "Clint got home yet?"

"Now you talk 'bout drunks—he's the prize one." Jack was back on the firing line. "Tell me him and old Doc Cheney been drunk since way 'fore the storm started."

"Clint's just mixed up, that's all, Jack."

"Yep, but he's your fav'rit mixed-up son-in-law."

"And yours, too."

"Yep, but no fav'rit by any stretch of a sow's tail. If Rende had any sense she wouldn't a even said hello to him, less 'lone marry him. Gits so it's the same every week or so. She comes runnin' here with them kids 'way from him and that ole shotgun."

Sarah was about to answer when Pastor Broadnap appeared at the screen door. "O-ho," he beamed, "caught you sittin' for supper!"

The rotund minister swept into the room, his long black preacher coat flapping at his knees. Little pods of sweat stood out on his forehead at the point where the hairline receded sharply, as if it were shaved. He scanned the table. "Just in time to share the gifts of the Lord," he said.

17

"Oh my," Newt mumbled, "there goes my chicken legs."

Prissy snickered and Sarah fired a glance at Newt. "Come on in, Reverend," she said, "and have some supper." Newt watched his mother push aside the legs he had hoped for, and he couldn't suppress a groan. "One more grunt out of you, boy, and up you git without any more supper at all," she whispered fiercely.

"Yessem," Newt chirped, his face plumped up in exasperation.

Space was made for the pastor, and Sarah heaped food on his plate and passed it to him. "Got any of your fine apple butter, sister Winger?" he asked.

"Right here in the cupboard," she sang out, reaching through the door behind her for the jar.

"Bless you. Bless you."

"Quite a blow we had today, Reverend."

"Yes 'twas—yes 'twas," he mumbled, reaching for a slice of cornbread with one hand and the gravy dish with the other.

"Any damage to the parsonage at all?"

"No, brother Winger, just the church steeple. Blowed off its base. Don't rightly know what's holdin' it up there. Good thing it stopped blowin' when it did, otherwise it'd shore be on the ground."

"Yep, we're lucky at that, I guess. Could'a been worse, a lot worse. Well, just gotta round up some members for straight'nin' it up, that's all."

"Bless you, Jack. Bless you." He was flooding the cornbread with gravy now. "Well," he continued, chewing, "I attach a very special meanin' to that storm. It's (Newt winced as Broadnap teethed the meat from the bone) a warnin' to the wrongdoin' of all these sinners round here. This place is poppin' with sin—people drinkin', cuttin', fightin' and doin' all sorts of things the Lord don't approve of; nobody comin' to church like they ought'a. Why, I'd say Chappie Logan's place got more drunks in it than we got members on Sunday mornin'."

Sarah Winger looked at the pastor and said, "For some reason it's the good ones who go first."

"Thinkin' 'bout Jim Pullens, huh, sister Winger?" Broadnap said, dipping into the jar of apple butter with his knife. "Well, it's hard to explain—hard to explain. Jim was a fine man. Always come to church and prayer meetin'. Only way I figger it is that the Lord takes the good ones like that so the bad ones'll hafta take more responsibility."

"Old Sam Wong got it too. They ain't found him yet, I hear."

"Naw, and with half that block on top of him they might not find him for a couple of days," Pete said. "And to think he was out safe, then went back for his cat and got killed."

"Well, you find out lots 'bout people in a big wind like that. Some proves weak, some proves strong." Jack Winger wiped his long mustache with his wrist and pulled his pipe from his pocket. "It's a easy time to cut lamb from sheep. Think God does prob'ly send things like this to test us. Wouldn't be surprised if he didn't git tangled up hisself tryin' to figger out these here folks in Cherokee Flats."

"Was you scared, Newt?" Prissy asked.

"Naw. Just sorry I killed the ants. That's all."

"If you'd been home choppin' wood like you was s'posed to, you wouldn't been in such a mess. Them anthills gonna be the death of you yet."

"Keep quiet and eat you supper, girl. You got no right to talk. You was just lucky to be home instead of gallivantin' somewhere."

"Yessem." Newt caught Prissy's eye, grinned impishly, snaked his tongue out at her and resumed his pious demeanor before she could bring his action to their mother's attention.

Broadnap picked up a bone and started gnawing on it. There was one leg and a rump left on the chicken platter, and both he and Newt eyed them. "How about another piece of chicken, Reverend?" Sarah volunteered.

Broadnap chuckled. Newt gritted his teeth and looked blankly at the wall ahead of him, sensing the maliciousness in Prissy's cough. Broadnap chuckled again. "You know one thing, sister Sarah, I think somebody else got their eye on that leg well as me, and I got a little proposition to make with him about who gits it."

"Oh," Sarah cut in, rolling her eyes at Newt, "that ain't a'tall necessary. You're welcome." She put the leg on Broadnap's plate.

"No no no, sister," Broadnap protested. "Now, Newt, you been studyin' your Sunday school lessons lately?"

Newt gulped, "Yessir, I—"

"Fine. Now if you tell me the name of the weapon Samson slew the Philistines with, the leg's yours." Broadnap grinned smugly.

Newt scratched his head in deep thought (Slingshot... naw, that was David... spear... naw...). "I got it!" he blurted out. "The jawbone of a—a—" He looked sideways at his mother.

"A what?" Broadnap snapped.

A wry smile wrinkled Newt's face. "Well, I cain't name it right out, but it's the same name as that part left on the platter."

"The ass," Broadnap grunted, dumping the leg on Newt's plate, "the jawbone of an ass."

Everybody laughed.

"Newt," Sarah admonished, "you shouldn't take that leg from Reverend Broadnap. Now—"

"Oh no, sister. The boy won it fair 'n square. I'll take what's left," Broadnap countered, spearing the chicken rump from the platter.

"You been over to see the little Johnson girl, Reverend?"

"Yes, sister Sarah. That child's lucky to be livin'. Hardly any hair or skin left on her. Doc Cravens says we got to ask for some volunteers in church Sunday."

"Volunteers for what?" Jack asked.

"Well, seems like Doc's gonna try to graft new skin on her. That means somebody's gonna have to give some'a theirs."

Sarah looked up in astonishment. "You mean Doc intends to strip skin off somebody else and put it on her?"

"That's what he's sayin', sister Sarah, if she's gonna live any kind'a normal life again."

"Poor child. It's a awful thing—a awful thing," Sarah said, shaking her head.

"Don't worry, sister Sarah, she'll be helped. Some good souls'll come forward."

"Hot coffee, brother Broadnap?"

"No, Jack. Ain't been sleepin' too well lately. Next time round, maybe. Got some more visitin' to do on my way to the parsonage. Sister Pullens and a few others." He got up. Those about the table started to rise, but he spread his arms above them. "Sit, my dear children, and bless you, sister Sarah, for the wonderful repast." He plucked several toothpicks from a bowl and picked up his black "preacher's" hat from the sideboard. As he passed Newt he patted him on the head. "Keep studyin', boy. Givin' the right answer meant that chicken's leg instead of the part that went over the fence last." He chuckled. Then he plopped the hat on his head and left as suddenly as he had come.

After supper the stove was fired, and soon its heat pushed the evening chill away. Pete slumped over a Western saddle,

20

stitching the flaps, while Prissy tended the kitchen. Jack Winger lit his pipe, leaned his chair against the wall and gazed at the ceiling. In the quiet of her bedroom, Sarah rocked back and forth patching overalls.

Newt lay on the dining room floor, swallowed up in the happenings of the day. The ants; the ugly sky; the flight; the fear; the pain; and the impassioned wedding of his body with Big Mabel's was an experience he felt he would never forget. And time and again his mind reached back beneath the warm, dusty blanket to grasp those sensuous moments.

Too, the storm had made him more aware of his family's importance to his existence. He admired certain things about each of them. He couldn't imagine anyone braver than his father; yet there were things about him Newt couldn't understand—why he resented Newt's wanting to play the piano, or why their talks together only dealt with tending chores. Newt thought of when his father was once sick and had sat around moaning, waiting for his mother to give him a teaspoon of medicine. But there he was, Newt recalled, out in that storm lookin' all over for me.

And Jack Winger was thinking it was good to have his youngest home safe and sound. He'd been pretty worried for a while, and he wished he could let the boy know about that. Why did he find it easier to pet a horse or a dog than one of his own kids? And why did he have to be so stupid when they needed help with their lessons? Well, he was glad he had Sarah to give them what he couldn't. Fact was, they'd all be in a bad way without her.

Newt's eyes rolled lazily to Pete's muscular arms and wide shoulders, and he started longing for the time when his own body and strength would match his brother's. Pete, who was twenty-six, had fought overseas in the World War. Newt remembered when he was reported missing during the Battle of the Marne; how his mother had refused to believe he was dead; the way she'd held back tears through the bitter winter, and then cried so hard when the telegram came saying Pete was safe. Now he was back working at odd jobs with his father, happiest when bucking wild broncos or wrestling steers during the local rodeos. He was discontented with Cherokee Flats, but saw little chance of ever leaving it again.

A plate broke on the kitchen floor.

"Save the pieces, Prissy," Newt hollered.

"Shut up," she shot back.

"Boy," Jack growled, "mind your own bizness."

"Yessir, Poppa."

21

Newt had no way of knowing it, but his sister had just been imagining his experience as he had recounted it to his mother before supper. Her subconscious explored his painful cuts and bruises, his fears, and then submitted to a moment of morbidness that fancied her brother lying dead somewhere in the stormy prairie. The apparition frightened her, and she had dropped the plate.

Newt thought of Priscilla as most boys his age thought of older sisters—meddlesome, tattlesome, scary, curious and unsociable. Prissy had once described herself in a letter to a distant cousin as "high brown, tall, gray-eyed, with long red straight hair," when actually she was dark brown, slightly dumpy, brown-eyed, with short curly black hair.

Sarah Winger rocked and sewed in her bedroom with an attitude of thankfulness. Newt's being in danger had shaken her more than she had realized. Her body and mind were spent. She had begun sewing to calm her nerves, gone to the back room in order to hide the anxiety still surging within her bosom. And she thought of her other children away from home. Less than a mile away the eldest child, Rende, no doubt sat fearful in her four-room clapboard, waiting for Clint—realizing that when he did come home drunk, cursing and threatening, she and her two children might have to run for the safety of the Winger homestead. And there was Roy in Chicago, and two other girls, Clara and Lucille, up north in Minnesota.

At fifty-two, Sarah was of unusual looks; smooth dark brown skin, with a sharp-boned face borrowing the high cheek and slanted eye of the Cherokee. A pinkish white scar the size of a quarter marked her left temple, resembling a flower in bloom. And this strange marking, inflicted by a thunderbolt during a long past storm, enriched the tone of her dark skin. A thin layer of curly black hair stretched to a ball at the nape of her longish neck, and her delicate ears, curving gently out from the back, seemed to be shaped of wax. She was short, wiry and quick-moving; and when her long skirt whipped out behind her, she gave an impression of forceful, almost perpetual motion.

Newt thought of his mother now (Wonder why she's back in her room tonight all alone?), and he tried to imagine their life without her. The warmth of the room, the serene images of his father and brother slid into a black void. He was as thankful for her presence as she had been for his safe return.

He pushed himself to his feet and limped through the parlor, dragging a finger over the battered piano keys.

" 'Bout time you was in bed, son," Sarah called out.

"Yessem—just comin' to tell you goodnight." He stepped into her room.

"Glad you did, boy—glad you did. How's the leg?"

"Okay, I guess. Well, goodnight, Momma."

"Goodnight. Sleep well."

"Yessem," he said, turning back to the dining room. "Night, Poppa."

"Night, boy."

"Night, Pete."

"G'night, Newt."

He limped quietly to the kitchen door. Prissy was hanging up the last of the cooking pots. "Boooo! Boooo!" he shouted.

Prissy shrieked, "Momma!" and dropped the pot.

Jack Winger jerked the pipe from his mouth. "Boy!" he shouted, "if you don't git to bed, I declare I'll skin your hide!"

Newt limped off to bed with a grin on his face. He was weary and sore, but happy to be home—safe from the storm.

CHAPTER ❦ 2

JACK WINGER climbed the tower ladder to within a few feet of the dangerously tilting spire of the African Methodist Episcopal Church. With trained eye he noted the damage, the angle of tilt, and instantly determined the number of jacks and cabling needed to hoist the structure back into position. From the ladder he swung to the floor of the upper loft. It was caked with a half century of feathers, twigs and bird droppings. He kicked away the top crust for surer footing, then, leaning precariously from the loft window, twirled a lasso in several wide looping motions, aimed it and let go. The circle of rope hit true and he pulled it tight about the two six-by-sixes jutting from the spire's base. He doubled the rope around an oak beam, knotted it, then slapped it for tautness. It shimmied like a tightly strung banjo string. Satisfied, he hollered to the men below. "Bring about ten jacks and all the tackle you got!" Another look and he yelled again, "Rope off a clearin' to the left and front!"

"Okay!" Pete hollered back from below.

The job started, Jack lit his pipe, rested his elbows on the window sill, and looked out over all Cherokee Flats from this perch. As he did, it came to him that contours of the village resembled those of an egg, the broader top half representing where the most well-to-do resided, and the lower half being where the poor and near-poor lived. The Frisco tracks, running north and south across the lower section, drew the social and economic line between the six thousand residents who made up the village. There were no well-to-do blacks, he reasoned, but there were poor whites who shared, to a certain degree, the status of their dark neighbors east of the tracks.

Far away on the north edge he could just see Flynn's River, the sun reflecting on its flat, slow-moving surface, snaking in and out of the craggy rocks and tall trees. Further beyond, where the water cut into the west, he saw the top of

County Hospital that perched on a knoll on the very outskirts of the village. He glanced toward the opposite end of the river where, off to the right of it, he recognized Jake Kiner's red farmhouse—barns, cattle pens and fruit orchards sprawling over the entire shank of the east hill. On up the gentle slopes the bright sun struck the white crosses and marble headstones marking the graves, and still further to the right of that the steep incline of Candy Hill down which the youth of Cherokee Flats raced their wagons and homemade vehicles in the summer, their sleds in the winter. All else outside the village perimeter, as far as he could see, was prairie, cornfield and brush.

He looked back to the center of the village. The stone courthouse and jail (squatting smugly, medieval-castle-like, in the square) stood out strong and unscathed in the bright Saturday morning sun. But the secondary business area, lying a block to the west behind it, had suffered the brunt of the storm. Talbot's harness shop was flat on the ground, its crushed sides jutting out from under the broken roof. Comstock's store front, peeping from beneath two huge maple trees, sagged, cock-eyed and windowless, against nine two-by-fours. Blake's general store, Davis' bakery, Carson's drugstore, Sam Wong's laundry, Mack's hamburger shack, snuggling together when the storm struck, were now hopelessly tangled in a half-block pile of crumpled roofs and smashed walls. Sam, the village's only Chinese citizen, was dead somewhere in the rubble of broken bottles, shattered plaster, torn clothes, spoiled hamburger and baking dough, pots, pans, hardware, ladies' accessories and such.

The Regency Theater (featuring William S. Hart this week—this month—this year) and the Mottsy Funeral Parlor stood together at the north end of the business section on Main Street. And a mile or so behind them Jack could see the two white people's churches and the two red brick schools for white children, all intact and standing relatively short distances apart. Too, in that area, smack in the middle of a terraced block, sat the big multicupolaed, red-shingled Cavanaugh house where Jack's wife worked.

A freight train puffed across toward the river, and he turned to watch its thick smoke curl in and out of the east side houses and shanties. After it cleared he noticed, for the first time, that the colored Shilo Baptist Church, half a block away, was missing several of its blue-purple-red windows, plus about fifty square feet of shingling; that the wooden colored grade school was askew on its concrete base. He noted

25

that aside from Jim Pullens' place, Mag Pullens' front porch, Booker Savage's old barn and the Winger henhouse, damage had been mostly in the southwest part of the village.

Jack had mixed feelings about this place. Like all other Kansas towns, Cherokee Flats wallowed in the social complexities of a borderline state. Here, for the black man, freedom loosed one hand while custom restrained the other. The law books stood for equal rights, but the law (a two-pistol-toting, tobacco-chewing, khaki-putteed, leather-legginged cop called Kirky) never bothered to enforce such laws in such books—"mainly 'cause I cain't read," he often bragged.

And though the white and black children were separated in the primary schools and the churches, they played together on the dusty streets, outlying hills and plains. The black boys and girls and the white boys and girls went to the same picture show—the whites downstairs and first balcony, the blacks in the peanut gallery or buzzard's roost. There was no written law against a black man's eating in a white restaurant or drugstore, but there could be trouble, lots of it, if he tried. So seldom, if ever, did he try—especially if he wanted one of the odd jobs that meant his existence.

To Jack Winger, Cherokee Flats and the whole state was a plateau of uncertainty. "Livin' here is like havin' a good lay with a woman you don't quite trust," he had boomed at the superintendent of schools one day. "My boy Pete got high grades in the white high school, and he was the best basketball player in the whole state, but he couldn't play on the school team 'cause his hide was black!"

"I know, Jack," Jess Hicks had sympathized, "but you know my hands are tied."

"And so's a black man's behind,'" Jack had countered.

Now his eyes turned back to the damaged church steeple. He, Pete and several of the other members had volunteered for this job without pay, to protect the church's dwindled funds. But in the rest of the village he calculated a month or more of steady work. He needed it, for his corn crop had done poorly the year before.

Jack could hear the other men making their way up through the tower now. At the same time he saw his son-in-law Clint and old Doc Cheney wobbling arm in arm through the door of Chappie Logan's Restaurant and Pool Hall, just a few steps east of the tracks. He watched them disappear behind the worn clapboard façade and wondered why this "den of hell," as he called it, hadn't perished in the storm.

The workmen were closer now, and the ladder creaked

under their weight. Pete was the first to the top and, though he could see only his father's back, he sensed his deep thought.

"What you lookin' at, Poppa?"

"Aw, nothin'. Just seen Clint and old Doc goin' in Chappie's."

"Rende says he ain't been home yet. She's got Newt out lookin' for him."

"Newt?"

"Yessir."

Jack paused. "It ain't right for that boy to be round Clint when he's drunk."

"He's gonna see a lot worse'n that before he dies, Poppa."

"Well . . . That Clint—Rende ought'a be glad he ain't home. I declare, I don't know what's gonna become of him. Doc and him are so drunk they gotta hold each other up."

Pete didn't bother to answer. He threw the block and tackle from his shoulder to the floor and jumped over it. "It's shore a long time since I was up here." He was changing the subject, for Pastor Broadnap was next up. "This ain't no time for a sermon on Clint's drinkin'," he thought.

A number of things attracted Clint to Chappie's—pool (which he always played with Pee Wee, the rack boy), whiskey (which Chappie made in his cellar) and the tall tales of the porters and waiters who "laid over" between their runs on the railroad. In their business, the railroaders claimed, one talked freely with the Morgans, the Rockefellers, the Vanderbilts and movie stars—even presidents. So Clint often explained to his wife Rende, "the pulse of the nation is at Chappie's more'n it is at the White House."

These men talked of big things, big people and big places, and this left Clint in a daze, for he had never even been outside of Kansas. At forty, he was a lean man of medium height, reddish-brown coloring and prematurely white hair. Half Negro, half Cherokee, he was a smooth blending of both. Despite Jack Winger's feeling, Clint loved his family. That his action now and then belied this fact was because of a weakness that came with his early hatred of Cherokee Flats. He had always had a desperate longing to leave it for good. His marriage to Rende prevented this, and from the day Butsy, the first child, was born, only liquored dreaming replaced the real adventure beckoning him from the bustling big cities. It was during such drunken reveries that he lost

27

control of himself and got the urge to destroy Rende.

And now he dreamed—deep and far—with old Doc Cheney in a stupor at his side. Lenox Avenue . . . State Street . . . Beale . . . Eighteenth and Vine. Chicago whirred past in one searing swallow. Seattle telescoped to St. Louis in less than a gulp. He drifted through New York against the round hot belly of a luscious brown girl. "Set 'em up!" he hollered. "Clint's in town! Set up the whole damn place! Hey, baby— come sit on Clint's knee! I'm loaded! Let 'em roll, fast and hard! Clint fades all fools—sky's the lim—"

"Quiet down, Clint! You want'a git the law on me?" Chappie Logan yelled, twisting his two-hundred-fifty-pound body around.

"—Tell the damn gov'ner to wait—cain't you see Clint's busy? Oh, you fine brown thing—shake—that—thing!"

Newt poked his head through Chappie's door just as Clint tried to stand, his head drooped nearly to his waist. Newt rushed over to steady him, but Clint reeled and crashed sideways to the floor.

"Goddam," Chappie grunted, "hurry up and git him out'a here 'fore he breaks up the joint." Then he helped Newt get Clint to his feet and out the door.

Chappie was surprised to see Rende in the shadow of the buggy canopy when he shoved Clint up into the seat. "Mornin', Rende," he said apologetically.

Rende didn't answer.

"Where'm I? What's this?" Clint mumbled, slumping to the floor of the buggy.

"Come on, Newt. Git goin'," Rende snapped.

Newt jumped up on the seat and popped the reins against the horse's rump. "Gitti'up," he commanded, and the buggy rambled off.

Sarah Winger had worked for Judge Jefferson Cavanaugh nearly twenty years—cooking, washing, cleaning, nursing, advising and generally running things. The Judge, a widower, lived with his two sons—Chauncey, who, at sixteen, had fallen far short of Jeff's hopes, and Rodney, just turned twelve. Sarah had predicted bad days for Chauncey early in his teens, and her prophecy had not gone denied.

Now she pulled back the faded green velvet drapes in the parlor and squinted against the morning sun. After a moment, her eyes conquered the glare and came to focus on the damaged church spire in the distance. She knew Jack and

28

Pete were beneath its dangerous leaning—and she hoped they would be careful.

Suddenly a groaning came from Chauncey's bedroom. She quickly crossed the hall and stood beside the door, listening. The groaning became louder and steadier, and her hand went to the knob, but she didn't twist it. "Chauncey." Her voice was low but sharp. "Chauncey, you all right?"

The groaning continued, and she gently turned the knob, inched the door open and peeped in. She adjusted her eyes to the dimness (He's stinkin' of corn liquor—) then she gasped, "Good gracious me!"

Chauncey was lying on the floor, and a blond woman (Looks like the Newhall girl—yes, 'tis), her head hanging off the side of the bed, hair streaming to the floor, shared his unconscious drunkenness.

Sarah stepped out hastily and shut the door with a resounding bang.

"Uh—uh—yeh—who's there? Who's—" Chauncey was stirring.

"It's me—Sarah. You better git that girl out'a here 'fore your paw comes for lunch. You hear me, Chauncey? You hear me?"

"What girl—what you—what you saying?"

Sarah's voice rose, and she banged her fist against the door. "Listen, boy! You better come to and git that girl out'a this house 'fore your paw comes!"

"Okay—okay—quit hollerin'—okay. Blanche! Blanche!"

Sarah grabbed the broom and swished down the long hallway. "Good gracious me—good gracious me—what won't that onery boy do next?"

By four-thirty the sun had sucked most of the wetness from the earth, and Newt, having got Clint home and helped him to bed, sat on the ground in the shade of an apple tree, reliving the high moments of the storm. A patch of muslin, soaked with hogfat and camphor, covered the sore lump on his head, and now and then he patted it to determine the decrease in swelling.

A grasshopper lit on his knee. He eyed it for a moment, then his left hand moved above and ahead of the insect. His other hand touched the tail lightly and the insect leaped into the trap. Newt held it between his fingers, his eyes squinting at the narrow forewings and the broad hind ones (no wonder you can jump so far), then, dipping its mouth to his fingers, he noted the tobacco juice (Poppa says you kill the crops), he tightened his grip, winced, smiled, then loosened it. The grasshopper sprang away.

He thought, "What are grasshoppers for anyway, and snakes and mosquitoes and flies and worms, wasps, potato bugs and things? Seems they ain't much good to the world, but God put 'em here. Seems they got as much rights as we have to live. If the grasshoppers didn't eat the crops, they'd starve. No worse'n us killin' hogs and chickens so we don't go hungry. Hogs and chickens and cows and rabbits and squirrels, possums and such must hate us much as we hate mosquitoes and gnats and flies. Dogs and cats and horses are 'bout the luckiest. 'Bout the only ones we don't go round killin' off all the time. The Ten Commandments say we oughtn's kill, then we come home from church and wring a chicken's neck for dinner—and Reverend Broadnap eats more'n anybody else." Newt stretched. "Too much for me to figger out," he said aloud.

Footsteps fell on the path behind him and he swung his head around to the sight of Beansy Fuller. Beansy, twelve, short and fat, shimmied as he walked. And because he was pigeon-toed, his motions resembled (according to Clint) "a pig doin' a foxtrot."

"How'ya, Newt?"

"Hi, Beansy. Sit down."

"Heard about you and Big Mabel gittin' caught in the storm."

Newt's eyes widened. "What'd you hear? Who told you?"

Beansy smiled slyly. "Big Mabel."

"What all'd she tell you?" Newt's eyes flashed to his bandaged leg.

"Aw, you know what she told me." He was grinning now. "She says you ain't got no cherry no more!" Now he doubled over in laughter.

"Shut up. Prissy and them'll hear you." Newt eyed the kitchen screen uneasily.

"Big Mabel got you, huh?" Beansy wiped the tears from his eyes. "How'd it feel, Newt?"

"How'd what feel?"

"Aw, come on—I'm your best friend. I ain't gonna snitch."

Newt glanced toward the kitchen again, then looked Beansy in the eye. "Don't go blabbin' to the rest of the fellas."

"Honest to pete, I won't. Come on, now."

"Come to think of it, I don't know just how it felt. Everything happened so quicklike. I knew I felt somethin' was 'bout to happen that I didn't know anything 'bout."

"Well, how'd it happen?" Beansy squirmed with anticipation.

"I don't know. We was both wrapped up in a quilt together."

"Naked?"

"Well, we didn't have no clothes on. Guess you'd call it naked. I was hard . . . so hard it was hurtin' . . . and she pulled me over on her . . . and I was feelin' warm . . . and she was groanin' . . . and all at once I had a shivery feelin' . . . like a hot chill . . . I started tremblin' and shakin' in my toes . . . and knees . . . and even my head . . . and everything was like a dream . . . then I went to sleep."

Beansy's knees pressed together tightly and his whole body rocked from side to side. "Boy . . . boy . . . boy . . . what else?"

"Ain't nothin' else. It just kind'a left me feelin' good, mighty good, that's all."

"You gonna do it again with her?"

"Come on. Quit askin' 'bout it. I told you everything."

They were silent, thinking. Newt's mind, awakened to the words of his first sexual experience, began searching for a deeper meaning of it. But his thoughts were no more explicit than his words had been. And his long legs, like Beansy's short fat ones, pressed together tightly; his slender body rocked slowly to the rhythm of his thoughts.

After Beansy left, Newt laid his wide young shoulders on the cool grass and watched the white clouds drift lazily across the sky. As he continued looking, the last of the clouds moved out of sight, leaving only clear, pale space. Still space. His arms came together and rested on his brow, excluding all other things from his vision (and in his mind the space became wider and deeper, easing him up into its mysterious nothingness and all about him was still except the buzzing of a single bee that after a while was joined by the sounds of violins many violins hundreds of violins and horns and drums many horns and drums and voices many thousands of voices freeing him from tasting smelling feeling seeing—no, a sparrow was specking the nothingness and it was coming down—no, a buzzard coming closer—no, a hawk a chicken hawk and the music is fading and the chickens are cackling and the hawk is swooping down) . . .

Newt jumped to his feet, hobbled to the chicken coops, grabbed a stick as the cackling grew louder. The big hawk started up, a chicken in its claws, but too late. Newt brought the stick down over its head, and it dropped the fat hen to the ground. The hawk fluttered up, claws flying. Newt struck at it again, but the bird jumped backward and up to the top of the henhouse. It wobbled for a moment, regained composure and swooshed off into the sky. Newt watched it disappear, then he cornered the frightened chicken, grabbed it and stroked back its feathers to see if there were any cuts from the claws. Then he released it.

Walking back toward the shade tree, he wondered of the strange music he had heard. He sat down again, tried to recapture the spell. But finally he realized it was one of those moments that would have to come unexpectedly—and without coaxing. And since there was nothing else to do, he felt the joints in his toes, examined the knuckles of his hands and wondered about the power that caused their workings. Ever who makes people is sure mighty smart, he concluded.

Not long afterward, his father and Pete came up the road, their flatbed wagon loaded with cables, jacks and rope. When they reached the alley, the horses slowed; Jack jumped to the ground, and the wagon continued to the barn. Newt noticed in a second glance that his father was coming directly toward him.

"Your momma home yet, boy?"

"Nosir, not yet."

"When she comes, tell her I'm over to the hospital."

"Yessir."

Jack ambled across the yard, and Newt watched him disappear into the pleasant landscape.

That evening Sarah and Newt took the river road to County Hospital. As she walked, her long skirt stirring the dust, Sarah mulled over all the possible reasons for Jack's going there. If he was sick, she reasoned, he would have said so. To her knowledge, no one was there who he would ordinarily choose to visit, and if there was, experience had taught her that he would not have gone without her. Her concern was deeper than she cared to let her young son know, and to hide it she hummed at times—a spirited hymn that gave a nonchalant rhythm to her motion.

Suddenly the humming stopped.

"Newt, you sure your poppa didn't say why he was goin' over here?"

"Yessem, just said to tell you he was goin', that's all."

She thought: "There's somethin' puzzlin' about this. He just wouldn't make off like that without some kind of word—some kind of explanation." And though she stretched her thought, no logic came of it. As they entered the hospital door, her hand went to Newt's arm; then, straining against fear, she spoke to the attendant.

"I'm here to see Mr. Jack Winger."

The attendant, newspaper in hand, looked at her in an un-acknowledging way, seeing but not seeing her. "He a patient here?"

"I don't know what he's doin' here. All I know is he's here." Her voice, steeled to a sharpness, brought the newspaper down and the attendant's eyes to focus on her.

"Jack his real name?"

"It's what he's known as. Andrew Jackson Winger is his full name."

"How long's he been here?"

"Came this evenin'." Her voice was losing its agitation.

"Just a minute, I'll check the records. Let's see—Wilson—Williams—yeh, here — Jack Winger." His forehead clouded. "You shore you didn't know why he was here?"

"Why would I be storyin' to you?" Sharply again.

"No harm. No harm. Just askin' 'cause he's in the operatin' room."

Sarah's heart skipped a beat. Her fingers pressed into Newt's arm. "Operatin' room, for what?"

"I don't know for shore. You better sit down and I'll check. You his wife?"

"Yes, and I want to know what they're operatin' on him for and who's doin' it." The attendant noticed her teeth grinding under her drawn cheeks.

"Take a seat. I'll try and find out. Card says he's Dr. Cravens' patient." A wave of relief swept over Sarah.

"Well, that's good to know," she said.

The attendant picked up the phone. Sarah motioned Newt to the seat, then they both sat staring at the wall. And Newt, sensing trouble, chewed his upper lip. The attendant's voice lowered and the two strained their hearing to it. "Lo . . . lo, Bertha . . . What's the Winger fella's trouble?" There was a long terrible silence. "Oh . . . naw, his wife. . . . Oh, I see (his eyes now no Sarah with a kind of new meaning) . . . yeh . . . yeh . . . okay . . . thanks, Bertha." He placed the receiver on the hook and stood up. "Missus Winger." He coughed. "Your husband's givin' skin to the little Johnson girl who was burned in the storm. He's under ether now and you won't be able to talk to him 'fore mornin', but they told me to tell you everything's gonna be all right, not to worry. Fact is, Dr. Cravens's comin' by to see you tonight to explain things."

33

A warmth came to Sarah Winger's face and her body relaxed in a certain relief. She thought for a moment, her eyes on the dusty hem of her skirt. "That's all right, that's all right," she said. "I understand."

The attendant remained standing. His voice came soft and unsteady. "Ma'am . . . that was a mighty fine thing for him to do . . . you ought'a feel proud of him . . . she'd a been messed up for life otherwise . . . they been askin' for volunteers all day . . . he's in good hands, ma'am. Doc Cravens'll take good care of him."

Sarah nodded to his words, arose. "I am proud, mister, and so's my son here. Tell Doc Cravens, for me, that I understand and I'll see him later." Pushing Newt ahead of her, she opened the door and they went out.

After walking for a while in silence, she spoke in a near-murmur. "Sure wish your poppa would let folks know what he's doin'."

Newt couldn't remember ever walking alone with his mother, just the two of them sharing moments as they did this evening. And for the first time, subconsciously measuring his gait with hers, he realized that even at twelve he was a little taller than she. He suddenly felt protective toward her, and his mind snatched at an illusion wherein he might defend her against an intruder on this lonely road, this very evening. And he envisaged doing so in the same manner as Hoot Gibson, Tom Mix or maybe William S. Hart. The last eventful forty-eight hours had nudged his imagination to a fertile awakening, and he was full of thoughts, ideas and questions.

Halfway home, he broke into his mother's humming.

"Momma, can I ask you somethin'?"

"Yes, boy. What you want to ask me?"

Newt pondered briefly, and Sarah slowed her pace. "Well, I don't know offhand, just about people and things like that."

Sarah smiled to herself, for she remembered that for the past year she had wanted to talk with Newt about "people and things" but thought him too young to understand the things she wanted to speak of. She had planned especially for him, her youngest, since the day he was born, but in the trials of living and caring for all the others she found it hard to clarify and formulate these plans. Now she welcomed the breakthrough. "Newt, you just ask me anything you want and I'll try to answer you."

"Well, after the storm, Poppa said that the storm and the people killed and everything was the doin' of God. You care if I ask you why he kills some people and not the others?

34

Poppa said hisself that Mister Pullens was a good man. And why did some of the town git torn up and the rest didn't?"

Sarah Winger came to a complete stop, and Newt was instantly afraid he had offended her. He took a step beyond his mother, his face pointed straight ahead, eyes lowered and cast sideways for the reaction. Her lips parted, but she didn't speak immediately; then she started moving again.

"Newt."

"Yessem."

"You know your poppa and me are religious people, don't you?"

"Yessem."

"Well, it would be real easy for me to say, you don't question the ways of God—and I was tempted to—but I know deep in my heart that there's more to it than that. It's true he guides us. But we cain't depend on him for everything. We gotta do things for ourself. Now, maybe if Jim had built himself a storm cellar or a stronger house, he wouldn't a got killed so easy. And if little Fannie Johnson's momma hadn't been drunk, she'd a held onto that lamp and her daughter wouldn't a got burnt. It's like I say, we got to do some things for ourself. If you got a battle to fight, you cain't rightfully ask the Lord to help you and not the other fella. Now can you?"

"No, ma'am."

"No, son, you got to fight and hope God likes the way you're using your fists. And that goes for the boy you're fightin'. Ain't neither one of you got time for prayin' while you're flingin' fists. Too many people, especially some of ours, boy, sit round waitin' when they should be out doin'. You got to always remember that, boy, always."

"Yessem. Are we gonna live here all our life?"

Sarah looked searchingly at him. "Don't you like it here?"

"I don't know, Momma. I ain't never been no place else."

"I hope you won't have to stay here all your life, Newt. It ain't a all-good place and it ain't a all-bad place. But you can learn just as much here about people and things as you can learn any place else. Cherokee Flats is sorta like a fruit tree. Some of the people are good and some of them are bad—just like the fruit on a tree. You know that, don't you, boy?"

"Yessem."

"Well, if you learn to profit from the good and bad these people do to each other, you'll learn a lot 'bout life. And you'll be a better man for that learnin' someday. Understand?"

"Yessem."

"No matter if you go or stay, think of Cherokee Flats like that till the day you die—let it be your learnin' tree."

"Do we all have to die someday?"

"That's one thing we all have to do, boy. No matter who you are. That's why it's so important to be ready when your time comes."

"You mean to be a Christian, like you and Poppa?"

"In a way—in a way. But it's even more than sayin' you're a Christian. It's a matter of givin' more to this world than you take away from it. So when you die you don't owe it anything. It's bein' able to love when you want'a hate—to forgive them that work against you—to tell the truth even when it hurts—to share your bread, no matter how hungry you are yourself. Dyin' comes easy when you know you've done all these things right."

"I'm gonna hate dyin'."

"Won't none of us like it, boy—none of us."

"I hate dyin' so much I wish sometimes that I wasn't even born."

Sarah blurted, "Why, I'm surprised at you sayin' such a thing." When she saw his face she knew he realized that she was stalling for time.

"Is there anybody who has ever come back from death that saw heaven?"

Sarah sighed. (Who's this boy been talkin' to? Where's he gettin' such notions?) "No, boy. Ain't no such thing as that ever happened, to my knowin'."

"Well then, how does anybody know there is such a place?"

Her mind's eye flashed frantically from Matthew to Revelations, criss-crossed ages of praying, of shouting and of preaching. And finally her lips betrayed her teaching, ages of it—made light of the blindness, broke with believers; with the mountains of ever-so-solid faith. "Newt." (And already her expression made him sorry he'd sprung the trap.) "Honestly, I don't know. Maybe there ain't no hell either. Maybe there ain't no gold thrones in the clouds and maybe there ain't no pits of fire tended by a devil with a pitchfork tail. I honestly think God made us and expects us to do some good while we're here on earth. I cain't even say that God's his real name, but it's good as any. It means Almighty."

Confusion disturbed her thoughts. "All my life I've been told there is a better place beyond this one, Newt. And I

36

guess I'll go to my grave believin' it. Such believin' has kept our family goin' when there wasn't much else to go on." She paused for a moment. Swallows, flying low and fast, fluttered the stillness. Then she spoke. "These are the things I was taught. It's awful hard now, this late, not to believe them." They didn't talk after that.

About nine o'clock that night Newt heard Dr. Cravens' Ford pull into the yard. "Doc's here, Momma!" he shouted.

"Well, let him in, boy. Let him in."

Newt swung the door open, and the lanky, bespectacled blond man stepped in. "Hi, Newt. Your mother in?" he asked.

"Come in, Timothy," she called from the kitchen. "Sit down. I'll be right out."

"How's Poppa doin'?" Pete asked from another room.

"Fine, Pete. He's hollerin to come home already."

Sarah came in, wiping her wet hands on a towel. Doc was stretched out on a chair, wearily pushing the fair, graying hair back from his forehead. "Jack's doin' all right, you say?" Sarah questioned.

"Oh, he's goin' to feel a bit of pain for a few days. Then it will ease off and he'll come along fast."

"Just wish he'd tell me when he's goin' to do such a thing."

"He's stuck with his own ways, Momma Winger." Doc Cravens pulled a cob pipe from his pocket and began packing it. "Not much use in our tryin' to change him now."

"You look tired, Timothy."

"You've told me that long as I can remember."

"Marryin' would help you more'n you think. Least you'd eat regular," Sarah said.

Doc Cravens chuckled. "You've been tryin' to marry me off for years now. I'm just thirty-five. Give me a chance."

"You'd better come by here and git a good meal now and then. You look like you ain't ate in a week. You'll be needin' a doctor if you keep goin' like you are."

"That I'll do, Momma Winger, the very first chance I get. It's been a long time since I ate as well as I did here."

Newt's eyes shot to the doctor. "You used to eat here, Doc—"

"None of your meddlin' now, Newt," Sarah cut in. "I want to know how long it'll be 'fore Jack's all right."

"Oh, he'll be up and around in another two weeks. He'll have to take it easy for a little while." He lit his pipe and puffed several times. "It was a great thing he did, Momma Winger."

"Well, yes it was," she agreed, "but he's not the kind to think of it that way."

"That's for sure," Doc Cravens answered, "that's for sure."

"What part of him did you take the skin from, Timothy?"

"His back, legs and arms, but—"

"Oh oh," Sarah grimaced. "Must be awful painful."

"It wasn't an easy thing, not at all. Not at all," Doc Cravens said.

Sarah asked him to have a sandwich and some coffee. He refused the sandwich but took the coffee. After he had finished it he looked at Newt's leg and the bruise on his head. "You had a busy day in the storm, Newt, a real busy day."

"Shore did," Newt replied.

He dressed both wounds, and Sarah poured him another cup of coffee. He gulped it down and got up to leave. He was so tall he had to duck to clear the doorway. "Don't worry about a thing, Momma Winger!" he called back from the car. He stepped on the starter. The motor whirred, caught, and he pulled off the path and into the dark street.

Later Sarah Winger lay in her bed, her arms above her head, her eyes turned sleepily to the blank dark of the ceiling. Cravens had assured her that Jack would be all right, and she believed him. After a while her mind returned to Newt, and a shiver of doubt creased her thoughts. "I wonder," she said aloud, "if I gave him the right answers today." Then her past was brutally before her ... the dusty Georgia road ... the three white men rushing in ... her sister Curtney screaming from the ditch ... and the fat red face above her, bleeding from the clawing she gave it. And later, her brother Tom's revenge with the rifle ... and the hounds tracking Tom down ... and his limp, tar-covered body sprawled in death, a lynch knot about his neck—in the same ditch where Curtney had screamed—and screamed—and screamed.

"I wonder if I told him enough." She sighed. Her question faded into a gentle snore and before long she was fast asleep.

As the first light of Sunday crept over Cherokee Flats, only the delicate chirping of birds tickled the morning stillness. But as the sun climbed, the hens cackled beneath the rooster's crowing, and stirred the pigs into grunting, the cows into mooing, bringing Newt awake.

He sat on the side of the bed, pulling on his overalls, listening to the hogs squeal their hunger, and he knew they wouldn't stop until their noses were deep in the swill. Eyes half closed, fighting sleep, he buckled one bib strap; but before he could fasten the other, his chin dipped to his chest and he dozed again.

Wham! The blast came as he fumbled with the other strap (sounded like a double-barreled shotgun . . .). He got to his feet, leaped over the bed, then, ever so cautiously, peeped out the window. It was Clint, on top the overturned chicken house, reloading the gun and hollering, "I'll git the son-of-a-bitch yet! I'll git him!"

Newt started for his mother's room, but she was already rushing to the kitchen door. Newt followed her. Pete's voice ricocheted against Prissy's. "Who's shootin'? What the matter? Momma! Momma! What's goin' on? Come back here, Newt! Somebody's shootin' out there!"

"It's Clint. He's still drunk!" Newt hollered, slyly enjoying the early excitement. And as he ran out behind his mother, he saw Clint blast away at the sky. Wham! "I'll get the son-of-a-bitch!" Wham!

Sarah Winger didn't stop until she was at the foot of the chicken house. "What you call yourself doin', boy? Who're you shootin' at?" Her tone was in keeping with the Sabbath.

Clint rocked around unsteadily, reloading the gun. "I'm gonna git him! Don't worry. I'm gonna git him!"

"Git who? Who you shootin' at, boy?" she shouted.

Clint wobbled precariously, pushing in the shells. "I'm gonna blow the ass off Jesus Christ, the long-legged white son-of-a-bitch! I burned him a little that last shot. I'll git him for shore this time!"

The others gathered about their mother now. "Put that gun down, boy, and come down from there 'fore you kill your crazy self!" Clint ignored her and started digging in his pockets for more shells. "I mean it, boy. Come down this very minute or I'm comin' up after you!" She fired the command this time.

"But, I'm gonna—"

"Git down, I said! I had enough of your foolishness for one mornin'!" Clint pushed the shells into the chambers, and Sarah motioned for Pete and Newt to boost her up on the house. Pete started to object but realized, soon enough, there was no use. "Quick. Shove me up like I tell you." He lifted her as Clint started to raise the barrels to the sky.

"Clint!"

He hesitated, and she snatched the gun and the flat of her other hand smacked against his jaw. He reeled drunkenly, then tumbled off the side, but Pete caught him and dumped him coldly upon the earth. Then he turned to help his mother

39

down. But first she broke the gun open at the chamber, removed the shells and pitched the gun to Newt; then she swung down in Pete's arms. "You boys take him in the house so's he can sleep that liquor off. I swear, I don't know what's to become of him." She took the gun from Newt, lifted her long nightgown and strode swiftly across the yard to the house, shaking her head as she went.

Clint rolled over on his belly, groaned and broke wind. Prissy tittered. Newt doubled in laughter. Pete, serious and unsmiling, looked down at Clint. "Ain't got a cent of his money left. If he had to pay for takin' a crap, he'd be forced to vomit."

There was tittering and laughter again. Even Pete managed a smile this time. Then he pulled Clint up and dragged him across the yard and into the house.

CHAPTER ✦ 3

NEWT, scrubbed and in his Sunday best, bends forward, elbows resting on his legs, chin saddled between his thumb butts, hearing but not seeing the Reverend Lucius Broadnap racing back and forth across the pulpit dripping sweat, his frock coat flying, spiking his sermon with the text, "What is my life?"

And "Yes, Lord! Yes, Lord!" fervent and wailing, answer the deacons.

"What's my life? . . . the storm! *. . . What's my life? . . .* the storm, it came! *. . . What's my life? . . .* and it left me safe! *. . . What's my life? . . ."*

"Amen! Amen! Amen!"

"And it came whirlin' over the hills! *. . . What's my life? . . .* and it twisted through the valleys! *. . . oh, God, what's my life? . . .* and it tore up the towns and the prairies and the people! *. . . yes, what's my life? . . .* and it blowed its warnin' smack against the dance halls and the whiskey dens (Broadnap pushes the tempo) *. . . what, what, oh, what's my life? . . .* um-um-um (and Newt feels the rhythm of the congregation pushing along with the new tempo) . . . um-um-um . . . and it ripped up time! . . . it ripped up space! . . . it ripped up our daily life! *. . . oh, what's my life? . . ."*

"Yes! Yes! Yes! Preach on, brother! Preach on."

"Oh yes! *. . . what's my life? . . .* it warned us of our sinnin' . . . um-um-um . . . warned of all your wrongdoin' . . . your stayin' away from the church! *. . . what's my life?* (lashing now with tearful frenzy) . . . and it blowed hard against those short flapper skirts! *. . . what's my life? . . .* and the devil-red lipstick plasterin' the mouths of our young girls. . . ."

"Amen! Amen!" (Newt looks up slyly toward Prissy, who sits biting her painted lips.)

"... deliver us—deliver us—deliver us from this sinnin', troubled world! *. . . what's my life?* um-um-um *. . . oh, what's* *my life?* . . . oh, stretch-stretch-stretch the bridge over Jordan!"

Emotion strikes the congregation like lightning. Newt feels the floor boards creaking rhythmically beneath him.

"*. . . what's my life?* . . ."

"Have mercy! Have mercy! Have mercy!"

"Give us patience! . . . oh yes! . . . *what's my life?* . . . um-um-um . . . help us endure our enemies! . . . give us strength to stand against those who want to destroy us! . . . cleanse our hearts and our bodies! . . . bring home the wayward husbands and the wayward wives." (Berthine Collins geysers up screaming, falls to the floor, the back of her hand plapping against Newt's forehead. Buford Collins, who everybody knows has been sparking lately widowed Emmaline Johnson, catches his wife's action from the corner of his eye.) . . . "*Oh, what's my life—my life—my life?* . . . um-um-um . . . open their hearts to their mates and their little dear ones! . . . stop the sufferin', drinkin', cuttin' and fightin' . . . *oh, tell me—tell me—what's my life?*" (Berthine is flopping like a chicken. "Save us! Save us! Save us!" They are pinning her arms back. And Maggie Pullens rushes over with her stinking camphor bottle. Buford's looking straight ahead. His face and back soaking sweat.) . . . "*Oh, what's my life?* . . . um-um-um."

Now from all over the church the shouting comes. Carrie Wells screams, "Go home! Go home!"

Emmaline Johnson: "Oh, my child! Please help my child!"

Martha Thompson, running up and down the aisle, hollering, "Yes! Yes! Yes! Yes! Yes!"

Deacon Henry Fuller moans, "Oh, thanks—thanks—thanks —for your blessin'!"

"*What's my life?*"

Jenny Crawford, strutting up and down the aisle, hands slapping against her thighs, intoning, "Have mercy! Have mercy! Have mercy!"

"And the storm rushes on, still takin' souls and buildin's! . . . and still we sin! . . . still we sin! . . . *oh, what's my life? Oh, Lord, what's my life?* . . . um-um-um . . ." (Now there's stomping all over the place, but Newt stays bent forward, elbows on legs—chin on thumb butts, hoping Berthine won't slap his sore head again.) . . . "Every soul here oughta feel blessed for bein' here this day! . . . this holy day! . . . for not bein' one of those that perished!"

Cornella Wade shouts, "Oh yes, Lord! Oh thank you, Lord!"

"*What's my life?* . . . to do better in the light of this day!

... and to serve God and the church! ... um-um-um ... *what's my life?"*

Beatrice Jones yells, "Amen! Amen! Amen!"

"Now, my good children, look at me. Cast your eyes upon the servant of the Lord! Look at me." (Newt feels his mother's eyes upon him—and his shoulders lean back to the time-polished bench, his eyes are stubbornly toward the pulpit.)

Suddenly Broadnap hunches his shoulders, extends his long arms from his coat sleeves, points his index fingers at the congregation. His head, hawklike and fierce, juts forward. His eyes, burning under sweat-drenched brow, search the upturned, hypnotized faces. "Look at me and tell me, my dear children, *what's your life?* ... think about it in the bright of day and the black of night! ... *what's your life?* (his fingers recoil into his fists—his arms drop; the tempo breaks and calm begins to return; the choir is singing, "What a friend we have in Jesus") ... . Thank you, dear God who giveth us life through our Lord, Jesus Christ ... bless you, my children, and lest we forget His kindness to us during this awful tragedy—let us pray." (The congregation, spent and still moaning, bows in silent prayer. Newt slumps forward again and brings his mind to the fried chicken that always comes with the Sabbath.)

Reverend Broadnap raises his arms again, this time for sinners and confessioners. Several are going forward—Fred Jenkins, Clara Brown and Otis Moses. Now everybody's curiosity is up, because Lester Saunders (he's wearing them white spats) is raising his head for confession. "What can God do to make me understand myself?" he asks.

Broadnap, mopping his brow, looks down at him. "What's troublin' you, son?"

"I don't like women." The church is very still.

"You don't like women?"

"No, I don't like women."

"How long have you been like that, brother Saunders?"

"Ever since I was a man."

Broadnap's thumbing his Bible. "Don't worry or be ashamed, brother Saunders. God acts in many ways. It may be your conviction." Now he stops and reads from the Bible —from Romans, 14th Chapter, " 'One man hath faith to eat all things; but he that is weak eateth herbs. Let not him that eateth set at nought him that eateth not; and let not him that eateth not, judge him that eateth: for God hath received him. Who art thou that judgest the servant of another? To his own Lord he standeth or falleth.' "

43

Lester is looking the minister straight in the eye. He turns and looks at the congregation. His left eye is damp. Now he is walking very fast, switching-like, down the aisle. Sadness is on his face. He's pushing through the swinging doors at the rear of the church. They swish back and forth—and he is gone. It is still very quiet. Reverend Broadnap raises his arms above the others and begins to bless them into the church—and again the choir is singing, "What a friend we have in Jesus."

After an early dinner, Newt slipped out to the cow barn and changed into overalls. Knowing his mother's feelings about such a change on Sunday, he hid his other clothes under a bag of grain and, when no one was looking, ducked out the back way to meet the four other members of his gang. As he jogged along, he spotted them sprawled beneath a giant oak at the edge of Logan's Grove.

Besides Beansy Fuller there was Jappy Duncan, a lanky, light-skinned thirteen-year-old, nicknamed for his slanting eyes; Skunk McDowell, also thirteen, dark brown, wiry and blusterous, with a white patch in his hair that resembled the markings of the animal he was named for; and Earl Thompson, thirteen and a half, chestnut brown, stocky, slow-moving, sloe-eyed and sullen, rarely speaking unless he was spoken to first.

"Git the lead out, Winger!" Skunk hollered.

"Take it easy," Newt shot back. "What's your big hurry?"

"Got a probl'm," Beansy said.

"What's wrong?"

"Savage wants to go 'long with us. Think we ought'a take him?"

"How'd he know we was goin'?"

"Skunk here—"

"Don't go blamin' me for it, Fatso," Skunk warned Beansy.

" 'Tain't no use in gettin' all steamed up 'bout it," Jappy cut in. "Nothin' we can do to stop him, anyway."

"What you think, Earl?" Newt asked.

"Don't make me no dif'rence one way t'other," he grunted.

"Aw come on, let's stop by for him," Newt said. And slowly they got up and walked toward the shanty where Marcus Savage lived. The boys weaved through the junk yard off which Marcus' father made his meager living, and as they approached the door they heard the older Savage's voice raised in anger. "You goddam black son-of-a-bitch!" he boomed.

"One more word out'a you and I'll whale you to a inch'a death!"

Then Marcus. "You winehead! You too damned drunk to stand up, less lone fight!" There was a moment of tense silence, then a banging against the wall, scuffling, cursing, and finally the door flew open and Marcus tore through the opening, blood trickling from his nose. "You old bastard! I'll git ya! I'll git ya yet!" he screamed back, ignoring the boys.

Big Booker staggered to the door. He was in his long drawers and held an iron skillet. He aimed and threw, but Marcus ducked it and ran. "Come on!" he yelled to the gang, "let's git the hell out'a here. The old bastard's goin' crazy."

They all moved quickly out of the yard behind him, and without saying anything to each other started toward Jake Kiner's, whose peach orchard they planned to raid.

Marcus Savage was black and tough. Not yet fifteen and motherless since birth, he lived with a father who spent most of his time drinking up what little money his junk gathering brought in. The ruggedness of a tough life added two years to his body, but his intellect barely matched that of any of the younger boys he now walked with. Yet, he was smart in the way that the desperate must be to survive, cunning in the way that the poor must be to cheat their misfortunes. The gang did not like him but tolerated him, and he felt big in their world—a small world that respected his strength an' demanded little of his brain.

They were nearing the orchard now, moving stealthily, watching for any sign of life around the Kiner house or barns. Then they were under the barbed-wire fence and into the peach orchard, snatching the fruit from the trees, filling their stomachs and pockets at the same time, unaware of Jake's figure creeping alongside the corral shed, dragging a long buggy whip behind him.

He crept, anger in check, biding his time, making surer his chance to lash one, or maybe more, of the culprits who were stealing his prize fruit. They would get away fast, he knew —so surprise and the whip would have to cut the difference between their youthful speed and his feeble jog. Jake pulled his wide-brimmed hat tight to his wrinkled forehead, kicked off his high-heeled boots and tiptoed the last two yards to the clearing.

Newt was the first to see the raging, whip-waving farmer bearing down on them.

"Run! Run! Run!" he hollered. "It's Jake!"

Beansy, a peach in his mouth and his pockets loaded, shimmied off to a fast start. Skunk tripped over Jappy, who had been munching contentedly on the ground, and they both scrambled to their feet, losing half the juicy loot in their getaway. In a few seconds Newt was outdistancing Beansy; and glancing back, he and Earl saw the whip lash Marcus Savage's waist.

"Ouch!" Marcus yelped. "Ouch!" Peaches flew from his arms in all directions as he desperately tried to evade Jake's cutting whip.

"Thievin' dogs!" Jake half grunted, half hollered as he struck again, causing Marcus to stumble to the ground.

"Stop it! Stop it!" Marcus yelled, but Jake kept thrashing him. The others, at a safe distance now, turned in time to see Marcus grab Jake by the heel and spin him to the ground. Then Marcus was on top of him, beating him about the face with the whip handle, and above him kicking him in the face and on the head until Jake lay still on the ground. At last Marcus threw the whip on Jake's prostrate form, filled his pockets with peaches and trotted toward the others. As they started toward Flynn's River, Beansy's scared voice stopped them cold. "Aw-aw, there comes his wife."

"You little heathens! You little heathens!" she screamed, shaking her fist in the air. "We'll git you for this! We'll git you!" Then she knelt over her husband and began shaking him.

No one ate any more of the stolen fruit except Marcus as the six boys made their way toward Flynn's River. And as he chomped viciously, his powerful black muscles flexed a warning to his companions: be with me if trouble comes, or suffer the consequences.

He broke his silence. "The old bastard pushed his damn luck too far. I tried to kill him. Goddam near beat his brains out with his own whip."

"What you think they gonna do?" Beansy asked.

"I don't know," Marcus growled, "and I don't give a shit. All of you saw him beatin' on me with that whip first." Nobody spoke, and this rankled Marcus. He stopped, his hands on his hips, red eyes burning like pools of fire in the blackness of his face. "Well! What about it? You did, didn't you?"

"Yeh"—"Uh huh"—"Shore"—"You're right, Marcus"— "Yeh—yeh," they chorused.

"Well, Winger, what about you? You with me or not?"

Newt sensed trouble and he didn't want it. "Yeh, I saw him hit you with the whip." He wanted to say more, and Marcus wasn't exactly satisfied with the tone of his answer.

"Well, anything else? Let's git everything straight now." He glowered at Newt.

"I said all I had to say—only—only I don't think you ought'a of beat that old man the way you did after you got him down, that's all."

"Well now, fellas, ain't that some fine bullshit for ya. He's feelin' sorry for that poor old peckerwood who was beatin' the hell out'a me, one of his own gang."

"We was stealin' from him. Don't forget that, Marcus."

Marcus' voice was foreboding as his mood. "So you gonna stick up for poor white trash. Hear that, fellas? Winger's gonna stick up for a peckerwood who beat up one of his own gang."

Newt bristled, partly from fear, partly from anger. He couldn't whip Marcus and he knew it. And he wasn't quite sure yet where the rest of the gang's sympathy lay. He chose his next words carefully. "I ain't stickin' up for poor white trash, like you say I am. All you fellas know old man Kiner ain't so bad. Jappy's paw works for him and so does Skunk's paw, sometimes. And he give us a whole barrel of cornmeal last winter when—"

Marcus clenched his fist. "I don't give a damn what he gave you last winter or nothin' else." (Newt felt Skunk and Jappy at his side. He knew he could count on Beansy.) "All I want to know is—you with us or not?" (Beansy moved in next to Newt, and Earl, getting the drift of things, halfheartedly followed.) "And I want to know it right now," Marcus went on.

"I'm always with the fellas—here," Newt answered, meeting Marcus' glare straight on, the word "here" spelling out his sudden support.

Marcus' eyes skimmed the opposition. "Okay. Okay. Let's all stick together," he snarled. "Let's stick together."

Newt had won, temporarily at least, and Marcus knew it —but he wasn't forgetting it.

During the next two hours, the slow-moving river cooled their naked bodies, and the impassioned tempers gradually drifted away with the gentle current. Meanwhile, they performed their specialties. Beansy comically portrayed a whale, floating head down in the water, his fat bottom protruding above the water, his feet close together and moving like a fish tail. At short intervals his chunky head popped up and he arched a stream of water from the wide space between his two front teeth, much to the delight of the others. Then Earl and Skunk sank out of sight together. Earl's feet went on Skunk's shoulders and the two shot upward. Near the surface, Earl catapulted from Skunk's shoulders and leaped out of the water like a flying fish. Jappy, swinging out high over the river on a rope knotted to an oak, let go and double-somersaulted, then executed a perfect swan dive, into the water.

Marcus climbed to the top of Rock Ledge and, to the envy of all, sprang his mighty body into space, barely missing the jagged lip below, and spiraled beautifully into the river. Then, adding to the drama, he stayed beneath the water, emerging far downstream. Newt, encouraged by the rest, portrayed a submarine—swimming submerged on his back, a string tied to his pecker, which he sometimes managed to stiffen and pull taut like a periscope skimming the water. When his pecker didn't stand, he substituted his arm, his hand curled into an eye that turned on his wrist, scanning the waterbanks for enemy ships.

When Newt went to dress, his overalls, shirt and socks were expertly tightened into one wet knot. Then he understood, quite clearly, why Marcus had departed earlier than the rest.

Between the river and home, talk went back to Jake Kiner and the beating Marcus had given him. Earl ventured a startling question. "S'pose he dies?"

"Dies?" Beansy squealed.

"You kiddin'?" Skunk grunted, his face screwed into fright at the thought.

Earl hadn't given much thought to the question when he asked it, but now he realized such a possibility and he began justifying it. "He's real old, ain't he? . . . and Marcus beat the hell out'a him, kicked him in the head and everything."

"Well, that's Marcus' tail, not ours," Jappy countered.

"Yeah," Newt said, "but don't forget, we was all stealin'. They'll blame all of us if anything happens to him."

"We'd be crazy to git in a mess over somethin' Marcus did. We all gotta stick together, fellas." Beansy had begun to mop the sweat.

"We just gotta tell it just like it happened, that's all. (Newt was fishing for a response.) Tell it just like—just like it happened." Newt repeated the last sentence as if it were foreign to him, as if he'd never intended saying it. "We just gotta tell the truth, no matter what happens."

48

And since the truth, in this particular instance, favored their position, they all agreed to tell the truth—knowing within their hearts (but not daring to say it) that no one would really suffer from it but Marcus Savage. They would defend him as far and as long as they could (even to saying old Jake was beating Marcus awfully bad), but after that Marcus would have to be on his own.

They split up at Logan's Grove. Newt slipped into the cowshed by the back way and changed again to his Sunday clothes. When he started toward the house, the sight of the dusty motorcycle leaning against the porch made his heart jump. His mind started racing—Kirky was looking for him. He wondered if he should go in now, or go feed the hogs like nothing had happened. And he backtracked in the direction of the barn.

"Newt." It was Prissy, speaking in a hushed voice from the kitchen window above him. "Boy, are you gonna git it! What you nuts doin' stealin' peaches and beatin' up old man Kiner? Boy, you shore gonna git it. Momma's mad as a wet hen."

"Kirky in there talkin' to her?" Newt whispered.

"Yeh, and he's lookin' for you and Marcus and the rest of them nuts. You better git in here, boy."

"Is that Newt, Prissy?" Newt's heart sank at the sting of his mother's voice. "Tell him I said to git in here, quick!"

Newt was in the room before she could call out again. He stood close to the door, his right toe stabbing the carpet, hands entwined behind him, gazing at the floor.

"Look up, boy!" Newt's eyes shot up at the heated command. "Now, I want you to tell me exactly what happened, every bit of it." She had been cleaning when Kirky had entered, and still clutched a feather duster in her hand. "Come on, boy. Out with it."

Newt avoided looking at Kirky, but his mind's eye saw the smirk on his red craggy face, the tobacco juice caked at the corners of his thin lips, the dirty khaki puttee-type pants and leather leggings strapped about the fat legs, spread now with vulgar authority; the crusty Western hat (off his balding head at Sarah's request) and his big, sweat-smelly torso, draped with two-gun Western holsters, each stuffed with an ugly forty-five revolver.

"We just stole the peaches and run, that's all."

"After you beat ole Jake Kiner damn near to death?" Kirky cut in, tobacco juice gurgling his question.

"You watch your tongue in this house, Kirky. We don't use cuss words here!" Sarah admonished.

Newt watched Kirky's lips curl apart, exposing his yellow-brown teeth. "Jake's layin' up in County Hospital, beat to a pulp. I'm just tryin' to git to the bottom of this mess." His voice lowered in a tinge of apology.

"Well, there's a respectable way in goin' about it," Sarah countered. "Now, Newt, tell me. Did you hit Mister Kiner? I want the truth and nothin' but."

"No, ma'am. I swear on the Bible I didn't touch him."

"Well, who did, boy?" Kirky shouted. "Who did?"

Newt was quiet for a moment, reconstructing the facts, weighing the gang's promises against Marcus' threats. "He was beatin' Marcus awful bad with a buggy whip, and he wouldn't stop. He just kept on beatin' him."

"Well, what you sayin' is that Marcus Savage did it. That right, boy?" Kirky urged. Newt looked toward his mother.

"Tell me, son. Was it Marcus?" Sarah's eyes held Newt's, searching them for the real truth.

"Yessem. It was Marcus—but—he was tryin' to keep Mister Kiner from hurtin' him."

Kirky was moving toward the door. "You shore none of the others touched him."

"Yes. I'm shore."

"Who was the others who was stealin' with you?" Kirky bit from a grimy plug of tobacco.

"It was me and Beansy Fuller and Earl Thompson and Skunk McDowell and Jappy Duncan and Marcus."

"Where's all of 'em now?" Kirky was putting on his hat, but by now he was in the doorway.

"Everybody's gone home, I guess."

"Your story betta check with the others', boy, or I'm comin' back for you." Kirky slammed the screen door and went out. He turned just before he mounted his cycle. "The whites round here ain't gonna like what happened to old Jake very much."

Sarah Winger's reply was fast and free of emotion. "We don't expect no trouble, but we can take care of ourselves if it comes."

Kirky grunted, kicked his motor to a start and roared off.

Sarah looked at her son. "Boy," she said, "don't you know it's a sin to steal, 'specially on Sunday?"

"Yessem."

"You gonna git it now, Newt," Prissy warned a moment later. And he knew she was right, for Sarah Winger was already out gathering switches from a small, sturdy elm tree.

"I've knowed them kids all their lives," Jake muttered to Kirky through puffed lips, "so it ain't the derned fruit I'm so mad about. It's that onery Savage boy. He's got bad blood—a born killer—ought'a be put away 'fore he murders somebody."

"I aim to do just that, if Judge Cavanaugh'll sign the necessary papers."

"Where's he now?"

"Locked up over at the jail. Feelin's runnin' kinda high 'mong the whites 'bout his beatin' up on you, Jake." Kirky snorted into a dingy blue handkerchief. "Like you say, the black bastard's born to trouble—broke into Sam Comstock's store last winter—slugged a usher that caught him sneakin' in the picture show the other night—tried to knife Doug Simpson for accident'ly bumpin' him on the street a couple months ago. Yeh, he's a nasty nigga all right. I'll put a slug through his ass one of these days. Wait'n see."

"Ain't he got no parents?"

"If you wanta call that likker-head paw of his such, he has. Ain't never had a maw that I know about."

Jake patted his swollen eye. "Well, no sense in race trouble over the likes of him. He's misery to the colored folks round here too. He's too young for Leavenworth, but there's reform schools that can take him, and—"

"Jake." Doc Cravens ambled through the door. "Got some visitors for you."

Jake's eyes rolled toward the door. "Send 'em in, Doc. Send 'em in."

Doc Cravens motioned in Newt, carrying a pie, warm from his mother's oven; Skunk, Jappy, Beansy (holding a bunch of flowers), Earl and Sarah Winger. The boys stood in awkward silence, petrified in their embarrassment.

"Go ahead, boy." Sarah pinched Newt into action and he thrust the pie forward like a robot.

"Well, what's this?" Jake raised on his elbows for a closer look.

(Another pinch.) Newt began mumbling the planned speech. "We're all here to say how sorry we are 'bout what happened—and—and—and that it won't happen again—" (Another pinch.) "And Momma made this for you—to eat." He put the pie on the old man's night table, and Beansy laid the flowers on the side of his bed.

After a jittery moment, Jake's sour face cracked into a

51

grin. "If them ain't my peaches in that pie, Sarah, I ain't eatin' it."

Relief swept through the five boys, and Sarah's smile answered Jake's. "Only two in there's yours, Jake. The rest are off the Winger tree, and that's why that pie's gonna taste so good."

"Thank you, Sarah. Thank you lots." Jake's shoulders fell wearily back to the bed. Then, sliding the wire-rimmed spectacles to the end of his bony nose, he peered seriously at the uneasy line of boys. His manner milked shame from each one's heart. "I'm forgivin' you on one condition. The five of you are comin' to help me, for nothin', come peach-pickin' time, and if I catch one of you chawin' my fruit, I'll skin you alive. Hear me?"

"Yessir—yessir—yessir—yessir—yessir."

"You heard that, Sarah." Jake kept his glare on the boys.

"They'll be there, Jake, if I have to pull all of them over by their dirty ears."

After that, Sarah and Newt went to visit Jack in the adjoining ward.

The next day, Kirky got Judge Cavanaugh to sign the "necessary papers" without too much trouble—the hearing lasting hardly thirty minutes. "You're a blight on your race and on society," the Judge scolded Marcus, his white mane trembling over his angry face. He signed the document that would rid Cherokee Flats of Marcus for at least a year.

"What's blight mean, Judge?" Marcus' query rumbled with violent sarcasm.

The skin around Judge Cavanaugh's knuckles tightened as his fist clenched, and he rose above Marcus like a mountain. "I'll tell you what it means, it means you are a disgrace to your people and to our town. And it also means that you're going to rot in Spit's Reformatory unless you rid yourself of the evil that's inside your onery hide."

Marcus smiled an ugly smile. "I ain't got no people and I ain't rottin' no place but in my grave, Judge. And by that time you gonna be long gone."

"Get him out of here, Kirky, before I lose my temper."

Kirky welcomed the order and, grasping his prisoner by the scruff of his neck, applied brute force to his removal from the Judge's chambers. At the cell door he gave Marcus a resounding kick in the behind. Then Kirky slammed the cell door and twisted the key.

Marcus turned and grinned evilly. "One'a these days it's

gonna be just you and me, you dirty, hairy peckerwood. You remember that!"

"I'm shore gonna remember that, boy. I'm shore gonna remember. I'm gonna remember that every day and every night you're in that hole where they're takin' you tomorra. And if you is ever unlucky enough to git out and come back here, I'll be waitin' and rememberin'. Don't you forgit. I'll be rememberin'!" Their eyes burned toward each other for a moment, then Kirky spat on the floor and stomped away.

Sarah Winger made a plea for Marcus while serving the Judge's breakfast the next morning, but to no avail. "The boy's dangerous, Sarah," he argued, wiping oatmeal from his lips, "and he'll be better off over at Spit's where he can learn some discipline." The manner in which he discarded his napkin and rose from the table convinced Sarah of the futility in pleading further.

During the evening of that same day, she had Pete harness a horse to the Winger buggy and the two of them with Newt drove to the hospital to pick up Jack Winger.

Dr. Cravens walked him to the waiting room. Pete and Newt, seeing that their father moved slowly and stiffly, went to assist him. After Jack was comfortably seated, Doc Cravens stepped back and spoke. "Well, Sarah—there he is. Be as good as new in a few weeks."

Sarah didn't answer. She just smiled.

"Okay, Doc," Jack said.

"Okay, Jack."

The reins slapped the horse's rump, and they drove off.

It was Saturday, a week later. Newt, Jappy and Beansy were down on the bank of the swimming hole, but they could hear the crap shooters up the hill behind them.

"That's Clint's voice, ain't it?" Beansy said.

"Sounds like him, all right." Newt knew it was Clint's voice.

"Your roll, Cheney."

"Seven—"

"Seven 'tis—keep rollin'."

"Seven baby—eight—eight's the point. Two I eight."

"It's a bet—got you covered. You takin', Sputter?"

"Two says you don't eight—you covered."

"Roll 'em."

"Eight baby—eight for ole Doc—eight honey, eight—for Doc. Goddam—seven!"

"Your roll, Silas."

"Seven come 'leven. Hit for Silas, baby—hit for ole Silas—'Leven!"

"I owe you five, Silas—roll."

"Six—not five, Clint. I ain't drunk as you think."

"Okay—six it is—roll."

Down below, Beansy grabbed Newt's shoulder. "Look. It's Kirky. He's sneakin' up on 'em from behind."

"Got his guns out," Jappy whispered.

Newt scooted back out of sight. "I'm gonna try'n warn 'em." He began crawling up through the brush on his knees.

"Careful, Newt. Watch out," Beansy cautioned, "he's liable to start shootin'."

Newt was near the crest of the hill now. "Clint—Clint," he said in a hushed voice, "Clint—look out, Kirky's comin'."

"What? That you, Newt?"

"Yeh. Run—run—it's Kirky."

Clint grabbed up his money. "It's Kirky," he warned the others. The men took off in all directions.

"Halt! Halt! Halt! or I'll shoot!" Kirky's warning came from behind a thicket.

Newt could hear the brush cracking all around him. Then someone hurtled right over his head. He looked back. It was old Doc Cheney, headed for the river.

"Halt! Goddam you—halt!"

Doc scrambled by Beansy and Jappy, drove into the water and started swimming downstream. Kirky ran out into the clearing. He fired a warning shot over Doc's head. Doc ducked under the water.

Beansy and Jappy huddled together in fright, watching Kirky take dead aim at the spot where Doc went under. He fired once—twice—a third time. Then he ran down the side of the river bank, puffing and sweating, watching for Doc to surface. Suddenly there was a big bubble, then some small ones. Doc bobbed up to the surface for a second or two. He wasn't swimming now—just floating.

"He hit?" Newt asked, coming alongside Beansy and Jappy.

"Yeh—shore is."

"He got him."

Doc sank under again, and Kirky stood looking. Doc bobbled up once more for a second, then he was gone for good.

"Damn," Newt said.

"He didn't git a chance." Jappy stood with his mouth open, his naked body trembling with fear.

"Poor ole Doc," Beansy moaned, "poor ole Doc."

Kirky holstered his guns and strode back up the incline to where the boys were. They looked away from him to the water where Doc had gone down. Kirky coughed. They kept their eyes on the water, still stunned.

"Well," Kirky said, "now you kin see what happens to crim'nals—'specially ones who don't halt when they're told to halt!"

The boys didn't answer. They just kept looking at the water.

"Shit," Kirky snarled. Then he scrambled back to the top of the hill and disappeared.

"What's gonna happen to Doc?" Beansy asked.

"Kirky's prob'ly gone to get the firemen," Newt said. "They'll have to drag for him."

"You gonna wait around?" Jappy said.

"Maybe we can keep a eye on the spot where he went down," Newt opined. "He's prob'ly trapped this side of the shallows there."

The firemen came back with Kirky and they dragged the bottom of the river from a rowboat for two hours without any luck. A small group of white people had gathered now, and they sat about the banks talking and laughing. The firemen rowed to shore and Kirky went down to talk to them.

Newt, Beansy and Jappy sensed they were the subjects of the conversation. "Prob'ly gonna ask us to dive for Doc," Newt said.

"How much'd he pay Skunk and Earl for haulin' up the guy that killed hisself that time, Newt?" Beansy questioned.

"A lousy quarter. That's all. And they dove a long time 'fore they snagged him."

"Here he comes," Jappy whispered.

Newt was right.

"You fellas want'a make two bits apiece?" Kirky grunted.

"Doin' what?" Newt asked.

"Divin' for Doc like your pals did for Mack Turner."

"Not for no lousy two bits," Newt said coolly.

"Okay, I'll give each of you ten cents extra."

"Nope."

"Well, what you want for doin' it? It's gettin' late."

"We won't do it for no less'n seventy-five cents apiece," Newt said.

"You gettin' real smart, ain't you, Winger? Could run you in for swimmin' naked out here, you know." Kirky was fumbling in his pockets to see if he had the price. He counted

55

for a few seconds. "Okay, you win. Go ahead." He turned to the firemen. "Okay, take 'em out. They'll do it."

Newt was scared. He hadn't thought Kirky would pay that much, and now he was stuck; but he couldn't back out now and save face.

The three boys got into the boat, and the firemen rowed them to a spot about three feet short of the shallows. They jumped into the river one at a time and splashed about for a minute or two. Then the firemen handed each one of them a grappling hook and they sank beneath the water together.

Newt lost sight of the others after he was about six feet down, but he kept pushing closer and closer to the wall of the shallows, thinking Doc might be caught there. He swam slowly, not knowing what he would do if he should see the body. His air gave out and he shot back to the top. Beansy was already up, and Jappy bobbed up right after Newt.

"See anything?" one of the firemen asked.

"Naw," Newt answered. Beansy and Jappy shook their heads. They hooked to the side of the boat for a few minutes and rested.

"Okay—try again!" Kirky hollered from the bank.

They waited another moment or two, then sank out of sight. Newt went straight down this time, and Jappy stayed beside him. They swam around together for a minute or two, then Newt felt Jappy's fingers in his side. Jappy was pointing. It was Doc, floating just off the bottom. Newt jerked his head upward and they swam to the top.

"He's right under the boat!" they called to the firemen.

"Which end?"

"Back end," Newt said, wiping the water from his eyes. Beansy popped up and Newt motioned him to the boat. "We found him," he said nervously.

"You see what he had on?" the fireman asked.

"Overalls."

"Good. That makes it easy. Now listen. I'm gonna push this pole down with these hooks on the bottom of it. You fellas get your hooks in his overalls and float him up over the end of mine. When I feel his weight on it I'll haul him up. Okay?"

They all nodded.

Doc was floating face down when they reached him. Then all together they hooked his overalls and started pulling him up toward the pole. Their air was giving out, but they wanted to get it over with. Jappy motioned and they floated

Doc the last few feet to the pole and placed the hooks under his overall suspenders. Then they quickly swam away.

Newt got a good look at Doc as the pole drew him up through the murkiness. The skin on his face, like bubbly clay, strained against the current. His eyelids, pushed back by the same pressure, left the dead white balls staring blankly in the slow-moving water. The arms and legs, limp as a rag doll's, swayed grotesquely—as if in a ballet of death. The corpse began a twisting motion, as though it were coming to life. A spasm of fear shook Newt and he knifed to the top. He sidestroked over to Jappy and Beansy, and the three of them bobbed about in the water until the head broke the surface.

"Okay! We got him!" a fireman shouted.

Their job done, the three boys started swimming toward shore. They climbed up the bank, collected their money from Kirky and dressed.

They didn't wait for the death wagon. They'd seen enough.

Newt had bad dreams all that night. He kept seeing the wet corpse of Doc Cheney floating all around the room. Fearfully he got up, went into the dining room and lit a lamp. About four o'clock Sarah awoke and saw the light. She too got up and went into the room.

"Why ain't you in bed asleep, son? What you doin' sittin' up here this time of the night?"

Newt sat shaking. "I'm—I'm scared of death, Momma."

She went to him and put her arms about his shoulders. "Why I never heard of such. A big boy like you sayin' he's scared." She was trying to kid him out of it.

"Cain't help it, Momma. I'm just scared of death."

"You have a bad dream?"

"Yessem."

"Bad dreams ain't never real," Sarah said.

"But this one already happened 'fore I dreamed it." Newt was shaking more than ever now.

"Your dream was 'bout death?"

"Yessem."

"Whose death?"

"Doc Cheney's."

Sarah stood for a while, thinking. Then she said, "Death's a long way off from you, son. Doc Cheney's gone. He cain't bother you. His soul's in peace—somewhere."

"But I keep seein' him. He keeps turnin' over and over in my dreams."

"But Doc liked you, always said you was such a nice boy. He wouldn't want to hurt you—even in death."

Newt got up. "Just a minute, Momma."

"Where you goin', boy?"

"I'll be right back."

"All right, son."

Newt went into his bedroom and fished the seventy-five cents from his overall pocket. Then, trancelike, he drifted past his mother and opened the door. After pressing the three quarters firmly together in his hand, he flung them far out into the darkness.

"What was that?" Sarah asked.

"Nothin', Momma, nothin'." He shut the door. "Maybe I can sleep now."

Sarah didn't question him further. She walked with him back to his bed, tucked him in and sat there beside him until he was fast asleep.

CHAPTER ❦ 4

AT FLYNN'S BALLPARK, Newt and his buddies sprawled on the hot bleacher seats, awaiting the first pitch of the game between the Fort Miles Hawkeyes and the Chanute Cornhuskers. One greasy box of popcorn disappeared rapidly among them. The total of the gang's purse (four nickels and five pennies) jangled in Beansy's left hand. This amount had been all they could rake up for a "peep fee" to Captain Tuck, a beefy, fortyish, razor-scarred, dark bully who scouted, for pay, beneath the grandstands for indelicate views of lady fans with wide skirts and no underpants. ("...u.p. looks, five cents—b.b. looks, ten cents. Take it or leave it," Tuck's husky voice whispered to his young male clientele.)

The gang had already voted on two b.b.'s (bare bottom) and one u.p. (underpants), which would absorb the purse; and since this arrangement eliminated two of them from any look whatsoever, a lottery, performed with concealed sticks, decided the winners. Earl and Beansy got the b.b.'s and Jappy won the u.p., leaving Skunk and Newt to the ordinary fate of just watching a ballgame.

During the bottom half of the third inning Sputter Duncan, a good hitter, was up, and two Hawkeyes were on base when Tuck came over and nudged Jappy. "One u.p., third row back, five people over—five cents."

"Hold it, Cap'n Tuck. Sputter's up," Jappy pleaded.

"Come on, right now. Cain't wait. Now's the time, while everybody's excited. They close up when things git quiet." Having no choice, Jappy ducked under the stands just as Sputter smacked a base hit, and the crowd roared.

Now Charlie Johnson was at bat with the bases loaded. At such a moment, Tuck motioned for Earl and Beansy; and, torn between both attractions, they noted Tuck's directions after ducking quickly under the grandstand. "A whoppin' b.b., four rows back, nine people over—twenty cents."

"Stee-rike one!" Beansy whirled to scan the field.

59

"Hurry up, boy. I ain't got all day," Tuck urged. "I got other customers 'sides you."

"Ball one!" (He's right, Beansy. Look, it's a whopper.)

"Stee-rike two!" (Man, she's got more fuzz'n a bear.)

Wham! "It's a homer! It's a homer!" someone yelled. And the b.b. jumped to her feet in the excitement, shutting out the view.

"Wouldn't you know it," Beansy pouted, "she's sittin' back down in a no-good position. Looks like we just gotta wait awhile." And they sat down and waited. Almost ten minutes passed before they got their full money's worth.

The game went two extra innings, giving Tuck an unusually good day, and afterward, as he walked across town to Chappie Logan's, jingling the take in his pockets, the boys followed—listening to Tuck's accounts of his adventures in things dearest to him: drinking, fighting and sex.

"See that!" He knotted his beefy fist. "I kin lick any bastard in the Flats with one hand tied!"

Beansy egged him on. "Where'd you git that long scar on your face, Tuck?"

"Son-of-a-bitch knifed me when I wasn't lookin', but you ought'a seen him when I got through. You'd a thought he'd been through a meat grinder."

Earl fed the next question. "Done any big screwin' lately, Tuck?"

"Haw—haw—haw!" Tuck threw back his thick head and laughed. "I got exactly four hens waitin' for me right now at Chappie's. Four of 'em. What'a you think of that?" He patted his bulging fly. "And you know what? They'll all go home satisfied. And what'a you think of that?"

"You're a helluva man, Tuck," Skunk ventured. "How much'd you make today?

"Damn near five bucks. And what'a you think of that?"

A quarter mile further on, Tuck patted his groin again. "'Member what I said. They're all gonna go home satisfied! Haw—haw—haw!" he roared, bumping open Chappie's door with his massive shoulder. The boys watched as he disappeared into the smoke and noise.

"Boy, Tuck leads a helluva life," Skunk quipped admiringly as they walked away.

"Shore does," Beansy agreed.

"If you ask me," Jappy said, "I'd say he's lucky to be livin', with all the scrapes he's been in."

"Poppa says he's got a charmed life," Newt added.

"He keeps bullyin' round like he does and that charmed stuff ain't gonna do him no good," Earl put in dryly.

Unless Big Mabel could be counted as four, then Tuck's story was untrue, for only she awaited his arrival at Chappie's. By ten o'clock, three of Tuck's five dollars had gone for two bottles of corn, and it was past midnight when they staggered out, arm in arm, and went up the road in the darkness.

They had gotten across the tracks and in front of Silas Newhall's house, where Tuck spotted Chauncey Cavanaugh's Maxwell roadster, idling and empty, at the curb.

"Wait a minit," he burped, rocking back and forth, his red eyes searching the blackness for the car's owner.

"Come on, baby." He pushed Big Mabel into the seat. "Let's you and me go for a little spin." Big Mabel grunted a mild protest, but Tuck shoved her over and slammed the door. Then he squeezed under the wheel and they started off.

Chauncey was slipping out the Newhall side door when he spotted his car rounding the corner. "Stop! Stop!" he hollered. But Tuck just grunted a laugh, jerked back the gas and spark levers—and the Maxwell roared off in a cloud of dust toward Flynn's River.

Chauncey started to holler again, but a light popped on in old Silas Newhall's window. So instead he sprinted the four blocks to the jailhouse and told Kirky what had happened.

"Who was it—what way'd they go?"

"Down the river road! It was too dark to see who it was."

"Come on. Prob'ly a likkered-up nigga. Let's git goin'."

A few seconds later they roared off on Kirky's motorcycle with Chauncey, his coattail straight in the wind, on back clinging to Kirky's Sam Browne belt.

Tuck was just slowing down for the "lover's lane" turn-off when the siren wailed in the distance behind him; and through the rear-view mirror he caught sight of the single headlamp bobbing in the darkness. "Goddam Kirky's chasin' us," he mumbled, nudging Big Mabel to life. "I'm gonna give him the run of his life. Now what'a you think of that?" He began coaxing the motor toward full speed.

"You better stop, Tuck. You just askin' for trouble."

But the dust was already blotting out the single light behind them, and Big Mabel began to sober as the trees from both sides of the road whirred in upon their light and whipped past into the blackness. The siren was closer now and Tuck's face, thrust out above the steering wheel like a gargoyle's, grinned in disdainful joy. "Come on, you son-of-a-bitch! Come on! Let's see how much you can do! Come (a shot rang out, and a crack marked the windshield just above Tuck's head) bastard's shootin' (another shot rang out) git low, way down—"

"Stop, Tuck! Stop! I don't want'a git hurt!" Big Mabel tugged at his arm.

"Just keep down! Keep down—you ain't gonna git (another shot, right behind them now) bastard's gainin' on me—this thing's wide open!"

"Stop, Tuck! Stop! Stop! (again the shot, and this time Tuck's head dropped onto the steering wheel) Help—hel—" Big Mabel felt the car twisting, sliding, hitting, spinning, then somersaulting, and suddenly she was flying free—only to sense, for a split second, the crushing jolt before unconsciousness and quick, merciful death.

Tuck's body, trapped within the hurtling machine, stayed on for the final, brutal crash against a tree, then it settled, from its own dead weight, to the floor of the crumpled wreck.

A peculiar sensation tugged at Newt's innards from the moment he heard of the deaths of Big Mabel and Tuck. It seemed impossible, but everybody was talking about it so it had to be so. He remembered how hot and firm Big Mabel's body had been when he lay against it during the storm. Now that she was broken up (as they were saying), memory of this moment was brought back with frightening clarity. He wondered why he hadn't tried for her again, and regretted not having done so. That evening, his twelve-year-old curiosity impelled him, with Beansy as a companion, to within a few steps of Mottsy's Funeral Parlor—where the bodies of Big Mabel and Captain Tuck lay.

Chris and Orville Mottsy stood talking at the body-receiving door, eying the boys as they approached. "Let's have some fun with those little nigger kids," Chris said in an undertone. Orville grinned at the prospect.

Chris was the first to speak. "Hi there, you-all. Want'a see Captain Tuck and Big Mabel?"

Newt and Beansy stopped dead in their tracks, Beansy a foot or two behind Newt. "Naw," Newt said, "we don't want 'you-all' to show us nothin'."

"Aw, come on. Don't git mad, boy. Captain Tuck'd be awful sore if you didn't pay him proper respects." Chris was inching closer to them as he spoke, but Beansy had already begun backtracking.

"Come on, Newt!" Beansy had sensed the trap and was already running; but Newt was pounced upon before he could follow, and the two pranksters carried him, screaming and kicking, through the entrance.

"Let go! Let go! I don't want'a see Tuck," he wailed.

"Aw, come on. Quit cuttin' up. Cap'n Tuck's gonna be so glad to see you, boy," Orville quipped.

"No! No! No!" Newt pleaded. But the door to the embalming room was being opened now. And quickly they shoved him into the smelly darkness, snapping the door shut behind him. Newt recoiled and scrambled back to the door, pounding, screaming, "Please! Please! Oh, please let me out!"

Chris pushed the light switch, and there before Newt was the naked, bruised gray-black corpse of Captain Tuck on a white slab, lit overhead by a bare fluid-smeared bulb. One eye stared at Newt with a baleful glare. And to his right lay Big Mabel, completely covered with a white sheet, her breasts raising the cloth tentlike above the rest of her broken body. Newt tried to yell out, but cold terror silenced his effort. Things began to swirl and he sank slowly to the floor, hysterically exhausted—and unconscious from an agonizing fear.

The sudden quiet on the other side of the door brought an uneasiness to the Mottsys, and their laughter gave way to apprehensive frowns. Orville opened the door and Newt, having fallen against it in his faint, rolled halfway through the opening.

Chris splashed three cups of cold water in Newt's face before his eyes opened and began focusing on the blurred figures above him. Suddenly reality came to him again and he screamed, "No! No! No!" Then, crawling from beneath his tormentors, he got to his feet and backed through the door. The air helped clear his thinking, slowly gave back his strength. He began running and didn't stop until he was all the way home.

Two days later, the Cherokee *Tribune* carried an item— only five lines long and almost undetectable on the back page—which read: "Chris and Orville Mottsy of Cherokee Flats were attacked and badly beaten last night by another local man, Pete Winger. The latter was given a brief hearing before Judge Cavanaugh but was released when the elder Mottsy, upon advice of his attorney, withdrew all charges."

CHAPTER ❦ 5

IN AUGUST, Newt began riding the Kiner land with Pete—
whom Jake had hired as a temporary foreman; and, to Pete's
satisfaction, Newt went about learning to mount his father's
quarter horse on the run, to ride with his head up and his
heels down, to swerve his mount easily in and out of a moving herd.

On Saturdays he peddled brooms with Rob Winger, his
blind uncle. During this time he came to marvel at all the
philosophies Rob imparted to him on their trips about the
village. His uncle talked to him of all the things his father
neglected to talk about. It was almost as if Rob, knowing his
brother Jack's shortcomings, tried in some way to make up
for them. And Newt, already perceptive enough to realize
this, looked with regret upon the September morning when
they would make their last walk of the year around Cherokee
Flats, selling a broom now and then, discussing the ways of
man and the universe.

A chill had come to the air and Rob, a sufferer of rheuma-
tism, decided the walks were becoming more harmful than
good. Furthermore, school was starting soon, and he felt that
Newt should spend his weekends preparing himself, especially
since he'd be entering the white high school in another year.

Crossing the Frisco tracks that morning, on his way to
meet Rob, Newt saw his uncle, brooms over his shoulder,
tapping the ground with his cane and approaching the crossing. Newt broke into a trot, trying to reach him before he
got to the drop-off leading down to the tracks.

"Wait up, Uncle Rob!" he hollered. "I'm comin'!"

Rob stopped and stood waiting until Newt came to his side.
"Hi there, boy. Thought I'd come to meet you," he said.

"Thought maybe I was late," Newt answered.

"Nope—I'm just a early bird."

"Which way we goin' today?"

"Well, think we'll try the upper west side," Rob said. "Ain't been there in quite a spell." He motioned with his head. "We'll start over on Mulberry Street."

They moved toward the tracks, Newt holding Rob's hand just above the nubs where the fingers had been blown off in an explosion years before. About twenty yards from the crossing Rob stopped, holding his cane to the ground, and Newt looked up at him, seeing his eyelids blinking rapidly behind the dark glasses.

Then the warning bell started ringing and the red signal arms started swinging back and forth. They waited a few moments, then heard the whistle, and before long the wheezing locomotive came pounding around the bend. As it rumbled by, pulling its eight coaches, Newt saw the images of the engineer and the passengers blurring past.

"Boy, I shore would like to be on there," Newt said as they started across the tracks.

"Why?" Rob asked.

"Oh, just to be goin' someplace far away, like them people are."

"Maybe they're people goin' back home or to places they don't want to be goin' to." Rob was smiling.

"Well, at least they been some place," Newt said. "Take me, I ain't never been out'a Cherokee Flats—'cept to Easton and Fort Miles."

"You're young yet. Got lots of time for that."

"You ever been any place else, Uncle Rob, 'sides here?"

"A trip up to Kansas City once when I was a boy many years ago. That's the only time."

"Mind if I ask you somethin'?"

"Go ahead."

"It's kind'a hard to say what I mean—what I wonder 'bout you."

"Try."

"Well, you told me how you got your eyes blowed out in a explosion. Well, that's been a long time ago—"

"More'n twenty-five years."

"Well, what I want to know is—can you remember what you used to see before that—can you remember what color the sky is?—what a bird looks like and things like that?"

They continued along in silence as Rob formed his answer and Newt waited to hear it. In a little while it came. "Yes, Newt, I do remember things like they were then. In fact, I think the colors are brighter in my darkness than they are in your light. I see blue and red and yellow and green and all the colors. And sometimes I have a little fun with color in

65

my darkness, like imaginin' you're green with pink ears and a blue nose and purple hair. Sometimes I fill up my dark world with people of all kinds of colors like these."

"Really, Uncle Rob?"

"Yep, boy, it's so. And you know what, Newt? I think sometimes if all the people in the world were made up of colors like that instead of just some black and some white, it would be a happier world. A wonderful world all mixed up with wonderful colored people, nobody bein' the same as anybody else."

Newt closed his eyes for an instant, trying to imagine such a world. Then he opened them again and laughed. "Maybe your world's prettier'n ours."

Rob smiled.

Throughout the rest of the morning they weaved in and out of the streets and alleys, selling their wares to the house-wives and small-store merchants. At noon they stopped to rest beneath a shade tree, and Rob pulled some sandwiches from his overall pockets. They ate, rested for an hour, then continued on. By three o'clock they had sold every broom but two, and they turned back toward home.

When, a short time later, they came upon a large white house, Newt said, "Maybe I can sell the last two here." He went up the walk, around to the back door and knocked. A blond boy of about thirteen cracked the door and looked him over. "What you want?" he questioned.

"Your momma want'a buy a broom?"

"A broom?" The boy opened the door wider.

"Yep, a broom," Newt repeated.

"Mother!"

"Who is it, dear? What do they want?" a voice asked from within.

"It's a nigger sellin' brooms! Want any?"

At the sound of the word "nigger," things became tangled for Newt. He threw down the brooms, pushed open the door and cracked his fist against the boy's face. The boy fell back, yelling, "Mother! Mother!" And Newt threw every ounce of his strength into another blow, knocking the frightened boy to the floor.

The woman rushed into the room, staring at Newt in utter disbelief. "What's this? What are you doing? You get out of here before I call the police!"

Newt turned and walked out the door, picking up his brooms. "You better tell your boy to stop callin' people nigger or he's gonna git worse'n that."

The woman jerked the door open and spat at him. He ducked, but her spittle caught him in the eye. Enraged, he rushed toward the door, but the woman slammed it and bolted it shut. "You are a nigger!" she shouted from the other side. "Nigger! Nigger! Nigger!"

Newt made his way slowly back to the sidewalk and Rob. He took his uncle's hand and they walked to the corner. "Step down, Uncle Rob."

They crossed the street.

"Step up, Uncle Rob."

They walked another full block in silence. Finally Rob spoke. "What happened back there, Newt?"

"Back where?"

"At the last house."

"Oh—nothin'."

"You're tremblin', boy. Tell me what happened."

"Oh—'twasn't nothin', I suppose—a peckerwood called me a nigger."

"What for?"

"For no reason a'tall—just bein' smart."

"Did you call him a peckerwood?"

"Didn't git the chance."

"What did you do?"

"I—I popped him upside his head, that's what."

"How big was he? Did he have a yellow nose and green hair?"

"A little bigger'n me, and he was white."

"Oh, then it was a fair fight." Rob chuckled.

"He didn't do no fightin'. His maw come runnin' out and she spit on me and called me nigger too."

A frown came to Rob's face. "You didn't hit her, did you?"

"Nope. But I think I would'a if she hadn't jumped back in and slammed the door."

"You satisfied?"

"Cain't exactly say I am. I'd a liked to give him a couple more good pokes."

"You keep goin' around pokin' my customers and I won't have any," Rob said, a smile creeping across his face.

"I'm sorry, Uncle Rob."

"Well, I'd take you right back there and make you apologize if that woman had acted more like a lady. But she didn't, so let's forget it," Rob said. "Take the rest of your anger out on the piano."

"If Poppa's home he won't let me play. Says piano playin's for girls."

"Best thing for you to do, then, is wait till your momma gits home from work. He won't run you up if she's there, will he?"

Newt grinned. "Nope, Uncle Rob. Like Pete says, Momma's got his bath water on."

"You're growin' up fast, boy." Rob was noticing his nephew's touch higher on his arm.

"Be thirteen come November."

"You ever think about what you want to be when you're a man?"

They reached a curb. "Step up, Uncle Rob—well, I ain't made up my mind just yet. Sometimes I think maybe I'd like to be a musician or an artist or somethin' like that—"

"Well?" Rob was smiling again. "Which one do you like best?"

"I like music best, I think. Prissy says the white teachers at high school tell colored kids to stick to bein' a carpenter or bricklayer or somethin' like that."

"So you like music. That razz-ma-tazz stuff?"

Newt laughed softly. "Aw, I know you make fun of jazz music. I kind'a like it, but there's somethin' else—when I'm in the prairie all by myself—when the wind blows a soft kind of sound almost like music, and I think I hear great big orchestras with lots and lots of people playin' all kinds of horns and violins, pianos, drums and things and it goes on for a long time—comin' and goin' with the wind—"

"How often do—"

"And sometimes I try to remember the tune so I can hum it to somebody, but I never do 'cause it's always so diff'rent."

They were quiet for a while after that, walking along with Newt's thoughts rambling and Rob's mind searching the future of his nephew. A quarter mile from the Frisco tracks Newt strained his ears but heard no sound. "She on time today, Uncle Rob?"

His uncle stopped, shutting his eyelids and rubbing the smooth handle of his cane, listening. "Yep. She's comin' right on time. You'll hear her whistle in a minute or two." Then they continued toward the crossing. In less than two minutes the shrill warning came as Rob had predicted, and as usual Newt looked at his uncle in awe.

"How do you do that, Uncle Rob? How do you always know?"

"Well, Newt, it's like this" (the 4:20 express was already upon them, rumbling and blowing through the crossing, and Rob waited its passing). "I know the rumblin' through my cane and feet. They took over where the eyes left off. Simple as that."

Newt looked both ways, then they crossed the tracks, and on the other side Rob continued. "Maybe the teachers think they're tellin' what's best. Maybe they don't understand that a youngster like you has got somethin' else in him that's tryin' to come out. Maybe they don't know you've got your mind set on bigger things. You've got to believe in yourself, Newt —don't let the teachers or anybody else hold you back. Learn all you can, so when bigger things come you'll be ready for them."

"Step up, Uncle Rob."

"You ever talk to your momma about any of this?"

"Just a little—sometimes."

"Well, you ought'a as much as you can. She's a good thinker, and she's got a peculiar kind of faith in you. She talks about you bein' born into the start of a new world. Maybe she's right."

"I git to feelin' like there are things I want'a say or do sometimes, but I don't know how to do it."

"Like what, son?"

"Oh, I don't know for shore. It's like just sort'a bubblin' over, like somethin's inside me tryin' to get out, but I just don't know what."

Talking stopped for a minute or two, and they passed over a wooden bridge and turned down a narrow lane.

"Step way down here, Uncle Rob."

Rob felt first with his cane, then he took the long step to the flat ground. "Well, Newt," he said, "I can make it from here." He fumbled in his pocket for seventy-five cents and put it in Newt's hand.

"Thanks, Uncle Rob."

"Thank you, boy. It's been a nice walk with you today."

"See you next week, maybe."

"Okay, but remember—study hard this year."

"Yessir, I'll try."

Rob Winger tapped on in the familiarity of his dark world, knowing easily the sudden humps and smooth leanings of the earth beneath him. A blue jay cawed and fluttered from tree to tree above his path as if to sound his way, and he smiled. It had been twenty-five years since he last saw this path on which he now walked. The deafening blast and the agonizing hours of near-death were long past. The awakening to blindness and the missing fingers, the slow recovery and painful readjustment—all this was long since over. Now he walked surely in his eternal night.

His cane bumped the first step of his porch and he cleared the other two, unlocked the door and entered. Standing the brooms in a corner, he walked to the window and pulled open the drapes, then sat in his rocking chair, gently pushing to and fro for a reflectful hour. When the tower bell rang in the Baptist church a mile to the east, he rose, ate some cold chicken and pie, closed the drapes and went off to bed.

The September rains came, and from his school windows Newt watched them weight the leaves so that, later, the winds of October easily blew them off and over the ground. By the middle of November frost was on the windowpanes, and the earth was hardening from the cold blasts that swept in from the north.

On the last Saturday of the month Newt awoke a little earlier than usual, because his father had predicted the arrival of a new calf during the night or early morning. With his breath fogging in the chill of the room, he dressed with speed, moving quietly to avoid waking Pete. When he entered the dining room, heat rushed upon him—and this meant his father was already up and out. The potbellied stove glowed, and Newt stepped bearably close to absorb its heat.

His mother had promised to let him accompany her to work, where he would visit with Rodney Cavanaugh, who had a big room to himself with books, microscopes, rifles, framed butterflies, bugs, stuffed animals, a Gramophone, and paintings of Greek statues on the walls. The two boys liked each other, and Newt often returned home wishing that both were either colored or white so they could spend more time exploring these wonders of Rodney's world. And Rodney was usually elated at Newt's coming, for he felt a superior satisfaction explaining the mysterious microscope and the enchanting world its thick lenses revealed.

By the time his mother's petticoats were cinched about her waist, Newt had fed the chickens, horses, and pigs; and he had stacked the firewood neatly behind both stoves. Then he went to the cowshed where his father had been since five, and his eyes lit up when he entered, for Jack Winger was busy pulling a newborn calf from its mother's womb.

"Gee, it's here—it's here!" Newt exclaimed.

"Git me some gunny sack, boy, lots of it," Jack grunted.

Newt raced to the corncrib for the sack, returning just in time to see the glistening calf ease fully into the world.

The mother began licking her baby's steaming body from head to hoof, while Jack gently rubbed it dry.

"Is it gonna be all right, Poppa?"

"Yep, boy, gonna be a fine one." He turned and looked at his eager son. "For a while I didn't think she was gonna git here on time for you. But here she is."

"She for me, Poppa?"

"Yep, son. Happy birthday."

"This my birthday? I forgot. Thanks, Poppa!" And he saw a real smile come to his father's face for the first time in a long while. Then quickly he was down to help rub the calf—but the mother, protective against his sudden move, butted him aside.

"Come easy-like," his father cautioned. "Come easy."

And Newt squatted gently to his father's side, and they rubbed and rubbed until the animal's thin coat was like velvet.

"What you gonna name her, son?"

Newt pondered a moment, trying to think of something that fit the occasion. "Well, I'm thirteen today, Poppa. I think I'll call her Lucky."

Jack lit his pipe and puffed the smoke into the early gray light. "That's good as any, son." He puffed again, and the blue smoke rolled up close to his face and under his broad-brimmed hat, causing him to cough. He repeated, "That's good as any." Then he took another close look at the calf, scratched his stubbly cheek and stood up. "We better be gittin' back. Your momma's prob'ly got breakfast on."

Then the two of them pushed their mackinaw collars up around their ears and went to the house, where Sarah gave them ten pancakes apiece—and presented Newt with a shiny silver dollar for his birthday.

After their breakfast, Jack and Sarah remained at the table while Newt went back to the barn for another look at the calf.

"That boy's growin' up—thirteen today," Sarah began.

"Worries me, sometimes," Jack replied.

"How?"

"Oh, with his daydreamin' and wantin' to play the piano and such things."

"He's different from the rest of the children, Jack. Might as well face it."

"Nothin' wrong with him as I can see. Just don't seem to have his two feet on the ground, that's all. He's all over the place doin' crazy things, dreamin' 'bout music, foolin' round anthills and such 'stead of doin' his work."

"He's a thinkin' boy, Jack. You should'a heard some of the questions he asked me about religion and death. I was hard put for the right answers, I'll tell you."

"Religion and death?"

"That's right, religion and death."

"I declare, he's gittin' crazy notions from someplace."

"His questions wasn't just crazy notions. They made me do a lot of thinkin' afterward. They were about things I used to wonder about when I was a girl, but didn't talk about just because I was scared to, for some reason or another."

"Well, one thing 'bout death, when your time comes you're goin', and that's that. Ain't very hard to answer that."

"It ain't just dyin' he wonders about. It's what comes after."

"He needs to go to church more, maybe."

"We been goin' to church all our lives, and so has he; still hearin' the same things we been hearin' since we was his age. The answers that used to satisfy us ain't goin' to satisfy Newt and the young ones comin' up now. They want proof. Some kind they can see and feel. And they're goin' to want more out of this world than we're gettin' out of it. Time's changin', Jack."

"This is a white man's world, Sarah. Ain't no time goin' to change that."

"No, maybe time won't, but this new crop of colored boys and girls will. You and me prob'ly won't live to see it, but these kids comin' along today are goin' to find a way to change things."

"The white man's got the money and guns—that spells power."

"There's more'n one way to skin a cat, Jack. Schoolin's more powerful than guns or money in the end. I honestly hope someday Newt'll git out of here and go where chances will be better for him. I pray for that."

Jack got up and poured Sarah a cup of coffee, then poured himself one. He gulped his down while standing. "Well," he concluded, "if daydreamin' was the ticket, he'd be gone tomorrow."

"Ain't nothin' wrong with dreamin', Jack. Dreams come true, often as not, if you work on 'em hard enough."

"Maybe so. Maybe so." He filled his pipe and lit it. "See you t'night. I'm gonna be at the smokehouse most of the day —and that's where Newt ought'a be 'stead of at the Cavanaugh's gittin' highfalutin ideas—"

"See you tonight," Sarah said, ignoring his remark. She

72

put on her coat and filled her shopping bag with fresh cleaning rags. "Newt!" she hollered out to the barns. "Come on, time to go!" She banged on Pete's door. "It's eight, Pete—git up! Prissy!"

"Yessem."

"Git up and fix Pete's breakfast. I'm leavin'."

"Yessem."

"Don't 'yessem' me. Git up right now, girl!"

"Yessem."

Later that morning, at the Cavanaugh house, Rodney's hand turned the focusing knob of a microscope and Newt, his eye glued to the eyepiece, watched fascinated as the blobs of brown sharpened to a huge animal-like head.

"Boy, it looks like a dragon or somethin', Rodney."

"That's a worker ant, Newt. They are females, but they don't mate or lay eggs."

"What do they do then?"

Rodney cleared his throat in a professorial manner. "There are several types. Some take care of the younger ants and the queens. Some find food—"

"What kind is this one?"

"He's a worker soldier. See the big strong jaws? This kind defends the colony against its enemies."

"Colony?" Newt looked up at Rodney. "You mean like a city?"

"That's right."

Newt's eye was on the eyepiece again. "How big are their colonies?"

"Oh, as big as an acre of ground sometimes, and as far down as sixteen feet in the ground. Fact is, there are as many of them in a colony as there are people in a big city like Kansas City or New York."

"Gee, really?"

"Yes," Rodney said proudly, "and what's more, there are more ants on this earth than any other insect."

"I guessed somethin' like that. I counted almost two hundred of 'em one time."

"Without a magnifying glass?"

"Yep."

Rodney gave him an admiring grin.

"What's those long things stickin' out of its head?"

"Oh, those," Rodney answered quickly, "are the antennas. Without them they couldn't taste, feel or smell." He removed his eyeglasses, much the same way he had seen Professor Radeaker remove his during science classes. "This particular

73

species finds its way to and from its nest by smell. In fact, it won't even pick up food unless it smells it first."

"Why cain't they use their eyes to see how to git round?"

"Some kind don't even have eyes, Newt. But even those that do can't see much more than light or dark. But let me show you something really fantastic." He nudged Newt aside, lowered the microscope and refocused the lens on the ant's eye. "Now look." He gestured Newt back to the microscope, his thin face glowing with eagerness.

"Looks like a diamond."

"You're right, but actually it's as many as one thousand little eyes."

"—and they still cain't see good?"

"Oh, maybe a bush or a rock or something like that, but not much more."

"Does this spe—kind bite?"

"She sure does bite, and her jaws won't let go even if her body is cut off."

"Poppa told me ants are awful smart and—"

"In some ways they are and in some ways they're a little dumb."

"How so?"

"Well, for instance—"

("All I want from you, Chauncey, is the truth!") Rodney's father's voice boomed from the outer hall. ("Did you or didn't you have that girl in this house?")

("And for the thousandth time I'm telling you, I didn't!") Chauncey's angry voice retorted. Newt's eyes shifted uneasily toward the slightly open door.

Rodney went on, seemingly accustomed to such outbursts, "—well, for instance, they have all kinds of places to store their food and put their trash, and they even have ant cows they milk, but—"

("Silas claims you did!")

("I don't care what he's claiming! I said she wasn't in this house and I'm sticking to it! Can't you take your own son's word for the truth instead of the town's prize bum? He's not pinning something like that on me! And Blanche is a lying so-and-so if she—")

Sarah Winger slammed the door, shutting off the battle from Newt and Rodney. (Blanche—must be Blanche Newhall, Newt thought.)

And Rodney went on, "—but put these ants in a circle, following one another around, and they'll die from exhaustion without having enough sense to get out of it."

After the lecture on ants, Newt heard about Rodney's collection of butterflies in such strange terms as Rhopalocera, Papilionidae and Lepidoptera. Then the two boys had a lunch of peanut-butter sandwiches and lemonade, which Sarah served them. And as Newt chewed and strolled about the room, he noted such book names as Hans Christian Andersen, Thomas Edison, Francis Bacon, Charles Dickens, Edgar Allan Poe, Marc Antony and even James B. "Wild Bill" Hickok. And there were just plain bugs under a glass neatly titled Coleoptera, with such names as *Eyed Elator, Ten Line June Beetle, Purple Tiger, DeGeer's Firefly, Blue Ground,* and a *Fifteen-Spotted Ladybug.* In the corner over Rodney's orderly desk, perched on an oak branch, were three stuffed birds, a *Road Runner,* a *Redheaded Woodpecker,* and a shiny-beaked *Yellow-Hammer.* There was a drawer marked *Chemical Symbols and Formulas;* another marked *Chemical Compounds,* and yet another marked *Inorganic and Organic Compounds.*

Rodney Cavanaugh's room represented a whole new world of knowledge for Newt—a world in which he suddenly longed to dwell; to know in a way that Rodney knew it; to be able to explain it to Beansy, Jappy and the others, in much the same way Rodney explained it to him. As he looked about, he felt that he had been somehow cheated. "After all," he reasoned, "Rodney and me are 'bout the same age, and I like all these books and things too." Then he thought about his home. He didn't even have a room of his own, much less microscopes, books, stuffed animals, pictures and such. And he wondered for a moment whether he would trade places with Rodney if he had the chance—and his decision was an emphatic No.

As he and his mother headed home in the crisp early dusk, tiny flakes of snow were beginning to fall.

Sarah said, "Did you have a good time with Rodney today?"

"Yessem, and he's shore a smart boy. He knows about everything—ants, butterflies, bugs, science and everything."

A strong wind brought the snowflakes in swifter, and Sarah pushed the scarf up close to her nose. "Yes, son, Rodney's very smart. He studies lots, and if you study the way you should, you can be just as smart as him. You'll be goin' to the white high school 'fore too long—there you'll have more things to read and work at."

By the time they reached home, snow covered the earth and trees; and, blowing wet in the strong wind, it smeared the night with its whiteness. Later, Newt sat at the front room window watching it pile up, feeling already the joy of a coming snowbound Sunday. He watched Prissy and Pete play checkers for a while, then started for bed. At the bedroom door he turned thoughtfully. "Pete?"

"Yep."

"Did'ya ever hear the word pap—papa-lon-i-de?"

Pete didn't look up from the move he was pondering. "Pappa what?"

"Papa-lon-nidi."

"Nope," he said, still figuring the move. "Why?"

"Oh, nothin'. Just askin', that's all." When he opened the bedroom door, cold air goose-pimpled his skin, and quickly he was out of his overalls and under the quilts (Pape-lion-i-die . . . pape-lion-i-die . . . is a insect with shingles—with scales—pape-lion-i-die . . . Rodney's prob'ly readin' . . . pape-lion-i-die), and before long he was asleep.

The next morning, as early sunlight cut across the land, the flakes sparkled like jewels in a world of pristine white. Unbroken brilliance lay over the fields, prairies and hills like a colorless blanket—reflecting, here and there, illusive spectral beams of fast-rising light.

Newt rose early, attended to his chores, and with his sled in tow was away to the slopes of Candy Hill before the rest of the family came awake. He met Waldo Newhall where the road bent into Logan's Grove, and they went on together. As usual, Waldo looked a little sad, and Newt often wondered if it was because his father was the town bum. But he liked Waldo, and enjoyed his companionship.

"Where's Beansy and them, Newt?"

"They ought'a be on the hill by now. I had to chop some extra wood for Monday mornin'."

A little further on, Rodney joined them in the final push toward the top of the gleaming hill where the others were already knifing the powdery slopes into fast, hard-packed trails.

Later, racing down with Beansy and Waldo, Newt saw the sled in front of him sideslip, then flip over, throwing its rider directly in his path. Newt's left foot dug quickly into the snow, skidding him sharply about. Then suddenly his sled was tumbling over and over, throwing him free and rolling, until he landed in a powdery heap with the rider who had sprawled before him.

Newt was up first. "Whyn't you look where you're goin'?" He began beating the loose snow from his clothes. "You almost got us both—" Two big brown eyes, set in a tan, dimpled face, stopped him dead. "Oh—I thought you was a boy."

"Well, I'm not, as you can plainly see." She, too, was smacking snow from her heavy woolen sweater.

Newt flustered an apology. "Oh, I can see now, all right. (Boy, she's pretty.) You hurt?"

"Nope. Thanks to you."

"Aw, wasn't nothin'." Six sleds whizzed by. "Just made a quick turn, that's all," he grinned, twisting his toe in a mound of snow. "My name's Newt—Newt Winger."

"I'm Arcella Jefferson."

"You ain't from round here."

"Nope. From Chanute, but I'll be living here for a while, I guess."

Newt's heart skipped a beat. "Well, well, boy, that's real keen news." Then bravely he assured her, "We can shore use some pretty girls round here."

"Use 'em?" Arcella's brow puckered. "What do you mean, use 'em?"

"Well, I—didn't mean it like you're takin' it. I just mean it's gonna be good just havin' you round."

Arcella seemed to know very well what he'd meant, and she smiled at his apparent discomfort before easing up on him. "Do you go to Booker T. Washington Junior High?"

"Yep. I'm in the eighth grade."

"So am I."

"Gee, we'll be in the same classes together."

By now they had retrieved their sleds, and Newt, somehow managing to pull them both, felt a new kind of warmth. And to him the snow they trudged in was no longer snow but just a necessary something to walk on in a world holding only two people, who walked alone in that something with not much to say—simply smiling or coughing without having to cough, wiping noses that needed no wiping. And by the time they reached the peak of Candy Hill, Newt was breathing heavily in the aching flush of first love.

But the crisp beauty of this fine Sunday was not only for Cherokee Flats. Seventy-two miles north, in a valley with postcard charm, the brown brick Spit's School for Wayward Boys rose from the white like a gingerbread cake. At 6 A.M. sharp, three clanging bells (one for each cell hall) broke the calm that lay over the morning.

"Okay! You bunch of fart-heads hit the floor!" Charlie

Crapper's voice bounced against the cold gray walls of Cell Hall One and echoed far into the other two sections.

"Shut up, you lousy bastard!" a voice shot back from the second corridor.

"What son-of-a-bitch said that?"

"Me, you stupid brass-ass!" Now a voice came from another direction. "It was me, your mammy's lover!" Laughter filled the halls.

"Cut out that goddam laughing—all you lunkheads! Cut it out and hit the floor—else I'll put my billy to you!"

Then the chorus started. Cell Hall One: "Anybody here seen Charlie's young daughter?" Cell Hall Two: "She can piss a mile and a quarter." Cell Hall Three: "And you cain't see her belly for the steam."

Charlie stalked up and down the halls, outraged into bitter silence, itching for a violator of the slightest demeanor. And the unlucky one was Marcus Savage, for he was the last, out of two hundred and three, to hit the floor.

"You like your rest, eh, Savage?" Charlie's voice was hot for revenge. Marcus, knowing his number was up, didn't answer. "I said, you like your rest, Savage!"

"I'm up, ain't I?" Marcus growled back sleepily.

"Yeh—and since you are, you black monkey, you gonna shovel the front path all the way to the county road—and before you git any breakfast. Now shake the stink out'a them sheets and then go grab a shovel."

Marcus was pulling on his overalls when he suddenly let them drop to the floor and, in a flash, his big fist smacked against Crapper's jaw, sending him crashing to the floor. Crapper struggled up and yanked out his billy club. Then bedlam broke loose. All the boys, as if on cue, swarmed through the corridor in crushing packs between Crapper and Marcus, bumping the guard from one side to the other. They were like bees tormenting a hapless fly. In final desperation, Crapper sounded his distress whistle, and six beefy guards jumped up from their breakfast and rushed in to his rescue; but by the time they came crashing into the area all the boys were standing stiffly, singing, with the most patriotic expressions, the first lines of "The Star-Spangled Banner." The six guards, clubs drawn for action, halted and stood contemptuously at attention as the voices droned painfully slow through the final line, "—o'er the land of the free and the home of the brave."

Standing before the warden, and aching from the private clubbing Crapper finally gave him, Marcus listened unemotionally to the punishment he was to receive: "—dry bread and water the rest of the day, and you git solitary confinement for the next two weeks. But first you're gonna shovel that snow like you was told. Take him away, Crapper."

And Marcus shoveled every back-breaking inch to the county road with Crapper standing over him all the way, avenging his soul with each shovelful. Marcus paused to rest a moment, then his shovel made the final scoop. But instead of throwing the snow aside, he sent it flying into Crapper's red face—and before the startled guard could clear his vision, Marcus slammed the shovel against his head and Crapper started falling; then, just as his big frame settled face down in the snow, the shovel caught him once again and he lay still. Marcus eyed him for a moment, started to strike again; but instead he ran across the road and into the brush.

He scampered through the forest of unbroken snow, fleeing aimlessly. He knew they would be hunting him soon, and, realizing how easy it would be to follow his fresh footprints in the snow, he cut back to a side road, mixing his tracks with others' that had come along before him. After a while the snow began falling again, and when it grew heavier he moved back into the forest, reasoning that the fresh flakes would hide the route of his flight.

At nightfall he was deep into the woods, cold, hungry and lost. He thought of his father and their shack, but no sense of warmth or safety came from those thoughts. So he kept moving along, avoiding the roads and open plains, traveling, without knowing it, in a circle that led toward the school rather than away from it. He saw a farmhouse a half mile off to his right, and his hunger automatically sent him in its direction. He tromped through the snow and crawled beneath a barbed-wire fence, but as he started up the cowpath two large dogs bore down on him, barking and blocking his approach.

"Come, boy. Come, boy," he whispered, trying to stop their barking; but they only barked louder.

He backed away and they followed, coming within a few feet of him. Scooping up some snow, he packed it into a ball and threw it, hitting one of them in the haunches. The dog yelped and ran back toward the house, its mate close on its heels. A shaft of light from the farmhouse blurred through the falling snow, and Marcus could make out the form of a man in the doorway. In his hand was a rifle.

"Who's there!" the man shouted.

Marcus stood silent, watching the man as he stuck two

fingers in his mouth and whistled. The dogs bounded past him into the house and he closed the door. After waiting a few moments, Marcus cautiously moved on to the edge of the forest from where he had come. He was strangely sleepy and chilled to the bone.

He stood freezing in the vast bleary darkness, too weak and hungry to stand straight, impulses welling up within him, bringing him to the point of tears. Even the cold reformatory room would have felt good to him now, and he thought of the other boys chattering away with their rude jokes and wild songs. "Maybe I should try to go back," he thought. "I'm gonna die if I try to stay out here." He rubbed his fingers together roughly, trying to get feeling back into them. His feet felt like painful nubs. He stumbled on from a last desperate will to survive; then his knees buckled under him and he slumped wearily into the deep snow.

Sometime later he heard the barking of the dogs and voices —Crapper's and the others—and felt their pulling him up and carrying him across the field to the farmhouse. The nightmare began to thin out, and he heard the farmer saying, "I had a notion it was the nigger boy missin' from the school my dogs was barkin' at." A half hour later they dumped him in his cell, and he fell into a fitful sleep.

The next morning he was told that the two weeks of solitary confinement had been stretched into three months. He didn't answer, either in protest or acknowledgment of the sentence. He didn't care one way or the other.

CHAPTER ❦ 6

IT WAS ABOUT eight o'clock on the first morning after school let out for Christmas vacation. Newt slipped into the dining room and cautiously opened his mother's fruit cupboard. Spying a Mason jar of apple butter, he lifted it, pulled the rubber collar gently so as not to stretch it, and unscrewed the top. Then, with a dull table knife, he expertly carved a circle an inch in from the edge and the full depth of the jar. This done, he upended the jar and dropped the middle section onto a newspaper, carefully recapped the jar and put it back. Finally he hid the filched preserves in a knapsack—and it was part of the food for a hunting trip he and Beansy had planned for the day. After that he finished his chores and awaited the arrival of his friend.

An hour later the two boys sat on the kitchen floor oiling their raccoon and opossum traps, hungering from the pungent smell of sausages sizzling in a skillet on the stove near them.

"Think we could sneak a couple'a extra sausages for our packs, Newt?" Beansy whispered.

"If Momma gits out'a the kitchen for a minute. They shore smell good. I cain't wait."

Their chance came when Jack Winger called to his wife for a clean pair of overalls. Newt and Beansy were up and over the meat by the time Sarah reached the middle of the dining room. Plucking two of the choicest sputtering patties, they juggled them frantically while Newt simultaneously forked the remaining ones into a position to hide the absence of the others.

Then, before they could know it, Prissy was coming through the door. And as she yawned away her drowsiness, Newt and Beansy shoved the hot sausages into their back pockets and backed against the wall.

Prissy stifled the yawn with the back of her hand and

looked at the boys wiggling in discomfort. "What you two nuts actin' so funny about?"

"What'a you talkin' about?" Newt shot back. He was standing the heat better than Beansy, whose plump behind was beginning to smart from the burning.

"You two are up to somethin'—I can tell." Her eyes were beginning to sharpen.

Beansy rocked against the wall, pressing the hot grease down to his tender thigh. "Ouch!" he yelled finally and burst through the door into the open, where he hurriedly slipped down his overalls, grabbed a handful of snow and applied it to his behind. Knowing nothing better to do, Newt rushed out after him. And Prissy, eyes popping, ran back through the dining room.

"Momma! Momma!" she yelled. "Newt and Beansy are pullin' somethin' funny!"

But by the time Sarah returned to the kitchen, Newt and Beansy had grabbed their packs, traps and other paraphernalia and headed for the woods.

They were nearly out of breath when they reached the foot of Candy Hill. And though it was very cold, they sweated beneath their heavy mackinaws.

"That Prissy would have to come buttin' in," Newt grumbled.

"'Tain't Prissy I'm worryin' 'bout now. My rump feels like I been sittin' on a blow torch."

"Still hurtin' much?"

"Hurtin'? It's killin' me."

"I'll take a look when we git over the top'a the hill. Maybe it's blisterin'."

"Now I know what a steer feels like when they brand his butt."

Newt laughed. "Now we'll be able to tell your rump from the hog's."

"'Tain't funny a bit."

On the other side of the hill they dropped their traps and packs. Beansy took off his coat and pushed down his pants so Newt could inspect the burn. "How's it look, Newt—red and puffy?"

"What'a you mean, red and puffy? A butt black as yours wouldn't git red if they fried it in red ink."

"Quit horsin' round, Winger. How's it look shore 'nough?"

"You're gonna live, Beansy. Don't git excited. Looks like a scorched ham butt," Newt kidded. Then he reached in his pack for a sausage, pressed some cold grease from it and coated the blister. "That ought'a help it some," he said.

A chilling blast of air swept down the slope, and Beansy jerked up his overalls. "Colder'n a Eskimo turd out here." His voice quivered as he snapped the bib hooks on his overalls and quickly got into his mackinaw. When he was thoroughly buttoned, they trudged through the deep snow to the frozen river, then scrambled up the bank and baited their traps. After setting them, they crawled into Rock Cave for shelter from the cold, got a fire going and settled back to enjoy its warmth.

"Wonder how Savage's doin' up at Spit's School?" Beansy said.

"Marcus?"

"Yeh."

"Funny thing," Newt mused, "I had a dream 'bout him last night, a real strange one." He bent forward, looking deeper into the fire, trying to recollect the details. "Seems like I was walkin' alone in a big forest and all of a sudden a big monster come out of the darkness at me—like a dragon or somethin'—and I had a sword, like the Knights of the Round Table. He had fire comin' out his nose and mouth. Seems like he had a lot of legs and I kept cuttin' 'em off when he come at me—but fast as I'd cut 'em off he'd have new ones. Then —then it wasn't a dragon no more but it was a bull, like they fight in Spain, only he had golden horns, and seems like his skin was made out'a one of them patchwork quilts like Momma makes."

"What's that got to do with Marcus?"

"Well, what's so funny is I was just 'bout to kill the bull with the sword when it began to cry great big tears and I stopped, and a voice kept tellin' me, 'Kill it! Kill it!' but I couldn't, and the voice said, 'Kill it 'fore it gits you!' and I started to run the sword through it but its head had turned to Marcus' head and he was cryin' too, great big tears, so big they turned into a river and he was drownin' 'cause he didn't have no arms, and I tried to save him but he was too heavy and he went under."

"That's all?"

"There was somethin' else—but I cain't remember—it was all so funny and strange-like."

"That wasn't no dream—that was a nightmare," Beansy said.

"I'd forgot all 'bout it till you called his name just now."

"When's he comin' back home?"

"I don't know exactly—'bout spring sometime, if he gits out when he's supposed to."

Beansy leaned back against the cave wall. "It's been kind'a peaceful since he's been gone, don't you think?"

"Yeh, it shore has. No fights or nothin' like that."

"He's gonna be surprised to see how big we all got when he does come back. You're almost tall as he is now, Newt."

"Yeh, but don't forgit he's gittin' bigger too."

"Trouble is, he thinks we didn't stick by him."

"I think it's mostly me he blames," Newt said.

"Maybe the school's gonna make him better. That's what a reform school's s'posed to do."

Newt poked into the fire with a stick, and the flame shot up. He squinted against the heat. "Momma says we all gotta try to help him when he comes out. Says he ain't never had much of a chance to be no better—never havin' a mother or a good home like you and me and the rest of the guys."

"Maybe so. Think the gang ought'a send him a Christmas card or somethin'?"

"Say—that's a good idea, Beansy! I'll ask Momma to git one, then all the guys can sign it 'fore we send it off."

Beansy pushed the conversation in another direction. "Whatcha gonna do next summer?"

"Don't know for shore. Rodney Cavanaugh says a professor at the high school is goin' to give some extra classes in science, free of charge, and he's goin' to ask his poppa to ask the teacher if I can come."

"What you want to go to a science class for in the summer?"

"'Cause I think it'll help me when I go to the high school next year. You ought'a think 'bout it too."

"Not me. I got other plans for the summer."

"It's only for a week."

"No, thanks—I don't care if it's for a day. I see a'nough of school all year 'stead of foolin' round it in the hot summer."

"Well, to tell you the truth we ain't eli—eligible till we go one year to the white high school. That's why Rodney has to git special permission for me."

"You gittin' some pretty high ideas from that Rodney," Beansy joshed.

"Ain't nothin' wrong with that, is it?" Newt's voice had a bit of pique in it.

"Naw—naw, I guess it ain't."

"Boy like Rodney might be President someday," Newt said profoundly.

84

"Yeh, and a boy like you might be a dog catcher some-day," Beansy chuckled.

"Ain't nothin' wrong with bein' ready when the big things come," Newt said, quoting his Uncle Rob.

Beansy was quiet for a moment. Then, "Remember the day old Prof Jones got after Earl for not havin' his homework, and Earl said, 'I ain't had no chance to study,' and old Prof said, 'You don't say I ain't had *no* chance to study. You say I ain't had *a* chance to study.'"

Newt laughed. "Boy, do I remember? We all busted out laughin' and he made us stay a whole hour after school writin' f-o-o-l-s on the blackboard over and over again."

"'Nother time he told Skunk that he must'a been sleepin' in the devil's privy when the Lord handed out sense."

They both laughed again. "Boy, we're shore gonna miss old Prof when we go to the other school," Newt said.

After an hour had passed they went back to their traps and found that three of them were still unsprung. Around the fourth was a smudgeon of red and part of a muskrat's tail. Beansy picked up the trap, its jaws still clamped to the flexible, gristly part. "Son-of-a-gun gnawed it off and got away clean as a whistle."

"Can't say as I blame him," Newt said.

"Bet he's got a mighty sore behind right now, though," Beansy countered.

Newt laughed. "Well, that makes two sore asses in these parts today—yours and that muskrat's."

"Yeh, but mine ain't cut off."

"With all you got back there, wouldn't hurt none if you got a little chopped off too."

"Wouldn't talk if I was you—skinny as your ass is." Beansy returned the laugh.

On the way back Newt decided to stop by Arcella Jefferson's house to see if she could go with him to a movie.

After inviting them into the parlor, Arcella said, "Sit down —I'll have to ask Momma," and she went into the kitchen.

"Gosh, she looks scrumptious today!" Newt exclaimed, forgetting Beansy's presence.

"Pretty as a speckled pup," Beansy agreed.

"Huh—oh—oh yeh," Newt answered in embarrassment.

Arcella fluttered into the room, pulling on her two long braids. "Momma said it'll be all right as long as we git home before nine."

"Okay. We'll go at six o'clock. I'll git by here 'bout five-thirty."

The two boys rose and Arcella walked with them to the door. "You coming too, Beansy?" she cooed.

"Well—maybe, I—"

"Nope," Newt cut in quickly, "he's got to patch a tail."

"Tail? What kind of tail?"

Newt giggled. "A blistered tail."

Arcella shook her head and closed the door.

Later, Newt and Arcella sat in the darkness of the "peanut gallery," the flickering light of the movie screen dancing on their faces. Newt took Arcella's hand and squeezed it (William S. Hart is closing in on the villain), then he withdrew his hand and eased it onto her knee, feeling the rolled top of her stocking beneath the gingham skirt. (Hart's lasso is about the villain's waist as their horses reach the crest of the hill.) Newt's other hand slid behind her shoulder (the villain is falling from his galloping mount) and his fingers pressed into the softness of her armpit (Hart jumps from his horse onto the villain), and Arcella pushed his hand down to her waist. (Hart and the villain are fighting at the edge of the cliff.) Newt inched closer (Hart gets it on the chin and goes down) and Arcella moved in closer too (now Hart is up and the villain is down), and Newt's cheek touched her braid (both Hart and the villain are rolling down the cliff) and she pushed her braid aside and touched her cheek to his (down and down go Hart and the villain in flying dust) and his knee squirmed toward hers (Hart and the villain are up fighting on their feet again, and the pretty girl they are fighting over gallops up just in time to see Hart silence the villain with a swift right), then their knees squirmed together (Hart runs back up the hill and embraces the pretty girl) and Newt felt Arcella's long eyelashes batting against his cheek (Hart kisses the pretty girl), then Newt pulled Arcella to him and they kissed (the word "End" is on the screen, the organ blares to a crescendo and the lights go on). Arcella sat up straight and pushed Newt away.

It was below zero when they got outside, so they hurried through the night without saying much. When they reached Arcella's house, her mother let them in and offered Newt some cake and hot chocolate, which he accepted. A half hour later Newt and Arcella were sitting on the davenport in the parlor, and Newt began where he'd left off in the theater, unaware that her father sat looking down on them from the darkness at the top of the stairs.

"Boy!"

Newt and Arcella jumped apart and sat stiffly in embarrassment.

"Seems to me that couch ought to be big enough for you and my daughter to sit on without bein' in each other's laps!"

"Yes—yessir, Mister Jefferson." Then he was up, fidgeting with his hat and coat. "I guess it's 'bout time I was headin' home," he mumbled to the blushing Arcella. "See you in church tomorrow."

"Okay, Newt," she said, scowling up at the darkness, "see you in Sunday school."

"Thanks for the cake and stuff, Missus Jefferson!" Newt called; then he glanced furtively to the top of the dark stairway and was gone.

He walked swiftly in the cold moonlit night, seeing his bulky shadow upon the snow that crunched under his weight. His thoughts turned to summer; to the warm soft breezes playing at Arcella's skirts, and the tender body-close evenings they would steal from the pleasurable months ahead. He drew his mackinaw collar closer about his ears and cut across a field to shorten his journey in the biting cold. He trudged through the deeper unbroken snow of Logan's Grove, leaped a narrow ditch and started into the yard of his home.

"Newt! Newt! That you?" It was his sister Rende—and her two small children, Butsy and Gin-gin—running toward him from the lower path.

He sensed their plight immediately. "Yeh! Yeh! What's the matter, Rende?"

"Clint's after me—with the gun. Momma home?"

"I don't know. She ought'a be—come on!" Newt grabbed Butsy and Gin-gin by their hands, and they all ran up on the porch.

Rende pounded on the door. "Momma! Momma!"

Sarah was darning socks when the shout came. Jack was cleaning his pipe. Prissy and Pete were playing checkers.

"That's Rende, Jack," Sarah said. "Open the door. Clint must be up to his Saturday night foolishness."

Jack got up and opened the door, and the four rushed in. "Momma—Clint's drunk again—he's got that gun!"

Sarah threw the ball of yarn to the floor. "Never seen it fail! Never seen it fail! Every time he gits a little money he tries to drink up half of Chappie Logan's," she said, going for her coat. "Just go on in the bedroom, Rende—nothin's goin' to happen. Quit your snivelin'."

And since this was an old thing to the Wingers, Prissy and Pete hardly stirred. "Your move, Pete."

"Keep your skirt on. I'm doin' a little figgerin' here."

"You want me to go with you, Sarah?" Jack asked, still cleaning his pipe.

"No—I'll handle him. You just gittin' back from the picture show, Newt?"

"Yessem. Missus Jefferson gave me some cake and chocolate."

"Hmm. If I catch you and Beansy stealin' sausage out of my skillet again, I'm gonna give you more'n cake and chocolate." She opened the door to go out.

Newt was at her heels. "Can I come with you, Momma?" Sarah gave him a look of refusal, then quickly reconsidered, thinking of her son's fondness for Clint. "Yes, come ahead," she said. Then they were out and down the path to meet her son-in-law.

They came upon him shortly. He was stumbling in the deep snow coming toward the house, the shotgun hanging from his hand at the barrel.

Sarah spoke crisply. "Where you goin' with that gun, boy?"

Clint stopped and rocked back and forth, the butt of the gun twisting about in the snow. "Oh—hi there, Momma Winger. Hi, Newt—"

"I said, where you goin' with that gun?"

"I—I'm gonna git Rende—tonight—shore'n hell. I'm—"

Sarah was within reach of him now. "Back, Newt," she said, "back out'a the way." Newt stepped to the side and watched his mother move slowly up to Clint.

"Now look out, Momma Winger—I mean what—I say—look out—" He was slowly raising the gun. "I'll shoo—"

The action was so quick Newt missed it. He heard the smack of his mother's hand against Clint's face and saw him go down; then he saw the dark form of the gun in his mother's hand.

"Help him up, boy. Git him to the house. He's so drunk he can hardly stand up, let alone shoot anybody." Newt bent down and helped Clint to his feet, and the three of them went back to the house.

As they entered, Newt saw Rende peeping at the bedroom door. When she heard her husband groan and collapse to the floor, she crept back into the parlor with Butsy and Gin-gin in time to see her mother hide the gun behind the china cabinet.

Jack threw some more coal in the fire and spat in the scuttle. "Just look at him," he said in a half growl, "his maw and paw shore wasted a night when they made him."

"Git to bed, Newt," Sarah said, ignoring Jack. "Don't forgit, you've got Sunday school in the mornin'."

"Yessem."

Rende went across the room and knelt by her husband. "Clint—Clint," she said, shaking him, "listen to me."

"Yeh—whad—you want—whad—"

"Clint, I'm goin' to have a baby."

The room went silent at her words.

"Me too," Clint mumbled. Then he turned over on his back and began snoring.

Rende wept. "What am I goin' to do, Momma? What am I goin' to do?"

Sarah put her arms about Rende's shoulders. "We've just got to pray over him, that's all. We've got to keep prayin'."

Jack blew out a ring of smoke. "I declare, prayin' ain't gonna do that varmit no good, none a'tall."

"Jack, I want you to stop talkin' like that. You know—"

"I'm tellin' you, Sarah—Clint's lost. God and the devil's both quit strugglin' for him, so it ain't much nobody else can do—I don't care how long and how loud they pray." He knocked his pipe on the coal scuttle and some loose ashes fell out. "He's lucky it's you who handles him. If it's ever me who has to take that gun away from him, he ain't gonna find it so easy. Fact is, he's gonna end up with a cracked skull."

"That's just why I made you stay in the house." She felt Newt's eyes upon her. "Boy, I thought I told you to git to bed!"

"Yessem."

"Don't yessem me. Just git goin'."

"Yessem."

Sarah turned back to Jack. "You've got to understand Clint. He ain't half as bad as you think. We've had some real nice talks together, and—"

"When he was sober."

"—and he's even promised me he's goin' to join the church."

"Well, I guess if anybody can drag him to the pulpit it's you. You got some kind of magic over him, or somethin'."

"Ain't magic at all. It's love, and Clint knows it."

"Well, I hope he don't ever try it when you're not around. He's in for trouble if he does."

Rende started sniffling again.

89

"You and the kids better stay here tonight," Sarah said. "You can sleep in Prissy's bed. She can make a pallet on the floor."

Jack stood up and stretched. "Got to git up early. Comin' to bed soon, Sarah?"

"Soon as I git Rende and the kids straight."

CHAPTER ❦ 7

"MERRY CHRISTMAS! Merry Christmas!" Newt shouted, rousing all the Wingers from their sleep. He had risen early, made a crackling fire and put on the coffeepot, knowing his father would be less grouchy if his insides were warmed up. By the time everyone was in the front room, bright sunlight was bouncing off the snow through the windows onto the tinsel and colored balls decorating the tree.

And as usual Prissy, with an overpoliteness that irked Newt, handed out the gifts, wearing a new middy blouse over her flannel nightgown as she switched about.

After Newt unwrapped his gifts he noted that they were more practical than ever before. He felt that the overalls, stocking cap, socks, book satchel and dictionary (this last from his mother) reflected his growing up. Proudly, he accepted them in this sense, letting go completely the tin soldier and wind-up car period in which he had found so much joy several Christmases before.

After thanking everyone for his presents, he began thumbing the dictionary (this pleased Sarah mightily) for the word *Papilionidae*. To his great surprise he couldn't find it. But he found *Papilionaceous,* and though he didn't understand one of the explanations for it, he immediately decided to learn the phrasing by heart and spring it on Rodney Cavanaugh when they met again. He jumped up, dashed to his room, grabbed pencil and paper and hurried back to the front room. From the book he scribbled: "Papilionaceous —having an irregular zygomorphic corolla somewhat resembling a butterfly." He copied the words over and over, filling the whole page with the new knowledge. Then he propped himself up on the couch and began memorizing it.

Pete sat on the floor rubbing up a pair of already shiny spurs. Prissy, preening before the mirror, tied and retied the handsome bow on her middy blouse. Jack sat admiring his new rough-grain pipe, and Sarah rocked back and forth fingering and praising the sewing kit that Newt, Prissy and Pete had chipped in to buy her.

"Pete," Newt said suddenly, his head still in the book, "did you or Prissy ever hear the word zy-go—gom, no, zy-go-morp-hic in high school?"

"Not me," Pete said.

"Not me," Prissy said.

Sarah looked up, puzzled. "What do you want to know about the word, son?"

"Just what it means."

"What you think that dictionary's for, lunkhead?" Prissy spouted out.

"That's no way to talk, Prissy," Sarah said. "Git over there and help him find the word and what it means."

"Yessem," Prissy answered, twisting the bow. "Oh, I just look sooo de-vine in this here lo-va-ly middy, so lo-va-ly." She flounced over to Newt. "Now, deah brotha, what is the word that you would have thou sista help you with?"

A common four-letter work beginning with *s* popped into Newt's mind, but his mother's eyes were on him and he answered, "Zy-go-morp-hic."

"Why are you worryin' about a word that you don't know anything about?" Prissy questioned facetiously.

"Prissy," Sarah said, "I'm listenin' to you."

"Yessem. Let's see—w, x, y, z—zy-go-matic bone, arch— oh, here it is. It's zy-go-mor-phic, not zy-go-morp-hic, nut."

"Well, what's the diff'rence, phic or hic. Just 'bout the same," Newt said.

"Oh my," Sarah said impatiently, "just tell him what it means and quit fussin'."

Prissy's cheeks dimpled to a mischievous grin. "It means," she said, "mon-o-sym-metric." She cocked her head at Newt. "That satisfy you, deah brotha?"

Newt was silent, temporarily defeated.

"Prissy, you're bein' smart," Sarah said. "Now, I—"

"No I'm not, Momma. That's all it really says." She took the book to Sarah. "See, look for yourself."

Sarah pushed the book away to a seeing distance. "Well, it must be more to it than that," she said. "Pete, come see if you can't help straighten this thing out."

Pete reluctantly dropped his spurs and moved over to his mother. He took the book and, without speaking, read from zygoma to zymurgy. "Newt," he said finally, "this thing's got me fuddled, but I think mostly it's about bones—cheek-bones. It says here to see sym-metrical."

"Zi-go this and zi-go that," Jack growled. "I declare, I wish Prissy'd git out in that kitchen and make some zi-go biscuits. I'm hungry."

"Why ah'd be glad to, Poppa deah," Prissy said, switching across the room.

Jack looked up at her. "That blouse is gonna git you into a mess if you don't watch out, gal," he muttered.

Pete laughed. So did Sarah and Newt. And they were all delighted to let the "zygomorphic" matter drop.

Arcella arrived shortly after breakfast, and when Newt opened the door for her she thrust a package into his hands, pecked him on the cheek and wished him a merry Christmas.

"Merry Christmas to you too," Newt said. "Come on in."

"Can't stay long. Oh, hello, Mr. and Mrs. Winger."

"Hello, Arcella—merry Christmas," they both answered.

"Same to you and to you, Prissy and Pete. I hope all of you have a nice Christmas."

"Very very very," Prissy cooed.

They stood awkwardly for a moment, then Newt motioned Arcella into the front room. "Santa Claus left somethin'—"

"Something," Arcella corrected.

"Sorry—he left something here for you under the tree." He picked up a small, gaily wrapped parcel from the floor and handed it to her. Then he pecked her on the cheek and said, "Merry Christmas, sweetheart."

Prissy started to join them, but Sarah motioned her back. "You just keep out'a there, girl. That's Newt's little party." Prissy shrugged her shoulders and went back to the breakfast dishes.

Arcella and Newt sat in the middle of the floor unwrapping their gifts, and Newt got his open first. It was a book of short stories by Edgar Allen Poe, Newt's favorite author. He flipped the first white page and grinned, for there was an inscription, "A merry merry Christmas to the sweetest person I have ever known. Love, Arcella. December, 1925."

"Thanks. Thanks very much," he said. Then he waited shyly as she opened hers.

"Oh, Newt!" she cried, "it's beautiful, just beautiful." She held the locket out to him, turning her back. "Fasten it. Fasten it. I can't wait to see it on."

Clumsily his fingers pulled the chain with the heart-shaped locket around her neck, and after some trouble he secured the clasp. "There," he said, feeling a warmth all the way to his toes.

Then they were both up before the mirror. "Oh, Newt," she repeated, "it's exactly what I wanted." She kissed him on the lips this time, and he leaned forward for another. There was a quick, breathless embrace, then another kiss, followed by hasty thoughtless chatter. "Got up early this mornin'."

"So did I."

"Then I called everybody and we gave out presents."

"Just about the same over at our place, only not as many people."

"There's five of us here."

"Only three of us. Mother, father and I."

"Well, that's the way it is. Some families are bigger'n others."

"Bigger than. Not bigger'n," she chuckled.

"Momma gave me a dictionary. There's lots of good words in it."

"So now you can stop talking like the rest of that gang of yours."

"They're not so bad."

"If they were as bad as their speech, they would all be in jail, Newt Winger."

"All of them ain—aren't as lucky as I am."

"And what do you mean by that statement?"

"I got you."

Arcella shook her head in playful disgust. " 'I got you,' " she mocked.

"I got you—I have you—I have got you. It all means the same. You're my girl—and that makes me real lucky."

She looked at him for a long nice moment, without saying a word. And he looked back at her, not saying a word. They both felt the need for an early spring, a warm, soft, kiss-luscious spring—each aware of the heat in the other's longing.

"I must go now, Newt."

"See you Saturday for the picture show."

"I hope so."

Arcella bid everyone merry Christmas once more and left. And Newt turned again to the inscription, kissed it and placed the book on top of the dictionary. He stood for a moment in the center of the room. "Momma," he called out, "when I get some more books can I have a shelf in my room like Rodney's?"

"I think that would be fine, son. I'm sure Pete and your poppa will help you make a fine one."

Christmas at Spit's School for Boys wasn't much different from any other day. A few of the exceptionally well-behaved boys were granted trips home for the holidays. The others received a pork chop dinner and a small bag of peppermint candies.

Marcus ate alone in the dimness of his cell. The card from Newt, Beansy, Jappy, Earl and Skunk was propped on the table beside his cot. He glanced at the scribbled names in the weak light, and his mind recalled their faces as they had looked when they stood against him on the road near the river. He thought it was Newt who had betrayed him. Then the face of Jake Kiner mixed with the others, and Kirky's and Judge Cavanaugh's. He began boiling within, and suddenly he took a vicious swipe at the card and it fluttered to the floor. It would be May—with no mishaps—before he could return to Cherokee Flats, and his mind wandered to the river, the open plains and the rolling hills. . . .

He had just settled back on the cot when Crapper hollered, "You got some visitors, Savage! Git up and try lookin' happy."

"Screw you," Marcus growled sullenly.

"Fool with me and you don't see nobody," Crapper warned.

"I don't give a goddam. Ain't nobody I want to see nohow."

But by now the visitors were coming down the corridor.

"Right this way, Rev'rend," Crapper said. He spoke with an exaggerated politeness that forced a grunt of disgust from Marcus. The cell door swung open and through it came Reverend Broadnap, Maggie Pullens—carrying a bag of fruit and candy—and Deacon Henry Fuller. Reverend Broadnap stepped over and touched Marcus on the shoulder. Marcus stiffened. He wanted to tell them all to go, but he held his tongue.

"We come to pray for you and to wish you a merry Christmas, son." He didn't answer, and Broadnap turned to the others and said, "Let's pray."

They knelt on the floor. Marcus' fingernails dug into the palms of his hands and his teeth ground together in an angry embarrassment. He kept his eyes low and straight ahead, as if ignoring their presence.

"Oh Almighty God," Broadnap began, "we come to you on bended knee prayin' for the soul of this young sinner." Marcus' muscles flexed and his gaze shot defiantly to the tops of their heads, then to Crapper, who stood in the doorway with an evil grin on his face. "Wash his black sins away in these white snows of your holy Christmas. Lighten the troubles he has brought to his young dark days. Bring peace to his tormented soul and help him to someday leave this place a cleaner and better young man. Oh God, show him the light. Show—"

"Shut up! Shut up!" Marcus shouted, "and git the hell out'a here!" He was on his feet now. "I don't want'a hear none of your Uncle Tom prayin' over me!" The three people rose, shocked beyond belief.

"You don't know what you're sayin', boy," Broadnap half whispered, trying to quiet him down, reaching again toward his shoulder.

"I know much 'bout what I'm sayin' as you do," he shot back, pulling away.

Maggie put the bag of fruit on his bed. Broadnap took out a Sunday school card with the picture of Christ on it and placed it on the table. "Read the scripture here on the back, son," he said, "and pray to the Savior. He'll hear you."

Marcus snatched the card, tore it in half and threw it at the preacher. "You and your white God git the hell out'a here!" he shouted. "I don't want no part of you soul savers —bendin' down, like Paw says you do, kissin' the feet of a poor white trash God." Tears were in his eyes now. "Look at Crapper there! He's white! Whyn't you git down and start moanin' and groanin' to him, so he can kick the crap out'a you like he does all us 'nigga' boys. Yeh, that's what he calls us—nigga! nigga! nigga! Tell 'em, Crapper. Tell 'em what you gonna do to me when they leave! Tell 'em."

"Son—"

"Don't son me. Just git goin'! So Crapper can tease me 'bout you niggas comin' here to pray over me!"

Broadnap, Maggie and Henry Fuller filed out, their heads shaking. Crapper slammed the door shut and followed them down the corridor. Marcus sat very still awhile, then suddenly he began to feel a deep sense of guilt, deeper than any he had ever felt in his whole life. He was bewildered. These people had come all that way to help him and he had hurt them, said things he didn't realize he could say. But what he'd said was more for Crapper than for them, he realized. If Crapper hadn't stood in the door with that silly grin on his face, things might have been different. But it was too late now. The harm was done. Yet, somehow, he felt he had got a point across to Crapper. He didn't know just what. Maybe he was really defending those people against somebody like Crapper, who had once told him, "All niggas are stupid and crazy." In a way he was telling him that they weren't, that he was on to his kind and their "lily-white God" that his paw damned when he got drunk.

He glanced up. Crapper was back. Marcus said nothing.

"Merry Christmas—nigga," Crapper said disdainfully, and turned back down the corridor.

Marcus was silent. His head fell back in the shadows and he closed his eyes, trying to form the image of a God with black skin, thick lips and coarse hair like his—but he couldn't. The image on the torn card at the foot of his bed had been implanted much too long before. It was difficult to erase that image now, or even substitute another one for it.

CHAPTER ❦ 8

"IT WAS AWFUL the way that Savage boy talked to us—simply awful," Maggie Pullens told Sarah as the two of them sat in the Winger front room that night.

Sarah thought for a while before answering, then she spoke what she knew to be the truth. "It ain't really the boy's fault, Maggie."

"Then whose is it, for the good Lord's sake?"

"That could've been Newt, Beansy, Earl or any of the other young ones around here. If we want to tell the truth about it, then we would say it's our fault—all the Christians, black and white, and teachers and officeholders and everybody who's supposed to have good in them."

"Yes—yes, you're right, Sarah. Guess you're right."

"Our young children's minds here are mixed up. This place with all its drinkin' and fightin' and murderin'—Jim Crow schools, picture shows and eatin' places is too much for these young ones to figure out. They've got bigger ideas about livin' than you and me had at their age, Maggie."

"We're in a rut for shore."

"We was born in a rut, and the reason we've been able to keep goin' is because we always thought someday we're goin' to git out of it. I ain't one to fool myself about my chances any more, but I'm goin' to do all I can to see that my children don't get bogged down here forever."

"It's a big problem, all right."

"Take that Savage boy—nobody's ever done anything big to help him. He should've been taken away from Booker when he was a little boy and put in a good home. There just ain't much good can come of him now."

"The only people tryin' to do anything a'tall is our church missionary society."

"That's true, Maggie, but it's mighty hard tryin' to push out misery and fill empty stomachs with the word of God.

Booker Savage asked me one day if we had a Jim Crow heaven waitin' for our saints.''

"That man's awful—just awful."

"Told me Chappie Logan was his god. 'Least he's black like me,' he said."

"Awful—just awful," Maggie moaned. A moment later she got up to leave. "Well, I have to be moseyin' on. Tired after that long trip up there."

"It's good you went, Mag. Don't feel too bad about what happened. I'm sorry I wasn't with you."

"Sarah!" Jack was calling and walking in from the next room. "Did you two see what's on the back page of tonight's paper?"

"No," Sarah answered. "What's in it?"

"Look here." Jack handed her the paper, and he and Maggie bent over her shoulder as she read: "Jess Hicks, district school superintendent, announced today that, beginning next year, Negro students who normally would enter Cherokee Senior High school as freshmen will not be admitted until their sophomore year. These students will be held over at Booker T. Washington school. Mr. Hicks said the action was taken because of overcrowded conditions and shortage of staff at the senior high school. Two substitute colored teachers, Callie Johnson and Fred Simmons, will be put on a full-time basis at Washington school. Asked if this was to be a permanent arrangement, Mr. Hicks replied that it would, unless the State allocated money for expansion at the high school. This, he said, was unlikely."

"Well, I'll be—" Sarah gasped.

"What's it say, Sarah?" Maggie questioned. "I ain't got my glasses."

Sarah sat rigid, biting her lips, her hands crushing the newspaper. "They're pushin' the colored kids—the freshman class—out of the white high school, the one Newt'll be in next year."

"What?" Maggie put both hands on her hips. "You don't mean it? What won't these white people do next? How can they call themselves Christian? Where's their religion?"

"Religion?" Jack scoffed. "A white man don't take his religion out of church. He locks it up there for safekeepin', so it's fresh and clean on Sunday mornin' when he comes to wash his week's sinnin' away."

"Well, I got to be moseyin' on," Maggie repeated. "But that's the best I heard yet. See you tomorrow. Goodnight."

"Goodnight, Mag," they both answered.

"Jack." Sarah was scanning the paper again. "We have to fight this thing. We just cain't let Jess Hicks and that crowd git away with this."

"Fight it—with what?" Jack bellowed.

"With the colored parents and teachers—that's what."

"I'm tired, awful tired," Jack said. "I want to live the rest of my life in some kind of peace."

"There ain't goin' to be no peace for you or none of us unless we make it for ourselves. Newt is—"

"Newt Newt Newt!" Jack was up now, pacing the room. "I declare, Sarah—you think that boy's gonna be President someday—the first black President of the United States?" He shook his head in disgust.

"I ain't worried about him bein' President. All I want for him is a better life than he's got here."

"You already got him thinkin' 'bout things he'll never git, believin' he can do anything Rodney Cavanaugh can do."

"If we give him the chance, he can. That's what the fight's all about," she snapped, "that's exactly what it's all about."

"Well—"

"Well, nothin'." Sarah was angry now. "You and me are goin' to git people together and fight this thing. And we're goin' to git those freshman kids back where they belong, if it's the last thing we do."

Jack turned and looked at her. "She's really got her dander up," he thought. And he said, "Looks like you're gonna stir up some trouble 'spite of my better judgment."

"And you're goin' to help me do it, Jack Winger."

"So be it, so be it," he concluded.

During the rest of January and all of February, Jack and Sarah spent what extra time they had marshaling all the Negro teachers and a sizable number of parents who had shown some sort of interest in "the fight." By the end of March the group, now thirty-five strong, was ready for action, and it met at the colored school. Professor Ebon Jones brought the meeting to order, and Sarah Winger proposed that they call themselves the Negro Parent-Teacher Association.

"That's a good idea, sister Winger," Ebon said, "but it raises a little problem with us teachers here. It's—well, what I'm tryin' to say is that we are sort of responsible to the superintendent's office, and—and—"

"And you're 'fraid to buck him—that it, Ebon?" Jack Winger asked.

"No—let's not get off on the wrong foot, Jack. You got to

remember that we teachers get paid by these people—and —and this can develop into a troublesome thing for us if we start snappin' too hard at the hand that's feedin' us."

"That's right," Myrtle Beasly cut in. "We've got a lot more to lose than some of the rest of you. What if—"

"Right, Myrtle." Encouraged by the sudden support, Ebon continued, "I think we better tread lightly and not get too excited about this thing." (Jack felt the restlessness in Sarah. He began squirming in his seat.) "They could cut off our pay just like that." Ebon snapped his fingers for emphasis. "By callin' it the Parents and Teachers Association—"

"Just a minute, Ebon." Sarah was up on her feet, her arms folded determinedly beneath her breast. "There ain't a one of us here in this dilapidated school tonight that don't depend on our bread and butter from the white people. Not a one of us." She defiantly scanned the group. "It ain't the teachers' jobs and it ain't the teachers' troubles that we're here for, so much as it is the problem of our children and what's goin' to happen to 'em in time to come, if they keep gittin' kicked around like they are now from school to school, whenever the white people feel like it. I—"

"Now, sister Winger, you—"

"You just keep quite a minute or two, Ebon. You said your piece. Now listen to mine."

"Go ahead," Ebon apologized.

"The more we let 'em kick us around, the more they're goin' to do it. There ain't no reason under God's sun why that freshman class shouldn't be in the high school where it rightfully belongs. There they can git all the things this school ain't got. Most of you mothers and fathers went to this same school—even you, Ebon. Do you see any changes in it? Same desks, same books, same windows, same old rickety stairs—nothin' changed in it but the kids. Meantime, the whites have built two new schools, gyms and made all kinds of improvements. And they did it off our taxes. But they keep our kids out of these schools and gyms for as long as they can."

Myrtle Beasly spouted, "But what's going to happen to the extra colored teachers, Callie Johnson and Fred Simmons, who were put on here to help teach the freshman class? They have to eat too."

"Like I said before, the children are the main worry. And I'm surprised at you teachers for takin' such a attitude. I had it in my mind you'd be leadin' the fight 'stead of hinderin' it."

"It's like Myrtle said, we got to eat," Callie Johnson spoke from the back of the room.

"You're worried about feedin' your stomachs and us mothers and fathers are worried about feedin' our children's minds. Seems to me it ought'a be the other way around. Ain't no reason why we cain't worry about both, but it's the young ones who're goin' to be facin' the hard years that's comin'— you teachers ought'a know it's goin' to be harder for them than it was for us. The world's goin' to be expectin' more out of 'em, and they're goin' to be expectin' more out of the world."

"We still have to eat, sister Winger," Ebon said.

"Eat! Eat! Eat!" Sarah shouted. "We hardly got enough to feed our own faces at our houses, but I swear if any of you git fired for fightin' for your rights, we'll all put some extra plates on our tables for you. Right, brother Fuller?"

"Right, sister Winger."

"Right, brother Duncan?"

"Amen, sister. Amen."

"Right, sister Pullens?"

"Shore will, Sarah."

"A little order, please!" Ebon said, pounding on the desk. "What do you feel about this, Reverend Broadnap? We haven't heard from you."

Broadnap stood, twisting his hands behind his frock coat. "Well," he said, "I kept quiet so far, 'cause I wanted to hear both sides of the argument. I know how you teachers feel 'bout this matter, but sister Winger's right. It's more to stake than the teachers' jobs, 'cause in the first place the law's against anybody takin' your jobs just like that. On top of that, these kids have got to be educated. That's the law, and we all know it. And we know these white teachers ain't comin' cross those Frisco tracks to teach our black children, so I don't see what you're frettin' 'bout. I think the only fair way is to take a vote on sister Winger's idea on a name for us, and those that's scared, git out—those that ain't, stay in. Just as clear as that."

"Amen, brother Broadnap."

"Well said, brother. Well said."

"I agree. I agree."

The vote was taken, and when it was over the group became the Negro Parent-Teacher Association of Cherokee Flats.

As Jack and Sarah drove Maggie Pullens home, Jack suddenly remarked, "I don't trust that Ebon Jones in this thing."

102

"I know what you mean," Maggie said. "He shore was pullin' back tonight."

"Well, you cain't blame the teachers altogether for feelin' the way they do," Sarah said. "But comin' down to brass tacks, they ain't no worse off than anybody else. As for Ebon, he'll be all right when the showdown comes."

It was April before the "showdown" came. At the start of the public meeting in Town Hall, Jess Hicks asked everybody to stand and pledge allegiance to the flag. Jack Winger grunted and mumbled to Sarah, "Think we was gettin' ready to throw over the gov'ment."

Jess sat at a table on the platform with Marshall Goodlander, the mayor, and Gordon Blair, the village treasurer, at his right. Miss Tilley Reeves, president of the white parent-teacher association, and Bart Phillips, the fire chief, sat at his left. Only twenty-one of the Negro group showed up. They were bunched near the rear on the left side of the hall. The rest of the room was filled with white parents, teachers and other village folk.

"We're a little outnumbered," Jack whispered to Sarah.

"Makes no difference," Sarah answered.

Jess Hicks rose and introduced his "guests" at the speakers' table; then he looked out over the audience to the blob of black faces to the rear. "My friends, both white and colored," he began, "we're here tonight at the request of a newly formed group"—he cleared his throat—"one involving colored teachers—and parents—that was formed without the knowledge of the school board, his honor the Mayor or myself. Mr. Blair tells me this group does not have a legal charter (Ebon Jones's eyes widened), but I felt it was in the good of the community to air such a protest as the group is about to make, in spite of this illegal procedure on their part."

Jess cleared his throat and paused, letting this information sink into the colored ranks. "Now I'm going to tell you very bluntly what their protest amounts to. They want the Negro freshman class moved back to the already overcrowded high school. Before I ask for their reasons, I'd like to ask Mr. Bart Phillips, our beloved fire chief, to tell us briefly what physical dangers this presents to the students themselves."

Bart, his red face growing redder, got up and said that the high school already held more students than it should, to comply with safety standards. Then Treasurer Blair, at Jess's request, rose and painted a dismal picture of state aid, saying in the end there was no money for building additional rooms at the high school to accommodate the overflow.

"Well," Jess addressed the audience again, "I have stated the protest and you have heard statements from Mr. Phillips and Mr. Blair, who have given much thought to the condition which is the basis of this protest." He cleared his throat and looked squarely at Professor Ebon Jones. "Ebon, are you the spokesman for this group?"

Ebon stirred in his seat, remaining there speechless for a moment or so. Then, feeling the eyes of his association—his illegal association—upon him, he rose slowly. "Well—well, yes—in a way," he stammered, "Mr. Superintendent."

"Fine, Ebon. Now, did your association take the fire chief's findings and the financial situation of the village into consideration when you planned this protest?"

"Well—no sir, we didn't."

"Why not, may I ask?"

"Because—because they didn't know about such conditions, sir."

"They—and you?"

"Yessir."

"Then you would agree"—he was looking toward the Mayor now—"that your group has acted unwisely, wouldn't you, Ebon?"

"Well, sir, in the light of such findings, I suppose. I—I feel maybe we were a little hasty, but the teachers and myself tried to—"

"Just a minute!" Sarah Winger pulled up out of her seat, ignoring Jack's tug on her coat sleeve. "How long ago was it you made these rules about safety and such stuff as you're tellin' us about?"

Jess gazed sternly at Sarah. She stared back.

"I thought Ebon Jones was the speaker for this group," Jess said flatly.

"I thought so too, until just now, but—"

"Well, if he's the spokesman I'd prefer listening to what he has to say."

"And I'd prefer you listenin' to what I've got to say."

Jess continued his bluff. "I'm going to have to ask you to yield the floor to your official spokesman."

There was a stirring in the back of the room. Judge Cavanaugh had risen very quickly to his feet. "Jess," he said rather heatedly, "I think you're being mighty highhanded in this matter, and I for one feel this lady has a right to say her piece."

"I—I have no objections to her speaking, only it's regular procedure to hear—"

"Don't tell me about procedure, Jess. I know a little about that myself, you know." The Judge was unrelenting.

"All right, sir. All right, would the lady give her name and speak up," he said, watching the Judge sink back to his seat.

"I'm Mrs. Winger. You know me."

"All right, Sarah. Speak up. We're listening."

"Mrs. Winger. Mrs. Jack Winger," Sarah repeated.

"All right, Mrs. Winger. We're still listening."

"I'd like to know when those rules were made you're talkin' about."

Jess turned to Bart Phillips. "Can you answer her question?"

"We've always had safety rules at the high school," Bart said.

"I know that," Sarah answered, "but I'm talkin' about the ones dealing with the number of people allowed in the school."

Bart looked up at Jess, then back at Sarah. "Well—during a recent inspection of the premises."

"Just lately then?" Sarah questioned.

"I suppose I'd have to say so."

"Did you inspect the colored school, too, Mister Phillips?"

"We intend to do it this coming week."

Sarah looked down at Ebon, then back to Bart Phillips. "Well, our association can tell you it's a lot more overcrowded than the high school, and that it ain't brick, and it ain't got a gymnasium or indoor toilets. And while I'm at it, I'd like to know why it was just the colored freshmen children who got pushed out and none of the white children."

Now Marshall Goodlander was on his feet. "I'd like the pleasure of answering this woman, if you don't mind, Jess."

"Go right ahead, Mister Mayor," Jess said.

"My good lady," Marshall began, "as mayor of this town, I have gotten to know these people here on this platform very well, and they don't deserve the insinuating remarks you're making against their wise decisions. We care just as much about the welfare of the nig—nigra students as we do the whites. Some of you folks, like Ebon Jones and others, know where my heart is. I know how you feel, my good lady, but you must have patience. You must give us time to rectify whatever wrongs there are in our school system, in our entire community. We love you and we want to help you, but we can't do everything in one day. You just have to—"

105

"Mister Mayor!" Jack was on his feet beside Sarah, holding her trembling arm. "Mister Mayor!"

"Yes—yes, Winger."

"You just said you know how we feel."

"Yes I did, and—"

"Well, let me tell you somethin', Mister Mayor"—Jack was standing at his full six-feet-four-inches now—"there ain't no white man in the world who knows, really knows, how a black man feels—"

"What do you mean?" Goodlander cut in.

"I mean just what I said. If you turned colored right now, they'd have you in a strait jacket up at Osawatomie by this time next week. You say have patience. Well, by God, if we ain't got it I don't know who has. We been waitin' and waitin' and waitin', since way 'fore Lincoln set 'bout tryin' to free us. The proclamation's layin' dusty on the shelves and we still ain't free—"

"Amen, brother," Maggie Pullens murmured.

"You say you love us. Well, it's a funny kind'a love. We pay taxes to you, we do your dirty work, we help fight for that flag you just had us pledgin' to, and you still walk on us—"

"Amen."

"Your young'uns suck the breasts of our womenfolk till they're strong and healthy a'nough to fly on their own—then you start tellin' 'em they're too good to eat by us—"

"That's enough of this, Jack Winger," Goodlander snapped. "I'll not stand here and take this abuse from—"

"Then sit down and take it!" Jack bellowed. "We're here to thrash this thing out once and for all. Did your boy Luke ever have to sit in that dirty peanut gallery at the Regency show house? My boy Pete here ain't gonna ever forget Bert Sampson askin' him to take a sandwich outside his drugstore to eat—the first day he got back from overseas, before he had a chance to shed his fightin' clothes. Did your boy Luke ever have to take such as that?"

"I won't listen to another minute of this!" Marshall Goodlander sat down.

"Winger—" Jess tried to interrupt.

"My wife here and me helped vote you into office. I heard you git up on a platform and talk 'bout how you was gonna do this and that. Now you keep hollerin', 'I won't listen, I won't listen.' Well, next time you're up on one of them stands hollerin' for votes, I won't listen to you either!"

"Amen, brother Winger—amen."

106

Jack sat down. Sarah eased down beside him, her fingers pressing into his thick wrist, expressing her feeling of pride. "Well done, Jack," she whispered. His eyes burned straight ahead.

Jess banged his fist on the table for order. "We aren't getting much accomplished this way," he acknowledged. "I suggest that the school board have time to study this protest, under more favorable circumstances, and that we have another closed meeting before this school year is over."

"With our association?" Reverend Broadnap hollered out the question.

"With your association, sir—your association," Jess answered wryly, "and if there is no more business I'll say that this meeting is adjourned."

Within fifteen minutes the hall was empty and dark.

"Charter or no charter," Sarah told Jack later that night as they undressed for bed, "we've got things stirred up—and everybody thought you did a mighty good job of tellin' Marshall Goodlander off."

"Just got a little hot under the collar, that's all," Jack mumbled.

"Those kids are gittin' back in that school, mind you. You watch what I'm tellin' you." She blew out the lamp and they went to sleep.

May had come. Booker Savage was slinging old automobile tires on his junk heap when a car stopped in front of his shack. He started to throw the last tire, then stopped at the sight of Marcus and a uniformed guard getting out of the car. He dropped the tire and walked toward them.

Marcus spoke first. "Hi, Paw."

"Hi there, boy." Booker pulled a cigar butt from his pocket and lit it. "Didn't know you was comin' today. Nobody told me."

"You his paw?" the guard asked.

"That's right."

"Okay, you gotta sign these papers on this line." He handed Booker a form and a pencil.

"What's this for?"

"To show we turned him over to you. Sign here."

Booker took the paper and marked an X where the guard indicated.

"That ain't no signature," the guard said.

"He cain't write," Marcus explained. "That's his legal way of signin'."

The guard grunted, took the paper and pencil back, got into the car and drove off. Marcus turned and watched the car churning away in a cloud of dust. "Well, I'm glad I won't be lookin' him in the face tomorra mornin','," he said. Then he turned back to his father and they looked at each other without speaking for a moment.

"Well, come on in, boy. Ain't much here to eat, but I'll stir up somethin'." Marcus picked up a small battered bag and they went into the shack.

Booker cooked some oatmeal and poured some molasses over it; then he piled cold biscuits on the table and they began to eat. "How'd they treat you up there, boy?"

"Like a dog."

"I meant to come up to see you, but things got busy."

"Yeh, I know."

"Well—well, you glad to be back, ain'tcha?"

"Anybody'd be glad to git out'a that stinkin' hole."

"They beat up on you?"

Marcus didn't answer. Instead he parted his coarse hair and revealed a long scar, a memento of Charlie Crapper's billy club. Then he turned his head and pulled down his shirt collar. There was an ugly raw scab on his shoulder.

"Them sons-a-bitches," Booker muttered, "I'm gonna kill one of them peckerwoods shore'n hell one of these days."

Marcus remained silent, spooning in the last of the oatmeal. Booker stirred uneasily on his chair, not knowing what more to say. "Goddam dirty bastards—dirty sons-a-bitches."

Suddenly Marcus stopped chewing. His jaws began quivering and he let out a guttural cry, spewing the food from his mouth over the table. Booker saw the tears coursing down his cheeks before he buried his head in his powerful arms—sobbing as if he were an overgrown baby.

"What's the matter, boy? What's the matter?" Booker was up and over him now. "You hurtin' or somethin'? What's the matter?"

Then, as if escaping some unforeseen doom, Marcus jumped up and ran from the house through the junk-strewn paths towards Flynn's River. He didn't stop sobbing until he lay on its banks, watching the river flow slowly past. He was free again, but his homecoming had left him nearly as empty and frustrated as he'd been during his imprisonment. He rolled over and propped himself against a tree. His hand felt the time-worn sides of a pebble. It was smooth and cool and sort of soothing to the touch. He rubbed it over his hot face, up his jaw and stuck the point of it into his right ear. He pushed a finger into his other ear, cutting off all sound. He was deaf to the world. Then he closed his eyes tight against the morning light. At first there was all darkness, then slowly he made out the image of the slow-moving river, still flowing through the blackness of his subconscious void. He remained that way for several minutes. The river image disappeared, then little flecks of white shimmered in the darkness. He opened his eyes and uncovered his ears. The point of the stone had some earwax sticking to it. He rubbed it off on his overall leg, then he stood and threw the stone toward the river. It splapped against the water, skipped twice and sank to the bottom. Marcus stood watching the ripples dissipate, then he turned and walked to the road—and on toward the center of the village.

CHAPTER ✦ 9

"GUESS WHAT, Momma?" Newt said at supper that night. "Guess what happened to me today?"

Sarah raised her head and smiled. "Somethin' good, I hope."

"The class voted for me to make the graduation speech. What you think of that, Poppa?"

Jack's mustache twitched slightly, showing he was pleased, but he grunted, "Uh-hu, uh-hu. Pass me the apple butter."

Sarah beamed. "That's wonderful, just wonderful, Newt."

"Good goin'," Pete said.

"Why'd they pick you? Nobody else want it?" Prissy teased.

Newt was too happy to banter with Prissy. "Goin' to be needin' a suit, Poppa," he said.

"What's wrong with the duds you already got?"

"Don't start that, Jack," Sarah said. "You know he's growin' out of all his clothes."

"Another year'n I'll be almost as tall as Pete."

"I'm six-three, boy. You're gonna have to do some real growin'."

"Polly's comin' soon as school's out," Sarah said.

"I know Polly, Momma?" Newt asked.

"You was very little when she was here the last time."

Prissy laughed. "You ought'a remember her. You went around tellin' everybody your white cousin was here."

"I did not."

"Aw yes you did. Remember, Momma?"

"He didn't know—he was too young," Sarah defended.

"Wasn't much wrong, at that," Pete said. "Polly's 'bout as white as anybody in town."

"Nice girl, good manners and all," Sarah said.

"Whose preserves, Sarah?" Jack was spreading them thick on his cornbread.

"Mary Kiner sent 'em over by Jake the other day."

"Speakin' of Jake—did'ya know Marcus was back, Newt?" Pete took the preserves from his father as he spoke.

"Yeh? You see him?"

"Nope. His old man told me."

"You don't call a boy's father 'old man,' Pete. You know better."

"Sorry, Momma. Didn't mean nothin' by it."

"He back for good, I wonder?" Newt's mood was changing.

"Long as he stays out'a trouble, I guess," Pete said.

Prissy got up and started clearing the table. "Maybe you better study boxin' 'stead of speakin', Newt," she chided. "Marcus don't love you very much."

"I ain't scared of Marcus, and I—"

"—And you don't have no need to be. Prissy, just go on. You're forever startin' somethin'."

"I ain't startin' nothin', Momma. I'm just tellin' him the truth."

"Go on, and quit yappin' so much."

"Yessem."

"High wind blowin' tonight," Jack remarked, getting up.

After Newt finished wiping the dishes, he got a pencil and pad from his room and came back to the kitchen. He waited until Prissy was through cleaning, then he turned up the lamp wick and began writing his speech.

Prissy dried the suds from her hands, hung up the dish rags and started out. Then she tiptoed back and peeped over Newt's shoulder. She read his first seven words, "Ladies and gentlemen, I am here to"—and she finished the sentence aloud—"to louse up this program." Newt sprang up and cocked his fist, but Prissy made off, slamming the door behind her. Sitting down again, Newt penciled out what he had written. Then he settled back and looked through the window into the darkness, trying meanwhile to construct another opening.

The wind had grown higher. It nudged the screen door back and forth, and its wailing sliced away at the quietness of the kitchen. Tree branches bobbed from the blowing, scratched the roof; their shadows suggested human movements at the window. The thought of Marcus Savage popped into Newt's mind, and he began pondering the evils Marcus' presence could bring. He tried to get back to the speech, but no words and thoughts came together in a fitting way. Before long he was slumped over the table, fast asleep—

111

his subconscious tangled in amorphous visions of swirling wind, dust and water; of Marcus; of fighting and death.

"Newt!" Sarah called from another room.

He bolted upright, rubbing his eyes. "Yessem." The lamp wick, bleary to his sight at first, gradually shimmered into focus. He batted his eyelids several times, blinking away the ugly, shapeless dream.

"It's late! Time for bed!"

"Yessem," he said hoarsely. He got up, blew out the flame, and stumbled off to his room with the pencil and pad in his hand.

The next afternoon, on their way home from school, Newt, Beansy and Jappy met Marcus. Having seen them first, he'd hid behind a tree until they were several feet past him.

"Hyee!"

The harsh voice came as familiar to them as a dog's bark. They turned as one in their surprise. "Hi, Marcus." "H'lo." "What'a you say?"

"Thought you guys forgot me."

"Didn't you git our Christmas card we sent you?" Newt asked.

"Yeh," Beansy said, "we all signed it and Newt mailed it. Didn't you, Newt?"

"Sure did," Newt admitted, "sent it two days before Christmas."

"Well, I didn't git no card," Marcus lied.

"Funny," Newt said, "I sure sent it."

"Callin' me a liar, Winger?"

"I ain't callin' you anything. I just said I sent the card. And I did."

"And I'm sayin' I didn't git it. One of us is lyin'." Newt kept still. "I say, one of us is lyin', Winger."

"Okay—okay. So one of us is lyin'."

"You ready to say which?" Marcus was inching in.

"Come on—let's go," Beansy said.

Newt was as eager to go as Beansy, but pride held him to the spot. "I ain't for any trouble, Marcus, but I ain't for runnin' either—that's for sure."

"Here comes Pete," Jappy said almost gleefully.

The words fell on Newt's ears like a blessing, giving him courage. He looked at Marcus squarely for the first time. He thought he still might have to fight him, even if Pete was coming, but he knew Marcus would have to fight fair with Pete around.

"I'll see you guys later—'specially you, Winger," Marcus snarled, starting off.

"What's goin' on, fellas?" Pete asked quietly.

"Nothin' much," Newt answered, his eyes still on Marcus.

Pete sensed the situation. "Glad to see you back, Marcus," he said.

"Yeh?" Marcus grunted. He turned and eyed Pete.

"Yep, I am—and I think the fellas here would be too if you'd just let 'em."

"Well, I ain't carin' what none'a you feel."

Pete turned to Newt, Beansy and Jappy. "You guys go on home. I'll see you later, Newt." The three boys slung their books over their shoulders and walked off.

Pete turned back to Marcus. "Goin' my way?"

"Nope."

"Okay," Pete said and started off. After a few steps he stopped and came back. "Marcus, the whole world ain't against you, like you think."

Marcus looked up curiously as Pete continued, "You're back now. Give yourself a chance and try'n forget 'bout what's happened in the past. I—we all know how tough you had it—we know it ain't been easy for you, but if you git into trouble again you're gonna land right back up there, and you know it. Why don't you git a job someplace and make a good start this time?"

Marcus' eyes widened. "A job? Where'm I gonna git a job? Ain't no place in town where they'd let me come in the door 'cept at Chappie's."

"Ain't many doors open to none of us round here, Marcus."

"You niggers is just as bad as the peckerwoods, far as I can see."

Pete chuckled. "I know how you feel." He thought for a moment. "Why don't you ask Chappie for a job?"

"Doin' what?"

"I don't know—washin' dishes, sweepin' or somethin'."

"Why you so anxious to help me?"

"I ain't exactly so happy to help you. I need a job 'bout bad as you—"

"—But you're the son of churchgoin' people and they wouldn't like you workin' there. But it's okay for me, huh?"

"In a way, I guess you're right. But if you want me to, I'll talk to Chappie 'bout you."

"I don't need no help from the likes of you."

Pete looked at him for a moment. "Well, I'm gonna talk to Chappie 'bout givin' you a job. You can go see him if you want. If you don't, it won't be no skin off my hide." He turned and walked across the street and around the corner. Crossing an alley, he entered Chappie Logan's through the back.

Marcus stood looking after him. "Chappie's wouldn't be so bad maybe," he thought. "Better'n nothin'. Least I won't have to eat that garbage Paw slings together." A little later he saw Pete come back around the corner. He kept out of sight until Pete was gone, then he went hesitantly in the direction of Chappie's.

"You come quicker'n I thought," Chappie said, as he waddled around the room with several bottles of corn liquor under his fat arms. "Pete Winger says you want a job. Do you or don't you?"

"Wish he'd tend to his own bus'ness 'stead of mine."

"Pete's a good boy, mighty good boy. Pay you to listen a little bit to him."

"I ain't listenin' to none of his holy talk—"

Chappie set the bottles on a table. "Look, I ain't got a lot'a time. You want a job or not?"

"Doin' what?"

"What I want you to do, that's what."

"What kind'a pay do I git?"

"Five dollars a week and grub when you workin'."

Marcus looked about the empty room. The crooked booths reminded him of cattle stalls, and the murky windows and mirrors hadn't been washed for years. The odor of stale smoke and alcohol hung in the air like an invisible mist. "I'll take it," he said. "When do I start?"

"Right now. You know how to make beds?"

"What you mean, make beds?"

"Change sheets and pilla-cases, stuff like that."

"We ain't never had no sheets and pilla-cases at home, but I had to make the brass-ass's bed up at Spit's."

"Okay." Chappie walked over to a big closet and jerked out eight sheets and eight pillowcases. "Here," he said, shoving the linen into Marcus's arms, "there's eight rooms up on the next floor. There's a broom and scuttle at the top of the stairs. Change all them beds and sweep the floors."

Marcus started up. "What else?"

"You git that done and come back down here and fix my room up." Chappie motioned him up the stairs. Then he turned. "Hold it a minute," he said, opening another closet full of hand towels. "You gotta put two of these under the pillows on each bed. Git me?"

"Yep."

"Okay. Git goin'." Then, "Hey, boy! The railroaders live on the third. Don't go near their rooms till I give you the word."

"Okay," Marcus hollered back.

The rooms were numbered from one to eight, and Marcus started in number one. He was up to room three before he began wondering about the sameness of their appearance. Each one contained a bed and a little stand with an ash tray on it. That was all. "Ever who stays in here don't have no clothes or nothin' else," he mumbled, smoothing out the clean sheets. Then he suddenly laughed out loud. "Goddam, what a dunce I am. This is the whore house Paw's always talkin' 'bout." He laughed again. "I'm a real dunce."

From then on he noticed the condition of the soiled sheets. Their disarrangement and the telltale stains backed up his new-found knowledge.

"Goddam," he chuckled to Chappie later, "ain't this a bitch? I'm workin' in a whore house for a livin'."

Chappie frowned. "Look, don't go spreadin' talk like that round. I told Pete Winger you'd be washin' windows and workin' round the kitchen. You go blabbin' off, and out you go."

"Ain't no need to worry, Chappie. I ain't sayin' nothin' long's I git my pay on time."

Chappie gave him a nasty look, shook his head and ushered him into what Chappie called his "den." The den held wonders the likes of which Marcus never new existed. The bed was canopied, and twice as big as any he'd ever seen. And though the room was very large, the candy-striped paper on the walls could hardly be seen for the great number of pictures plastering it. And what pictures they were, Marcus thought, craning his neck in awe as he awaited Chappie's orders.

"Now, I don't want you to touch nothin' in here but my bed, the floor and that face bowl over there in the corner. Wash that every day. Git me?"

"Yeh."

"Don't fool round with none of the pichures or go in my drawers or fool with none of these papers layin' round here 'less I tell you. Git me?"

"Okay."

After Chappie left, Marcus walked about in this world of strange photographs, circus posters, lurid drawings and sketches. Most of the subjects were nude or close to it, and there were bearded circus ladies, female impersonators, show girls and a motley of others. Almost all of the photographs were autographed to Chappie. One said, "To Chappie, the big daddy with big things. Yours, Poppy." Another, scrawled over the huge breast of a buxom nude, said, "The breast of everything to Chappie. Yours, Cleotopa." And yet another: "To Chappie, from the gal with two beards." Her pose made her meaning clear.

"Damn," Marcus kept saying to himself as he walked about. Finally he came to a corner that was closed in by red velvet draping. He looked cautiously to the door, then peeped behind the drape. There was a makeshift altar, covered by the same velvet, with a crucifix standing on it. Above it hung two ornately framed, tinted photographs. "His maw and paw," Marcus decided. Up in the left corner was a cluster of small half-burned candles. To the far right of the crude altar was a Bible in which were pressed some dried rose petals, sticking from the closed pages like faded parchment. A strong odor of incense clung to the enclosure.

"Paw'd shore be put out to see this in Chappie's own bedroom," Marcus mumbled as he closed the drape. Turning, he drew back at the sight of two pinkish eyes staring from the darkness of the floor at the side of the bed. "What the hell—?" he gasped. It was a huge, moth-eaten bearskin, its bared fangs showing fierce in its massive head, its long claws seeming to dig into the varicolored carpet it lay on.

Now he studied the bedpost with the clusters of cherubs and angels carved into the mahogany. The canopy and the bedspread were made of the same red-wine chintz material. In between the two head posts, and nailed to the wall, was a faded picture of a she-monster with a goat's body and a lion's head that vomited flames. Upon its back rode two unhappy figures clutching one another.

"One hell of a joint," Marcus muttered, "one hell of a joint." He took the broom and swept his way over to a huge oak closet lining the far wall. He peeped into the labyrinthine inner structure. Hanging there seemed to be hundreds of silk shirts, twice as many ties, and almost as many checkered, striped and tweedy suits with caps to match—all lined up neatly, and obviously not worn for years. There was row upon row of sharp-pointed shoes that Chappie couldn't possibly squeeze his big feet into now. "Goddam," Marcus muttered again, "look at all them overcoats. Same color as all the suits."

The room was lit by candles and two red-chimneyed oil

lamps with porcelain peacocks for bases. These sat on an ornate dresser. There were photographs on the dresser too, but they were of Chappie in his younger and thinner days, dressed in some of the finery that now hung neglected in his closet. Too, there was one of him as a baby, sitting in a white lace dress on the lap of the same woman whose portrait hung above the velvet altar. Another one showed him in short pants, a middy blouse, a straw sailor hat, black ribbed stockings and high-button shoes. He wore this outfit as he proudly straddled a white donkey in some long-forgotten backyard.

Marcus inched a drawer open, and there were more silk shirts. As he ran his hand beneath the stack, trying to determine the number, his fingers struck a metal object. His touch curved to the shape of it. It was a pistol. He slipped it out quickly, rubbed the long barrel admiringly, then he heard footsteps. He put the gun back hastily, shut the drawer, grabbed the broom and started sweeping.

"How you comin'?" Chappie asked as he came through the door.

"Okay—okay," Marcus said briskly.

"Told the cook to give you a sandwich and coffee after you git through here." Chappie picked up something from the dresser, and Marcus watched his big hulk move back through the door.

"That bastard must weigh three hundred pounds," Marcus said under his breath.

The following Saturday morning, Pete, without explaining why, got Newt up rather early. "How'd you like to do a little boxin' this mornin'?"

Newt looked surprised. "Boxin'? With you?"

"Yeh, with me."

So right after breakfast Pete took Newt behind the henhouse and gave him his first serious lesson in self-defense— teaching him to lead with the left, feint with the right, double-jab with the left, send home the damaging right and roll away, keeping balance with the left foot forward.

"That's it . . . that's it . . . feint . . . come on . . . two left jabs . . . cock the right . . . feint . . . jab again . . . throw the right." Newt swung the right—hard.

"Try again . . . you missed . . . come on . . . left, left . . . right . . . feint . . . jab . . . throw it!" Newt aimed for Pete's chin. But the blow never reached its target.

"Uump!" Newt grunted as the wind shot out of his mouth.

Pete's big fist had crashed into his midsection, caving him in. "Ho-hold it a-min—minute—I'm—out of breath."

"Let that be a lesson to you," Pete said. "Don't ever forget to cover your gut. Keep your elbows lower when you come in for the kill."

And the rest of that month Newt worked as hard on the art of self-defense as he did on his speech.

"You comin' along all right," Pete confided about two weeks later. "Keep it up and I'll have to git a few lessons someplace myself."

To Newt, this was like receiving a high school diploma, for Pete, though he wasn't a bully, had gained a lot of respect with his fists through the years. "Pete don't ever pick a fight, but he don't ever lose one either," Jack Winger was quick and proud to tell anyone who misconstrued his son's easygoing manner.

Graduation came on a most beautiful night in June. Sarah Winger took off work that day. "I've got butterflies in my stomach, Judge," she explained to Jeff Cavanaugh the night before. "You'll just have to do without me tomorrow." The Judge understood, predicted that Newt would make a fine speech and begged her not to worry.

Just before the exercises commenced, Ebon Jones stepped from behind the curtain on the stage and, with a broad grin on his face, shouted, "We have been victorious! We have won our fight! This class graduating tonight will enter the high school!"

Applause and shrill whistling shook the auditorium. Sarah pinched Jack in her excitement, and Jack managed a broad smile.

"Well, you made it," he whispered to his wife.

"We made it," she whispered back.

Ebon continued, "The superintendent of schools regrets that he won't be able to be with us tonight. But he sent his greetings along with that good news. I want to thank you all for the courageous effort you put forth. I thank you."

Newt sat proudly, but a little nervous, in the front of the auditorium with the other members of his class. There were in all six girls and six boys—the girls dressed in white, the boys in blue. Newt's father had scraped up enough for a suit two days before.

Arcella sat next to Newt, and every now and then they would accidentally rub each other with a hand, leg or shoulder. After several minutes Professor Ebon Jones stepped again from behind the curtain. This time he spoke to the

118

graduates about the role they would someday play in the world. He droned on about the possibilities that lay ahead for them. Newt hung onto every word he said, binding himself solemnly to their meaning. Then he heard Professor Jones ending with, "and finally I say to you, get as much learning as you possibly can. You will need every bit you can possibly grasp for the long journey ahead."

The class play, with Beansy playing the lead, was Shakespeare's *Comedy of Errors*. And Beansy did justice to the title, bringing the audience to a howl when he accidentally tripped and sprawled in the middle of the stage.

Now it was time for Newt's speech. With a glance at Myrtle Beasly—who had helped him with the construction of it—he walked to the front of the stage, sweat coursing down to his toes. Sarah twisted uncomfortably in her seat until he started:

"Pro—Professor Jones, parents, friends and fellow students, our class's motto has been 'Look back only when you can find something to help push you ahead.' We know that long after we leave Washington Junior High for good we will look back to her, because it is she who has given us the things we need to go forward. She has prepared us for this difficult journey that Professor Jones has told us we must face. (Sarah heaved a sigh of relief.) Our days here have been happy ones, ones we will always remember. They have been days filled with hope—longing for a better world to live in. (Newt fumbled the paper, and Sarah caught her breath.) But we know that we have been sup-supplied with the materials to help us move forward with con-confidence and courage.

"We hope for a better world and we also hope to have a part in making it a better world. Nobody knows better than we do what a country filled with hate and bi-bigotry can do to the people who must live in it. All we have to do is ask our brothers and our fathers who not so long ago faced death overseas. (Pete felt a lump in his throat.) We all hope and pray that those who didn't come back didn't—die in vain. (Newt dropped the paper to his side and spoke from his own heart.) We, our class, never thought we would be going to the high school next year, but we had made up our minds to study all the harder if we didn't. (He read again.) We are all thankful for our parents and teachers who are fighting—who can make you proud of us when we get there.

"As the school year ends, our need for knowledge gets more important. We will be stepping into higher education

119

but also into problems that have faced our people for many years. Our race is not the best liked in the world, and we know it, but our class is de-determined that this will not keep us from going forward. We are proud to be black. And (The applause, something he'd never anticipated, stopped him momentarily; he lost his place then found it again), and we have seen the end of a terrible war. But this is in the past. We look back only to take a lesson from it. What happens in the future will be determined by what we learned from the past. Our class does not expect life to be easy. We only expect it to be better, and we are determined to help make it so by con-trib-uting something to it ourselves. Using some of the words of Abraham Lincoln, I end by saying that our future is piled high with difficulty, and we must rise to this difficulty. As our problems will be new, so we must think anew, and act anew. Thank you." He bowed stiffly and turned about.

It was over, days of rehearsing, nights of fearing he would "flub-de-dub," as Prissy had warned he would. He bounced back to his seat in a hail of applause—hardly knowing what he'd said on that stage that seemed as big as the whole world itself. And Arcella complimented him when he sat down, even squeezed his hand. "Oh, Newt, it was marvelous," she whispered.

Next, they filed up and got their diplomas. They held them on their breasts as the school chorus and orchestra joined in a stanza of "America," then they marched off into the arms of their proud parents, who by now had rushed to the bottom of the steps to meet them.

Later, Newt and Arcella walked home behind their families, and Newt said shyly, "I'd like to take you some place for some ice cream if your momma would let you."

"Let's catch up and see," Arcella said.

They caught up at the next corner and got permission. Pete slipped Newt fifty cents before they took off across the tracks to Sampson's drugstore.

Most of the graduates from the white junior high school were there when they went in. They were jammed around the soda fountain, in the booths and on the floor. Newt made his way to the counter and ordered two banana splits.

"To take out?" the soda jerk asked.

"Two banana splits," Newt repeated.

The soda jerk gave him a distrustful glance, but he turned and dished up the splits—on cardboard plates. "Here you are!" he hollered above the noise. "Thirty cents." Newt gave him three dimes and turned away, his face burning from embarrassment, his whole evening beginning to hint of a bad dream.

"Come on, Arcella—let's go."

"Newt—Newt Winger!" It was Waldo Newhall and his girl. They were sitting at a table, still in cap and gown. "Congratulations on your graduation!" Waldo shouted. "Come sit with us!"

"Like to, Waldo—but we gotta be goin'."

"Aw come on, Winger," he said, nudging Arcella into the seat beside his date. "Kate, this is Arcella Jefferson. You know Newt."

"Yeh, we know each other," Newt said, "but look, Waldo, we can't sit here with you like this—"

Waldo was beside himself with gaiety. "Who says you can't? This is a free country, Winger. Sit down. Come on now."

"Maybe it'll work," Newt thought, "with a white boy invitin' us to sit with them." He decided to try it. "Okay," he said shakily.

Things went well for a few minutes, then Newt saw Bert Sampson, the owner, making his way through the crowd, and his heart sank. Bert came up to the table and tapped Newt on the shoulder. "Okay, buddy, you and your girl'll have to finish eatin' outside. Sorry."

"What you mean?" Waldo said. "These are friends of mine."

"Then go outside and eat with 'em, if they're friends of yourn."

"I ain't goin' anywhere!" Waldo snapped, "and they ain't either! We paid for this slop and we're goin' to eat it here, right here!"

"Forget it, Waldo," Newt said. "We're goin' to a party anyway." The place was dead quiet now. "Come on, Arcella. Goodbye, Kate. So long, Waldo."

Neither of them answered. Kate turned and looked up at Bert Sampson. "You big slob," she said. Bert looked at her sullenly, but he didn't answer. "You big slob," she repeated. Bert turned and walked back to the end of the counter.

Newt jerked the door open and they went out, walking briskly to the corner as if they really had some place to go. They stood there on the curb under the lamp light for a few moments. "Oh, Newt—" Arcella began to cry.

"It's okay," Newt said, putting his arms around her, "it's okay. We'll show 'em someday. We'll show 'em." He threw the remains of his banana split on the sidewalk. Arcella smiled and did the same. Then they walked slowly, arm in arm, to the tracks, across them, and into the darkness of their side of town.

CHAPTER ❦ 10

JULY FOURTH at Peaceful Park was always a big day for Newt. This particular one had special meaning because he was taking Arcella. With Prissy and Pete, he stopped by that morning to pick her up; and after helping her into the buggy, he plopped down beside her in the back seat. Catching a lilac fragrance, he said, "Guess you're wearin' the toilet water I gave you for your birthday."

"That's right," she said, smiling.

He inhaled deeply and moved closer to her—and within a block they were rubbing hands and touching knees.

The sputtering and popping of firecrackers sounded as they neared the park entrance. "They're startin' early," Pete said.

"I don't want those things goin' off around me," Prissy remarked.

"You scared of fireworks?" Newt asked Arcella.

"I don't like setting them off. I think the sparklers are prettiest."

"They'll be shootin' the rockets off over the water after dark."

"That should be lovely," she replied.

"There's Earl, Jappy and Beansy," Prissy said, pointing at Newt's friends walking alongside the lagoon.

"Where's Skunk!" Newt hollered out to them.

"Comin' later!" Beansy hollered back.

"What an awful name," Arcella said, shaking her head. "Why don't you call him by his right name?"

"I did once and he thought I was tryin' to kid him." Newt laughed.

"Oh, well," Arcella remarked gaily, "if he ever gets married, his wife will change that. You won't call her Mrs. Skunk."

"You don't know Skunk. He says he's goin' to stay single all his life and have lots of babes."

"Ha ha," Arcella scoffed. "So you think that's smart?"

"Not me—not me," Newt said, correcting her quickly.

After Skunk arrived, Newt departed with his friends to shoot off cannon crackers, leaving Arcella with Prissy. Though Skunk kidded him about going back after an hour, as he had promised, he returned on time; and then he and Arcella went off in search of wild flowers. They tromped on through the woods, picking a flower here and there, leaving the noises and the voices of the others far behind.

"Oh, look—a cluster of violets," Arcella cooed, "and what a lovely setting—like a garden in the forest." She took Newt's hand and they sidestepped down the incline to the spot. "Oh, they're so beautiful here I hate to pick them."

"Then don't," Newt said softly. "Let's just sit here and look at them for a little while."

"Oh—that would be silly, wouldn't it?"

"But you just got through sayin' it was a beautiful settin', didn't you?"

"Of course, of course, but—"

"Aw, come on. Let's sit just for a little while," Newt said, coaxing her down to the mossy earth.

Then they sat there, still holding hands, gazing at the violets as if they were the only flowers in the world.

"We must always think of this as our garden, Newt—our private garden in the forest."

"We could come and see it every now and then."

"Maybe—who can tell?"

They inched together, joining their warmth. And Arcella's lilac fragrance hung heavily in the fresh damp of their "private garden." Her cheek was suddenly against his. He took her in his arms and gently pressed her back upon the earth. Her lips parted and he instantly leaned over her and covered them with his own. Then they both closed their eyes to the dim-lit woods, their ears to its faint noises—and she began squirming beneath his trembling.

"Arcella—Arcella."

"Don't—don't, Newt, I—"

"Please—please—"

"No—no—no. Let's just lay here like this."

"Oh—Arcella."

"Stop—st—st—stop—I can't—I can't—not now—please—please." She pushed herself free of his body.

"What's the matter? What's the matter, Arcella?"

"I don't know. I want to, but I just can't—not just now. Not now."

"But I love you."

"And I love you, but something might happen."

"But I want to marry you someday, Arcella. It—it ain't like I just wanted to have a good time or somethin'."

"I know—I promise, but let's wait."

They sat up. Neither of them looked at the violets now.

"Guess the barbecue's 'bout ready," Newt said.

"Hope so," she answered softly. "I'm awfully hungry."

Newt helped her up and they retrieved the flowers Arcella had dropped earlier. Putting their arms around each other, they kissed again, scrambled up and then strolled off, hand in hand, toward the picnic grounds.

That night, as the two of them sat watching the rockets burst high over the lagoon, Newt began thinking seriously of the day when he would really marry Arcella. They wouldn't live in Cherokee Flats, he thought. And she'd probably insist that he finish college—if he could get the money someplace. His mother and father could never send him, he knew. At that moment he resolved to save every penny he could put his hands on.

A rocket shot up, burst and sprayed its red, white, green and blue over the silvery dusk of the lagoon.

"Arcella."

"Yes."

"Would you marry me if I didn't go to college?"

"Oh, Newt, we've got years to think about such things. Let's watch the rockets."

"But I gotta know now," he insisted.

"You mean you have to know now." She smiled.

"I have to know now—then," he agreed.

"Well, I don't think it would make any difference, but I sure hope you'll try to go just the same." She pinched his arm tenderly.

"I'm sure goin' to try—I—can I say we're sort of engaged now—like—well you know, like we're goin' to get married for sure?"

"One doesn't become engaged with hundreds of people around them shooting off firecrackers, Newt Winger."

"Then I'll ask you again later."

"Prissy tells me your cousin Polly's coming soon, and that she's real pretty. Maybe you'll want to marry her instead."

"Marry my own cousin?"

"Some people do," she said. "Better look out!"

"Don't worry—not me."

Two days later, when Polly Bates stepped off the train, Newt was looking in the opposite direction. "There she is! There she is!" Prissy shouted. "Polly! Polly! Here we are!"

"Where's she?" Newt said, jerking about. Prissy was already running to meet her.

"Come on, Newt," Pete called, "that's her in the red straw hat."

"Golly, she is white," Newt mumbled to himself.

After hugging Prissy, Polly ran and threw her arms around Pete.

"It's so good to see you again," Polly cried out.

Newt hung back. He noticed the whites on the station platform, especially the men, poking one another—saying things he couldn't quite hear.

"Is that Newt?" Polly stretched out her arms. "Boy, how you've grown. Come gimme a kiss."

Newt stepped forward and they embraced and kissed. "Good to see you, cousin Polly," he found himself saying.

"You're almost as big as Pete," she said as the porter handed down her two bags.

"Thanks," Newt replied, not knowing what else to say. He grinned, then he stood back and took a good look at her as she identified her bags. "It's true," he thought, "like Pete said, she's as white as anybody in town." He noticed, too, that her hair was almost blond and that she had a few freckles, and that her eyes were a greenish-blue. "She's downright pretty." He imagined she was about the same age as Prissy. And they were about the same height.

"You gonna stay all summer?" Prissy asked.

"If Aunt Sarah'll let me. I sure hope so. How is she and Uncle Jack?"

"They're just fine," Prissy said. "They're both out workin' now. Otherwise they'd be here too."

Pete and Newt took her bags, and they all got into the buggy and drove off. Newt saw the whites still looking as they pulled away. He held his chin up smugly and ignored them.

The most Newt got to know about Polly's coloring was that she got it from her father. He found this out from little snatches of talk that flitted about the house during the first week Polly was there. ("Your momma used to call your paw 'poor white trash' when she got mad with him.") ("Paw used to get so mad when people took him for white.") ("Your momma Curtney used to kid him. 'Jonas,' she'd say, 'if they ever have a race riot, you're gonna have a hard time provin'

126

you're one of us. Better start paintin' a sign for your back now.'")

What Newt didn't know—nor, for that matter, did Pete or Prissy—was that Jonas Bates was the offspring of a Negro servant woman and a white Georgia plantation owner. As a boy he had been brought from Georgia to Pennsylvania by his mother—so the story went. When he was a man he had met Sarah's sister, Curtney, who was living in Philadelphia. He fell in love with her and married her after a three-day courtship. Curtney died when Polly was ten, and Sarah had gone to attend the funeral and bring Polly back to Cherokee Flats until Jonas was able to get someone to care for her while he worked.

After a month he had come for Polly, saying he had found someone. A year later he wrote that he had married that someone and that they were moving to Topeka, where he had found a better job. This made Sarah very happy, for again Polly had a mother. But Polly became ill two summers later. And Sarah, having gone to see her, was surprised to find that Jonas had married a white woman. Sarah had no objections to his marriage, but secretly she was upset for a few days. Her brother-in-law was rather matter-of-fact about the whole thing—and honest too. "It makes things easier for me," he had said.

"Bud what about Polly?" Sarah had asked.

"Don't worry, Sarah, she'll adjust to things."

"In other words you're gonna bring her up white."

"That's about it," Jonas replied, "but," he added hastily, "you're always welcome at my house."

"And you at mine," Sarah had replied.

But one day she heard Jonas telling his white neighbor that "Aunt Sarah" used to work in his family back in Georgia, and that he had her up now and then for a visit. And "Aunt Sarah" packed her things that minute and took a train back to Cherokee Flats. She hadn't been in Jonas' house since. And she vowed she would never set foot in it again. Polly never knew about the incident; and Sarah had no intention of ever telling her, for Polly was still as dear to her as she was to Polly.

Polly had never really adjusted to the white life Jonas dumped her into. And it was a relief, she felt, coming to Cherokee Flats where she could be herself. One night she confided to Sarah that if anything ever happened to her father, she would come to the colored side for good.

"Fact is, Paw doesn't know that I'm planning to do just that when I'm twenty-one," she told Sarah.

"Now, Polly, be careful. Don't wind up hurtin' your paw," Sarah had warned.

The circus came to town on its own railroad train during the third week in July. Newt, Earl, Beansy, Jappy and Skunk met it at the outskirts and got jobs watering the elephants, feeding the camels and helping the roustabouts rig up the tents. For this they got free passes to all the shows, free rides on the ferris wheel, merry-go-round and roller coaster.

Newt enjoyed mingling, backstage-fashion, with the clowns, spielers, cowboys, Indians, sword swallowers, fire-eaters, snake charmers, strong men, bearded ladies, midgets and tightrope walkers—feeling himself a part of these people and in tune with their environment. He worked hard through the day— so hard that Spikey, the chief roustabout (a reddish, fat, balding man with little pink ears), offered him a steady job. But Newt refused, saying proudly, "I'm goin' to college and then get married." At night he and Arcella used up the passes in the side shows and the big tent.

On Friday, Beansy got carried away with the art of the sword swallower, and he nearly choked trying to duplicate the trick with a table knife—up-chucking all over the side of the bearded lady's tent. The experience upset Beansy so, he gave Newt and the rest of the gang his free rides for the day and went home. But he was back bright and early the next morning. Newt, Earl and Skunk came across him helping Spikey erect a platform in the middle of the grounds.

"What'cha buildin', Beansy?" Skunk asked.

"A free-for-all-ring," Beansy shot back authoritatively.

"A what?" Newt said.

"Free-fo'-all—free-fo'-all," Spikey cut in. "It's a Missa'sippi spoht. You guys kin make yo'selfs some extra dough today. Whyn't you all sign up?"

"How's it work?" Skunk inquired.

"Simple," Spikey advised, his big shoulders edging a plank into place. "Ten of you in da ring at a buck a head. At da gun shot ever'body starts sluggin' away. Da last two standin' in da ring git a three-minit rest, den go for da big prize. Da winnah gits eight and da losah two—and any extra da crowd throws in da ring."

"Everybody has to git knocked out but the last two?"

"Aw naw—if you git knocked down you gotta stay down—

dat's all." Spikey took a slip of paper. "Here, you guys kin sign up fo' da one-fo'ty to one-fifty de'vision."

"You game, Newt?" Beansy said.

"I don't know." Newt looked at the rest of them. "You fellows want to try it?"

Skunk winked at Newt. (He must have a plan, Newt thought.)

"Well, what y'all say?" Spikey had a pencil in hand now.

"It's okay," Skunk cut in, "we'll git Jappy. That'll mean we only have to git five more."

"Dat'll be like duck soup," Spikey said, shrugging away, "here, all y'all sign up right now—even fo' yer buddy Jappsy, or evah what his name is. We'll git da rest out'a da crowd."

They all signed, and Newt signed for Jappy.

"Y'all be heah at three sharp, now. Heah me?"

They all agreed. And Skunk did have a plan. He revealed it to the others after they found Jappy. "Look," he began, "ain't none of us gonna git hurt if we use our heads right— it'll be like takin' candy from a baby."

"What's your plan?" Jappy asked.

"Well, it's like this. There's ten bucks, ain't it? Well, that means two apiece for us with nobody gittin' hurt."

"But—"

"Hold it, Beansy. Listen me out. Well—we gang up on the other five real rough like—I mean really let 'em have it. That'll git the crowd all steamed up. By then they'll think it's a real mean fight. Now here's the twist. Winger, you and Beansy are the best duckers 'cause Pete's been showin' you things. Everybody goes down then but you two. You two put 'em on a good show and one of you go down—then," Skunk shrugged his shoulders in much the same way Spikey had, "then we go off and split the dough."

"Not bad—not bad," Jappy said.

"Okay, fellas?"

"Yeh." "Guess so." "Okay." "All right by me."

At three o'clock the five boys climbed into the ring, all of them stripped to the waist. Spikey strutted about in a striped turtle-neck sweater and a derby, a cigar slanting from his crooked mouth. "Step right up, ladees and genal'mon! See da fight of da yeah. Step in—step in closah—fine-fine!"

Newt and his friends stood around the ring trying to appear tough, their muscles flexed and their chests poked out. Spikey continued, "Now we need jus' five mo' hundred-fo'ty-five to hundred-fifty pounders, da two winnahs take all."

He spied two Mexican boys. "How 'bout you two—yeh—you two wid da young lady dere—fine-fine, come on up! Now we need three mo', jus' three mo' and we's ready fo' da big go 'round—winnahs take all! How 'bout you two fine-lookin' young roosters?"

The two Mexican boys had climbed through the ropes and pulled off their shirts."

"You two a'comin' to join yo' friends? Fine—fine—now folks, we only needin' one mo'—jus' one mo'—how 'bout dat strong young buck 'hind da old man wid da specs. You—you—come on, boy—git some'a dis fine money we givin' out heah!"

The two other Mexican boys climbed in the ring, stripped and stood next to their friends. "They all look puny and skinny," Beansy whispered to Newt.

Spikey went on, "You 'fraid, boy? You 'fraid, a big buck like you? Okay! Okay! Gotta be anotha he-man 'mongst dis crowd—jus' one mo'—jus'—"

"I'll go with 'em—I'll go with 'em!" Marcus Savage was pushing his way through the crowd.

"Oh, shit matittle," Beansy mumbled.

All the flexed muscles began to droop.

"Fine! Fine! Fine! Now we kin staarrt da greeatest fieeght on dis heah earth—da Missa'sippi free-fo'-all!"

Marcus had an evil grin on his face as he climbed through the ropes. He stripped off his shirt and shuffled up close to Newt. "We gonna be the last if I have to hold you up with one hand and beat all the rest with my other," he growled. Fear spread through Newt as if it were injected through his pores. He kept quiet, thinking back to the lessons Pete had given him, trying to fasten them clearly in his mind.

Now Spikey was in the middle of the ring. "Now, dese are da rules. When you fall, scoot off da platform and onto da ground—da last two standin' gits a three-minit rest. Den dey go afta da big swag. Now when ah fire dis pistol ah wants y'all to start swingin'. Heah we go! Ready!"

Newt's skin was stretched as taut as a drum over his knuckles. Beansy was trembling so much his teeth were chattering. He was ready to fall at the first blow. Skunk was ready to fall with him. Earl and Jappy had decided to work on Marcus together—to soften him up for Newt. They inched to either side of Marcus. Newt was scared, but ready to face the test.

Spikey pointed the pistol at the sky.
Bang!

(Newt swung and a Mexican went down with the first blow.)

A roar went up from the crowd.

"Kill those niggers!"

"Bust his gut!"

"Git them niggers!"

(Beansy was being ganged by two Mexicans. Newt spun over to help him.)

"Kill that fat black bastard! Kick him in the balls!"

(Earl and Jappy were banging up Marcus. A Mexican cracked Jappy behind the ear and he went down.)

"Yea! Yea! Yea! Git them greases!"

"Git the big bastard!"

"Bust his gut! Bust his gut!"

(Skunk and his Mexican went down at the same time. Earl's chin caught Marcus' brutal right. He tried to fight back. Another right from somewhere knocked him senseless. He sank to the floor.)

"Watch that grease!"

"Kill him! Kill him!"

"Watch that big black bastard!"

(The last two Mexicans were beaten down by Newt, Beansy and Marcus—all punching desperately together.)

"Yea! Yea!"

"Now git the big nigger! Git 'im!"

"Kick him in the nuts!"

(Newt slammed a right to Marcus' jaw. He reeled, catching Beansy with a light left at the same time. Marcus stayed on his feet but Beansy plopped to the floor.)

"Yellow black bastard! Yellow bastard!"

"Now git that big bastard! Let him have it in the balls!"

(Marcus steadied himself and lunged toward Newt, but Spikey jumped in between them.)

"Hold it! Hold it!" He grabbed their hands and held them above his head. "Da winnahs! Da winnahs, folks!"

The first round was over—in less than two minutes.

Newt and Marcus stood scowling at each other. All the others had rolled from the ring to the ground. Some held their swollen eyes. Some grasped their bloody noses. Above them Spikey was hollering, "Three minits to the main go! Jus' three minits! Make yer bets! Make yer bets!"

Suddenly Newt looked out at all the grinning faces, those that had called them niggers; called the Mexicans greases. He looked below at his fallen comrades and the hapless Mexicans. He wanted to run from there—not from Marcus. He

131

would rather have fought him alone in a quiet alley; rather have been beat to a pulp in some private place than win from Marcus here in front of these people who suddenly reminded him of animals—dirty, white, vicious, grinning animals about to bet on two "nigger boys" who would try to beat each other's brains out.

But he was trapped.

The crowd had grown ugly and boisterous. They were already making their bets. If he quit now no one would understand, and everyone would think he was a coward. If he didn't fight, he might take a worse beating from the crowd than he would from Marcus. He wanted to ask God to help him fight to win, but he suddenly remembered his mother's telling him on the river road, many nights back, that God couldn't favor one fighter against another. He thought next of Pete, wished he were there. The lesson began to come through (cock the right—jab with the left—feint him out of position—jab—throw the right—).

"Alrighty—righty—folks," Spikey said, strutting around the ring, "how 'bout a few nickels and dimes fo' dees gallant fightas who shed blood fo' you. Show 'em you 'preciate it."

Pennies, nickels and dimes began clinking into the center of the ring. Spikey hopped about picking up the money and putting it into his derby.

"Okay, let's git on with the fight!" someone hollered from the crowd.

"Let's go!"

"Three minutes is up! Let's git goin'!"

Marcus had been sizing up Newt in the meanwhile. He was surprised at the hardness of his body and the bulging muscles. "He's growed a lot since I been away," he thought.

"Okay! Okay! Heah we go fo' da main bout, folks. Da winnah gits eight—da losah two. Ah want a clean fight. Da one who goes down first loses. Unnerstan'?"

Marcus and Newt nodded their heads. Spikey lifted his gun.

Bang!

The crowd let out a bigger roar than before.

Newt and Marcus circled cautiously, eyeing each other.

"Hit him, boy!"

"Hit the big bastard!"

They continued to circle. Newt kept his left out, pawing with it as Pete had taught him. He kept his left foot forward —his right cocked—elbows low. Suddenly Marcus lunged with a vicious right. It went over Newt's shoulder, and he sent two hard jabs home to Marcus' jaw and jumped back.

"That's it, Sambo! Kill him! You can do it, Sambo!"

"Git him, Newt!"

"Come on, Winger!"

Newt was feeling more confident. Marcus was fighting off balance. He didn't even have his left foot forward and he was holding his elbows too high. Newt feinted with his right and sent home a couple of stinging lefts, and he saw Marcus blink in surprise.

"Atta boy, Sambo! I got money on you!"

"Good goin', Newt!" Beansy hollered.

"Keep goin', Winger!" Skunk hollered.

Suddenly Marcus rushed him like a gored bull, flinging both fists in uncontrolled rage. Newt felt his jaw sag under the blows. He spun free as Marcus tried to rough him up, tasting the fresh blood in his mouth. The crowd was one big roar now. Marcus lunged again and they rocked each other with hard rights. Newt felt himself losing control. He danced back, trying Pete's method once more. He feinted with a right, slipped in two good left jabs instead; then, taking the big gamble, he followed through with the right. He was so frightened when he threw it he didn't look up. He only remembered seeing Beansy's frightened face. But he felt right at that instant, the way Pete told him he would feel. His left foot was forward and his right shoulder had swung around—and his elbows fortunately were low, for they kept Marcus' terrible right from his stomach. His blow landed. He felt it in his right shoulder and he was still going forward. There seemed to be no one in front of him.

"You got him! You got him!"

"Good, Sambo! We won! We won!"

"Atta boy, Newt! You did it! You did it!"

Marcus was flat.

Newt felt his hand being pushed up in victory. Then he looked down to Marcus. Blood was running from his nose and he was holding his left eye. He suddenly felt ashamed again. He reached down to help Marcus up. Marcus raised his head and let go with a bloody glob of spit. It caught Newt in the face. Then Newt tried to kick Marcus, but Spikey stepped in and pushed him aside.

"Let him at the black son-of-a-bitch!"

"Booo! Boooo! Booo!"

"Kick his balls out, Sambo! Kick his balls out!"

"The black bastard spit in his face!"

Marcus got up, grabbed his shirt and ducked out the back

133

way, holding his eye with one hand and the two dollars Spikey had given him with the other. Newt and his gang made their way back to the mess tent. Newt clutched the eight dollars as he walked, spitting out blood every now and then. A little white boy about seven years old came running up from behind and patted Newt on his bare back. "I'm glad you won, Sambo," he said, smiling.

Newt whirled and started to hit the boy. "Get out'a here! Get out'a here!" he said through clenched teeth. The boy drew back, surprised. Newt dropped his arms, handed the money to Jappy and started buttoning on his shirt. "Divide it up equally," he said.

"But it's all changed now, Newt. You did all the fightin'."

"A bargain's a bargain," Newt said through puffed lips. "Split it up like I said."

Spikey came up. "Good goin', fellas—y'all put on a good show for 'em."

"What happens to the money they throwed in the ring?" Skunk asked.

"Aw, dat. Dat's fo' da pr'moter. Dat's fo' ole Spikey."

"Bullshit," Earl grumbled. And they all went home. They didn't even go back to use their passes for the rides that night.

By dawn the next morning the circus had packed up and gone.

For several days Newt hated any white face he saw. Time, it seemed, couldn't erase the jeering, inhuman voices that had goaded him to such an indecent victory. They kept coming back, screaming him into bitterness and deep shame. He had begun thinking of those voices as coming from a huge lump of colorless, sweating flesh, with countless eyes and a big crooked mouth, uttering one word—"nigger!" He sat dejectedly on the porch now, wanting to run from this place to some unheard-of-land where such a word didn't exist, wanting to shed the ridicule that cloaked his conscience; wanting to tear the hurt, the puffed eye and the busted lip from his body. He didn't want to see his gang or anyone who might have seen the fight.

"Newt! Newt!" It was Mag Pullens calling from the road.

"Yes-mam!"

"Your cousin Polly's on the telephone. Wants you to meet her at Kress's and help her with packages!"

"Yes-mam! Tell her I'll be right there!"

He met Polly soon after.

"You got a lot of stuff," Newt said, looking at the packages.

"Things for Aunt Sarah and the house. Didn't know it was

134

going to be so much," Polly answered. Then they started off.

They were within a half block of the Frisco tracks when three white boys approached them. Newt recognized Delbert Mottsy but he didn't know the other two. Delbert and his friends kept their eyes on Polly, stopping almost, then single filing as they passed. After a few feet they stopped and looked back.

Newt sensed trouble. It came quickly.

"What'cha doin' walkin' with a nigger, blondy?"

The packages fell from Newt's arms as he swung around.

"Newt—Newt—come on now—"

Polly might as well have remained silent, for Newt was already upon the boys, swinging wildly. Delbert got it first. He was down before he realized what happened. The other two drew back for a second, then came charging in together, knocking Newt to the sidewalk. Then the three of them pounced on him, kicking and beating with all their might.

"Help! Help!" Polly screamed. "Help, somebody!"

Newt fought his way to his feet again, but the others were up with him and he went down under another hail of blows.

"Help! Help!" Polly continued to scream. She ran over and tried to pull the boys off, only to be knocked down herself.

Then suddenly Newt heard Delbert holler, felt one of the other assailants jerked from his back. Someone had come to his rescue. He didn't know who, nor did he have time to find out. A foot was headed for his face. Newt's arm caught the blow of the foot, then he snatched that same foot, upended its owner and pounced on him, flailing him with his fists. The boy scrambled up, pulled loose and ran.

Polly was up, running across the tracks for help.

"Look out, Waldo!" Newt hollered, seeing it was he who had come to help.

Waldo ducked. But not in time. Delbert cracked him across the head with a stick and Waldo went down. Then Delbert and the other boy ran. Newt started after them, but stopped and trotted back to Waldo, who was sitting on the ground, stunned from the blow. Newt helped him to his feet.

"You okay, Waldo?"

"Yeh—guess so." He shook his head. "I'm okay. I'm gonna get that little Mottsy bastard."

Newt began picking up the packages, and Waldo, still a little groggy, helped him. A small group of Negroes had gathered and were coming with Polly to meet Newt and Waldo.

"You really saved me that time," Newt said. "I was havin' a hell of a time for a minute or two."

"What'd it all start over, anyhow?" Waldo asked.

"Over Polly. They thought she was white, I guess. But I sure want to thank you, Waldo. They had me goin'."

"Ain't nothin', Newt. You'd have done the same for me." He blew his nose. "Crazy bastards. I knew she was a nigger all the time."

Newt was ahead of Waldo. He shut his eyes, grimaced and went across the tracks to meet Polly and the others.

Sarah Winger heard about the incident that evening. After supper she had Jack drive her to the Mottsy home on the other side of town, and she gave the elder Mottsy a piece of her mind.

Three nights later, after Polly and Prissy had experienced more trouble on the streets, Sarah called her niece to her room.

"Polly," she said, "I hate to tell you this—but—but I think it's goin' to be better for everybody if you go back home. I—I don't want to do this, but—but—" Sarah stopped abruptly and leaned forward, nearly falling from the chair.

"What's the matter, Aunt Sarah? Uncle Jack! Uncle Jack!"

"What's the trouble—what's the matter?" Jack said, stepping into the room.

"Aunt Sarah's sick or something."

"You sick, Sarah? You—what is it?" He eased her back in the chair. "You want me to call Timothy?"

"No-no Jack. I'm all right. Just had a little dizzy spell—that's all."

"You shore?"

"Just a little dizzy spell," she repeated.

The next morning Polly started packing her suitcases. Prissy sat on the floor watching her. "Sure hate to see you go, Polly. We were just beginnin' to have fun."

"Yeh—I know, Prissy, I know."

"It's a crazy world, Polly."

"It ain't the world, Prissy. It's the people in it."

"Comin' back next summer?"

Polly stood up. She held a calico blouse under her arm. "One of these days I'm coming back for good. I—I—I—oh, Prissy. Oh, Prissy." They embraced and both of them began to cry.

Newt had been listening outside the door. A lump came to his throat and he went out to hitch the horse to the buggy.

Two hours later Polly took the train for Topeka.

CHAPTER ❦ 11

FOR WEEKS after the circus fight Marcus kept out of sight. His feelings had been hurt worse than his body. There was no way he could explain his defeat to the other boys, so he shrank from their presence, feeling more alone than ever. Though he went sullenly about his work at Chappie's, he liked the privacy the job gave him. But he went to bed angry and he got up angry. He was overly sensitive to anything his father said during the few hours they were together. It got to a point where he hardly spoke to anyone—and did not care whether they spoke to him. He cared only about one thing—getting even. But he controlled his impulse to act openly against Newt, being content to store this impulse within the design of hatred that was building stronger and stronger inside him.

The gang welcomed his absence. They had all come to feel the embarrassment of the "Missa'sippi free-fo'-all" and were as eager as Newt to forget it. Only once, undressing at the swimming hole, had they talked about it—and then only briefly.

"That Spikey sure made nuts out'a us," Beansy had said.

"Bastard had more money in that derby for hisself than all of us had together," Earl grumbled.

"Bet right now he's got some other suckers beatin' their brains out someplace," Newt said.

"That damned Mexican shore bopped me upside the ear," Jappy complained.

"What happened to you, Beansy?" Skunk asked slyly.

Beansy got flustered. "I—I slipped, just 'bout the time—"

"Just 'bout the time you saw Savage's fist headin' your way," Skunk cut in.

They all laughed. Then Skunk shouted, "Follow the leader!" and they scrambled over the bank and plunged into the river.

Newt's bitterness gradually lessened as the summer waned.

He had lived the experience and now, he told himself, he must forget it. High school was ahead, and he looked forward to the wonders it would offer him. He daydreamed himself into the classrooms with the big windows and roomy desks; the laboratories with the microscopes; the huge gymnasium and auditorium he had heard Prissy talk about.

When opening day arrived, he dressed in the same suit he had worn on the June graduation night. The pants were already too short, but he solved that problem by slipping his belt down over his hips. Then he shined his shoes and slicked his hair back tightly with "Pluko"—a thick, yellow, smelly hair dressing that he and Beansy had obtained from a Chicago mail order house.

He gulped down his breakfast and set out for Arcella's. She was already in front of her house when he arrived, so he took her books and they made off across the tracks—happy as could be on this bright September morning. About a block from the school they met Chauncey and Rodney Cavanaugh, and Newt introduced them to Arcella.

"That Chauncey's kind of cute," Arcella murmured after the two boys had gone ahead of them.

"He's a senior in junior college here," Newt said rather dryly. "He'll be leavin' for the University next year, I suppose—had to make up some work, Rodney says."

"Well, he's sure cute——curly hair and—"

"I heard you the first time," Newt said, a hint of anger in his voice.

Arcella smiled. "Why, Newt Winger," she cooed, "I do believe you're jealous!"

Newt said nothing. They had reached the school door now, so he opened it and followed her into the spacious, clean-smelling hallway.

The first week of school was exciting for Newt. It was a pleasure for him to walk up and down the long corridors flipping hellos to the new friends he was making. He found his teachers generally likable, and he came to like Professor Radeaker the best. He taught science, and at the start of each class he usually had a joke to tell, often at the expense of one of the students.

The white students were friendlier than Newt had expected them to be. One of them, Zack Spears—who sat in front of him in French class—filled him in on lots of things that were not generally known. For instance, Zack and several other sophomore boys had failed French I, not for lack of ability to grasp it, but for a far more impressive reason. Zack said,

138

"Ever notice Miss Purvelle sits all the boys up front and the girls in the back?"

"That's right, she does," Newt agreed.

"Well, let me tell you somethin'. She don't mind you lookin', if you git what I mean."

The next day Newt borrowed Zack's seat in front, and found the story to be true. And it was also true that the boys with the choice seats were sophomores who had failed the year before. There was one notable exception. Carson Bigelow, who sat dead center, was a junior.

"Hell," Zack said, laughing in his horselike way, "Cars ain't even had a textbook for two years."

Newt's guidance teacher was Miss McClinock, who taught English and American History. She was a large, full-bosomed, red-haired woman with a long nose, who wore black crepe dresses and high-laced shoes. There were no shenanigans in her room, and Newt found out, soon enough, that anyone coming to her class without homework properly done paid rather dearly. For such a misdemeanor she made Newt stay an hour after school three evenings in a row. For those three evenings he missed walking home with Arcella—and this hurt.

"What are your ambitions, Newton?" she asked just before he left on the last day of punishment.

Newt looked up, surprised at the suddenness of the question. "Ambitions?"

"Yes, ambitions," Miss McClinock repeated.

"Well—well, I think I would maybe like to teach English —like you," Newt lied.

"No apple polishing, Newton. Tell me the truth. I'm your guidance teacher."

Newt thought he'd better come clean. "Well, I just don't know, Miss McClinock."

"Haven't you ever thought of what you would like to do when you leave high school?"

"Oh. Yes-mam, of course. I'd like to go to college."

"College?" She spoke as if he'd said an obscene word. "Are you serious?"

"Yes-mam."

"Who put such notions into your head?"

"I—I put them there myself, I guess. I—"

"What does your father do? Where does he work?"

Newt began rubbing his hands nervously. "Oh, odd jobs mostly—and we raise corn every year."

"Your brother Peter attended this school, didn't he?"

"Yes-mam."

"Did he go to college?"

"No-mam."

"Why not?"

"I—I don't really know," Newt said.

"Well, I'll tell you why—for the same reason that ninety-nine percent of the Negro students don't go to college. They aren't college material," she said bluntly. "The few who are—and are lucky enough to get the money—usually wind up as cooks or porters anyway."

Newt felt his anger mounting, but he kept quiet.

"That, I feel," Miss McClinock went on, "is going to a lot of trouble just to become a servant."

"Well, I won't be nobody's servant—college or no college," Newt shot back.

"Don't become angered, Newton. I'm your guidance teacher. I'm here to advise what is best for you. You had best take a general course next year instead of a college preparatory. It will be easier for you, and much wiser."

Newt looked Miss McClinock straight in the eye. He noticed that her long nose was twitching and that there were little beads of sweat on the end of it. "I don't understand you," he said finally.

"You will someday," she said archly.

"Am I excused now?" Newt asked.

"You're excused," she said.

He picked up his books and went out. Closing the glass-paneled door, he saw that Miss McClinock was up and walking toward the window. He went to his locker for his other books. When he passed her room again, on the way out, she was still at the window gazing blankly at the campus.

Newt was confused. He walked slowly toward the front door, his footsteps echoing through the empty corridor. Miss McClinock had given him something to think about.

Newt got a start when he reached home. Doc Cravens' Ford was parked in front of the house. Somebody must be sick, he thought. He walked quietly through the open door and put his books on the dining room table, then he peeped into the front room. His father sat in the rocker moving to and fro. He looked up when Newt's head appeared.

"Somebody sick, Poppa?"

"Nothin' serious. Your momma had a dizzy spell at work and had to come home. Nothin' serious."

"Prissy been home from school yet?"

140

"She's gone to the drugstore for a pr'scription. You better fetch some wash water from the hydrant."

"Yessir." He went off to get into his overalls and mackinaw.

A moment later, Doc Cravens came out of Sarah's bedroom, and Jack asked. "Well, how's she doin'?"

"All right—but she'd better take the rest of the week off, I think." Cravens was taking a small bottle of pills from his satchel. "Have her take one of these every four hours. It's marked on the bottle. Prissy back with the other medicine?"

"Not yet."

"Those will be pills too. Have her take one each night before goin' to bed." He was moving to the door now, and he motioned Jack out after him. He stopped at the edge of the yard.

Jack was uneasy. "Anything serious?" he asked hesitantly.

"Well—it could be if she doesn't take it easier. It's her heart."

"Her heart?"

"Nothin' to get excited about, Jack. She just needs to take it a little easier, as I said. She should be up and around in a day or so. Nothin' to go gettin' excited about."

"She goes too hard, Tim—too hard."

"I told her about that. Now just follow the instructions. I'll be around again in a couple of days."

Newt approached them with two buckets of water. "Hi, Doc," he said. "How's Momma?"

"Hi, Newt. She's going to be all right. By the way, how do you like your new nephew?"

"New nephew?"

"Didn't you know Rende had her baby this mornin'?"

"Nobody told me," Newt said, looking at his father.

Jack cleared his throat. "Forgot 'bout that," he said.

Doc Cravens smiled, then got into his car and drove off. Jack walked slowly back to the front door. Newt watched him for a moment, then continued on to the kitchen, emptied the buckets in a tub and went back for more. Prissy came through the alleyway as he hurried along. "Miss McClinock told me about you!" she hollered.

"So what?" Newt shouted back.

The next morning Professor Radeaker stood before his class with the usual overly serious expression on his face. "Students," he said, "a certain young man in my class, occupying the third seat from the front on the far right" (all heads turned toward Newt) "is indeed quite a comedian."

Newt grinned and squirmed in his seat, realizing that he was about to be honored as the butt of one of the professor's jokes.

Radeaker continued, "Well sir, the other day, after grading one of his papers, I asked this young man if he had taken physics at the last school he attended. What do you think he answered, class? He said, 'Why, nosir, Professor—I never had any trouble with my movements.' "

The class burst into riotous laughter.

"All right. All right. That's enough guffawing for one day," the professor said solemnly. "Let's get down to work." And since it was his custom to ask the victim of his joke the first question of the day, Newt braced himself.

"Newton Winger, you look bright this morning, so you get the first question." Radeaker removed his glasses. "Have you ever heard of a gentleman, notable to science, with the name of Einstein?"

"Yessir."

"His first name, please."

"Albert, sir."

"He presented us with an important theory. Can you tell us what it was concerned with?"

"A—a—"

"A?" Radeaker questioned. A few snickers came from the class. "Quiet, numbskulls!" he shouted. "Well, Winger?"

"A—rel—relativity, sir."

"In what year did he present this theory?"

"Nineteen hundred and—and five, sir."

"Mmmmm. Can you explain it in detail, Winger?"

"No, sir. I don't think I can."

"Well—thank God for that," Radeaker exclaimed. "In case you could, I was going to take a seat and let you teach me. You get an 'A' for honesty. Sit down."

Newt felt very proud of himself and he turned to beam at Arcella across the room. Then his heart sank, for she was gazing out the window, looking as if her thoughts were far away. They met briefly in the hallway after class, and Newt said, "See you for the picture show Saturday."

"Not too sure. I'll let you know later," she answered. He shrugged his shoulders and headed for his French class. When he arrived he found Mr. Faulkner occupying Miss Purvelle's chair. She was out sick, he explained to the class.

Midway through the period, Carson Bigelow became quite ill—so ill, in fact, that Zack Spears had to help him from the room.

"Carson really misses his regular teacher," Mr. Faulkner quipped. Newt guessed from his expression that Mr. Faulkner also knew the score.

As the days went by, the relationship between Newt and Miss McClinock became considerably worse. He got his homework done and it was acceptable, but she never asked questions of him. And though he thought he deserved a B on the midterm test in October, he received a C. He went to see her about this one evening, asking her bluntly why he didn't get a higher mark.

"Are you telling me how to grade, young man?"

"No-mam, I'm not. I just think I should have got a higher mark."

"Well, there seems to be some difference between what you thought and what you got, doesn't there?"

Newt felt the anger rising again. He decided he had better leave and he started for the door.

"You come back here. Don't you dare walk out of here without asking to be excused. Do you hear? Come back here this minute!"

Newt stopped and faced Miss McClinock—and he said what he had been wanting to say to her for a long, long time: "You know one thing. You don't like me or any of the rest of the colored kids. I found out you told my sister and brother the same thing you told me—that we'd wind up porters and maids, and you been tellin' all the other colored kids the same thing for years and years. That's why they always make you their guidance teacher and—"

"You shut your filthy mouth—"

"—and we all hate you—every last one of us!"

"Why, you impudent thing! You're going before Mr. Hall next week. I'll see to that. You wait and see. I'll—"

Newt stormed from the room and slammed the door.

When he got outside, Arcella had already gone, and this added to his disappointment. But he found Beansy waiting for him on the building steps. Newt didn't feel much like talking now and Beansy seemed to understand, so they walked along in silence. Finally they stopped at the athletic field, where the football team was going through a scrimmage.

"Sure wish they'd let us colored kids go out for football," Newt said.

" 'Fraid we'd rub some black off on 'em," Beansy answered jokingly.

"Suppose you're right," Newt agreed. They stood watching a minute or so longer, then walked on.

Beansy said, "One thing, though—you can play on the colored basketball team."

Newt shrugged. "Well, I'm tryin' out for it."

"Aw, you'll make the squad for sure."

"Hope so. It's a lot better, anyhow."

"Yeh."

They lapsed into silence again, walked on to the tracks and crossed over. "Ain't seen you with Arcella lately," Beansy said, failing in his attempt to sound casual.

Newt failed just as badly with his answer. "Oh—old lady long nose has been keepin' me in lately. The old witch's got it in for me."

"Arcella just rode off with Chauncey."

"Yeh?"

"Goin' to the show Saturday?" Beansy was still pushing.

"Guess so—why?"

"Nothin'. Takin' Arcella?"

"Sure. Why not?"

"Nothin'—nothin'. Just thought I'd ask, that's all."

The answer did not completely satisfy Newt, but he was accustomed to Beansy's way of saying and not saying something at the same time.

Newt went by to pick up Arcella on Saturday, but her mother told him she had gone over to Chanute to visit her grandmother for the weekend. So rather than face Beansy and the others at the movie without Arcella, Newt went back home. He stayed close to the house all that weekend—and sadness was upon him like a plague.

"What's the matter, son?" his mother asked him, having noticed his mood.

He wanted to tell her everything—even about Arcella—but he settled for his problems with Miss McClinock, spilling out the whole story almost without stopping. Sarah was thoughtful for a few moments. "You should've told me about this a long time ago," she said finally.

"Poppa said we shouldn't worry you much, so I didn't."

"I'll be goin' to school with you Monday," she said. "You shore you've told me the real truth about this?"

"Yessem—what I told you was the honest truth."

But Sarah Winger wouldn't be able to accompany Newt to school as she had planned, for she took to her bed again Sunday night. It was more than dizziness this time. Newt could tell that by the deep, persistent frown that creased his father's face after Doc Cravens left.

"Your momma won't be goin' back to work for quite a spell," Jack said. "We all better try and help git things in order tomorrow." He moaned despairingly and shook his head. "Rende's goin' to help with the cookin' and washin' for a spell, while you kids are at school. But with that new baby it's goin' to be hard on her—so Prissy, you and Newt start gittin' home soon's you can from now on."

At school Monday morning Newt noticed that Arcella's seat was vacant. He now had reason for double concern, for he had already been told to be in the principal's office during the coming lunch hour. He hardly knew what went on throughout the morning. Though Miss Purvelle was back from her brief illness and the front-and-center boys were happy again, Newt didn't bother to look up. But he did notice, during the English period, that Miss McClinock avoided looking his way.

When the lunch bell sounded, he headed straight for the principal's office—expecting the worst. "I might even be expelled," he thought. When he arrived he was told to wait in the outer office until Mr. Hall could see him. And so he sat fretting, having no planned defense; only a feeling of determination burned within him. Before long Miss McClinock arrived. In somewhat of a flurry she swept into Mr. Hall's office without seeming to even notice Newt.

"Gettin' her story in first," Newt mumbled under his breath.

About five minutes later the secretary's buzzer sounded. She went to the principal's door, then turned to Newt. "You can go in now," she said.

Mr. Hall, a rather youngish, open-faced man wearing steel-rimmed glasses, leaned back in his swivel chair when Newt entered. Miss McClinock sat beside his desk, her fat hands resting firmly on her knees.

"Howdy do, sir," Newt said.

"Hello, Newton. Sit down there," Mr. Hall ordered. Newt sat down, and Mr. Hall twirled his chair in half circles for a few seconds before he spoke again. "Miss McClinock tells me you were rude and impudent last Friday. What have you to say for yourself?"

Newt picked nervously at a scab on his forefinger, looking at the principal. "Well—I guess it's all in the way you look at it, sir."

"What do you mean by that?"

"Well—I didn't mean to be rude when I went to see her. It was just because of things that happened between us a long time ago."

"As I distinctly remember, it was about your mark on the midterm test," Miss McClinock snapped. "You felt I had down-graded you."

"That right, Newton?"

"In a way, yessir. But that ain't—wasn't all there was to it."

"What are you trying to say? Out with it."

"It's just that we—Miss McClinock and I—had a little fuss —or I don't know whether you call it fuss or not—but we didn't see things the same way after the first week or so."

"Miss McClinock happens to be your instructor—as well as your guidance teacher."

"I know, sir, but I didn't like the way she wanted to guide me."

Mr. Hall made a few more half turns, scratching his head. "This caused you to tell Miss McClinock that you hated her?"

"I didn't say I—"

"Don't lie, young man," Miss McClinock cut in, her cheeks glowing red. "You know you said it."

"I didn't say I did, alone. I said all the colored kids hated you—and they do."

"Why do you say this, Newton?" Hall asked.

"Because they all say so."

"Do they give reasons?"

"Yessir, they do. They say she tells them all the same thing—that they shouldn't go to college—that they're all goin' to turn out to be porters and cooks and maids. That's sure what she told me."

A frown came on Hall's face. He turned from Newt and Miss McClinock and looked out the window at the tree tops. "This true, Miss McClinock? Do you tell the Negro students such things?"

"Mr. Hall," she began, her nose twitching, "you've been at this school for just two years. I've been class advisor to these colored students for the last twenty years. What I've said to them was what I've been instructed to say to them."

The principal had turned to face her, and his frown was deeper now. "So this accusation of his is true?"

"To a certain extent—yes."

"Who instructed you to say such things?"

"Mr. Hornsby, our former principal. He—"

"Just a moment, Miss McClinock," Mr. Hall said, "just a moment, please. Newton, wait in the outer office until I call you."

Newt got up and went out, then Mr. Hall rose and shut the door behind him.

As he sat there on the bench, Newt began trying to imagine the conversation as it would go between Mr. Hall and Miss McClinock. He had been aware of the principal's surprise when she had confessed to the truth of his accusation, and he felt this was in his favor. His tension had eased somewhat, but he had already taken a pessimistic view of the outcome. He had decided that if he were expelled, he would say even more about what he felt was an injustice. If he won, then nothing more needed to be said. "But any way it goes," he decided, "Miss McClinock's goin' to have it in for me."

He sat there, time going slowly, recalling Washington Junior High, comparing it with this school of big, airy, sun-splashed classrooms, auditoriums and gymnasiums, remembering that there had been no microscopes and no chemical labs, and that their outdoor playground had been no more than a deserted garbage-strewn field adjoining the school property; retaining the memory of the little gym, the way it was used for just about everything, and the odor of stale sweat and smelly tennis shoes that clung to it even on graduation night—despite the thorough airing it was given the afternoon before.

His stomach growled from hunger, and the secretary glanced in his direction.

But he had known some wonderful moments back there too, warm, intimate and gay moments of easy pleasure and unrestrained laughter—moments that had not yet come to him here. He wondered, as he had often done before, what the whites' real reasons were for denying them a part in the school's athletic and social affairs. "Why does our color make such a difference? ... Didn't God know that we'd have a lot of trouble if he made us black? ... Since he's white, maybe he don't care either." He smiled wryly. "Never seen black angels ... even the chariot horses are white."

He gritted his teeth in defiance of the conspiracy he felt Miss McClinock and Mr. Hall must be forming against him; of the scorn he felt she held for his coloring. "If I turned white before they called me back in there, 'twould be a different story altogether...." He knotted his fist and watched the skin lighten under the pressure of the knuckle bones. "Wonder if you tore all the skin off, if it would all come

147

back black? Guess it would...don't think I'd like bein' white, anyway."

He dug into his pocket and brought out three large raisins; after picking lint and pocket dust from them, he popped them into his mouth. Then he got up and started across the room to the water cooler. At that moment, the door to the principal's office opened and Miss McClinock bustled out past Newt and into the hall.

"Come in, Winger," the principal said, and Newt followed him back into his office.

Mr. Hall began very slowly—uncertainly. "I just don't know —well, this is all sort of an unnecessary mistake—or maybe a misunderstanding. I'm speaking of Miss McClinock's attitude toward you and other Negro students—and her advice to you about college and so forth. For an explanation to make sense to you—or me—one would have to go much further back, to a period—a tragic one—before you or I existed." Hall walked to the window and gazed out at the campus, much the same way Newt had seen Miss McClinock do that evening after their argument. "Although she must share the blame for this awful wrong, Miss McClinock is somewhat a victim herself—having been eased into this wrong channel of thought many years ago, not only because she thought it to be right but because it was a truth that existed during those same years."

Hall talked on, seeming to Newt to be addressing some unseen audience. "Mr. Hornsby was more to blame than she—but then, so is my father, my mother, Miss McClinock's father and mother and millions of others who helped shape the ideas that Miss McClinock so unwisely passed on to you—forgetting that time and progress must shake away such ideas." He turned slowly. "Are you following what I am saying? Do you understand, Newt?"

"Yessir—I think I do."

"Frankly, I was shocked at Miss McClinock's confession, but—" He shrugged, then paused for a second. "The valedictorian of my graduating class at college was a Negro, Curtis Mathews. But—do you want to know the ironic thing about this, Newt?" Hall shook his head. "When I came through the New York train station from a New England vacation last summer, there was Curtis Mathews—bearing out Miss McClinock's prophecy—asking me if I would like help with my bags. He was a redcap—a redcap, carrying bags for people who couldn't begin to compare with him in knowledge

148

or social worth. 'What a waste!' I remember thinking when I left him that day."

"Did he know you, Mr. Hall?" Newt asked.

"Oh, yes. Yes indeed. He stopped work and we talked for nearly a half hour." Hall was quiet—remembering again. "He had seven children by then, Newt. I'll never forget it, a man with a master's degree, carrying bags, with seven children—and no hope."

They were both quiet for a moment.

"There are some things here at my own school that I don't like, son. For instance, I feel badly about the school board's keeping you boys off our football and basketball teams. It's a stupid, costly thing. Our white basketball team hasn't made the state championships in the last ten years. The colored team has not only done this, but it's held the championship of Kansas, Oklahoma and Missouri four times during the same period. Believe me—if it were left to me, or Coach Dennison, this would stop, but we are powerless."

"Yessir, I understand."

"I hope you do. And another thing—what I've told you is strictly between us. I had a long talk with Miss McClinock and I'm sure her thinking and attitudes will be different from now on. You continue to work hard. She will do the rest."

"Yessir."

"If you have any more problems, bring them to me. You're excused." As Newt started out, he added, "And you are to show Miss McClinock the highest respect. You understand that, don't you?"

"Yessir. Thanks, Mr. Hall."

"You're welcome."

Newt stopped by Arcella's on the way home from school that same evening. Mrs. Jefferson opened the door for him and said, "Come in, Newt. Arcella's been ailing a bit. I'll call her."

An uneasiness crept over him as he saw Arcella walking slowly down the stairs. She didn't look ill, he thought, but she was puffy around the eyes. He assumed that she'd been crying.

"Sorry you've been sick," he said.

"Oh, it isn't anything—just headaches and head colds," she answered dryly.

"I've sure missed you," he said, taking her hand.

She drew back. "Mustn't get too close—you'll be getting a cold too."

149

"How long will you be out of school—you know?"

She shook her head wistfully. "Don't know for sure. I hate missing all the classes."

"I can bring your homework to you every evenin'," he volunteered.

"Oh, that would be fine, Newt. If—if I'm not here—downstairs, I mean—you can just hand them to Momma."

She didn't ask him to sit down, as he had expected, so he said, "Anything I can do for you—before I go?"

"Oh, no no. Thanks a lot. I'm going back upstairs and lie down."

Newt touched her hand and looked into her swollen eyes. "What's the matter, Arcella? Tell me what's the matter."

"I told you—I told you. I tol—" She looked as though she were about to cry. Then, turning on her heels, she rushed back up the stairs.

Newt stood looking after her as Mrs. Jefferson came in from the kitchen. She listened to Arcella's door slam, then she turned to Newt. "Did you and Arcella have a falling out, Newt?"

"No-mam." He looked up the stairs. "Why?"

"Well, she's been acting like she was mad with somebody or something. Bad enough tending to the cold she's got, let alone her stubbornness and meanness. Just thought maybe you two had a little spat."

"No-mam, we sure haven't had no spat at all."

"Oh well, she'll get over it soon. Don't worry, son. Women are like that, you know." She was smiling now.

As he walked toward home, Newt had an odd feeling—one of melancholy; of loneliness and futile longing.

Arcella was slipping away from him—and he knew it.

CHAPTER ❧ 12

NEWT MADE the colored basketball squad, traveled with it to Pittsburg, Chanute and Parsons, where they won each of their games. Coach Ebon Jones put him in during the second half of the third game, and he emerged the second highest scorer. When he got home from school the next evening he saw his picture in the paper for the first time in his life. He raced to his mother's bedside with it, bubbling with happiness.

"I'm mighty proud of you, son," she said. "Have Pete pick up some more of these at the newspaper office."

With his spirits thust bolstered, Newt went about his school work more earnestly than ever. And he found that Mr. Hall had been right about Miss McClinock. After the first week she began asking Newt to recite as much as she did the others, and her whole manner became gentler. She even told him that his work was improving. And it was, because he worked extra hard in her class.

As he had promised, he took Arcella's homework to her each day—but he never saw her. She had taken to bed and refused to see anyone. There were rumors that she had tuberculosis; that she had a sleeping sickness. Newt wrote her two notes, but they weren't answered, and his heart became sad again. He wouldn't eat and he couldn't sleep, so finally, in desperation, he went to his mother with his problem.

She was propped in her bed drinking tea when he entered. Sensing that he was troubled, she spoke first. "Somethin' botherin' you, son?"

He nodded gloomily. "Yessem—might as well tell you. It's Arcella. You know she's been sick?"

"Yes. I've been hearin' about it. How is she?"

"That's the trouble. I don't know. I've been to see her several times, but she won't see me. I wrote her twice and she didn't even answer my letters."

"Maybe she's too sick, Newt. Maybe—"

"It's more'n that. Even her mother wouldn't talk to me when I went by there this evenin'."

"Did you do somethin' you shouldn't have?"

"No-mam, nothin' I know about."

"Well, give it time, son. It'll all blow over. Give it time."

But time came and time went, and he got no word.

The Christmas holidays were approaching again, but it was apparent they would not be the same as before. Jack couldn't find much work and neither could Pete. Prissy, who had been working at Judge Cavanaugh's on weekends, took to working full time for the holidays. Newt went about with Beansy and Jappy shoveling snow, or tackling any other odd job they could find.

A few days before Christmas, Newt returned home, cold and low of spirits, to find his father waiting for him outside the door. The scowl on his father's face told him that something was amiss.

"Hi, Poppa."

"Come on in the house, boy," Jack said, "I want to talk to you private. You got some explainin' to do."

What could it be? Newt wondered, following his father into the dining room.

"Boy," Jack started, "that Jefferson girl's father was over here to see me today."

"Yessir."

"Well, don't that mean nothin' to you, boy?"

Newt looked up, surprised at the question and his father's manner. "I don't get what you mean," he said. "Is she worse or somethin'?"

Jack Winger looked long and hard at his son before he spoke again. "Mr. Jefferson says—he says Arcella's gonna have a baby—that's what he says."

Newt felt as if a stick of dynamite had exploded in his stomach. He was stunned beyond speech.

"Well—do you know anything 'bout it?"

He turned away, but Jack spun him back around, whispering fiercely so as not to disturb Sarah. "Tell me—tell me, boy—did you do somethin' to that girl?"

"No, Poppa! No, Poppa!" he cried. "I didn't! I didn't!"

"Quiet. Quiet—"

"Jack!" It was Sarah. "What's goin' on? What's the matter?"

Newt broke from his father's grasp and strode into his mother's bedroom. "Oh, Momma—oh, Momma—" he said.

"What is it, son? What is it? Jack, what's goin' on?" Her hand was about Newt's wrist.

Jack went slowly to her bed. "I didn't want to bother you with this right off—but—but Bob Jefferson was over to see me this afternoon 'bout his daughter."

"Well—what about her?" Sarah asked nervously.

"She's gonna have a baby."

"A baby?" Sarah's grip tightened. "He thinks Newt had somethin' to do with it?"

"Yep—that's what he's thinkin'," Jack moaned.

"Did you, Newt?" Sarah looked into his eyes for the answer. "Did you, son? Tell me the truth. Don't be afraid."

Newt was shaking now—with unutterable hurt. "No, Momma, it wasn't me. But—but—I wish it was."

Sarah looked up at Jack. "He's tellin' the truth," she said, "he's tellin' the truth." They were quiet for a moment. "What does Arcella say?"

Jack shrugged. "She won't say who it was—won't say a'tall."

"Well, Jack, only one thing to do. Take him over there to face the girl and see what she says in front of him. No sense in them thinkin' it's him when it's not."

"Yep. Guess that's the only thing to do. Come on, boy. Come on. I declare, you'll be the death of me yet." Newt turned and followed his father from the room.

A few minutes later, when Newt entered Arcella's room with his father and her parents, she angrily pulled the covers up over her head. But her father snatched the covers back to her shoulders and said, "Now I want you to tell us, here and now, if this boy is responsible. You hear me, girl? Speak up!"

"I told you a thousand times he wasn't!" she shouted. "Why do you keep bothering me with it?"

"Then who is it if it ain't him?" Bob Jefferson hollered back.

"Bob—Bob." Arcella's mother was on the bed beside her. "Tell us, honey. Tell us—and get it over with. Momma'll help you."

The room was extremely quiet for a minute. Mrs. Jefferson wiped the tears from Arcella's eyes with the top of the sheet. Arcella turned over in the bed, then she reached for Newt's hand. "Come sit beside me—you'll try to understand, won't you, Newt?"

"Yes, I'll understand—"

"I'm awfully sorry, Newt—awfully sorry."

"Yes." He was silent after the one word.

"You will forgive me, won't you?" Newt nodded his head, and after sniffing a couple of times she said, "Well, Poppa— it's going to shock you, I know—and all the rest of you too. I told you not to go and get Newt mixed up in this, but you wouldn't listen."

Newt had a sudden desire to run from the room, not wanting to hear the rest. He tried to get up, but Arcella pulled him back to her.

"It was Chauncey," she said, "Chauncey Cavanaugh, Poppa —not Newt, like you said."

She released Newt's hand and he got up, walking quickly out of the room. He rushed down the stairs and out into the cold, senseless day. As he walked along, he kept repeating, "Chauncey—Chauncey—" softly to himself.

On Christmas morning Newt got up especially early and made the fire; but he didn't call the others. Instead, he stood beside the dining room door, looking at the tree, remembering the Christmas before when he and Arcella had been so happy. He had a present for her now among the few others under the tree. He picked it up and went out the door. It was snowing heavily, so he turned up the collar of his mackinaw and walked slowly toward Arcella's house. He had decided to place the gift on the porch, and he didn't want to be seen.

As he approached the house he wiped the wet snow from his brows and peered ahead. Then he moved quickly to the porch, pulled back the storm door, and placed the gift on the threshold. Turning to leave, he noticed the window shade was up. He glanced through it, expecting to see the Christmas tree—and caught his breath. The room was bare. Pressing close to the window, he was able to see through most of the house, and there wasn't a stick of furniture anywhere. The Jeffersons must have slipped away in the darkness of Christmas Eve, he concluded.

So Arcella was gone from him—forever. For a moment he stood gazing at the small red and green parcel of lilac water settling in the moist snow between the doors. He started to pick it up, then decided to leave it there. He closed the storm door gently against it, turned and headed for home.

"Wonder why she did it? Must have lost her head for a minute ... thought she could go to the other side of the tracks for good ... Chauncey's big car and his money and big house and everything ... but who knows, maybe she really liked him ... maybe he really liked her ... she was pretty

154

enough for anybody to like ... only thing wrong for her with Chauncey was her color."

When he arrived the family was still asleep, so he went back to the living room and took another look at the tree. It seemed dull compared to the one of the previous year. The scarcity of presents on the floor spoke of the hard winter. Outside the window the whitened land seemed gray under the thick curtain of tumbling flakes. Newt gritted his teeth, swallowed the lump in his throat, then tromped through the house, shouting, "Merry Christmas! Merry Christmas!" Then, as on other Christmases before, he put on the coffeepot—knowing, as always, his father would be less grouchy if his insides were warmed up.

It snowed on for two days and part of another night. When it stopped, the cattle barns could hardly be seen from the house. The big snow was a blessing for Jack and Pete, for they were hired by the County to help clear the outlying roads. On the last Saturday of the month Newt went along. Sitting between his father and Pete on the big plow truck, he watched the snow churn up and off to the side, where in some places the drifts were higher than the cab of the truck. Halfway between the swimming hole and Jake Kiner's place on the river road, Pete stopped the truck and braced for such a drift; then he revved up the motor and knifed the plow blades into it, sending the snow up over them and in all directions. There was a sudden jolt, and Newt and his father slammed forward into the dashboard. The truck bounced back and stalled.

"What'd you hit?" Jack boomed.

"Don't know!" Pete hollered back. The three of them jumped down and started kicking away the snow from the object buried in their path.

"It's a car!" Newt yelled. "It's a car, Poppa!"

Pete grabbed three shovels off the truck and they began uncovering the car. It was an old Model-T Ford, and it took them five minutes to dig their way to its windshield.

"Careful now," Jack cautioned. "I hope and pray ain't nobody in it."

They dug slower, inching their way.

"Poppa!" Newt hollered, "I hit somethin' on the runnin' board!"

"Git back. Let me see." Jack felt the object with his shovel and carefully scraped away the snow. He stopped suddenly. "Good Lord—it's a man! He's stiff as a board."

"He dead, Poppa?" Newt questioned.

"That you can be shore of," Jack said solemnly.

"Anybody we know?" Pete asked.

"Ain't never seen him before," Jack said.

Newt peeked and said, "Me either."

"It's a Missouri plate," Pete said, brushing the snow off the raised numbers.

Jack turned to Newt. "You better hike back to town and git Kirky. Just tell him what we found. We're gonna keep diggin'. Might find somebody else here too."

When Newt returned with Kirky in Doug Simpson's Ford car, his father and brother had dug the car completely free of the drift. Kirky strode over to the corpse, kneeled down and wiped the loose snow from the face. "Hell," he said, "that's Bats Oliver. He's a bootlegger from K. C." He got up, forced open the back door of the car and yanked a tarpaulin off the back area. "Look here, he's got the whole assend loaded with booze!" He inspected the cache more closely. "Hell, must be more'n fifty bottles in there. Want some, Jack?"

"Nope," Jack said, "nothin' I can do with that stuff."

"Well, he shore won't be needin' it," Kirky said. He and Doug loaded the bottles into their car, stepping over and around the body as if it were a log. Then Kirky said, "You all stay here. I'm goin' to git the dead wagon. Be right back." And with that Doug turned the car around and drove off.

On New Year's Day, Sarah had a visit from Judge Cavanaugh. She had expected him for some time, so his coming was no surprise. He brought food packages and a few gifts for everyone, and Rodney had come along to help with these as well as to see Newt.

After a while, in the quiet of Sarah and Jack's bedroom, the Judge told them what he suspected they had known for days. He spoke his regret, and said that Arcella would be taken care of. He didn't say in what way—and Jack and Sarah didn't ask. Of course, Chauncey had denied everything, but to no avail. "He will work this summer—if he has to dig ditches—to pay for all this and more," the Judge said.

He and Rodney ate black-eyed peas and pig's feet with the Wingers for good luck, then they got into their big shiny Maxwell and went off to their big house on the other side of the town.

Five days later Prissy came home and said that Chauncey had packed his clothes and slipped away while the Judge was in court. "All he left was a letter for the poor Judge." Prissy sighed.

January, February and March were equally cold, desolate and hard for Jack Winger and his family. With the feed bins running low and the icebox nearly empty, Jack had to kill off most of his chickens and slaughter two of his best hogs. One cow died, and a horse was crippled from a fall on the ice. Jake Kiner had brought in feed a couple of times when he had needed it desperately. And though Jack couldn't pay for it, he had noted the amount in his soiled account book. "You'll git it back soon's I'm able," he told Kiner.

Yet all was not bad. Jake promised to hire Pete for some spring cattle driving, and Sarah finally got permission from Doc Cravens to return to work on the first of April. In addition, Prissy announced she had a beau—though she never revealed who he was.

Newt, in spite of his loss, had been doing extremely well in school; and he had become a regular on the basketball team, being the third freshman in the history of the school to do so. As the months wore on, the pain of his wound gradually lessened, and every now and then he would completely forget the bittersweet affair. Still, naturally, there were times when, catching the scent of lilac water, or scanning the inscription in Poe's book of stories ("Love, Arcella. December, 1925"), he felt life wasn't worth living. He had inquired of her when his team returned to Chanute after the holidays, but no one he asked knew of the family's whereabouts. It was as if they had disappeared from earth without leaving a trace.

Later, in the early part of April, he dreamed of lying with Arcella on the mossy earth near the violets in Peaceful Park—but he awoke only to a rooster's crowing. And his heart, which had seemed to thump on Arcella's breast, beat only against his lumpy mattress.

CHAPTER ✿ 13

SPRING! Birds darting about—singing in trees and over the prairies. Overhasty flowers popping up from the damp earth. And only two more weeks of school!

Things had got back pretty much to normal for the Wingers. Sarah was at the Cavanaughs again, working hard as ever, and Prissy helped her on Saturdays with the heavy cleaning. Jack was busy in the fields, and every so often he drove a steam-roller for the County. Pete rode the herd for Jake Kiner Monday through Friday. And every day after school Newt joined Beansy, Earl, Jappy and Skunk in the ritual of testing the water at the swimming hole.

On the first Saturday morning in June, Newt went over to the Kiner farm looking for work. He met Jake at the barn door and said humbly, "Mornin', Mister Kiner."

"Mornin', Newt." Jake pushed his spectacles to the end of his bony red nose. "No peaches yet, you young scallywag. What you want?"

Newt grinned and said, "Want some extra work this summer."

Jake grunted. "Extra, huh? None of you young'uns wants anything steady."

"Got to get my swimmin' in, you know that. You was young once."

"I ain't none too happy 'bout it, though. Wasted lots of time—like you're doin' right now. You ought'a be a good hand like your brother Pete,' stead of cavortin' all over the place swimmin' and stealin' peaches and such."

"Oh, them days are over for me, Mister Kiner. I got to make money for college. Only got three more years."

"Sounds good. Prob'ly lotta hot air, though."

"Nosir—I'm goin' for sure. Ask Momma."

"Well, what you want'a do 'sides sleep and eat?"

"Oh, some hoein' and feedin'—helpin' anywhere—maybe ridin' with Pete when he'll let me."

"Just a minute." Jake pushed open the barn door and hollered, "The Harvesta' man bring the plowshares yet, Silas?"

"Said he'd be out this afternoon round three," Silas called back.

"Mister Newhall workin' for you this spring?" Newt asked.

"Well, I'm tryin' him. Don't know how he's gonna work out—quite a boozer." Jake studied Newt for a moment. "Okay, young fella, you come round next Saturday. See if I cain't put you to doin' somethin'."

"Thanks, Mister Kiner, thanks. School'll be out next Friday, so that'll be just fine. I'll be here bright'n early."

On the last day of school, Mr. Hall called Newt to his office. "Newton," he said, "I want to congratulate you on your final marks—and especially on the good report Miss McClinock turned in."

Newt had been nervous when he entered, but now he beamed brightly. "Thanks, Mister Hall. I tried hard."

"Your report card shows you did. See you next fall. Have a good summer."

They shook hands, then Newt made a special trip down the hall to say goodbye to Miss McClinock. She smiled stiffly and told Newt that she appreciated his coming to her. And he felt good as he walked out of the door toward summer and vacation. He joined Beansy, Jappy and Earl on the steps, and they all started across town, comparing marks. As they reached the tracks they met Skunk.

"How'd you git over here so early?" Beansy asked.

"Got a new babe with a big new car," Skunk lied. "You ought to see her. She's got hair down to her ankles and a keester that would make old Rev'rend Broadnap throw his Bible in a privy hole."

They all laughed and continued across the tracks. The rest of the afternoon they wandered aimlessly over Candy Hill and along the road leading to Rock Cave and the river—happy in the freedom of summer that lay ahead.

When Newt entered the house that evening, Prissy handed him a letter—and his heart jumped. "It might be from Arcella," he thought. He tore it open and began reading.

"Who's it from?" Prissy asked, peeping over his shoulder.

Newt kept reading, and a big grin came on his face. "Hot dog! Hot dog!" he shouted.

Prissy was beside herself with curiosity. "What's it say? Who's it from?"

" 'Professor Radeaker invites you to participate in the

special science seminar he will conduct for a week this summer,' it says. Wait'll I tell Momma! Won't Rodney Cavanaugh be surprised? He'll be goin' too."

"Huh—you think you're somethin' great," Prissy said.

"It's a big honor, because he only invites the ten best students every year. They go on field trips and everything." He danced about the room, waving the letter. His summer was shaping up.

The next day Newt went to work on the Kiner farm, and Silas Newhall was four hours late. Jake stormed about the place damning himself for having given Silas a chance. "Should'a known better'n to trust that likker-head!"

"Anything I can do, Mister Kiner?" Newt asked.

"Naw. Just you keep cleanin' up that tack," Jake snapped. Pulling out a bunch of keys, he unlocked a door near the barn entrance. He went in, and a short time later shouted, "Come here, boy!"

Newt dropped the saddle and reins, went over to the door and found Jake stacking bottles on a shelf. He climbed atop a box and motioned to Newt. "Hand me them bottles out'a that tub there," he said. Newt began handing them up as Jake placed them on a higher shelf.

"Look out!" Jake shouted, as one of the bottles toppled from the shelf and broke on the floor. "Hit you?"

"Nope," Newt said.

"Pint'a good peach brandy gone," Jake mumbled. "Okay, keep shovin' 'em up." Newt kicked the broken glass to the side and began handing Jake the bottles again. He was just picking up the last two when Silas staggered into the barn and came over to the brandy closet.

"Mor-mornin', mornin',," he mumbled. "Uh—look'it all the hooch—no wonder you—keep that—big ole lock—on that there door, Jake," he added groggily.

Jake placed the last two bottles and climbed down. A mixture of anger and disgust was on his face as he stood regarding Silas. "What you mean 'mornin' '?" he growled finally. "It's past twelve—and you're soused to the gills!"

Silas giggled. "Jus' a little spir-its, that's all—a little spir-its —" He wobbled closer, and Newt caught the reek of liquor that seemed to come from his clothes.

Jake reached in his pocket and pulled out some money, sorted out several bills and shoved them into Silas' hands. "Here—you're fired," he said. "Now git off my property."

"Now wa-wait a minit, Jake—you cain't do this to me."

"Git out, I say!" Jake started shoving him toward the door.

"Okay—okay—" Silas stopped and counted the money. "Lis-sen here, this ain't a'nough—this's a day short." He stood rocking in the middle of the floor.

"That's all you're gittin'. You ain't got a cent comin' for today," Jake said, "not a cent. Now out you go!" Jake pushed him on through the door and into the open. The door banged shut behind them.

Newt went over and started cleaning the tack again. He could hear the two men outside screaming at each other:

"You owe me 'nother day, you ole ba-bastard! I want the money what's comin' to me!"

"Go on, git out! Git out!"

A few minutes later Newt went outside for lunch, and he could see Silas far across the field, stumbling toward the village. "Poor Waldo," he thought. "What a guy to have for a father." He took a paper sack from his overall bib, unwrapped a ham sandwich and began eating. After a while Jake came out with a cup of milk. "Somethin' to wash it down with," he said, then walked back toward the house.

Later that evening, at the Winger supper table, Newt remarked about Silas' being fired. "Jake was plenty mad too," he said. "He just shoved some money at Silas and told him to get goin'."

"Silas drunk?" Pete asked.

"He sure was. Couldn't hardly stand up."

"Shame," Sarah said. "I feel so bad for Waldo. He's such a nice boy at heart."

"Cain't say the same for Blanche, though," Jack put in.

"Well, Silas shore ain't set no great pattern for neither one of them to go by," Sarah retorted.

A knock came on the screen door. "Newt—can you go?" It was Beansy and Skunk.

"Just a minute," Newt answered, and looked at Sarah. "Momma, you care if I go to the early show with Beansy and Skunk?"

"Long's you git home before nine, it's all right. No later."

"Yessem." Jumping up from the table, he grabbed his cap and joined his friends.

On their way to the Regency Theater they passed Chappie Logan's place, and Newt spotted Silas Newhall coming out the door. He was still drunk, leaning on the arm of Booker Savage. Newt tried to hurry past without being seen, but he wasn't fast enough. "Hey, boy!" Silas hollered. "You tell that ole goat Jake I'm comin' for my money. You tell'm now, hear me?"

"Yeh—yeh," Newt answered, still moving.

"An' tell'm he better put more'n one lock on that booze he's hidin' in that barn, too. You tell'm, hear?"

"Yeh—yeh," Newt repeated.

As the boys went on down the block, Skunk quipped, "Them two are the ass-ends of nothin'."

"What's Silas talkin' about, Newt?" Beansy asked.

"Jake Kiner fired him today for bein' late and drunk."

"Su-prised me he hired him in the first place," Skunk said. "I wouldn't trust him behind a mosquito's pecker."

They walked on to the tracks, where a freight train stood blocking their path. "Come on, let's go over the top," Skunk urged, "else we'll be late for the show." He jumped on the bottom step and began scaling the metal rungs of the boxcar. Newt and Beansy hesitated a moment, then followed. They had just reached the top of the car when the brakeman spied them.

"Git off there, you bastards!" he shouted.

"Screw you, red balls!" Skunk hollered back.

They scurried down the other side, leaped to the ground and made off toward the Regency.

CHAPTER ✤ 14

NEWT ARRIVED at the Kiner farm early the next Saturday morning. There was a note from Jake tacked to the barn door saying that he and his wife would be away until afternoon. Newt stuffed the note in his pocket, wishing now he had gone to see Pete ride in the rodeo at Parsons.

He cleaned tack for the first hour, then swept the floor and went out to the fields, hoeing weeds until nearly twelve o'clock. Finally, tired from the half day's work, he swung the hoe to his shoulder and looked about for shelter from the burning sun. There was a tree close by, but he found it too skimpy for shade; so he walked back to the barn—figuring to get a good hour's rest before Jake returned.

He entered the barn, stood the hoe against a wall, and settled on a box. Then, changing his mind, he climbed the wooden ladder to the loft and stretched out in the hay. It took him several minutes to devour two sandwiches, then he rolled over on his back and gazed idly at the ceiling until his eyelids got heavy. Before long he was fast asleep.

More than two hours had passed when he sprang awake to a squeaking noise down on the floor beneath him. He scooted quietly to the edge of the loft and peeped below, fearing that Jake had discovered his absence. Then his breath caught in his throat. It wasn't Jake. It was Booker Savage— and he was ripping the lock off the door to the room where Jake stored his applejack and peach brandy.

Afraid of what Booker might do if he saw him, Newt just lay quiet and watched. The bottom hinge was loose now, and Booker wedged the crowbar under the top screws. With one powerful jerk he wrenched the lock and hinges off and they clattered to the floor. Then, hooking the crowbar on the back pocket of his overalls, he placed a gunny sack on the floor and slipped into the dark room. Within seconds Newt saw him loading pint bottles in the sack.

Booker stopped at the sound of Jake's angry voice coming

from the barn door. "You ain't gittin' one penny more out'a me, Silas! Now git out'a here, you drunken bum, 'fore I throw you out!"

Silas Newhall staggered in after him. "I ain't leavin' here till you pay me what's comin' to me, you goddam old pinchpenny!"

Jake's face screwed up in anger, and he reached to the wall for his bull whip. "I'm warnin' you for the last time to git out!" he hollered, threatening the reeling Silas with the heavy end of the whip.

"You don't scare me, you old son-of-a-bitch!" Silas grabbed Newt's hoe as he yelled back, but before he could swing it Jake stepped to one side and clouted him on the temple with the butt-end of the whip. Silas fell unconscious to the floor.

Jake had stumbled on the sack of bottles as he swung, and now, as he steadied himself, he saw the awesome figure of Booker Savage peering from the dark of the doorway. Bewildered, he paused a moment with his mouth open—then he snapped the whip and struck. Booker flinched and raised the crowbar. Jake drew back again, but before he could swing, the crowbar smashed against his head. He went down without uttering a sound. With the first blow the beast seemed to have been loosed in Booker, and he smashed the crowbar time and again into Jake's bloody head.

Finally Booker stood over the two forms on the floor, looking about, breathing heavily. Silas moaned. Booker stooped, pulled the whip from beneath Jake's arm, and beat the moan to a stillness. He dropped the whip by Silas' head and started away; then he turned back, picked up the crowbar and placed it in Silas' limp left hand. After that he lifted the sack of bottles, stepped warily through the door and fled across the field.

Newt hadn't moved during the swift, brutal assault, and when he did it was in a maze of nightmarish thought. It was as if he'd had a bad dream and, not yet fully awake, believed he was still dreaming. He crawled to the back of the loft and pinned his eye to a crack in the wallboards, watching Booker make off into the nearby woods.

Suddenly he knew he had to get out of there himself. He started for the ladder, then stopped and crouched back, for Mary Kiner had appeared at the barn door. Catching sight of the forms lying in the shadows beyond the doorway, she stepped in further, an apprehensive look on her face. Then she threw up her hands and ran screaming toward the house. "Oh my Lord! Oh! Help! Help!"

When she was gone, Newt clambered down the ladder, crept toward the door, glancing timorously at the two men sprawled like ragamuffins on the floor. He peeped out the door, then burst through it and loped over the furrowed earth toward home. He slowed down as he approached Logan's Grove. He was shaking now, so instead of going to the house he cut across to the cowshed, staying there until the shaking stopped.

Though fatigue was upon Newt like an opiate this night, he couldn't sleep. He had slipped off to bed at nightfall, dinnerless and faking an upset stomach. Jack Winger sensed more worry than ailment in his son's complaining, but he was wrong about the source. "That boy's heart shore must be heavy if he goes off to bed without eatin'," he confided to Sarah, slapping a fly on his forehead. "Must still be thinkin' 'bout that girl."

"Well, it was a pretty hard blow for him to take at his age," Sarah said. And then they had dropped the subject.

Twice during the night the harrowing scene ran through Newt's mind and flushed him to a fearful awakening. He lay in what seemed like never-ending darkness, wondering whether he should tell...

By church time Sunday morning the news of Jake Kiner's death and Silas Newhall's arrest had swept across languid Cherokee Flats like a storm. Every minister in town sparked his sermon on the tragedy, but the Reverend Lucius Broadnap preached a half hour overtime, ending finally by shouting, "—the devil got in here yesterd'y afternoon and undone all the good the word of Jesus been spreadin' among us for years! Bless the sorrowful widow of this poor man whose life's blood lays cold this minute on the floor of his barn. Bless us all, dear Jesus—amen."

Later, an uneasy calm lay over the Winger household while Sarah and Prissy spread the Sunday table. Uncle Rob, heavy eyelids batting behind dark glasses, sat in the shadow of the chimney pipe. Pete stood at a window, gazing into the distance, watching the slow turn of the weather vane atop the Kiner barn. Newt sat on the floor, his back propped against the sideboard, staring into space. And Jack leaned against the wall in a straight-back chair, smoking his pipe. He was the first to break the silence. "Powerful sermon Broadnap preached today, Rob."

Rob's head lifted and his lids blinked even faster. "Yes, it was. Yes, it was." His right little finger was nervously rubbing

165

the nubs on his other hand. "And his words about Jake sure touched the heart." He paused, then went on, "Jake was a good sort—a little cranky maybe, but he did lots of good things too—like the time he donated the stain-glass window for the church."

The talk about Jake brought a new agitation to Newt, and he began rocking back and forth in little inconsistent rhythms, glancing furtively at his father, uncle and brother. And before he could halt the words, they were flowing from his mouth: "You know, Poppa, I did some hoein' for Mr. Kiner yesterday."

Jack was coughing out smoke and Newt thought his father hadn't heard, so he added, "I left his place early, though."

Rob inclined his head toward Newt. "What did you say, boy?"

"Oh, I just said I'd done a little work for Mr. Kiner lately, a little hoein'."

"Oh, you did."

Pete eyed Newt curiously, and Newt had the feeling that his brother was aware of his cover-up.

Sarah entered the room and placed a platter of chicken on the table, and Prissy followed with hot bread and vegetables. Jack took his brother Rob by the arm and led him to his seat at the table. After they were all in place, Sarah called on Newt for the blessing.

"Lord, make us thankful for what we are about to receive, for the nouris-nourishment of our bodies. Amen."

Sarah heaped food on Rob's plate and sat it before him. "There you are, Rob," she said.

"Thanks, Sarah."

"Leg, Newt?"

"Yessem, guess so."

"Prissy?"

"Same, please."

"Pete, you and your poppa help yourselves."

Jack stuffed a napkin in the collar of his white shirt. "I declare, I cain't for the life of me understand how Silas Newhall could do such a thing."

"Whiskey'll make a man do lots of crazy things," Rob said.

"Got Silas over at the jail?" Sarah asked.

"From what I hear he's at the hospital—pretty well banged up himself."

"Heard they'd been fussin' about a week over some money Silas claimed Jake owed him."

"Who told you that, Pete?" Jake asked.

"Talk about town."

"Coffee, Rob?"

Rob dropped his fork. Newt picked it up, wiped it on his napkin and placed it in his uncle's hand. "No thanks, Sarah."

Jack chomped the white off a scallion. "Well, I'm shore glad 'twasn't a colored man who done it," he said. "It'd be trouble shore enough."

"Yep. We can all be thankful for that," Pete agreed.

"Poor old Jake," Sarah sighed, "he had enough trouble in the last couple years."

"Yeh," Jack replied, "with the beatin' the Savage boy gave him and all."

"What about Mary?"

"They say she's been out'a her mind ever since it happened."

"Where's she, home by herself, Sarah?"

"Nope. She's—eat, Newt—she's over at the hospital under Timothy's care."

"Well, it's a shame—downright dirty shame. Who'd ever thought it could happen right here under our very noses?"

"Sin's got no respect for time or place, Jack. You know that."

"Silas'll prob'ly git life, won't he, Poppa?" Pete said.

"Don't see how he can 'scape it. Seems to me they got him dead to rights. Found him layin' right 'longside of Jake, drunk as a loon."

Rob's face lifted before he spoke, and Newt could see the whole table reflected in the black lenses. "They still have to prove he's guilty first. Never can tell. Silas's liable to plead self-defense or somethin'. Never can tell till it's all over."

"Ain't you hungry, Newt?" Sarah questioned. "Whyn't you eat your chicken?"

Newt shot a side glance at Pete, then picked up the leg and began chewing listlessly. Pete looked away. "Got any more coffee, Prissy?"

"What does it mean, 'gettin' life,' Poppa?" Newt popped the question while Jack had his mouth full of food.

Rob sensed his brother's long delay and cut in, "Means he'll go to prison for the rest of his life, Newt."

"Till he dies?"

"Till he dies," Jack finally answered.

"Lucky he ain't in Missouri—he'd git death," Pete said, shaking his head.

"Don't mention such a thing, Pete," Sarah said, getting up. "It's awful just to think about such a thing."

Sarah served hot mince pie and poured the grownups more coffee. And after everyone was finished, several minutes of quiet fell over the table. Newt was apprehensive. Things were worse than he'd thought.

Then his mother was up, taking the dirty dishes off the table. "Come on, Prissy," she sighed, "let's clean off the table."

At three o'clock Rob asked for his hat and cane. Jack, who had been dozing on the front porch, called Newt to walk his uncle home, and it was a welcome duty for Newt. Sarah wrapped some cold chicken and pie in a grocery sack and gave it to Rob. "You might git hungry this evenin'," she warned.

Rob took the package and smiled. "I might, at that," he said, "I might, at that. Thanks, Sarah." Newt gently took his wrist, helped him off the porch, and they went on their way.

A half hour later, as Newt sauntered back across town, he wrestled with his harsh dilemma (If I tell on Booker, there could be lots of trouble . . . and all the colored people might call me a snitch . . . and I'd sure have trouble with Marcus all the rest of my life . . . but it ain't right for Silas Newhall to go to prison for somethin' he didn't do either . . . still, Silas is white and he might get off easy . . . if I tell on Booker, lots more people might get killed . . .).

As he drifted down the quiet road he suddenly envisioned the blacks and whites of Cherokee Flats fighting each other—Pete and his father swinging clubs at the Mottsys and Simpsons and Stocktons, and all the houses burning and people screaming and fighting with guns and knives and himself fighting Waldo hitting and hitting his head with a rock and Kirky and some others dragging Booker through the streets with a rope around his neck and Booker screaming for help and Marcus trying to get him loose and being knocked down and his mother rushing in trying to stop all the fighting and yelling stop it! stop it! and Prissy hiding in the bedroom with Rende and Butsy and Gin-gin—and Rodney Cavanaugh hiding and crying in his big house on the hill with the blacks burning it down. . . .

"Hi, Newt." ,

He looked up, surprised. It was Waldo Newhall on his bicycle. "Hi—hi—how you doin', Waldo?"

"Want a lift home? Get on."

Newt thought Waldo looked very sad. He straddled the seat. Waldo shoved off, stood up on the pedals and pumped the last blocks to the Winger house. Newt got off, thanked him and started into the yard, wanting to leave Waldo as quickly as possible.

"Guess you heard about all the trouble Paw's in, huh?" Newt paused and turned back, wide-eyed. "Yeh—oh yeh—what's gonna happen?"

"Don't know—don't know."

"I'm awful sorry, Waldo."

"Think your maw'd let you drive me and Blanche over to the hospital to see Paw in a little while? Blanche ain't got no way to get over there."

"Why—why sure. I—I can ask her—for you, Waldo. I—"

"Okay, I'll go in with you now so Blanche'll know for sure."

Sarah was glad to help, so she told Newt to hitch up the horse to the buggy and drive them over. And in less than an hour Newt found himself standing with Blanche and Waldo outside Silas' room. Blanche had cried on the way over and Waldo had wanted Newt to go in with him.

"Not in the room," Newt had said.

"You can wait outside the door."

Blanche knocked and a nurse peeped out the door and said. "Yes?"

"I'm here to see my father," Blanche said tearfully.

"Oh," the nurse said. "He's just now come to, and I don't think you—hold on just a minute." She turned back into the room, leaving the door cracked.

"What you gittin' at, Kirky?" It was Silas' voice.

"You know what I'm gittin' at. You know well's I do—Jake's dead. And you kilt him!"

"You must be out'a your head. Why'd I do such a thing?"

The nurse came back with Doc Cravens, who stepped outside and closed the door behind him. "You're the Newhall children?"

"Yes," Blanche sniffled.

"Hello, Newt. What you doin' here?"

"He drove us over," Waldo answered quickly.

"Well, your father's been under sedatives most of the day. He's comin' around now. You wait out here for a few minutes and I'll take you in to see him." He opened the door and went back in. Kirky's voice came through the opening: "—and you done too much blabbin' 'fore you pulled it off. That's your trouble, Si—" Cravens shut the door behind him.

Blanche started crying again, and Waldo, not knowing what

169

to do, spread out his hands in a helpless gesture and looked at Newt.

It was nearly twenty-five minutes before Doc Cravens called in Blanche and Waldo. While they were inside, Newt sat on the floor and propped himself against the wall. This thing was growing too big for him. Twice in the buggy he'd been inclined to blurt out the truth, to relieve Blanche and Waldo of their anxiety. But confusion, more than anything else, stopped him. Now his thoughts were becoming even more jumbled, and suddenly he didn't trust himself on the ride back. He got to his feet and started toward the exit.

He was about to go through the hall door when he heard Blanche crying again as she and Waldo came toward him. "Kirky's stayin'," Newt thought.

It was pitch dark when they got back to the buggy, so Newt and Waldo lit the side lamps. As they rode along in the country darkness, Newt glued his mind to the sound of crickets in an effort to shut out any other thoughts whatsoever. The three of them were quiet all the way to the Newhall house, and then it was only after Blanche had gone in that Waldo spoke. "You know one thing, Winger?"

"What?" Newt asked nervously.

"I don't believe Paw killed anybody."

"Did he say he didn't?"

"Yeh. And I can tell when he's tellin' the truth, 'cause he lies so damned much."

"What'd he say?"

"Not much. He's still kind of dizzy from those drugs they been givin' him for pain. But he kept sayin' he thought he saw somebody else there besides Jake—thinks for sure he did."

Newt began chewing his lips. "Did he say what he looked like?"

"Said he looked colored."

"He said that sure enough?"

"Yeh, he said it, all right. But I don't think anybody much is gonna believe him. He's in a tough spot—a real tough spot."

"Maybe somethin'll happen, Waldo."

"Can't tell."

"Can't tell," Newt repeated.

Waldo jumped to the ground and thanked Newt, then moved on toward the house. Newt gazed after him a moment, then drove off. As he rode along he looked up at the sky. The moon was out. It was full, and the man in it was smiling.

Later that Sunday evening Marcus Savage was at the stove, heating leftover beef stew, when he heard Kirky's motorcycle screech to a halt at the front of the shack. He kept on stirring the greasy chunks in the bubbling gravy. (Wonder what that son-of-a-bitch wants here—somethin' to do with the killin', I bet.) A knock came on the door. "Yeh! What'a you want?"

The knob creaked, then Kirky was in the room. "Well, well—look who's cookin' Sunday dinner—Mista Savage's little innicent chile."

Without turning, Marcus spat in the coal bucket and kept on stirring. "What the hell you want here, brass-ass?" He spat again. "You come to give me a ride to church?"

"Watch your goddam trap, boy," Kirky snarled, "or you might have to dig my foot out'a your black ass!"

"You ain't got no biz'ness here, so git out! I had enough trouble out'a you."

"Well, you gonna have a lot more if you ain't got the right answers to some questions I'm gonna ask you."

"Yeh?"

"Yeh. Where was you b'tween one and four o'clock yestidy aftanoon?"

Marcus pulled two tin pans from the shelf above him. A cockroach jumped from the top one onto his arm. He shook it to the floor and squashed it with his foot before it could get away. He planked the tins on a nearby table, scraped the boiling stew equally into each one, pushed back a curtain and called out, "Come on to dinner, Paw!" Then, kicking a small barrel in place, he sat on it and began to eat.

"You hear my question, boy?" Kirky asked.

Marcus chewed out his retort. "How old you have to be in this stinkin' town 'fore white trash quit callin' you 'boy'?"

"Oh, ah begs yo pardon, Mista Savage, suh. Now would you mind tellin' this po, humble white trash where your sweet, noble black ass was yestidy b'tween one and four, please, suh—and what you did with all them green bottles'a peach brandy and applejack you stole out'a Jake's."

Marcus shot up like an uncoiling spring. "I was at your mammy's, you—" Kirky cocked his fist and moved forward.

"What's goin' on in here? What's all this fuss?" Booker Savage's big menacing frame, naked from the waist up, ambled through the doorway.

Kirky's arm dropped to his side. "I'm just tryin' to clear

171

your hotheaded son here from some trouble that's brewin', that's all. I'm tryin' to find out where he was when Jake Kiner was killed."

"Jake Kiner? Jake Kiner's dead? You kiddin'!"

"You ain't heard?"

"Naw—I been here all day, sleepin'."

"Well, he was killed yestidy in his barn."

Booker shook his head. "Ain't that somethin'." Then he turned on Marcus. "Well, where was you, boy? Where was you?"

Marcus grumbled. "I cleaned at Chappie's in the mornin', then I went to Blanche Newhall's and helped Waldo clean out her basement from 'bout twelve to five. That's where I was at. If you don't believe me, go and ask her yourself." He pulled a silver dollar from his pocket. "Right here's the money she give me for doin' it. Every goddamn bit of it."

"All right, boy, I'll ask her," Kirky scowled. "I'll sure ask her." He went out the door and banged it shut.

Marcus was still eating when, a few minutes later, Booker left the kitchen, went into the bedroom and returned with a blue shirt. Dark stains were on the lower sleeves. Booker lifted the stove lid and shoved the shirt in the fire. "Goddam chicken got blood all over me."

"What chicken?" Marcus asked.

"One I killed for Mag Pullens t'other day."

"Oh—"

Booker got drunker as the evening wore on, and eventually he stumbled to the other room and flopped down on the soggy pallet that he shared with his son. Before long he was snoring, groaning and cursing. Marcus couldn't stomach the racket, so he pulled two chairs together for a bed in the kitchen. They didn't suit him. Then he lay upon the floor for a few minutes, rolling from side to side, straining for comfort. Finally he remembered an old mattress he'd seen in the coal shed; he lit a lantern and went outside for it. He had already lifted the mattress and was turning back when his light struck the green bottles sticking up from the gunny sack (Where in hell'd the ole man git all that booze, I wonder . . . must'a stole it someplace . . .). He pulled the door to and started up the path, then he turned quickly and re-entered the shed, holding the light close to the bottles (Goddam . . . Kirky said somethin' 'bout green bottles . . . wonder if the ole man . . . goddam, this is somethin' . . . I cain't believe it . . . goddam . . .). He tossed an old quilt over the

172

bottles, shut the door and headed back toward the shack (Ain't this a bitch . . . ain't this a bitch . . .).

He was breathing heavily by the time he reached the kitchen door. Pushing it open with his shoulder, he closed it quietly behind him and dumped the mattress on the floor; then he put the lantern on the table and sat on a chair listening to the fitful snoring in the next room. Finally he jacked up the lantern chimney and blew out the flame, then leaned on the table, his arms crossed beneath his head. . . .

"O! O! O! loog out! loog out! Naw! Naw! Naw! . . . lemme go . . . lemme go . . . Aaaaw . . ." Marcus' head lifted to Booker's hollering, then dropped back wearily on his arms. He couldn't sleep—and he didn't try. He just closed his eyes and tried not to think.

The next morning, as Marcus peeped into the icebox, Booker staggered in holding a half-empty bottle of peach brandy. "You ain't gonna find nothin' to chaw on in that thing—ain't even no ice in it."

Marcus spoke without looking at his father. "I'm so hungry I could eat the bark off a tree."

Booker grunted, lifted the bottle to his mouth, took two hefty swallows and wiped his lips with the back of his wrist. "Well, 'less you spend that dollar you was showin' off when Kirky was here, you betta start skinnin' that big cottonwood 'side the house. It's got plenty bark." He grunted again and turned back toward the bedroom.

"Paw—where'd you git all that booze you got hid out in the shed?"

"What booze you talkin' 'bout, boy?" His red eyes were glowing with meanness as he wheeled drunkenly to face Marcus. "What booze you talkin' 'bout?"

"That booze in them green bottles in the gunny sack that was under this mattress, like the bottle you got in your hand now."

"What you been snoopin' round like a filthy black cat for? Spyin' on me or somethin'?"

"I wasn't snoopin'. I wanted the mattress to sleep on. You was hollerin' and fartin' all night, so I went out to the shed to git it—and come across all them bottles."

"Ain't none of your biz'ness where I got it. Keep your goddam trap shut or I'll put my fist in it." His body trembled under the fury of his threat.

Marcus eyed the bottle in his father's grasp. "Okay, Paw. Guess you know what you're doin', but if you don't, you betta

173

ask somebody. And you know well as I do, ain't too many round here hankerin' for your askin'."

"What you gittin' at, boy?"

"I'm tryin' to say that if you got some kind of trouble, you ought'a tell me 'bout it. I'm your son, ain't I?"

"I had to take your maw's word for that, boy."

Marcus bristled. "Why, you—" He weighed his chances against the burly two hundred and fifty pounds, decided against finishing the sentence. Instead, he stood looking at Booker, feeling a hatred that even he thought himself incapable of possessing. All at once he shuddered, burst into a frantic sob and lunged toward his father with both fists flying—expecting to go down under a hail of blows and really not caring. But Booker just grabbed him about the waist and held him as if he were in a vise.

"Simmer down, boy. Simmer down—" He had become unexpectedly contrite. "Your ole man's sorry for sayin' such a thing. Honest, boy, I'm sorry." Gradually he released his hold and Marcus stood free, stunned at the first kind words he could ever remember his father speaking to him. And the tough shell that for years had shut him off from tender emotion gave way for an unusual moment—and Marcus gave himself to this rare instant in a flood of tears.

"You think I killed ole Jake, don't you, boy?" Marcus was silent. "Well, boy—I—I did kill him. I didn't mean to, but he caught me breakin' in his place and it was my only way out—and he hit me with that damn whip, same as he did you. You believe me, boy?"

"Yeh."

"It's our secret, ain't it, boy? Don't be forgittin' I'm your ole man. It could git us both in lots of trouble round here. You know that, don't you?"

"Yeh."

"Then I kin depend on you, huh?"

"Yeh."

"Good boy. Good boy." His hand went toward his son's shoulder, but Marcus avoided it and went out the door.

"Where you goin', boy?"

"Over to the bak'ry for some stale buns."

"Atta boy—atta boy. Uh—Marcus."

"Yeh?"

"Git a little coffee on your way back."

"Okay—okay."

Booker watched his son turn from the front path into the road. He rubbed his stubbly chin in a moment of thought, gulped another mouthful of brandy and returned to his greasy pallet.

That same morning Newt was scraping down the hog troughs when he heard Pete's voice at the barn door. "Must'a been workin' extra hard on Lucky. Coat's smooth as silk."

"She's a good girl—be two this fall."

Pete asked the question more directly than Newt had anticipated. "You know anything 'bout that killin'?"

"The killin'?" His mind was racing.

"Yep, the killin'."

"Naw—naw, I just said that—"

"Remember, I'm your brother—your own flesh and blood. You gotta tell me the honest-to-god truth."

Newt had thought at first he might be able to confide in his older brother. Now he felt it would be impossible to compromise Pete's honesty. "He'd tell Momma for sure," he thought. "What makes you think I ain't goin' to tell the truth? You ain't givin' me the chance to answer you."

"Okay, now you got the chance. Go ahead."

"Okay then." He feigned anger, stalling for time. "Let me say what I want to say."

"Go ahead. I'm listenin'."

"All I said before was I'd been doin' some hoein' for Jake lately."

"Not lately, Newt. Saturday. Ain't that right?"

"Yeh, that's right—but I left real early in the afternoon, 'cause I didn't think Jake would get back before five or six. And since Silas was fired and Missus Kiner was away, I sort of took off."

"Well, why'd you git so shaky yesterday when you told Poppa and then tried to back out of it the next minute?"

"I thought you caught on to what I was doin'—I got to thinkin', real quick, that Poppa would give me hell for sneakin' off the job like that. You know how he is, Pete. And you know as well as I do that it's crazy to get messed up in somethin' like this if you don't have to."

"Then you don't know anything 'bout the killin'?"

Newt's look of innocence contrived his answer. "You know doggone well I don't. I was just scared stiff 'cause I knew how close I was to it."

"Okay—okay—I see your point now. But if you're gonna go round tellin' people you was there on the day of the killin', you're gonna find yourself right in the middle of it."

Relief swept over Newt. "You're right there, Pete. I'm

175

keepin' my mouth shut from now on." He watched Pete stroll back toward the house. The matter was closed—and he felt that he'd given the right answers.

A few minutes later he had finished his chore. He went to the house, got his books and went off to school.

CHAPTER ✤ 15

A GRAND JURY indicted Silas Newhall for the murder of Jacob Elijah Kiner, and he spent the rest of June and all of July in the county jail at Fort Miles. During the first week of August he was brought back to Cherokee Flats to stand trial.

The prosecuting attorney was Stewart McCormack, a flamboyant, portly, white-maned lawyer from Fort Miles. McCormack had senatorial ambitions, and a conviction in such a case as this could further those ambitions. The defense was to be carried by Harley Davis, a red-haired young man from Cherryvale. He had finally accepted the unfavored case after Blanche Newhall traveled to his office twice in one week to persuade him. A need for money and experience, and his belief in Silas' innocence—after a three-hour talk with him—influenced his decision.

It was Tuesday, a very hot day, and the townspeople milled about the square, mopping sweat and talking about the trial. The jury had been picked and court was due to reconvene within an hour. Silas lay on his back watching a fly buzz about the top of his cell, darting in curving patterns from one wall to another. It started down, spun into a looping dive and struck his forehead. He swatted at it. The insect buzzed away, and Silas watched it sail between the iron bars to the outer room. He covered his eyes with his hands and lay waiting.

And while Silas lay there, Newt Winger was squirming in his seat during the science seminar, his mind wandering in a world of death, guilt and fear, with Professor Radeaker's voice puncturing his thoughts: "... the sciences include mathematics and logic, the physical sciences, such as physics and chemistry..., then there are the biological sciences, such as botany and zoology... fourth, there are the social sciences, such as sociology and anthropology. Now, scientific study may be divided into these different categories ... and pure science summarizes and explains the facts and principles discovered about the universe and its inhabitants. Applied science uses these facts and principles to make experiments . . . so both pure and applied science are necessary to bring the benefits of scientific research to—Newton Winger!"

"Yessir."

"Are you observing something of scientific nature out that window?"

"Aaa—yessir—I mean, nosir—"

"Well, in that case it might do you well to make notes, same as the rest of the class!"

"Yessir."

"Let's see now, where were we? Oh yes—we were on the necessity of both applied and pure science—"

Just about that time, Silas Newhall's cell door opened and Kirky entered with Harley Davis and a tray of food. Silas sat up.

"Here's your lawyer, and some victuals," Kirky drawled. "Looks to me you need 'em both purty bad."

Silas reached for the tray without answering, and nodded for Harley to sit beside him on the cot. The two didn't speak until Kirky left.

Harley placed his hand on Silas' knee. His tone was low and friendly. "Silas," he began, "I'm going to ask you a few questions—some I have asked you several times before. Answer them truthfully. I want to know exactly what I'm fighting out there this morning—the truth or a lie."

"Go ahead," Silas said, still chewing.

"Did you kill Jake Kiner?"

Silas lowered his eyes and stopped chewing. "It's like I told you before—I just don't know."

"Do you honestly feel that you didn't?"

"Yep. I feel that all right. I shore feel that."

"Why?" The question was fast and sharp.

"Well—"

"Why?"

"Well, I just wouldn't ever kill anybody, 'specially over a day's pay. I just wouldn't—that's all."

"But you went after him with the hoe."

"That was only to pr'tect myself 'gainst his whip."

"Would you swear you saw someone else there, besides Jake?"

"No—I don't s'pose I could swear to it."

"But you honestly think you did see someone else?"

"Yep."

178

"Do you remember what this someone looked like?"

"Nope. It just seemed like a dark form."

"You're sure now, Silas—you're sure?"

"Shore as I can be, since I was half out and drunk."

Harley rose to his feet and began walking slowly back and forth. "Eat, Silas. We don't have too much time." He continued pacing. "You know one thing, Silas?"

Silas looked up. "Yeh, Mister Davis?"

"Call me Harley—I believe you, Silas. I believe you're innocent. Now you've got to start believing in yourself. Do you understand?"

"Yep."

"You've got to believe that you didn't do this thing, and I've got to prove that you didn't do it. Do you understand?"

Before Silas could answer, a shattering sound came at the window and glass showered over the cell floor. Someone had thrown a rock through the bars from the street. Silas started to get up, but Harley motioned him back on the cot and inched toward the window.

"What bastard did that?" Silas asked nervously.

Harley was peering into the street from behind the wall now. "It's some young—" He ducked, and another rock banged against the bars and dropped back to the ground. "It's some young dudes whooping it up down in—"

"We gonna git you! You killin' bastard! We gonna git your ass! You ain't gonna git off with life, you bum!" someone shouted from below.

Harley grabbed Silas' spoon and banged it against the bars of the door for five minutes before Kirky finally came. "You still got another twenty minutes 'fore trial time," Kirky protested as Harley bounded past him toward the outer door. "Where you goin' in such a hurry?"

"To the Judge's chambers," Harley snapped back, "that's where I'm going."

Twenty minutes later, Jeff Cavanaugh was standing high on the flat base of Thomas Jefferson's statue in the center of the town square, and a crowd had closed in to hear what he had to say. Kirky and the two lawyers were directly beneath him and Mary Kiner stood just in front of them. Jeff remained erect and unruffled, looking very much like the man with whose image he now shared the marble platform. After a considerable wait, he raised his long arms above the crowd for silence.

A stillness came over the crowd as Jeff began:

"Fellow townsmen, I am going to speak to you—not as a

179

judge or as a member of the legal body of our State—but as a friend. A few minutes ago some irresponsible persons threw stones through a prisoner's window from the street. You all know who the prisoner is, and why he is in there. In case you don't, let me inform you. He is Silas Newhall, a citizen of our town, who is about to go on trial for his life. A reliable jury of twelve people has been picked from amongst you." (Jeff wiped the sweat from his face.) "If he is found guilty, I will, in the name of our State, pronounce sentence to fit his crime. Not a soul here would be denied the same chance we are about to give Silas Newhall. The widow of Jacob Kiner, for whose death the charges in question were brought, stands here below me. She is a woman who is as anxious as anyone —even more so, I should say—to see that justice is done. But she asks that there be no violence of any sort and that you leave it in the hands of your courts to decide the fate of the man there in that cell. This woman has suffered more than any one of us here. Let none of us do her or our country the disservice of denying her that simple request. We here must yield to the right that is within us. There is none here who hasn't erred. And all of us, at one time or another, have been wrongly accused when we were innocent. Such injustice leaves a terrible scar. If we were not to give Silas Newhall an unbiased trial, our crime would be far greater than the one we are about to explore—one which I promise to preside over in all conscience, in all fairness and without favor or fear of anyone. I have the power to bring in U. S. troops, if necessary, to carry out Mary Kiner's request, but my faith in you is as solid as this base on which I stand. Please, I beg you, do not destroy that faith." He stood for a minute looking into the faces of the crowd that stretched out to the street, then he said, "That is all," and got down.

A few minutes later, Kirky returned to Silas' cell with Harley. He unlocked the door and said, "Silas."

"Yeh."

"Time to go." He opened the door, motioned Silas out and shackled his wrist. Then the three of them started down the corridor toward the courtroom.

"Well," Harley smiled, "here we go. Are you okay?"

"Reckon so, Harley. Reckon so."

"Don't get excited now."

"Too late for that now, Harley. Too late for that."

"There's going to be a lot of people in there. Keep your head up and face them. Don't start off looking guilty."

bring home to you, more than any statement of mine, the vileness of this offense against heaven and humanity."

Silas' head lifted and he saw the crowbar on the table for the first time. He stirred nervously and Harley's hand pressed against his leg.

During his pause, McCormack's eyes swept the courtroom in hypnotic glare, falling at last on Silas. "—And there, ladies and gentlemen, sits the beast who—"

Harley was on his feet. "I object, Your Honor, to such reference to this defendant."

"Objection sustained. Watch your language, counsel."

"I'm sorry, Your Honor. We intend to prove that he (his left hand pointed at Silas) did with premeditation and willfulness, murder the deceased with (his right hand reached for the crowbar and he waved it through the air) this instrument—in cold blood!" Silas winced and shut his eyes against the outburst. "We will prove that he even boasted publicly of his intentions before actually committing the crime! We will prove that he attempted to steal from the premises of the deceased, after being befriended and hired by this very same man he so heartlessly bludgeoned with this iron (he smacked the crowbar against the table) instrument of death." He paused again and looked about the hushed room.

"But I didn't steal nothin' from—"

"Quiet, Silas—take it easy. We'll have our turn."

McCormack wiped the sweat from the creases in his neck and continued. "I am here, as your servant, to emphasize the meaning of this indictment against one whose guilt is as clear as the charge. It would indeed be difficult for the State to produce a more damaging piece of evidence than this iron crowbar, used for intended burglary and eventually murder, found, mind you, in the defendant's hand—only a few feet from the man who had been beaten to death with it. Jake Kiner's blood is still on it and so are the fingerprints of the accused. This too we will prove in due time. In fact, during his arraignment, the defendant readily admitted boasting to half of Cherokee Flats that he was going to 'git'—yes, that's the very word he used, 'git'—Jake Kiner. Unfortunately, he made good his boast, and it is up to the State to see that he pays the ultimate penalty."

McCormack clasped his hands together beneath his chest. His head dropped forward and his voice was very low and wavering. "I would have liked to spare this woman and you, ladies and gentlemen of the jury, the gory details of this vile crime, but duty prevails upon me, in the interest of our society, to lay the facts, cruel though they are, before you. And it is better that I did. For when at last the penalty is extracted, we can all say and know that justice was indeed triumphal."

Silas watched as McCormack's face swept the jury. The back of his white linen suit was soaked with sweat. "It is my intention, as Prosecuting Attorney for this State, to prove, beyond a reasonable doubt, the charges we have brought—we are going to show that when the body of Jake Kiner was found there was evidence of considerable bleeding and severe wounds; that the man was a victim of burglary and robbery; also that this death was not only committed in a brutal manner—repeated beating over the head, showing deliberate intent to kill—but also that it was committed with unwarranted vengefulness.

"Ladies and gentlemen, you will hear about Silas Newhall. You will hear reliable people testify to statements he made, and we ask you to pay particular attention to these witnesses, to all of the evidence, and we know you will withhold your judgment until the entire case is concluded and then render a verdict according to your conscience and good common sense, and according to the evidence in this case. I thank you."

A rumbling of the crowd began. Silas stole a side glance at Waldo, who sat next to Blanche. Waldo was biting his fingernails. The Judge's banging gavel snapped Silas' head around. "The attorney for the defense may now address the jury if he so wishes," Cavanaugh said.

Harley rose.

"Your Honor, Mr. Foreman, ladies and gentlemen of the jury. On behalf of the defendant, Silas Newhall, I want to let you know we are cognizant of the sacrifices that you are making to be here, and the deprivations of your own families, but it is our jury system that is the bulwark of our judicial order in this country, and without it our system of equality and justice would suffer; so I am sure that this morning each of you is aware of your responsibility in this case. As the Honorable Justice has informed you, both Mr. McCormack and myself will attempt to prove certain things to you. We will make statements contradictory to one another's, I am sure, but in the end it must be you who will decide the truth.

"We, the defense, do not come here this morning seeking pity or sympathy. We simply ask that you give us your open minds, and our evidence your considerate appraisal. We will show that on the day in question, this defendant, unarmed,

184

at some hour in the afternoon of June fourteenth, went to the farm of the deceased with no intent to burglarize or kill, but solely for the purpose of business—namely, to collect monies that were owed him by the deceased.

"We will show further that when the defendant did not leave as quickly as the deceased thought he should have, the deceased attempted to forcibly evict him, that it was at this point that he, the deceased, attacked the defendant and repeatedly beat him about his face and head; that it was therefore after this defendant was attacked, while he was in fear of his own safety and when he had no other alternative, that the defendant picked up a hoe, not the instrument exhibited, and attempted to defend himself; but that before he had a chance to use it he was knocked down by the deceased, then beaten to unconsciousness while he was on the floor, not regaining consciousness until he was in the Fort Miles County Hospital, where he found himself handcuffed to a bed.

"We indicated in our questioning of you that our defense is and will be based on a plea of not guilty of any of the charges made in the indictment. We intend to show you that the wounds and abrasions on this defendant were inflicted by the deceased in a fit of violent temper. We intend to show you that the deceased, not the defendant, was the aggressor.

"We intend to show you that the wounds inflicted on the deceased, causing his death, were not inflicted by the defendant's but by another's hand.

"I say in conclusion that the defense feels confident, from the questions propounded to you and the forthright answers you made to questions, that you intend to be fair in this case, and that is all that we ask. We do beg you to listen to the evidence carefully and judge this defendant's guilt or innocence solely upon the events as presented in this case—and with that, we leave the fate of this defendant in your hands. Thank you."

Harley returned to his seat.

Cavanaugh spoke now. "Due to the late start, the court will be adjourned until one o'clock. Can we begin hearing testimony from the State witnesses at that time, counsel?"

"Yes, Your Honor. We will be ready," McCormack answered forthrightly, as he popped to his feet.

Back in his cell, Silas tried eating a piece of ham and some string beans which had been brought to him. But the ham was too tough and the beans too raw, so he pushed them aside and gulped a couple of swallows of steaming black coffee. Then he sat there, staring at the wall, seemingly defeated. He had already confided his fears to Harley after what he considered a "damagin'" speech by Stewart Mc-Cormack.

The hour passed swiftly, and he was taken back into the courtroom. During the first few minutes there was a conference, in secretive tones, among the lawyers and the Judge. When Harley was back beside him, Silas asked, "How's it goin'?"

"Okay—okay," Harley answered.

"The State will now call its witnesses!"

McCormack was up, a look of confidence on his face. "Yes, Your Honor. Will Officer Jason Kirky please take the stand?"

"Yessuh," Kirky drawled. He got up gingerly and strode toward the witness stand. As he stepped up, he stumbled— and faint laughter flitted through the courtroom. He stood up straight, raised his hand and was sworn in.

"Officer Kirky, you visited the scene of the crime immediately after it was committed, didn't you?"

"Yessuh, I did."

"What did you find when you arrived?"

"Jake and Silas was both out on the floor."

"Would you please elaborate—or describe more fully the situation as you found it?"

"Well, Jake was layin' in a pool'a blood—"

"Was he dead yet?"

"Aw, yessuh. Dead as a door nail."

"Go ahead, Officer Kirky."

"Well, Silas there was sprawled out and moanin' somethin' crazy-like. I shook him but he didn't make no sense a'tall— jest kept moanin'.'"

"Did he have anything in his hand or close to his person resembling the weapon we have there on the table before the court?"

"I object, Your Honor!" Harley said. "Mr. McCormack is leading the witness."

"Sustained. Counsel, please rephrase your question."

"Sorry, Your Honor." McCormack paused. "What did you see other than the deceased and the defendant on the floor?"

"That crowbar that's layin' there. It was layin' under Silas' hand when I got there."

"Did you find anything else irregular?"

"Irreg'lar?"

"On the prem—in the barn. Near the dead man."

"Oh—oh, yessuh. The door to the little room where ole Jake kept his peach brandy and stuff was yanked off the hinges."

"In other words, it appeared as though the defendant used the crowbar to rip the door off its hinges and—"

"I object, Your Honor. The prosecuting attorney is putting words in the witness's mouth. The witness is being questioned for facts and not what appears to be fact," Harley protested.

"But, Your Honor," McCormack intoned, "I'm trying to establish a likely situation developing out of an additional motive here—"

"Objection sustained. Defense counsel is correct. Personal conjecture is not expected of the witness here."

"Very well, Your Honor, I am indeed sorry. I will phrase my question differently." McCormack patted his wet brow with a handkerchief, then continued, "Officer Kirky, was the crowbar used for breaking into the room the same as the one used as a murder weapon?"

"Well, the grooves in the wood that was smashed, they fit the same size crowbar. I found out that much."

"That's all for now, Officer Kirky. Thank you."

Judge Cavanaugh pulled off his glasses and looked down. "Would the defense care to cross-examine?"

"I would, Your Honor." Harley got up, approached the stand and said promptly, "Officer Kirky, what was the condition of the defendant when you found him?"

"He was layin' out on the floor like I said, and he was groanin'."

"You say he was groaning. Was he bleeding from any parts of his body or face?"

"Well, not so much when I got there, but you could see where the blood had been runnin' out his nose and down over his lips and chin."

"What condition was his face in?"

"All black and blue-like."

"Would you say he had been beaten rather severely about the head and face?"

"Yessuh, he took quite a wallopin', all right."

"Did the defendant smell of alcohol at the time?"

"Yessuh. He smelled like he'd been dunked in a keg of it."

"You testified that the crowbar was laying under the defendant's hand. Which hand was it?"

"Let me see—uh—the left hand. That's right, the left hand."

"Did you later inspect it for fingerprints?"

"Not me. We had a expert do that—Mr. Wiggins from Fort Miles, there in the second row."

"Did you find the article which the defendant had been beaten with?"

"Yessuh."

"Where?"

"By Jake's body."

"What was it?"

"A whip."

"Are you saying that a whip could inflict the kind of bruises that were on the defendant's head and face?"

"It was the heavy handle part, so Doc Cravens said."

"Were there indications of a violent struggle—that is, apart from the condition of the deceased and the defendant?"

"Not so much. There was a hoe on the floor and a few scuffle marks showin' on the boards."

"Thank you, Officer Kirky. That will be all for now."

McCormack's next witness was Clarence Wiggins, the fingerprint and blood expert. His testimony was brief, establishing the fact that Silas' fingerprints were on the weapon and that the blood on the crowbar was that of Jake. Then Harley faced him. "Mr. Wiggins, you say you inspected the crowbar in question and found the fingerprints of the defendant on it."

"Yes, sir, I did."

"Which hand?"

"The prints of the left hand were the only ones found on the instrument."

"Only the left hand?"

"Yes, sir."

"Did you find other fingerprints on the same crowbar?"

"Yes, there were some weaker impressions that I believe to have been those of the deceased. I also found a stronger impression of two other hands."

"Two others?"

"Yes, sir."

"Did you find out who they—these other two hands—belonged to?"

"No, sir, I haven't."

"Have you tried?"

"Yes, sir."

"Would you say the two foreign sets of fingerprints belonged to the same person?"

"Yes, I would say they did."

A murmur came from the crowd, and Harley said, "Thank you, Mr. Wiggins, that will be all."

During the remainder of the afternoon McCormack brought several witnesses to the stand. Silas knew all of them but two—a shaggy-haired, unshaven man named Dilly Case, who claimed he had heard Silas threatening to "git" Jake for not paying him the money he had coming; and a Mrs. Betty Link, a blond woman, who said she had only moved to Cherokee Flats three days before the murder, but that she had seen Silas drunk the night preceding the slaying and had also heard him make threats against Jake's life.

"Now, Mrs. Link. It is Mrs., isn't it?" Harley cross-examined.

"Yes 'tis. My husband ain't livin' here—but I'm still married to him."

"Fine. Now, Mrs. Link, you said you heard the defendant making threats against the life of the deceased."

"Shore did."

"Just exactly what did he say, word for word?"

Betty Link sat up straight as though she was starched from the middle upward. Pursing her highly rouged lips, she pulled her tight skirt down over her knees before answering. "He said somethin' like—"

"Not something like, Mrs. Link. We want to know exactly what he said. Try hard now. Stop and think."

She was silent for a second or two, then she said, "First off, he was drunk and his words was kind of slurry—"

"Slurry?"

"Yeah, sorta runnin' into each other, but I heard him say, 'I'm gonna git my money from that old skinflint or die tryin'.' Yeah, that's exactly what he said—and somethin' about 'over my dead body.' "

"Mrs. Link, can you remember ever having said such a thing as 'I'll die trying' or 'over my dead body' when you were very determined to accomplish or prevent something you felt strongly about?"

McCormack was up. "Your Honor, I object. The inference is irrelevant and of no consequence in this case."

"Your Honor, I intend to establish that common use is made of such a statement by many of us in normal everyday conversations."

"I see no harm in this question, Mr. McCormack."

Harley turned back to the witness. "Do you remember ever having made such remarks as these, Mrs. Link?"

" 'Course. When Charley—my husband—told me he was

gonna git a divorce from me, the first thing I said was 'over my dead body.' " Laughter filled the courtroom.

Jeff's gavel banged for quiet. "If quiet isn't maintained here, this room will be emptied of all spectators. Proceed, counsel."

"To whom was the defendant speaking when he made these remarks?"

"I don't know who the man was. All I know was that he was colored and that he was drunk too."

"Where did all this take place, Mrs. Link?"

Betty Link's face turned noticeably pink. "Well—well—I'd heard about this late-hour place called Chappie's and thought I'd drop in to see what it was like."

"Chappie Logan's?"

"Yeah. That's what they call the joint—place—or—"

"What time was this, Mrs. Link?"

"Oh, about two-thirty in the mornin' or a little later."

"Did your escort hear the threat also?"

"Escort?"

"Yes. Didn't someone accompany you there?"

"Nope. I was just sorta driftin' round by myself that night."

"One more question. Did you hear the defendant call the name of the deceased at any time?"

"He just kept callin' him an old skinflint."

"Then how do you know he was referring to the deceased?"

"Well, it all came back to me when I heard about the murder and saw his picture on the front page of the paper."

"Whose picture?"

"His. The Newhall man."

"Thank you, Mrs. Link. That will be all."

"Can I git down now, Judge?" she cooed.

"You may, Mrs. Link."

After the evening adjournment, Harley went along with Silas and Kirky to the prisoner's cell. Kirky said, "Your dinner'll be comin' in soon's I git mine. Take it easy. You stayin', Mister Counsel?"

"For just a little while. Come back in about ten or fifteen minutes, Kirky."

Rain was beginning to fall outside, and Silas moved to the broken window and peered out at the square. He could see people ducking in and out of buildings. And as the humid warmth of evening drifted through the window he wiped the sweat from his bony face. "I'll be glad when all this is over." He plopped down on his cot. "How long do we have to listen to that flour-headed old goat paradin' that bunch of lyin' dogs

190

up to that witness chair? Why don't they just go on and give me life like they're gonna do anyhow?"

"That's no way to feel, Silas." Harley's answer was given without much feeling. His mind was groping for something more important.

"I don't much care how I feel right now."

Suddenly Harley reached into his satchel and pulled out some loose papers. "Here, hold these a minute, Silas. I figured out something a while ago."

Silas' hand went out for the papers. "What's these for?"

Harley closed his satchel. "Now hold this for a second."

"What's all this for?" Silas asked, shifting the papers to his other hand and taking the satchel.

"Are you left-handed or right-handed, Silas?"

"Why, I'm right-handed. Why?"

"That's just what I thought. We've got a little something working for us, old boy. Just a little something."

The trial droned on, and on Thursday night of the second week Newt tossed about in his bed, trying to fight off the secret weighing so heavily upon him. At the dinner table he'd heard his father size up Silas Newhall's chances. "He's goin' up for life shore as I'm sittin' here. He's got 'bout as much of a chance as a feather in a wind storm."

"Too bad—too bad all the way round—for Mary, for Blanche and Waldo—and Silas. I'll never understand why he did such an awful thing," Sarah said.

Three o'clock came, and though Newt closed his eyes against the night his thoughts boiled on. "A man's whole life is at stake. But if I tell the truth, a lot more people might git killed, even some of us right here in this house."

He continued rolling and thinking. It was four-thirty by the time he decided to lift the weight from his shoulders, and he went through the darkness to his mother's room.

He touched her gently on the shoulder. "Momma." She stirred slightly and rolled over toward Jack, who snored like a fog horn. The next moment Newt was against telling her, but as he started toward the door a board creaked under his weight and Sarah came awake.

"Who's that?"

"It's me, Newt, Momma."

"What's the matter, boy? Havin' bad dreams?"

"It's lot worse'n that."

Sarah was sitting upright now. "Come here and sit down by me," she whispered. "What's troublin' you, son?"

Newt sank to the bed and started telling his story. "Wait a minute," his mother said. "We'd better go out in the livin' room. We don't want to wake your poppa." She rose and wrapped a blanket about her, and they went in and sat together on the divan.

Newt, his mind unraveling like a ball of yarn, poured out the nightmare hurriedly, as if he couldn't wait to rid himself of it. When he was finished, the two of them just sat there until dawn without saying any more to each other. Toward six o'clock the room gradually filled with a soft light. Sarah was still awake, but Newt was sleeping peacefully now, his head against his mother's shoulder, his mind free for the first time in two months.

When Jack awoke later, Sarah told him Newt's story and the three of them decided that nothing further was to be said until Sarah talked with Judge Cavanaugh.

She told Jeff just before he sat down to breakfast, and then he slumped down to his chair, rubbing the mahogany arms. "This is fantastic, Sarah! Do you think the boy is really telling the truth?"

"I know he is. I know he is," she sighed.

"Does anyone besides you and Jack know about this?"

"No, no one."

"Good—good. Now Sarah, this is a ticklish situation. As a judge trying this case, it would be highly improper for me to divulge this information. You must do it. And the proper person to receive such information is the Prosecuting Attorney. You'd better prepare to come to court today with Newt and Jack. I'll call for a two-hour recess so you'll have sufficient time with Mr. McCormack. I would rather he didn't know you told me. In case he asks if you told me, I would advise you to say that you did. But don't volunteer it. Do you understand?"

Sarah said she did and that she would get Newt and her husband and appear at the trial. "Do you think he—Mr. McCormack—will listen to me, Judge?" she asked.

"You just hand him a sealed note when I call for a recess and tell him you are supposed to wait for an answer. Just write that you have some very important information concerning the case and that you would like to talk with him in his office during lunchtime. He'll listen to you. Don't worry."

"You'd better tell me just what to write, Judge. I may not say just the right things."

Jeff dictated the note. Sarah sealed it in a plain envelope and stuffed it in her apron pocket. "Another thing," Jeff added, "try not to let anyone see you hand him the note. Come through the side door. I'll have the bailiff save seats for you."

After that, Justice Jefferson Cavanaugh had his breakfast and then went off to open the morning session of the trial.

After serving Silas a breakfast of lumpy, lukewarm oatmeal, cold biscuits and black coffee, Kirky said, "You look pale, Silas. Somethin' gittin' your spirits down?"

"Naw, but this slop you feed me is ruinin' my insides."

"Well now, ain't that somethin'! Our celebrity's complainin' 'bout his victuals." Kirky chuckled. "It's a lot worse at the big house, a lot worse. You take my word for it."

Later, when court reconvened, Harley noticed the dark rings under Silas' eyes and he attempted to cheer him up. "Blanche and Waldo told me to tell you that they are pulling for you, Silas."

"I got a feelin' they'll need a twenty-mule team to help pull me out'a this."

"We're all doing the best we can. Keep up your faith."

"I'd be glad to if I had any left, Harley. I know you're tryin', but there just ain't much to go on."

"It'll work out. Don't worry."

All that morning the witnesses kept coming. And in spite of Harley's frequent objections, a picture of Silas emerged, portraying what the town had known him to be over the years, when he wobbled up and down the streets and alleyways of Cherokee Flats, swearing to himself in his drunkenness. An official of the welfare agency told of his children being shunted from one house to another after their mother's death. And the black picture grew blacker.

Sarah, Jack and Newt Winger arrived in the middle of the morning session, and the three of them squeezed into a spot the bailiff had reserved upon instruction of the Judge.

Jack Winger leaned close to Newt, whispering, "You all set?"

"Yessir." Newt was looking away as he answered, his face gone ashen, his heart constricted at the sight of Booker and Marcus Savage sitting unperturbed in the middle of the room.

"What's the matter, boy?" Jack noticed Newt's tenseness.

"Booker and Marcus are here."

"You shore?"

"Yessir, right in the center there."

"Well, I declare," Jack muttered to himself.

When the noon recess was called, Sarah felt the Judge's eyes upon her and her hand automatically squeezed the envelope in her pocket.

Quickly Sarah was at the lawyer's side, the note held close and low to her side. "Mister McCormack."

"Yes—yes. What can I do for you?"

"Here is a note for you."

McCormack took the envelope and slipped it in his pocket. "Well, thank you, lady. Thank you." He started to move away.

"I'm supposed to wait for a answer."

"An answer? For whom?" The courtroom was emptying now. Only a few stragglers, lagging behind in gossip, approached the exit. Newt and his father stood by the wall on the far side of the courtroom.

"You'd better read it now, sir," Sarah said. "It's awful important."

McCormack looked at her, then glanced at Jack and Newt waiting on the side. "Those two waiting for you?"

"It's my husband and son."

He tore open the envelope and read the note. "What's this all about, lady?"

"About this case—and it's awful important."

McCormack pulled out his watch and checked the time. His impatience was mounting. "Well, hurry—come on in this side room over here."

"I'll need my son and husband, too."

"Okay, but let's hurry. It's lunchtime."

McCormack listened impatiently for a half hour, then he grumbled, "Why didn't you volunteer this information earlier, boy?"

"He was scared of race trouble," Jack cut in.

"That's no excuse—no excuse whatsoever. I hope, for your sake, you haven't told anyone about this except your parents."

"Nosir, I didn't."

"Good—good, because, whether you know it or not, you could be seriously implicated yourself. You might even wind up behind bars too."

"What you think I should do?"

"Only one thing. Since you've waited this late—keep your mouth shut and let me handle it from here."

"But—"

"No buts, boy. You're lucky you came to me instead of someone else. Now don't, under any circumstances, reveal this to anyone else . . . Understand?"

"Yessir—I understand."

"Fine. Now I must be off to lunch." Then McCormack was through the door and gone. Sarah, Jack and Newt moved slowly into the corridor. Silently and nervously they ate some sandwiches Sarah had prepared.

Meanwhile, Booker and Marcus devoured two bowls of chili in the backroom at Chappie Logan's. Later, heading back toward the courthouse, Booker told Marcus the trial would probably be over in less than a week.

"Yeh," Marcus agreed. "Looks like old Silas's gonna git it."

"Yeh, shore does."

Ten minutes later they mixed into the crowd that was flowing back into the courtroom.

Stewart McCormack called Sam Stockton to the witness chair, and he told of seeing Silas, in a drunken condition, going in the direction of the Kiner farm that fatal afternoon. Two other witnesses testified to about the same and Harley declined to cross-examine them.

The rain had stopped. The late sun was splashing against the drab courtroom walls, and Newt sat nervously awaiting the moment when he would be called to give the testimony that would perhaps free Silas and maybe at the same time set off a racial explosion worse than he dared imagine. Then, unexpectedly, McCormack turned in the direction of Mary Kiner.

"My dear Mrs. Kiner, if it isn't too much for you, the State would like for you to take the witness chair." There was a stir in the room as Jake's widow rose slowly and made her way to the chair.

"Now, Mrs. Kiner, we won't hold you long or ask you many questions. God in heaven knows you have suffered enough. But it is my duty as the State's Attorney, to leave no stones unturned in our relentless search for the truth. Now, Mrs. Kiner, will you please tell the court why your husband hired the defendant, knowing too well that he was an habitual drunk and of unsavory character?"

"I object!"

"Objection sustained."

"Sorry, Your Honor. I will rephrase the question. Now Mrs. Kiner, why did your husband hire Silas Newhall?"

"Well—Jake was like that. He believed in givin' everybody a chance. Silas asked him for such a chance because everybody else turned him down, and Jake gave it to him."

"How long did he work for your husband before he—uh—this unfortunate thing happened?"

"Oh, 'bout two months, I guess. I don't recall the exact day he hired him."

"Did he do his job well?"

"Well, yes he did till up near the end when he started drinkin' again."

"You and Mr. Kiner were very happy together, weren't you?"

"Oh my, yes. We had our little fusses now and then, but I loved—" Tears welled in her eyes.

"Do you wish to stop for a while, Mrs. Kiner?"

She reached beneath the veil and dabbed at her eyes. "No —no—I'm sorry—I can go on now."

"Do you feel, or know rather, whether or not your husband owed the defendant any more money—that is, after he had fired him?"

"I just don't know 'bout that part of it. But I cain't imagine Jake not payin' anybody he owed. He just wasn't like that. And everybody round these parts knows that."

"Where were you when this awful thing happened?"

"I'd come into town for shoppin' in the mornin' with Jake, then later in the day I went to have his glasses fixed. He had busted the ear-piece on one side of them. Silas was at the gate when we got back and he started arguing with Jake—and I went on in the house to fix some lunch. Then I went to the barn to call Jake to eat."

"Now, Mrs. Kiner, we are just about through with the questions. I sincerely hope this will be the last of this, but it is very important to tell the court what you saw when you went to the barn to call your husband in for lunch. Just take it easy and tell us as simply as possible."

She paused for a moment, wiped at her nose, braced herself by placing her elbows on the arms of the chair and brought her hands together in a firm grip. "Well, I came across the field—the barn door was hangin' open—and I first caught sight of Silas, on the floor. I first thought maybe he was just drunk—but then I saw Jake's hand—I was afraid to look in—but I did and—"

"Go on, Mrs. Kiner."

"—and there he was—all bloody and everything—"

"Yes?"

"I could tell from the looks of him—that he was dead—"

"What did you do then?"

"I—I—I—"

"Easy, Mrs. Kiner. Easy now."

"I just run back across the field to the house and called

the operator—and told her—my husband—oh oh oh—" She had lost complete control now, and McCormack whipped out his silk handkerchief and put it in her trembling hands.

"That will be all now, Mrs. Kiner—unless the defense wishes to cross-examine." Harley motioned negatively. Then McCormack walked slowly back to the front of the courtroom. He stepped squarely in front of the jury and stood looking at them for a few seconds, as if trying to gauge their compassion, their sorrow, their hatred for this man upon whom they would soon be called to pass judgment. Then he turned toward the bench and said, "Your Honor, the State closes its case."

Jeff Cavanaugh's eyebrows raised and he stared at McCormack as though in disbelief.

There was silence. Since it was late, both counsel awaited the familiar words of adjournment as Jeff continued staring at McCormack. Finally, he asked, "Will the defense present witnesses tomorrow?"

"Yes, Your Honor."

"Then court is adjourned until eleven o'clock tomorrow morning." Jeff then closed his notebooks and stood up.

On the way out Sarah whispered to Jack that she was surprised that Mr. McCormack hadn't called Newt to the stand. "Oh, he's prob'ly got somethin' up his sleeve. He'll prob'ly call him tomorra sometime."

"But you don't understand, Jack. He said that the State rested its case. That means he's through prosecutin'."

"Aw, you must be wrong, Sarah," Jack said. "These legal doin's ain't easy to understand. The Judge'll explain it all to you tonight."

Newt didn't venture an opinion. He was relieved at not having been called to the witness stand. He and his father walked Sarah to within a block of the Cavanaugh house. Then they turned back toward home.

Sarah had just come through the door and was putting on her apron when the Judge called from his study, "Sarah! Sarah! That you?"

"Be there in a minute, Judge!" She scurried along the hall, sensing urgency in his voice.

He met her halfway. "Didn't you tell Mr. McCormack what you were supposed to tell him?"

"Yessir, I did."

"Everything?"

"Yessir, we talked to him for—"

Rodney came through the front door loaded down with

school books. "Hello, Dad—Sarah. Why wasn't Newt at the seminar today?"

"Hello, Rodney."

"H'lo, Rodney. He had to stay home today," Sarah said.

Rodney continued on to his room. Sarah and Jeff moved into the study. "As I was sayin', we talked to him for over a half hour."

"What did he say after you told him?"

"Well, he just thanked us and told us not to say anything to anybody else about it."

"Well, so help me—this thing's really got me puzzled."

"His closin' the case without callin' Newt to the stand?"

"Exactly. Exactly. Well, you are going to tell somebody else. You're going over to Mr. Davis, the defense lawyer, and take Newt with you. And you're to tell him the same thing you told Mr. McCormack." Jeff was red with fury. "By the way, does Mr. McCormack realize that I know about this information?"

"No, your name wasn't called at all, Judge."

"Fine. Now you be on your way. Go pick up Newt. Rodney and I will make out for supper."

"Where's he stayin', Judge?"

"Oh—over at Jennie Brighten's place. You'd better call and make an appointment with him before going there. His number's in my book there." He picked it up and thumbed through some pages. "Let's see—here it is—4437. Better call him right away."

Sarah telephoned Harley and he asked her to come to his place at eight. Later, the attorney sat facing her, Newt and Jack, finding it difficult to believe what he was hearing. During the full twenty minutes of Newt's story, he took notes and asked Newt to repeat now and then. When Newt had finished, he took him over the same ground, step by step, trying to find some discrepancy or weakness in the fabric of his astounding story. But the words were too solidly stated, the events too logically placed. Harley was convinced he was telling the truth.

"Why didn't you come forth with this information before now, Newt?" Harley asked softly.

"I was afraid—afraid that there might be a lot of trouble between the colored and white people if they found out Mister Savage did it."

"I understand," Harley said. "I think I know how you felt." He looked at the boy long and hard. "Newt, how do you feel now about the possibility of such trouble?"

"I don't know—I just don't know—"

"Are you afraid?"

"A little." Newt looked Harley square in the eye. "Are you, Mr. Davis?"

"One truth deserves another, Newt. I'm a little afraid too, but not so afraid that I won't do what I know to be right."

"Well—you're white. You ain't got much to worry about—"

"Newt," Sarah interrupted, "I—I don't—I don't think Mr. Davis feels no different than we do 'bout this." Her eyes were upon Harley. He knew they expected a truthful answer.

"Thanks, Mrs. Winger. Naturally, I'm interested in seeing justice done in this case, and—as much as it is possible for a white man—I understand Newt's concern for what his testimony could do to racial relations in this town. Feelings have run rather high around here. I was with Silas the other day when those rocks came smashing through his window." He paused. "And it wasn't a very comfortable situation for a while—but I think Judge Cavanaugh's plea for calm was well taken by the townspeople."

Jack Winger spoke now. "I hope so, but if they can give a threat to a white man like that, what won't they do when they find out it's a colored man?"

"We have to have faith in the people," Sarah cut in, "that's all that's left to do."

"That's my feeling too, Mr. and Mrs. Winger. However, Newt here is the one the burden is on. Will you be willing to repeat what you have told me in court tomorrow morning?"

Newt looked toward his mother and she answered for him, "He'll be there tomorrow mornin', and so will my husband and me."

"Fine. Fine. Fine." Harley was on his feet. "This is going to make all the difference—all the difference." He walked up and down the room, banging his fist in the palm of his hand. Sarah, Jack and Newt rose and prepared to leave.

"Mrs. Winger."

"Yes, Mr. Davis?"

"Pardon me for asking again, but you did say you spoke to Mr. McCormack about this?"

"Yes, I did," Sarah assured him.

"Incredible—incredible," Harley repeated. "One other thing —who told you to come to me?"

"Do we have to say that, Mr. Davis?" Jack asked.

"Not if you don't want. Believe me, that's unimportant, so unimportant."

199

"Well, we'd rather not, if you don't mind," Sarah added.

Long after the Wingers' departure, Harley was busy taking notes and checking Newt's statements. It was well past midnight when he finally went to bed.

The moment Newt made his appearance in the courtroom the next morning, Harley beamed. Silas sat gloomily beside him, unaware of the turn of events.

Harley nudged the defendant, but Silas barely reacted. "Yeh?"

"Perk up, Silas, things look good—very good."

"Yeh?" Silas moaned.

"Lot of colored people here today again, Silas."

"Yeh."

"You know most of them?"

"Yeh."

"Do you know Booker Savage?"

"Yeh, that's him sittin' over there in the middle. He ain't hardly missed a day."

"You mean the big husky fellow with the red shirt?"

"Yeh, and that's his boy alongside him. Why you askin'?"

"Oh, I just heard some talk about them last night."

"Stay 'way from 'em if you don't want'a git hurt. They're bad actors," Silas warned.

Court convened at eleven sharp. And, after what seemed like an eternity to Newt, Jeff called out, "The counsel for the defense may now present evidence and witnesses."

Getting up, Harley whispered, "I may have to call you to the stand today, Silas. In case I do, give the same answers in the same way—exactly as you have in the past—and don't be nervous." Then, he walked up front.

Harley pulled out his watch and noted the time. There was less than an hour before noon recess. The trap would have to be sprung before then.

"Would Officer Jason Kirky take the stand," Harley said. Kirky strode forward and plopped down in the chair.

"Officer Kirky, would you tell us, in which hand did you find the crowbar?"

McCormack jumped to his feet. "I object, Your Honor. Officer Kirky did not say that the crowbar was found in the defendant's hand. He stated that the crowbar was found beneath one of his hands."

"Correction, Officer Kirky. Under which hand did you find the crowbar?"

"The left hand."

"Officer Kirky, did you know the defendant was right-handed?"

"Nosuh, I didn't."

"Now you heard Mr. Wiggins testify that only one set of the defendant's fingerprints were found on the crowbar—the left ones."

"Yessuh, I did, suh."

"Now, in the light of this disclosure, and taking into consideration the slight build of the defendant, do you think it was possible for this defendant to bludgeon the deceased, to the extent that you testified he was bludgeoned, with his left hand and still show only one set of weak fingerprints?"

McCormack was up again.

"Your Honor, I object strenuously to Mr. Davis' question! The witness has not professed to know the limits of the defendant's physical prowess."

"Objection sustained."

"One more question, Officer Kirky," Harley said. "Did you find any of Mr. Kiner's bottles of brandy in the defendant's possession?" Marcus shivered a little at this question.

"No."

"That's all," Harley said.

A low buzzing filled the courtroom. Harley, a look of confidence on his face, noticed that McCormack was mopping sweat from his brow. And Silas, seemingly encouraged by this last bit of testimony, took a more dignified posture. A slight smile even came to his lips. Blanche and Waldo whispered to each other, and the Wingers exchanged confidential glances.

Now Harley was ready. "Your Honor," he said. "I would like to request a short consultation with the bench."

"Request granted. Will both attorneys please come forward?"

The buzzing grew louder as McCormack rose with a quizzical expression on his face and joined Harley in front of the bench. The consultation was very brief, and when it was over McCormack looked unhappy as he went back to his seat.

The Judge then called Kirky and the bailiff to the bench and whispered something to them. The two men nodded and went in opposite directions, the bailiff to the side door on the right, Kirky to the one in the rear. They locked these doors —and the buzzing now turned to excited talk, which rose higher until Jeff's gavel banged for silence.

Jeff spoke first. "Ladies and gentlemen of the jury, the

court has found it necessary to undertake a rather unusual procedure at this time. Due to the nature of the next witness's testimony, no one will be allowed to leave the room unless he is accompanied by a court officer. I hope this is thoroughly understood so that there will be no trouble. The court sincerely hopes that no one is inconvenienced by the action—which it deems highly necessary. You may call your witness now, Mr. Davis."

"Thank you, Your Honor," Harley said. "Will Newton Winger please take the stand?"

For Newt the moment of truth had arrived, and with a belly of nerves he drifted across the front of the courtroom and mounted the platform, feeling the crowd leaning toward him, sensing their stares—especially those of Silas, Booker, Marcus, Stewart McCormack and Mary Kiner. A wave of murmuring rose, then died, and everything was quiet.

Newt found himself repeating after the bailiff, "—to tell the truth and nothing but the truth, so help me God." He asked strength of something, be it God or whatever, to carry him, his family and the rest of the colored people safely through the trouble he now imagined his testimony would bring.

Stewart McCormack twisted in his seat again, mopping his brow, as Harley began his questioning. "Would you give the court your full name?"

"Newt—Newton Buchanan Winger."

"How old are you, Newton?"

"Fifteen in November."

"Did you know Jacob Kiner, the deceased?"

"Yessir, I did."

"How long?"

"All my life, I guess."

"Did you ever work for him?"

"Yessir."

"What kind of work did you do for him?"

"Hoein', weedin', pickin' fruit and stuff like that."

"When did you last work for him?"

"On June fourteenth."

"Of this year?"

"Yessir."

"Then you worked there the day Mr. Kiner was killed?"

"Yessir."

"How long did you work that day?"

"Well, I was supposed to work from eight to five, but I didn't."

"Why didn't you work out your full time?"

"I got tired and sleepy."

"What did you do then?"

"I sat under a tree to rest, but it was too hot so I went inside the barn and went to sleep."

"Where in the barn did you sleep?"

"In the hayloft."

Booker Savage flinched.

"What time was this, Newton?"

"About twelve noon."

"How long did you sleep?"

"About two hours."

"Did you wake naturally, or did someone wake you?"

"Nosir. I woke up when I heard some noise downstairs."

"Noise? What kind of noise?"

"Somebody was rippin' off the door to where Mr. Kiner kept his peach brandy and cider and stuff."

Booker stiffened and nudged Marcus, who screwed his right fist in the palm of his left hand, squinting his eyes in burning contempt toward Newt.

"What was this person using to break into the room?"

"A crowbar."

"Like the one here on this table?"

"Yessir. Just like that."

"Did you say anything to this person?"

"Nosir."

"Why not?"

" 'Cause I was scared. I didn't know what he might do to me."

Silas was now leaning forward in his seat, his mouth agape, following every word.

"What happened then?" Harley asked.

"Mr. Kiner and Mr. Newhall came through the door, fussin' at each other."

"What were they fussing about?"

"Well, Mr. Newhall was claimin' Mr. Kiner owed him some money and Mr. Kiner claimed he didn't, and he told Mr. Newhall if he didn't get out he would throw him out, or somethin' like that."

"Go on. What happened then?"

"Well, then Mr. Kiner got real mad and hit Mr. Newhall over the head with his whip handle—and Mr. Newhall grabbed a hoe, but Mr. Kiner hit him and he went down before he could get a blow in."

"Mr. Newhall went down?"

"Yessir."

"Did Mr. Newhall appear drunk?"

"Yessir, he was pretty tipsy."

"What was the person who broke into the room doing all this time? Or had he left?"

"Nosir, he hadn't left. He was hidin' in the dark."

"Then?"

"Well, when Mr. Kiner stepped back, after hittin' Mr. Newhall, he saw this other man and started hittin' him with the whip too, but the man raised the crowbar and got him across the head—and he kept hittin' Mr. Kiner on the head after he fell down."

Mary Kiner started crying, and Sarah moved over quickly and put her arms about Mary's shoulders. "Poor Jake, poor Jake," she cried. Silas sat as if in a trance, showing no sign of emotion. Booker looked about nervously, and Marcus whispered, "Take it easy, Paw. Take it easy."

"Go on, Newton. What happened after that?"

"Mr. Newhall started groanin', like he was comin' to—and the man took Mr. Kiner's whip and beat Mr. Newhall over the head with it till he stopped groanin', then he put the crowbar in Mr. Newhall's hand—"

"Which hand?"

"I don't exactly remember. Then he picked up this gunny sack full of bottles and left."

"So this man beat both Mr. Kiner and Mr. Newhall?"

"Yessir, he did."

"What did you do when it was all over?"

"I started to get down and run, but Mrs. Kiner came to the door and looked in—"

"Yes—go on."

"Well, she started screamin' real loud and ran back toward the house."

"What did you do then?"

"I got down from the loft after I was sure she was gone. Then I went home."

"Now, Newt, I want you to tell the court why you didn't come forth with this information before now."

"I—I was scared—that's all."

"Scared of what?"

"Well—I don't know—I guess I was scared of what the people might do—"

"You mean—well, what do you mean by that?"

Newt hesitated. "I—I thought it might bring on some kind of race trouble."

"I see. Now, Newton, I want you to look carefully around this room and tell the court if you see this man—the one who broke into the room and then beat Mr. Kiner and Mr. Newhall."

Newt saw his mother's eyes on him now, demanding the truth. His own eyes shifted, and every head in the room turned and followed his gaze until it rested on Booker Savage.

"That's the man. There in the red shirt. It's him—Mr. Booker Savage."

"He's lyin'! He's lyin'! He's lyin'!" Booker sprang up, shouting above the mumbling crowd. And Newt closed his eyes, trying to shut out the scene from his mind. All things he had seen before him, the faces, walls, floor, ceiling—all floated in a jumble of gray nothing. He was limp with fear. But he was free now, free to meet violence if need be, as he had met the truth—without guilt smothering his conscience.

"Git the nigger killer!" someone shouted in the back.

"Order! Order!" Jeff pounded his gavel until it was quiet. Then he said, "Proceed, counsel."

"That's all, Newton."

McCormack waived cross-examination and Newt was told to step down. He opened his eyes, stepped off the stand and rejoined his mother and father on the other side of the courtroom.

"Your Honor," Harley said quietly, "the defense requests that this man Booker Savage take the stand."

"Officer Kirky, escort Mr. Savage to the stand," the Judge commanded.

Kirky stepped gingerly into the aisle where Booker sat and motioned for him. Booker got up, patted Marcus on the knee and moved his big frame into the aisle. Then he lumbered up toward the front, towering over Kirky by a head.

"Lynch that black bastard!" someone shouted. "Kill him!" the echo came from the opposite side of the room. Booker flinched at the shouts and whirled around. Newt gritted his teeth and shut his eyes again.

"Order! Order!" Jeff shouted, banging his gavel. "I want the persons who said that to——" He didn't have a chance to finish his words, for just in front of him Kirky was sinking to the floor from a swift, powerful left-handed punch that Booker had shot at his chin; and somehow Booker had grabbed the gun from Kirky's right holster.

There were screams, and Booker shouted, "I'll kill anybody who tries touchin' me! I'm gittin' out'a here, Judge—right through your chambas!" He swung his legs over the railing, brandishing the weapon nervously toward the spectators. Kirky rose to one knee, his right hand inching toward his remaining gun. "Flatten out, you bastard!" Booker bellowed. "Keep your hands free and flatten out to the floor!" Kirky plopped down and Booker backed quickly past the bench, motioning Jeff Cavanaugh to one side.

"You won't get away with it, Savage!" Jeff hollered. "Put the gun down—nothing's going to happen to you!"

"Git back! I'll plug you too!" Booker threatened. Then he leaped through the door and slammed it behind him.

The crowd was on its feet. Then Kirky jumped up, whipped out his other gun and a bunch of keys and leaped over the railing. Now a bunch of whites was pressing forward.

"Lynch him!"

"Kill him!"

"String the black bastard up!"

"It's started—it's started," Newt said to himself. "I knew it would happen."

Kirky fished about for a key on the ring. Finding the right one, he twisted it in the lock, then holstered his gun and started waving the angry crowd back. "Hold it! Hold it!" he shouted. "He's trapped—the door to the outside's locked too! Hold it!"

"Naw—let's git the bastard!"

"Quiet! Quiet! Quiet!" Jeff hollered, beating a tattoo with his gavel. "Back to your seats! Order! Order!—"

A shot rang out from inside the Judge's chambers.

Several women screamed. Kirky, gun still drawn, slowly twisted the key in the lock. "Stand back," he cautioned. Then, standing sideways, the gun pointed, he eased the door open and peeped in. After a moment he holstered his gun and pushed the door fully open. He motioned for the Judge, and Cavanaugh stepped down from the bench, went forward and looked into his quarters. Booker Savage lay mortally wounded—a bullet hole in his temple. In a few moments he was dead.

Marcus rushed up, pushed by the Judge and went in. For a while he stood looking down on his father, then he began sobbing. Jeff Cavanaugh shook his head and closed the door. When he was back on the bench he waited until everyone was seated, then he rapped his gavel several times. Quiet was finally restored, and he said, "Stay with him, Officer Kirky." Then he turned to McCormack. "I think it's your move, counsel," he remarked dryly.

Stewart McCormack rose and in an extremely low voice said, "Your Honor, in view of what has taken place—here before us—I think it no more than proper to—to withdraw all charges against the defendant, Silas Newhall—if the court will permit."

"The court will permit," Jeff answered sternly. "And the court wishes to thank the jury for its patience, unselfishness and admirable duty to the people of this state. I now order the defendant released. The case is closed—but let me say this—" He turned to face the spectators and went on. "A man lies dead at the feet of his son in this room behind us, and you who hollered out for his life a few minutes ago have your wish. You are as much—or more—responsible for his death as he himself. In less than five incredible minutes you judged him and screamed for his black life, because you assumed he had killed a white man—forgetting, in your senseless moment, that a black boy had just saved a white man's life— right here before you. It took courage, a lot more than those of you who shouted have, for him to do it. It was what this boy feared of you that kept him from divulging earlier the information that might well have prevented this second tragedy."

Jeff Cavanaugh paused and looked about the room. "We have a judicial system in this country which gives any man the right to a fair trial when accused. You who yelled so barbarously frightened him out of that right. You pulled the trigger. You sent the bullet tearing through his brain. This moment should haunt your minds forever. Go home—and pray to Almighty God that you be forgiven for your sin."

The doors were unlocked and the crowd rose quietly, turned and headed out. Marcus Savage emerged from the Judge's chambers and stood stiffly by the door; then he moved away, walking slowly toward the exit. Newt intercepted him and said, "I'm sorry, Marcus."

"Yeh?" Marcus answered surlily. They stood eying each other in cold silence for a few moments, as Jack and Sarah stood off to the side watching with Waldo, Blanche, Silas and Harley Davis.

"Come on, son," Jack said finally, and Newt turned away.

Marcus walked on with his head down, muttering to himself, "I'm gonna kill that Winger son-of-a-bitch if it's the last thing I do."

When Newt rejoined the group, Jack said, "You did the most you could, boy."

"You certainly did, Newton," Harley agreed, "and all the Newhalls are grateful to you—and so am I."

"You can bet'cha life on that," Silas said, pumping his hand.

"I'm sorry you had to go through so much, Mr. Newhall—but I was in a spot—didn't know what to do. I hope you understand."

"He understands," Harley cut in quickly. Both Blanche and Waldo patted him on the arm reassuringly.

"Jack—Jack—"

"What is it, Sarah?"

"We'd better—we'd better—" She couldn't finish the sentence, and she was slumping toward the floor. Jack caught her in time, lifted her up and laid her on a bench.

"Run git Doc Cravens, Newt—fast as you can! She's fainted."

Sarah had lapsed into a complete coma by the time they finally got her home to bed. Doc Cravens stayed in the bedroom with her for more than an hour. When he came out he took Jack aside. "I hate tellin' you this, Jack," he said, "but I don't think she's goin' to make it this time. You'd better notify the rest of the children."

Jack's voice trembled when he asked, "Any—chance a'tall?"

"As long as she's breathin' there's a chance, Jack. But I don't want to get your hopes up. I have to give you the truth—it's a severe heart attack. She never should've attended that trial."

"With that boy on the stand, you couldn't'a kept her away. You know that, Timothy."

"I know, Jack."

"Well, what do we do now?"

"Just wait—that's about all we can do." Doc Cravens closed his valise and started toward the door. "I'll be at the hospital in case you need me. Otherwise, expect me about nine o'clock. Just keep things very quiet around her."

That evening Prissy sent telegrams to her brother and sisters and cousin Polly.

CHAPTER ✿ 16

THERE WERE some Negroes in Cherokee Flats who criticized what Newt had done, but the majority felt he had done the right thing—and they said so openly. Some outside newspapers called his testimony sensational, courageous—even heroic.

"I was just scared," Newt told a reporter from Kansas City, but his statement was glibly translated by his interviewer as an expression of great modesty. "Surprise Witness, Modest Hero," the sub-headline read in bold print in the following Sunday edition.

Newt, still shaken by the trial and aware of the talk that was making the rounds, stayed close to home for the first few days. Beansy, Jappy, Earl and Skunk hung around the Winger yard, sensing Newt's reluctance to go out. After the third day they tried coaxing him off to the swimming hole, but he refused. "Got to stay around the house," he said. "Momma's awful low."

"Maybe he's scared of meetin' Savage," Skunk suggested to the others, as they headed toward the river.

"He's just all upset," Beansy defended.

"Winger ain't yellow," Jappy said, "you ought'a know that, Skunk."

"Didn't say he was, did I?"

"I wouldn't've wanted to be in his spot," Earl said grumpily. "Bet you wouldn't either."

"And to think he knew it all the time," Beansy remarked, scratching his backsides. "Boy, I'd'a been scared to death."

"He's had a tough time," Jappy said, "Arcella and everything."

"He says he forgot all about her," Beansy cut in.

"He ain't forgot—that's a lotta crap," Skunk said. "He'd take her back if she showed up tomorrow."

"You wouldn't run from her yourself," Earl said.

"She ain't done nothin' to me," Skunk said flippantly.

"'Tain't your fault." Earl's retort was loaded with sarcasm.

By now they were at the river, and they started undressing on the run. "Last one in's a donkey turd!" Skunk hollered. And one by one they plunged into the water.

Bitterness, fed by frustration and loneliness, ate deeper into the soul of Marcus Savage. Two days after his father's death, he had stood by himself as they lowered the body into a pauper's grave on the far side of Candy Hill. Mag Pullens, Deacon Fuller, Chappie Logan and Reverend Broadnap stood in the background watching. Broadnap had offered to say some last words, but Marcus had told the undertaker, "I don't want nobody prayin' over my old man—nobody." And Broadnap, respecting his wishes, did his praying silently as the cheap box disappeared beneath the earth.

"Okay, Chappie, let's git goin'," Marcus said, after taking a final look. He brushed by the others as if they weren't there and made for Chappie's big Dodge.

Chappie turned and waddled behind him. "Don't you think you ought'a say somethin' to those people who was kind a'nough to come?" Chappie asked softly.

"I didn't ask 'em to come, did I?" Marcus snarled.

"But, boy, you—"

"Hell with 'em. If you don't want to ride me home, I'll walk."

"Git in," Chappie said.

As the others made their way to the undertaker's car, Mag Pullens moaned, "What can you do for a boy like that?" No one had an answer.

Chappie and Marcus drove along without speaking. "I'm all by myself now," Marcus was thinking. "Ain't a soul carin' if I live or die." Then he said aloud, "I know one thing—I'm gonna git that Winger bastard."

Chappie gave him a quick glance. "Aw, come on—you're doin' all right now. Don't go foolin' around and git yourself in a lot of trouble."

"He's the cause of my old man bein' in that grave right now."

"Take my advice and stay out'a trouble," Chappie said. "Want to stay at my place tonight?" They had turned off the highway.

"Naw—reckon not."

"You're welcome, you know."

"Want to git home. Got lot'a thinkin' to do for myself."

Chappie was quiet after that. They drove on the last few

blocks and stopped in front of the Savage shack. "Want to-morrow off?" Chappie asked.

"Naw—be in early." Marcus got out of the car, slammed the door and walked off. Chappie sat watching him. Suddenly Marcus stopped and turned around. "Thanks," he said gruffly.

"It's okay, boy." Chappie shifted the gears and the car rattled off.

Marcus took off his coat as he walked down the path between rows of rusting junk. He pushed open the door of the shack, threw his coat to the floor, then stripped off the shirt and tie Chappie had given him for the burial. "The old man died without friends and he got buried without 'em—that's prob'ly the way he wanted it," Marcus mumbled. He threw the shirt and tie on the table and stood in the middle of the room for several minutes—a great loneliness seeping into him. There was nothing—no today, no tomorrow, not even a cursing, drunken father any more. It was as though he were an abandoned piece of charcoal, dropped dead-center of an empty, slow-turning world—one without people, air, light, dark or sound. He wanted to cry but couldn't. Instead he began laughing, and he laughed and laughed until tears rolled down his rough cheeks and his hot neck, and his arms crossed and his fingernails cut into his skin until it bled and he felt the blood and the punctured flesh at his fingertips.

He began, at last, to cry.

On Friday of that same week, Earl drove his father's car up to the Winger yard. Newt was sitting on the front porch, and Earl got out and came over to him. "Gotta drive over to Fulton to pick up a saddle for Paw. Want to go along for the ride?"

"Comin' right back?"

"Yeh—right back. Come on."

Newt climbed in and they took off in the Model-T Ford. They reached their destination by eleven o'clock, picked up the saddle and headed back toward Cherokee Flats before noon.

"Damn!" Earl said suddenly. "I'm 'bout out of gas!" They had been riding quite a while now.

"Ain't no station between here and home!" Newt hollered above the popping motor.

"I know it." Earl looked at the little white needle that indicated his supply. "Guess we can just 'bout make it!" he shouted.

They putted on through the outskirts of Easton, churning up dust from the dry road. And as they bumped along, Newt slumped in his seat, watching the parched corn stalks moving lazily in the gentle wind. They stretched ahead on both sides as far as the eye could reach.

"Summer's goin' fast!" Newt hollered.

"Summer, hell!" Earl bellowed. "More worried 'bout this damn empty tank! We still got more'n three miles to go yet!"

"Aw, we could walk from here."

"You could—not me!" The motor coughed once, and Earl shot a quick glance at the trembling needle. "Don't stop here, baby! Git me home!" Then he quit talking—as though conversation, itself, might drink up the gasoline.

Newt welcomed Earl's quietness, for now he was thinking back four years to Big Mabel and the storm. His mind wandered over the corn and across the prairie to her grave on the slopes of Candy Hill and reshaped the dust of her remains into the firm, rounded figure it once was. The image held for a moment, then faded—she was only dust again. "What a waste," he thought. "Big, good-feeling Mabel is just a pile of dust."

The Flats were growing dull to him now, and within him stirred the possibility of leaving them for good. The thought caused him to open his eyes and look down the road. He could see that they were approaching the Easton railroad tracks. Then, in the distance, he saw the warning arms swinging—and above the sound of the motor he could hear the clanging bell. About a hundred yards from the crossing, Earl slowed down and looked to the curve at his left, then to his right.

"I don't see no damn train! Do you, Newt?"

Newt popped up, his ears straining for the familiar sound. "Seems like I hear rumblin'. May be a slow freight, but no tellin' what's around that curve. You better slow down!"

Earl pressed in the clutch and braked the car to a near-stop. The tiny white needle trembled wildly. He eyed it quickly, then once more shot looks in both directions. "Must be a freight! Curve or no curve, I can beat a freight here. Always done it before." Suddenly he jerked down the gas lever and the car shot ahead. "Damn, I cain't run out'a gas here!" he yelled.

Fear gripped Newt as they roared over the last few yards to the crossing. Then both of them froze at the frightening sound of the engine whistling in from the left.

"Damn!" Earl yelled.

It was the Katy Express, not a freight, and it was blowing hard as it came barreling down on them. Earl slammed the brake and clutch in together just before the engine reached the crossing. The car shuddered to a stop, but the nose of it was just touching the track.

"Jump! Jump!" Earl screamed. Newt was already rolling in the weeds when he heard the crunching sound and saw the car somersaulting alongside the speeding train. At the same instant he saw Earl in a flying plunge just ahead of it. By the time the Express screeched to a halt, a half mile away, the car was aflame. Newt jumped up and ran over to drag Earl away from it.

"You hurt, Earl? You all right?"

"Yeh—just shook up a little. Help me up." Newt bent over to help him—then drew back and screamed.

"Your foot's gone, Earl! Your foot's gone!"

Earl kept his eyes on Newt. "You're crazy—you're crazy, Newt! I don't feel nothin'!" Then slowly he turned his head and looked down at the chalk-white splintered bone sticking through his bloody pants leg. "Oh no no no! Good God no! No no no—"

Newt looked beyond the burning car and he could see people running toward them. "Help! Help! Over here!" he shouted, cupping his hands around his mouth. "Help! Help!"

The big fireman arrived first. His red puffy face was streaked with coal dust and he was sweating. "What you two niggas tryin' to do—kill us all?" he raged.

Newt stood and bristled.

"My Lord! His foot's off!" It was the engineer. He brushed the fireman aside and bent over Earl. "Git the first aid kit, Rufus! Hurry! I'll try a tourniquet. Gimme your shirt, sonny." Newt ripped off his shirt, handed it to him. "Now git me a good strong stick, boy!"

"How big, mister?"

"About so-so—" he said, spacing his bony hands apart. "Hurry, boy! Hurry!"

Newt returned with a stick, and the engineer broke it across his knee. After tying a loop in the shirt, he thrust the stick through and began twisting it above Earl's knee. Earl was quiet now.

The engineer said, "Here, sonny, hold this in place. Hold it tight, now."

Newt took the stick, then looked down at Earl. "Does it hurt much?"

"Not too much," Earl said.

"Didn't you boys hear the bell ringing?" the engineer asked.

"Thought we could make it. Thought you was a slow freight."

"You ought never try beatin' a train," the engineer said, "freight or whatever."

Newt was aware of more people around them. They were passengers from the train. A conductor began asking questions. "What's your name, boy?"

"Newt Winger."

"And his?"

"Earl Thompson."

"Where you live?"

"Cherokee Flats."

"Him too?"

"Yep."

"Whose car was it?"

"His—his paw's."

"You hurt any?"

"Naw."

A short fat man in a checkered suit, wearing rimless glasses without ear-bars, looked down at Earl's leg. He just kept looking, with his mouth open. A tall, birdlike woman peeped over the fat man's shoulder, turned white and grabbed him by the arm. "Come, Gerald," she said. "How can you bear to look?" They left, and others closed in.

"You people have to stand back now," the engineer said. "Give us some air." He turned to Newt. "There a doctor close by, sonny?"

"Over at the Flats. Doc Cravens is about a mile and a half from here. He's got a ambulance."

"Well, you better run for him. I'll take the tourniquet now. Hurry on!"

The better part of an hour passed before Newt and Doc Cravens pulled up in the makeshift Model-T ambulance. Newt watched Doc fill a glass tube with liquid, attach a needle to it and stick it in above Earl's knee.

"That's a good tourniquet you tied there," Doc said, and he and the engineer nodded to each other. Then they lifted Earl into the ambulance. Newt got in beside him and closed the door.

They were a good half mile down the road before Earl spoke—and to Newt's surprise, he was grinning. "Anybody back there ever bother to look for my damn foot?" he asked.

214

Newt managed a weak smile and, looking through the back window as they bounced down the road, he could see the Express picking up speed. Then suddenly it was out of sight. The warning arms stopped swinging, and he saw only smoke from the gutted Ford in the distance—curling slowly over the cornstalks and the desolate crossing.

While Doc Cravens was operating, Newt sat in the waiting room, wrapped in a wrinkled intern's jacket, explaining the accident to Earl's parents. He mumbled the details in much the same way he had once related a bad dream to his mother, after running to her bedside in the dark of a wintry night. Throughout his disordered narration he listened to Martha Thompson's soft crying, interspersed with the consoling voice of her husband, Fred.

After a long wait, Doc Cravens came. "Earl's sleepin' now," he said. "His condition's serious—but he's goin' to be all right." He looked to Martha Thompson. "I saved as much of the limb as possible, Martha. No sense in any of you worryin'. What's done is done." His eyes moved to Fred. "He's alive. Be thankful for that much."

"We are. Believe me, we are."

"He should sleep through the night, so you'd better come back in the mornin'." He turned again to Martha. "Remember—no worryin'."

They were leaving the hospital now. "You takin' Newt home?" Fred asked.

"Yep," Doc said. "Got to call on Sarah. Haven't seen her since this mornin'."

"How's she doin'?" Fred asked.

"Seems to be holdin' her own. Well, goodnight. Come round in the mornin' after eight."

"After eight."

"It'll be that late before I can tell you anything."

Fred put his arm about Martha's shoulder and they walked slowly to their buckboard. He helped her in, untethered the horse and climbed in beside her. As they rode off, Doc put his hand on Newt's shoulder. They watched the wagon as it disappeared in the darkness—and listened to the clomp, clomp of the horse's hoofs and the creaking of the dried-out wheels.

"Momma any better, Doc?" Newt asked.

They looked at each other for a moment, then Doc said, "Your mother's in bad shape, Newt—you might as well know."

"She'll be all right sometime, though, won't she?"

"Only time will tell, Newt."

They went on to Doc's car, got in and drove off. As they rode along, Newt wanted to ask more about his mother but he didn't know how to form the questions. Too, there was an inner fear of facing the fact that she might be dying. So he contented himself with what little he had been told, and he watched the road come up blurry and whitish from the edges of the country darkness.

His mind shot back to Earl. It seemed ages since they had started out that morning. Poor Earl! No more basketball for him—no swimming at Flynn's River—no more races over Candy Hill. If only he'd listened! That chalk-white bone sticking from his bloody pants leg, a white person's bone couldn't be any whiter.

The car slowed. Two deer, caught in the gleam of the headlamps, stood transfixed, readying their leap toward the sudden brightness. Doc Cravens quickly switched off the lights. A moment later he turned them on again. The deer had fled into the brush, and the car picked up speed.

They were halfway to the Winger house when Doc finally spoke again. "Newt."

"Yessir."

"My father died when I was just about your age. You're fifteen, aren't you?"

"Almost."

"Well, soon after he died, my mother ran off to St. Louis with a fellow from Kansas City." Newt turned and looked hard at him. "Surprised, huh?" Doc said.

"Well—"

"I was alone, so your mother took me in and cared for me like I was one of her own."

"You mean you used to live at my house?"

"Before you were born. Durin' that time I came to know the way people could really live on this earth if they only tried." He twisted the steering wheel and they turned the corner into Logan's Grove. "It wasn't easy for her, either. Folks, black and white, did some talkin' against her takin' in Sadie Cravens' white son, but their complaints fell on deaf ears. I didn't miss a day of school or go without eatin'—for two years, mind you."

Newt was quiet.

Doc Cravens reflected for a moment or so. "Early in the third year my mother died, and your mother paid my way to her funeral in St. Louis. I stayed there and went to school

216

on money my mother managed to leave me. I don't know where she got it."

"Why'd you ever come back here?"

Doc pulled up alongside the Winger yard and stopped. "I can't exactly say why, Newt. It's as good a place as any to help people who really need helpin'. . . . Let's go in. Oh, by the way—your sisters and brother came after you left this mornin'."

Newt followed him into the house, and Doc went on into Sarah's room. Clara, Lou and Roy got up smiling as Newt crossed the hushed parlor to greet them. He hugged and kissed his two sisters and shook hands with Roy. Lou looked about the same, but Clara—who Jack called "the marryin' one"—had changed. She looked skinnier to Newt, and she was dressed in fancier clothes than when he had seen her several years before. Roy looked the way Newt felt all sharp Chicagoans should look—hair parted to the side, striped suit, striped tie, white spats and needle-nosed shoes. "He'll be tellin' us some wild tales about Chicago," Newt thought as he pumped his hand.

The next day Newt, Clint and Roy were lying in the yard beneath the big apple tree. It was hot, and Roy lay face down in a clump of cool grass, the other two flat on their backs. Newt held a string tied to the leg of a huge June bug that spun lazily about their heads. Clint said, "What's that June bug doin' hangin' round here in August?"

"I've seen 'em later'n this," Newt said.

They were silent for a while, then Clint said, "Tell us 'bout the Windy City, Roy. Anything happen to you lately?"

"Not much. Got robbed last week—that's about all."

Clint and Newt raised to their elbows in simultaneous motion, and Clint's eyes popped. "Robbed? Hell, man! Tell us 'bout it! What happened?"

"Wasn't nothin' out of the ordinary, Clint. Guy just stuck a big forty-five at the back of my head and told me to fork over."

Clint cocked his head to one side. "Well, come on—what'd you do?"

"What'd I do? I gave him the dough. What else could I do?" Roy chomped off the end of a blade of grass, winked slyly at Newt and suppressed a grin. "I was lucky he didn't slug me. He had me in the clutch, and I wasn't about to give him no back talk."

"Didn't you say nothin' to him, at all?"

"Sure. I said, 'Here you are, sir—have a pleasant journey.'"

Clint shook his head, chuckled and fell back on the ground. "Boy! You shore lead a hell-of-a-wonderful life, Roy."

"Wonderful? What's so wonderful about a gun pointin' at the back of your head. Naw, you're lucky to be here away from all the crap you have to take in a big city. Right, Newt?"

Newt sensed the whole tale was a lie, but he was flattered by the confidence. He winked at Roy. "Right you are, Roy. Right you are."

"Just the same," Clint said dreamily, "it must be terrific. Action and dames and everything. Nice—nice dames. Boy—"

"You kiddin'? A bunch of money-grabbin' chicks lookin' to take you for everything you got. Nice dames. Boy, some of them would steal the white off rice. Naw, Clint, you better be thankful you're here in the Flats."

"What else happened you ain't told us 'bout?"

"Couple other things. Ain't got time now. Maybe tomorrow." Roy jumped to his feet and walked away.

The June bug lit on Newt's nose. He watched with crossed eyes as it crawled up the bridge of his nose to his forehead, dragging the dirty string over his lips. Suddenly the bug took off with a jerk, leaving its leg on the string.

Clint propped himself up on his elbows, watching the insect's crazy flight to freedom. Then he said, "If I was that goddam bug I'd fly straight to Chicago without stoppin'!" He got to his feet, brushed the dirt from his behind and moved over to the porch where Jack Winger sat smoking. "How's Momma Winger doin', Poppa?"

Jack puffed a couple of times, removed the pipe and spat. "Seems to be holdin' her own." Then he went on puffing.

Clint pushed his hands deep into his overall pockets, kicked the side of the porch, looked to the sky and spat. "Rain for shore way back there, Poppa Winger."

"Yep—does look like it."

Clint's hands jumped from his pockets to the shoulder straps near the bib. "It's hot," he complained. Then he turned abruptly, his mouth twitching nervously, and hurried down the path toward his shack. When Jack turned in puzzlement to look after him, he had already disappeared below the hill.

Newt remained in the shade of the tree, squinting toward the mirages of shimmering heat that hung over the cornfields and plains beyond. The small talk had relaxed him and left

218

a warm and special feeling. But now a sense of guilt crept over him, so he got up and called, "Poppa, I'm goin' to the hospital to see Earl!"

"All right, boy. Tell him I'll be to see him 'fore long."

Clint was right about the rain. It started around six that evening, and by seven-thirty the creeks and rivers were reaching their watersides. Marcus Savage had been rummaging through the junk in the yard when the first downpour came. He scurried into the shack, leaving the door cracked to let in fresh air. Then, sitting on the floor with his back to the wall, he watched the silver rain coming down in sheets beyond the opening.

He pondered his circumstances. "Ain't got nobody now. All on account'a that Winger son-of-a-bitch—couldn't keep his trap shut—helpin' white trash 'stead of his own kind. 'Course Paw killed Jake—the dirty bastard had it comin'— I spent a year in hell on account'a him." He plucked a small ant crawling over his knee, held it for a moment, watching it wiggle helplessly; then his powerful black fingers rubbed it into nothingness.

He took a raw turnip from his pocket and pulled a knife from his overall bib; pressed a tiny metal button at the end of it and a huge blade popped from the groove. He peeled the skin, tossed it aside and sank his teeth into the starchy white meat, chewing viciously. "But I'll git Winger. He's been stickin' close to home. Sooner or later he'll come down to the river and—" He sensed a movement at the door. It was a big field rat, seeking shelter. As it slithered through the opening, Marcus sprang up. "Git! You son-of-a-bitch!" The frightened rat bared its yellow fangs and backed off cautiously, then whirled and fled back into the wetness.

CHAPTER ❦ 17

NEWT SAT on a barrel in the corner of the kitchen, listening to the downpour vibrate the tin roof above him and watching Lou and Clara ready the evening meal. Realizing that if his mother died he might have to live with one or the other sister, he observed them closely—trying to decide which one he would rather be with. He liked them both, so he sat mentally sifting their habits and dispositions, applying them to his own simple, yet important, personal plans and desires. "Clara's a little bossy," he thought. "She'd prob'ly want me to stay in all the time—want to pick all my friends, too, but she likes to dress fancy—prob'ly help me get some keen things to wear. Lou's easygoin' and easy to fool. I like the way she fries potatoes, but she'd prob'ly want me to go to church all the time. Sure had enough religion to last me a long time."

"Newt, put some wood on the fire. Hurry up, now!"

(Yeh—Clara's mighty bossy, all right. . . .) "Okay, okay." He went to the outer shed adjoining the kitchen, came with the wood and stoked it in above the glowing grate. Then he returned to his perch on the flour barrel. Glancing into the dining room, he saw Maggie Pullens rise and walk toward the front of the house. When she came back she said to Jack, "Sarah's breathin' easy."

"Doc Cravens seems to think she's gainin'," Jack said.

"Glad to hear it," Maggie sighed, " 'cause I don't mind tellin' you that a white dove come and set on my window sill this mornin'—you know what that means—I thought the worst had come. Well, I dressed and grabbed this camphor bottle and got here fast as I could."

"Supper's about ready, Poppa."

"Git me some buttermilk, Prissy."

"Yessir." Prissy switched back to the kitchen. "You want some buttermilk, Newt?"

"Huh?"

220

"Whyn't you wash out your ears? I said do you want some buttermilk?"

"Sure I want some buttermilk—and I wash my ears more'n you wash your a—"

"Newt!" It was Clara. "Don't you dare use such language with your momma on her dyin' bed!"

"Aw, I ain't said anything, yet." He slid from the barrel and started for the dining room. Reaching the doorway, he turned to Prissy. "You know one thing, twitchy pants, one of these fine days you're goin' to turn up missin'."

"Save your bluff for Marcus Savage, big boy. You don't scare Prissy none."

"All right. You two cut it out and get to dinner!" Clara whisked past them, carrying a big platter of chicken. "Come on, Poppa. Come on, Miss Maggie. There's plenty here for everybody. Pete—Roy—come on!"

A short time later Jack began blessing the table. "Lord, make us truly thankful for—"

"Help! Help!"

Newt sprang to his feet. "It's Rende, Poppa."

"Sit back down, boy!" Jack ordered. Then he got up and went to the door. "I'll handle this." He jerked open the door and peered into the darkness, the rain needling his face and arms. "Rende!" Rende!"

He could see her vaguely in the pouring black waterscape, carrying the baby, coaxing Butsy and shoving Gin-gin up the slippery path. He rushed out to meet them. "What's the matter, girl? What you screamin' 'bout now?"

"It's Clint, Poppa! He's got the shotgun!"

"I declare! Where's he at now?"

"Followin' us up the path," Rende gasped.

"Git in out'a the rain!" Jack said, ushering them into the room. He looked back toward the dark path. "Why'd he pick a time like this to booze up?"

Everyone was standing when Rende and the children scrambled through the door, soaked to their skins. Jack came in behind them and quietly forced the door shut. Lou took the baby, and the two small children stood there big-eyed, shining in their wetness, until Clara moved over and began wiping their faces with her apron.

"Now don't start that bawlin', girl," Jack said to Rende. "Git your momma excited."

Prissy stayed close to the older women, while Newt, Pete and Roy stood watching their father. Suddenly Jack seemed to realize that he was confronted with Clint for the first time.

221

He turned to his sons. "I don't want your momma hearin' a fuss and gittin' upset, so you boys stay out'a this. Git my hat and raincoat, Newt. Rende, you and the kids go in Prissy's bedroom—and stay there. Rest of you sit down and finish your supper. Now, everybody do as I say. Hurry up, Newt!"

Newt bounded across the floor with his father's hat and black rubber raincoat. He helped him into it, then grabbed his own overall jumper and started putting it on.

"Take that jumper off, boy," Jack snapped.

"Yessir." Newt dropped the jumper and moved to the table.

Jack watched Rende hustle the children into Prissy's room, then he finished buttoning his coat and started for the door.

"Better be careful, Poppa," Pete cautioned.

"Don't worry, boy." Then he was out the door. He was pulling it shut when he felt the double barrels of the gun push firmly against his belly.

"Where's Rende?" Clint drawled menacingly.

Jack's voice was steady and low. "Boy, this ain't no time for trouble and you know it, no matter how drunk you are." The gun pushed harder, and Jack backed off the pressure. But quickly it was upon him again, forcing him into the room where the others watched, horrified.

"There won't be no trouble if you just git me Rende, Poppa Winger." A grin was set on Clint's face. "Where's she hidin'?"

"Close the door, boy. It's rainin' in here."

"We'll just leave it open. I aim to be goin' pretty quick." The gun moved up and down. "I ain't foolin'. Both these barrels is loaded—and there's plenty for reloadin'. Where's she, in the bedroom?"

Maggie Pullens dashed out the kitchen door. "I'm callin' Kirky," she cried.

"Git back here!" Clint shouted, his eyes shifting toward her. But she was gone. His eyes were on Jack again and he pushed him on toward the bedroom ahead of the gun. Pete, Roy and Newt stood by the table, tensed for action.

"Clint, you oughta be 'shamed of yourself," Clara scolded, "you know Momma's breathin' her last."

"Keep your fancy mouth shut, Clara, or you might git it too!" The gun raised to Jack's chest. "All right, Poppa Winger—move away from the door."

"You gonna have to kill me first, boy." Jack's right hand inched toward a flatiron on the pressing board nearby.

"Okay! Hands up high!" Clint barked. The gun was against

Jack's forehead now, fuzzing his view of all except the long black steel barrels through which the blast would come. They seemed to spread across his entire forehead. He could see Clint's wet knuckles, shining and trembling beneath the finger on the trigger.

"Okay, Poppa, I'm countin' to five," Clint said, "if you ain't out'a the way by then, off goes the top of your head! One—"

Pete had motioned everyone back, and they were all on Clint's right now.

"Two—"

Pete grabbed a plate from the table and threw it at the door. It struck with a startling crash. As Clint wheeled toward the noise, Jack felt the barrel rims tearing across his forehead —heard the blast, the splintering door and the screams.

Everyone had fallen to the floor except Jack. He grabbed the flatiron and threw it just as Clint bounded out through the door. The iron missed Clint and sailed into the open. Clint sprinted for the cornfield, emptying the smoking shell chambers as he ran. He continued several yards in among the stalks, then stopped to reload.

Sarah had awakened with the blast and Jack had rushed to her bedside, sopping blood from his gashed forehead with a dish towel.

"Oh my—he's been doin' fine till now," Sarah said. "Wonder what got into him?"

"The devil—what else?" Jack answered.

"Where's Rende and the kids now?"

"In the bedroom till Kirky comes."

"Kirky?"

"Yeh. Maggie ran out and phoned him."

"No more shootin', I hope."

He patted her arm. "Don't you go gittin' excited, Sarah. Everything's gonna turn out all right."

"Where's Newt?"

"In with his brothers guardin' the doors."

"Keep him out of the way, Jack. He might try somethin' foolish."

"I'm watchin' him. Don't worry." He pulled the cover up under her chin. "There's Kirky's 'cycle. I better git out there."

Kirky came stalking through the rain with two pistols drawn. Doug Simpson and Bull Terry, his hastily formed posse, flanked him, each of them carrying a high-powered rifle.

These two had come in Doug's Ford. The rain had slackened, but they were all wearing slickers.

Jack and his sons met them in the yard.

"Where's Clint hidin', Jack?" Kirky's tone was brusque and mean.

"Don't know for shore. He made for the cornfield there."

Thunder rumbled in from the west, and lightning streaked across the black sky.

"I'll bring him out—if I have to drag him out by his goddam heels!" Kirky growled. He turned toward the field, "Come on, men. Keep low and be careful. This bastard's crazy when he's boozed up. We'll go in 'bout ten feet apart. I'll take the middle. Doug, you take the left—and, Bull, you cover from the right. When we spot his position, blast in his direction—not to the side. We'll go in ten steps at a time and stop. Wait till you hear me 'fore goin' any further. Got it straight?"

"Yeh, we understand."

"Okay, let's go."

Jack touched Kirky's arm. "Lemme call him first. Maybe he'll give up."

Kirky shook his head. "I'm callin' signals now, Jack. You and your boys better git out'a the way now——" He motioned them aside with his guns.

Jack ordered the boys into the house, and Newt said, "If only Momma wasn't sick. Kirky won't give him a chance, Poppa."

"Ain't much we can do now, boy. It's all Clint's doin'."

Kirky and his men were at the edge of the cornfield. "All right, Clint! It's Kirky!" he bellowed. "You comin' out or do I hafta come in and drag you out?"

Except for a low rumble of thunder, and rain beating on the cornstalks, there was silence. Kirky motioned toward the ground with his guns, and he and his deputies crouched low, took ten steps into the field, then stopped.

"Okay, Clint! You better yell out your position so we don't shoot!" Silence. "Okay, men. Ten more." He was speaking softly now. They had just taken the third step when thunder and lightning cracked above their heads—and at the same time Clint let go with a blast, shearing the corn tops above them. The three men dropped to their bellies and returned the fire—crack—bam—bam—crack. Then there was silence again.

Suddenly Clint's voice chided from another part of the

field. "What you waitin' on, Kirky? You red-neck son-of-a-bitch! You scared?"

The posse crawled ten paces toward the direction of the voice. Boom! Clint blasted again. The three flopped to their bellies, and their guns fired back into the wet, swaying corn. "All right, men," Kirky said, "crawl out to where we started. We gotta track from another position." They scooted back to the edge of the clearing.

"This ain't the jazzy little party you told us it'd be, Kirky," Bull said, wiping the mud from his face. "That black bastard's shrewd as a fox."

"Don't worry. We'll git him. Don't worry." Kirky was wiping his gun.

A light had appeared in the doorway, and through it came Pete and Roy, carrying their mother into the yard. She was heavily wrapped in quilted blankets. Clara and Lou held umbrellas over her head and body.

"What's this?" Doug motioned toward the house. Kirky and Bull turned to look, and Kirky dropped his guns to his sides.

"Who's that they're carryin'?" Bull asked.

"Jack's wife. Must be out'a their minds. She's half dead." Kirky started waving them back, but they kept coming.

Jack walked over to Kirky and said, "He'll come out if he knows she's out here."

"You're crazy, Jack! Git her back to bed. Clint's gone loco. He'd kill anybody now!"

"Try it her way," Jack said.

"Naw—"

"Call out to him," Sarah said, and Newt cupped his hands around his mouth. "Clint! Momma Winger's out here! She wants you to come in! Can you hear me, Clint?"

After a moment, Clint's voice came from a new direction. "You're lyin', Newt! She's in bed! You git back out'a the way!"

"Honest, Clint—she's here! We'll turn the car lights on her so you can see for yourself!"

"Naw—don't you turn them lights on!" Kirky shouted.

"Maybe we ought'a let her give it a try," Doug urged. Kirky shrugged, and Doug rushed to the car, started it, and switched on the headlamps. Then he drove up the path and stopped, with the lights flooding the group.

"Here she is, Clint!" Newt hollered. "See for yourself!"

There was a slight rustling in the field, and Kirky's hands tightened on his guns. Everyone else stood rigid and quiet.

"Don't try no monkey business!" Clint called out. "If it ain't her, I'll shoot! Turn her to the light!"

Roy and Pete turned their mother into the beams of light. "Come on, before Momma gets soaked!" Pete yelled.

Clint was on his belly now, snaking his way in, the gun barrels parting the stalks before him. He halted a moment, then continued in a crawl, stopping finally within a few feet of the clearing.

"That you, Momma Winger?" The question was almost whispered.

"Yes—Clint. Come ahead. Nobody's goin' to harm you."

"You shore?"

"I'm sure. Come on."

Clint wriggled quickly to the edge, then jumped up and burst from the cornfield toward Sarah.

"Drop that gun!" Kirky bellowed.

Clint ran for the refuge of the group, dropping the gun in the mud—and Jack's fist cracked against his jaw, sending him to the earth. He got up groggily.

"Git in the house—you lunatic," Jack said heatedly, grabbing him by the scruff of his neck. "I declare—I ought'a—" He shoved Clint into the house.

They carried Sarah back into her room, where Lou and Clara removed the wet blankets and covered her with dry ones. Clint came in, dropped to his knees and started praying. Rende observed him a moment or two, then she moved over and knelt beside him. But Kirky stepped up and grabbed Clint's shoulder. "Come on, Clint—you're goin' in."

"Leave him—to me—Kirky," Sarah said. "You didn't git him—I did."

Kirky looked at her, then at Jack. "Okay," he grunted. He motioned Bull and Doug from the room, and they stomped out of the house without looking back. "I'll git that bastard yet," Kirky growled as they crossed the yard.

Doc Cravens met them near the end of the walk. "What's goin' on?" he asked.

"When you find out, tell me, Doc. I'd like to know too," Kirky snorted as he mounted his motorcycle.

Newt was undressing for bed when Pete called, "Momma wants you, Newt."

"Somethin' wrong?"

"She's askin' for you—better come right away."

Newt walked slowly to the bedside. He sensed the others in the room, but he looked only at his mother—noting the sunken cheeks, the pallor lying like silk over her deep brown skin, the dullness of her eyes beneath the half-closed lids.

"Come close, son." Her face twitched to a faint smile as she spoke.

Newt dropped to his knees and touched his lips to her cheeks; and through his hands, resting on her thin arms, he realized the full extent of her suffering. "How are you feelin', Momma?"

She looked at him for a moment before answering. "I'm goin', son—just wanted a few words with you."

Newt's eyes began to water.

"Now don't go puckerin' up," Sarah said, smiling. "I'm ready—I'm happy and I don't want cryin' from any of you."

She was silent for a few moments, seemingly gathering strength. Doc Cravens pressed a damp cloth against her forehead, propped an extra pillow behind her neck, and took her pulse. Rende, Lou, Clara, Prissy, Roy and Pete stood off to the side. Jack was in front of them, his smokeless pipe hanging from his lips. The rims of his eyes were swollen and red.

Sarah went on. "Your sisters are takin' you back north with them. Promise me you'll mind them—and keep out of trouble."

"I promise."

"It's another kind of world up there, Newt—hope and more promisin' things. Put—put somethin' into it—and you'll git somethin' out—simple as that."

"Yessem."

"Make a good man of yourself up there. It's a dream of mine—for you—make it come true."

"I'll try."

"You'll do it."

"Yessem, I will."

"Do the ri—right thing—not always the easiest—"

Her eyes were closing and Doc Cravens touched Newt's shoulder. He started to move away, but stopped as his mother spoke once again. "Believe in somethin' and live up to it. Be good, son. Be—" Her hand dropped to the side of the bed.

Doc Cravens lifted Newt up. "She's sleepin' now," he said. "You better get to bed."

At the parlor door Newt turned for one more look, then went off to his room.

Lying in the darkness of his room, he began absorbing the full measure of the tragedy now facing the Winger family. For the first time in his life he realized it was his mother

227

who had really kept things together; who performed the miracles—such as she had done with Clint this very same night—that insured their existence; who calmed the fears that came with the trials of long, bitter winters. His father, though he would be willing, could never shoulder the burden. Newt knew it, Jack Winger knew it, and so did everyone else.

It had already been decided that Prissy would go with either Lou or Clara, as he would. He began thinking of his family as a shrinking tree. His mother, part of the trunk, was withering away. His brothers and sisters, like leaves, would soon scatter in all directions. Now his mind wandered to the faraway place up north—where his mother expected him to bring flowering to her dream. He couldn't conjure up a clear image of it, but his heart, he knew, was already racing there. Soon he would join it and go in search of the "promisin' things" she had just spoken of, just a few minutes before.

He tossed and turned in his bed, got up twice for water, and made a trip to the outhouse. It was nearly three when he finally slept—and his dreams were as frightful as his day had been. One dealt with a huge chunk of peanut brittle he was trying to keep from sinking to the bottom of Flynn's River. After a couple of violent twists in the water, it was no longer peanut brittle, but Marcus Savage. Marcus had only one leg, and when Newt grabbed it to pull him ashore, he was horrified to find his hand wrapped around a hot, double-barreled shotgun.

His dreams were of such substance when he stirred to a hand on his cheek. "Newt. Newt. Wake up."

"Who is it? What you want?" He could just make out Clara's dark form above him.

"It's me. Clara."

"Yeh. What's the matter?"

"Newt—" she said softly.

"Yeh?"

"Momma's dead."

CHAPTER ✤ 18

DAWN ARRIVED painfully slow, and Newt, as if in a trance, lay gazing out the window through the dank lace curtains. He watched the sky pale as the sun climbed to the foggy horizon and brightened the upper reaches. His mind, with unaccountable calm, explored the reality of this hour over the deep, uneven snoring of Roy and Pete, sleeping beside him.

Their mother was dead, he knew, but it was hard to believe. Suddenly he wondered if, somewhere up there in the pale blue nothingness, her soul—free of tortured body and earthly things—was already floating silently about, knowing at last the real purpose of its sojourn on a complex and troubled earth. What if she had found that all the praying and religious rites were just a lot of folly; that her soul floated with no more righteousness or dignity than that of Doc Cheney, Big Mabel, or even Captain Tuck? What a shock it would be to her!

He now thought uneasily of such a possibility, and he couldn't help but feel that this was more than likely the case —and the feeling shamed him. Then he softened his shame with the reasoning that if such were true, she would never begrudge anyone such equality. Whatever judgment settled upon her, he thought, would surely be the best that eternity could possibly extend.

As Newt dressed quietly, the sun burned through the fog, warming the wet rooftops, drying the leaves and grass. And the moist cool earth took in the heat and in return gave forth little curlings of cloud that quickly disappeared in the clean morning air.

He entered the dining room and looked around. Everything was just about the same, except the door which the shot had blasted. Stepping to it, he ran his fingers over the splintered surface. Daylight leaked through it now, and a sudden fright gripped him, for he realized that this destruction was actually meant for Rende. Remembering the gun against his father's head, he shivered and stepped back involuntarily (this could've been Poppa's skull), then he moved warily across to his mother's room. They had already taken her to the undertaker's.

The odor of camphor and medicine still hung in the air, and a bouquet of withered posies lay on the rocking chair in the corner of the room. The sheets had been removed, and the mattress was doubled upon the sagging springs. Above the antique dresser hung an oval-shaped photograph of his father and mother, framed in a polished, worn wood. It had been taken their wedding day, and both stared straight ahead—unmindful of this faraway moment when their last child would stand silent, alone and uncertain in this room of death.

Almost in every sense, Newt had come to link death with violence. Even his mother's passing, he thought, couldn't escape a brush with it. Nearly everyone he had known intimately, and who had ceased to live, met their demise in bloodshed. And it was probably for this reason that he feared death so much—and this fear, he reasoned, was childish. His mother's easy, tranquil and unflinching acceptance of death enhanced his respect for her. Now, this morning, it was creating within him a near-fanatical desire to rid himself of this stigma that had dogged his soul since the day of Doc Cheney's death.

Turning from the room, he channeled his thoughts into an imaginary rectangular hole that someday would be his grave. And his whole being reacted against the eternal blackness, the unending airlessness, the unchangeable recumbent position of his body—never to eat, taste, feel, speak or hear again. He shuddered. Now he envisaged the others reposing about him, acre after acre; worm-bored coffin sides, everlasting decay, dust piling forever upon eternal dust—entombed in the still, suffocating blackness.

Why, then, was life given, and for no logically explained reason taken away again? He recalled the rolling, wearisome voice of Pastor Broadnap. "—From dust you came and to dust you must returneth!" Newt remembered his authoritatively hollering such things over Big Mabel's coffin. He remembered, too, his swing about the pulpit, frock coat flying, sweat dripping, screaming of immortality—"of the spirit, of the soul"—not the good, solid body.

Newt opened the front door and stepped out on the porch. As his bare feet moved over the clammy boards, he heard the creaking beneath them and noted that they would soon have to be replaced. Sunlight bathed the edge of the porch, so he went to stand there, warming his body in the brilliant glow.

Morning eased into afternoon, evening, night, restless sleep—then there was morning again. The gray, simple casket arrived in the early afternoon. It was placed in the parlor by the window, resting on six silver wheels, and by late evening the room had become filled with flowers.

Twice during the day Newt went to look at his mother, once with his father and then with Prissy and Pete. Prissy cried, but he didn't; and as the three of them walked from the coffin, he placed his arms consolingly about her shoulders—this for the very first time in his life. And she cuddled to his touch. It gave him a good feeling, a good, big-brother and close-family feeling; one that demanded swift growing up, in mind and body alike. His entire body and his mind reacted to this demand, and he seemed to grow on the spot, feeling the expansion in his muscles, his thighs and belly—and heart. On impulse, he said to himself, "I've got to prove somethin'—to myself."

"What'd you· say?"

"Nothin'. Just thinkin', Prissy. Just thinkin'."

Later, walking through the backyard toward the hog pens, he had a certain notion, and as he worked this notion grew. He would sleep this night on the floor beside his mother's coffin, in the very presence of death. If during the night his fear left forever, the purpose would be served. If it remained . . . His thoughts juggled the possibility for a few seconds, then he shrugged it off. "Mornin' holds the answer," his voice sighed to the crimson evening, "mornin' holds the answer."

As night raced upon him, all else—funeral plans, mourning, telegrams, arriving kinfolk—passed as would trifling scenes in a powerful drama. He was caught in an impulse that denied significance to anything but that impulse. And though he existed in the land of the living, his mind was unrelated to it.

By one-thirty in the morning he was lying in his bed hearing nothing but the deep, unrhythmed sleep of the household; his heart pounding, the finger of fear touching it, the challenge calling from the dark room where his mother's body lay. The reality of the moment grasped him like steel claws. Dreamlike, he rose as if pulled from the bed and draped a blanket about his shoulders. The immense underground of death took its place in his mind, but he moved on toward the room through the ever-so-quiet darkness. Reaching the parlor door, he stopped, breathing heavily. He felt that he had awaited this moment all his life, and now that it had arrived, he could not fail it. He pushed the door open gently, paused, then stepped in—leaving the door ajar behind him. In the dimness he could see the shape of the coffin. His heart sank, and he wanted to run from the room; but he realized he had to go through with it after coming this far. Sweat dripped from his armpits, and he could feel the moisture in the palms of his hands. He made another small step toward the coffin (the lid's down), one more step—driplets of sweat coursed down the sides of his face. He gently eased up the lid, shivered, trembled, looked. The dark form of his mother lay deep in the cushion of crinkly white. (I made it, Momma—I made it—give me strength to stay on—give me strength.) Bracing himself, he took a final steady, muscle-taut, teeth-grinding look, dropped the blanket to the floor, spread it, lay upon it, jerked it about him, closed his eyes tightly—sealing off all blackness except that of his own inner being. After a while the heartbeat slowed, the trembling eased. He commenced the struggle with sleep. Though his eyes were closed, all the counterparts of fear tried forcing their way into his vision; but he helped his mind form the image of his mother as it had existed in reality, before death—and he held onto that image with great tenacity. (...I ain't afraid...I ain't afraid...) An owl hooted in the nearby woods; crickets chirped in brittle unending chorus; and in this hour Newt heard the forlorn cry of the whippoorwill. (I ain't afraid no more, Momma... I ain't afraid....) He was easing into weariness now. (I ain't afraid....) At last, as if in answer to his courage, sleep came. Before long, he was snoring softly. His dreams, unafraid.

Here, Jack Winger found his son in early morning. At first, the sight of Newt curled up on the floor alongside the open coffin shook him. But he quickly understood. He knew his son better than his son thought. And the look of peace on the boy's face signified something more important than his just sleeping there. He started to rouse him and put out his hand, then suddenly drew it back, tiptoed out and softly closed the door. Then he went through the foggy morning to appease the hunger of his squealing hogs.

"...Ashes to ashes...dust to dust...from dust we came and to dust we returneth." The petals of the broken rose fell from Pastor Broadnap's fingers, twisted and dipped in blurred confusion before Newt's tear-filled eyes, then came to rest on Sarah Winger's coffin. ". . . may this beloved mother and wife rest, forever, in peace. May God have mercy on this family . . . amen."

Newt felt his Uncle Rob's hand ease to his shoulder, pressing home the end of the rites. Grief engulfed him as he stood staring into his mother's open grave. (Goodbye, Momma—I won't forget your dream.)

"Come on, son—let's go," Rob said.

"Okay, Uncle Rob, I just want to stay a little longer."

"It's all right, boy. Take your time." Rob waited as the others started filing out toward the waiting cars.

Newt's eyes swept the grave for the last time, continued on to two chalk-white headstones, lined up stiffly to the left of his mother's final resting place. Time and weather had worn the once crisp lettering:

CLARINDA WINGER   MILLER WINGER
Born May 12, 1901   Born December 16, 1897
Died May 12, 1901   Died June 14, 1909

A warm gentle breeze licked his ear. He turned at its touch and took Rob's hand and they walked away. As he neared the car, he noticed two workmen sitting beneath a giant oak tree. Picks and shovels lay at their sides, and they were eating from tin lunch pails. (. . . grave diggers . . . they'll be coverin' Momma soon's we leave. . . .) The thought began overpowering him, and he screamed inside. He hurried Rob the last few yards to the car, helped him in beside his father and slammed the door.

"Everything all right, boy?" Jack asked.

"Yessir, Poppa. Everything's all right now."

The big black funeral limousine moved slowly through the huge wrought-iron gate, turned onto the highway and rolled smoothly into high gear. Newt heard its tires singing on the hot macadam, drowning out the stifling silence of anguish and sorrow. He closed his eyes and his thoughts, slumped down into the seat and completely surrendered his body to the car's gentle, surging motion.

The following day Newt began packing for his trip north. As he neatly arranged his meager belongings, Beansy sat on the dining room floor, his back to the wall, harboring a regret at Newt's leaving.

"Hate to see you go, Newt. Won't be the same round here without you. But it's prob'ly best this way."

"Maybe yes. Maybe no." Newt paused and gazed blankly at the candy-striped pajamas in his hand. "Who can say—I'll miss you and the fellas—but I'll be comin' back for visits—and who knows, maybe you can come see me before long. It ain't really like we won't never see each other again." He pressed and held his weight upon some wrinkled overalls.

"Wonder what it's like up where you're goin', Newt?"

Newt folded his gray bell-bottomed pants on top of the overalls. "I don't know for sure. Clara and Lou say you don't have to sit in the buzzard's roost at the picture shows, and you can even eat in some of the white places and play on white school teams like everybody else."

"You think that's just a lotta talk?"

"Don't know."

A grin stretched Beansy's rubbery, fat face. "What about the white girls, Newt?"

"I ain't worried about *them* none. I ain't for kickin' 'em out if they get in bed with me. But like Roy says, 'All behinds feel the same in the dark.' "

Clara strutted in and stood above them, her hands wet with washing suds. "Newt, you ain't takin' those bell-bottom pants nowhere."

"What's wrong with 'em?"

"You just ain't takin' 'em, that's all." She picked up the end of one of the spreading legs. "Why, that cold air'd git up under them things and freeze your tail off. You're goin' north, boy—not south." She wiped the suds off on her dress. "Take 'em out now, like I say." She switched off to the kitchen.

"Crapmafittle," Newt said under his breath, exchanging grins with Beansy. He glanced toward the kitchen, took the pants, hid them in brown wrapping paper and squeezed the package in at the very bottom of the pasteboard suitcase.

"She's gonna be bossy, Newt."

"Her growl's worse'n her bite. Anyway, I'll be on my own soon's I get myself a job." Roy had given him two shirts and a tie. He cocked his head to one side and proudly observed the presents and placed them on top of the pile. He exhaled deeply, then pushed the bag into the corner. "That's about all I can do now—finish the rest in the mornin'."

"Prissy gonna live with you?"

"No. She's gonna be with Lou, but we'll be in the same neighborhood. Poppa and Pete are gonna stay here for a while. They may come up later."

"What time we meetin' the gang over at the river?"

"About four," Newt said, "I went over to the hospital to say goodbye to Earl this mornin'."

Aware now of their possibly never seeing each other again, Newt and Beansy casually ambled into the open, and for the next half hour they sat quietly on the edge of the porch, swatting flies, pitching rocks, whittling sticks—their thoughts saddened by the waning hours of comradeship.

" 'Bout time to meet Jappy. He'll be at Logan's Grove at a quarter to four," Newt said.

"Where's Skunk?"

"Cuttin' grass—be over later."

Marcus had an armful of dirty sheets when he saw Newt and Beansy from the second story window at Chappie's. "Must be headin' for the river," he thought. "Now's my chance."

He dropped the sheets and walked casually, but swiftly, down the stairs. He saw the back of Chappie, who was sprawled in a big chair talking to the cook. He moved quietly past the big bar, entered Chappie's room and opened the drawer in which the gun was hidden. He broke it open and eyed the breech. It held one bullet. He shoved the revolver into his pocket and, feeling for more ammunition, upended the shirts. Finally, his hand struck one bullet lying on the very bottom. He dropped it in beside the gun and kept hunting—to no avail. As he attempted to straighten out the shirts, a stack of loose bills slid out of one of the sleeves.

"Damn," Marcus whispered. He fingered the money quickly. "Must be two hundred bucks here—'nough to git anyplace on." As he crammed the bills into his back pocket one peeled off and fluttered to the floor. He closed the drawer and crept into the barroom, then slipped out the front door and headed toward the river.

Chappie got up and looked through the door. "Seems like I heard somebody come in," he said to the cook. He looked around the room and up the stairway. "Savage!" he shouted. "You up there?" He wobbled over to the foot of the stairs. "Savage—you workin'?" Chappie wearily climbed the stairs, the boards creaking under his tremendous weight. "Savage!" he called out angrily, seeing the sheets lying on the floor. He went back downstairs and crossed to his room. "Savage!" He saw the ten-dollar bill on the floor, and his eyes shifted to the drawer. He pulled it open, seeing the ruffled shirts. His hand felt for the money, then the gun. "That bastard!" He

235

grabbed his hat and started out the door, then he called to the cook, "Potsy, I'm goin' over to the jail!"

"What's up!" the cook hollered back.

"That goddamned monkey's stole my money and gun! Watch out till I git back!" He piled into the car and shot off over the tracks. He met Kirky coming out of the door and told him about the theft.

"Where's he now?" Kirky asked.

"How'd I know?" Chappie said heatedly. "Prob'ly gonna try'n shoot that Winger kid 'fore he skips out!"

"Prob'ly right," Kirky agreed. "See if you kin round up Bull and Doug for me—tell 'em to meet me over to the Winger place."

"Okay," Chappie said, and Kirky hopped onto his motorcycle and bolted across the tracks. Two blocks away he spotted Skunk pushing a lawn mower down the street. Kirky skidded to a stop.

"Seen the Winger boy?" he shouted.

"Naw," Skunk answered.

"Betta tell the truth, boy. It's for his own good."

"Somethin' wrong?" Skunk asked casually.

" 'Twill be plenty wrong if I don't git to him 'fore that Savage boy does. Come on now—where's he at?"

"At the river—goin' swimmin'. I'm meetin' 'em soon's I put this mower up."

"You stay 'way from there!" Kirky shouted as he roared off.

Newt, Beansy and Jappy had crossed the river road now and they were trooping through the brush toward Rock Cave. Jappy carried a heavy stick, and now and then he would stop and swing at a stone, bottle or tin can in a golfer's manner. The river was in full view now, and Newt subconsciously noted the pinkish-gray coloring upon it in the distance where the watersides curved again into the forest. "It'll prob'ly be the last time I'll see this place—be on the train this time tomorrow," he was thinking. They were passing the cave now and heading down toward the bank. Beansy walked over and knelt beside the water and pushed his hand against the current.

"Gittin' colder," he observed.

"Yeh, won't be long now before you guys'll be trappin' down here again." Newt was remembering his and Beansy's last trapping expedition, when he stole the hot sausage from his mother's frying pan. It seemed like years had passed since then.

"You guys goin' in?" Beansy hollered.

"Let's wait up for Skunk," Jappy said.

"Okay by me," Beansy answered, "he ought'a be comin' soon."

They continued along the bank, filling their last hours with small talk. Three sparrows darted about in hot pursuit of a crow. The boys watched the big bird wheel, rise, drop, rise again and shoot into the tall trees, the sparrows still on its tail.

"Nest robber," Newt said.

There wasn't much left for them to say. The world had suddenly grown quiet. The sun was lowering into a pink haze. A cracking of brush came from about twenty yards behind them. Beansy turned. "Skunk must be com—" The rest of the word froze in his mouth.

"Winger!" Marcus hollered.

"He's got a gun!" Beansy yelled.

Newt, Jappy and Beansy scrambled into the woods between the road and the river. Marcus aimed toward Newt and fired.

"Ow!" Jappy screamed. He had caught the bullet in the leg. Marcus was running toward them. "My leg! My leg!" Jappy hollered, as he kept stumbling toward the road. Newt and Beansy looked back, horrified.

"He's after me! Help Jappy, Beansy! Help Jappy!" Newt fell to the ground and grabbed the stick Jappy had dropped; then, terror-stricken, he rolled behind a thicket, got to his feet and ran off in another direction with Marcus close on his heels. Beansy pulled Jappy up and helped him out to the road. "Oh God—oh God," Beansy kept saying.

"Run for help, Beansy! Hurry! Hurry!" Jappy shouted. "I can make it from here! It's just my leg!"

"You shore?"

"Yeh—hurry!"

Marcus was closing in fast, and Newt, feeling it useless to run any more, stopped—the stick clutched tightly in his hand. He stood against a tree; will shattered; body tensed; wanting to cry out for mercy; for help; ready to fall whenever the bullet came ripping through.

Marcus aimed and pulled the trigger.

Click—click—click—click—

Spasms of fear shot through Newt's body.

Click—click—click—click—

"You bastard!" Marcus shouted. Then, inflamed at the misfire, he threw the gun at Newt with all his might. Newt

237

ducked. The gun smacked against the tree and bounced off his shoulder to the ground. Looking back to Marcus, he saw him pull his knife, flinched as the blade popped out. Newt backed toward the road as Marcus circled to the right. Marcus lunged. Newt swung the stick. The blow aimed for Marcus' head, caught him on the shoulder, knocking him off balance; but the momentum of the charge brought them into contact, and the knife, aimed for Newt's heart, sliced his left shoulder instead. Newt felt the blade tear through his skin. He hollered, jumped back and frantically swung again. The stick found its mark this time, and Marcus dropped to his knees. But quickly he was up—blood running from his nose to his chin—stalking Newt like a wild animal. "You son-of-a-bitch! You gonna die! You gonna die!"

Newt felt the warm blood at his elbow, but his eyes stayed on Marcus and the glistening blade. He circled backward, being careful not to stumble, his fear mixed with a great desire to survive. Marcus crouched, sprang again, low this time, and Newt swung—but missed him—jumped to the side as the blade slashed through the denim of his overalls just above the knee. Marcus plunged onto the ground. Newt started in, hesitated; then Marcus was on his feet again, cussing, circling, cussing. "You son-of-a-bitch! You black bastard! I'm gonna cut your fuckin' heart out!" The blood rolled thick over his lips now.

"Come on! Come on! I'm ready for you!"

The courage in Newt's voice enraged Marcus. He spat a gob of blood, stuck out the knife and charged. Newt's aim was true, and as the blow smashed against Marcus' skull he went down with a howl and a thud, the knife flying from his hand. Newt dropped the stick and dived for the knife, beating his dazed assailant to the weapon. But Marcus was not finished, and his hand coiled Newt's wrist in a powerful effort to shake the knife from his hand. But Newt held on, and they wrestled to the side of the road, their bodies rolling as one in the dust, the knife extended beyond their heads. Finally they landed in a ditch with Newt on top, and with a last burst of strength he yanked his wrist from Marcus' grasp. Then the blade was up, the hand trembling, the arm tensed for a downward thrust. But the look of helplessness and fear beneath the bloody mask that was Marcus' face stopped Newt's arm cold. For a split second their eyes burned into each other's.

"I ought'a kill you, Marcus." Newt breathed heavily, the knife still up. "I ought'a kill—"

A siren sounded, and they both started. "It's Kirky, Newt! Gimme a chance! He'll shoot me to pieces!"

Newt glanced up the road, then back at his frightened enemy. "Okay, git goin', and don't never come back." He released his hold, and Marcus staggered up and started running toward the rocky ledge. Newt pushed the dirty wet blade into the groove, felt his arm. It wasn't as bad as he had thought. The next minute he was secretly hoping, even praying, for Marcus' escape.

Kirky's motorcycle skidded to a stop in a cloud of dust. He jumped off, eyed Newt quickly and drew his guns. "Where's he at? You hurt?"

Newt looked toward the opposite direction from which Marcus ran. "He went into the woods."

"Which way?" Newt didn't have to answer. Kirky suddenly spotted Marcus loping toward the rocky ledge. He fired and shouted, "Halt! Halt!" Then he started running, firing and shouting at the same time. "Halt! Halt!"

Newt pocketed the knife and followed. (Run, Marcus, run, run, run . . .).

"Stop, you black bastard! Stop, goddam you!" He was firing both pistols now, and Marcus was trying to reach a safe diving position from the ledge. It was obvious he was going to attempt the river—under water, downstream. Kirky fired again, and the bullet chipped the stone above Marcus' head.

Suddenly Newt yelled, "Look out! Oh God! Oh God!" Marcus had slipped and was falling down toward the stone apron, screaming as he plummeted through space. Kirky's mouth flew open and he held his fire. Newt slapped his hands over his eyes as Marcus' body smashed and crumpled against the jagged lip, stayed for a moment, then began a grotesque end-over-end plunge downward. When it splashed into the calm river, great ripples swelled from the entry point, then began wasting themselves in their own motion. The head bobbed up a couple of times, the body rolled over like a slow-moving fish, then spiraled to the bottom of the river.

Kirky holstered his guns, mopped his brow with the back of his hairy hand and spat. "Well, Winger, you kin rest easy. You won't be bothered with him no more."

Newt stood gazing into the easy-moving water. "Ain't we goin' to try and get him out?"

"Not now. Pull him out tomorra mornin'. Be dark soon. It's a cinch he ain't goin' nowhere tonight." He took a plug of tobacco from his puttees and bit off a chunk. "He cut you deep?"

"Not too bad."

"Git on. I'll give you a lift home."

"Nope. I can make it by myself."

"Okay by me, boy," Kirky grunted. He mounted the machine and stomped the pedal with his foot. The motorcycle pop-popped to a start and belched off in a cloudy roar.

The last of the sunlight was gone now, and the crickets had already begun rubbing at the evening dampness. Newt started off then stopped, his mind jumping back and forth between home and Marcus' body, wallowing now somewhere at the bottom. For an instant he thought of going back, not knowing why; then he reasoned against it.

Newt turned for a last look at the river. The pink coloring was gone, and the gray was edging into blackness. Marcus was just a memory. He felt his arm, shivered, then slowly turned homeward over the dusty road.